I CANNOT
GET
YOU
CLOSE
ENOUGH

By Ellen Gilchrist

In the Land of Dreamy Dreams
The Annunciation
Victory Over Japan
Drunk With Love
Falling Through Space
The Anna Papers
Light Can Be Both Wave and Particle
I Cannot Get You Close Enough

I CANNOT GET YOU CLOSE ENOUGH

THREE
NOVELLAS BY
Ellen Gilchrist

BACK BAY BOOKS

Little, Brown and Company

BOSTON   NEW YORK   TORONTO   LONDON

FIRST PAPERBACK EDITION

The characters and events in this book are fictional. Any similarity to real persons, either living or dead, is purely coincidental and not intended by the author.

The author is grateful for permission to include the following previously copyrighted material:

Excerpt from "Slow Hand" by John Bettis and Michael Clark. © 1981 Warner-Tamerlane Publishing Corp., Flying Dutchman Music and Sweet Harmony Music, Inc. All Rights Reserved. Used by permission.

"A Daylight Art" from *The Haw Lantern* by Seamus Heaney. Copyright © 1987 by Seamus Heaney. Reprinted by permission of Farrar, Straus and Giroux Inc. and Faber and Faber Ltd.

Excerpt from "This Be The Verse" in *High Window* by Philip Larkin. Reprinted by permission of Faber and Faber Ltd.

"The Hawkweed" by Edna St. Vincent Millay. From *Collected Poems*, Harper & Row. Copyright 1928, © 1955 by Edna St. Vincent Millay and Norma Millay Ellis. Reprinted by permission of Elizabeth Barnett, Literary Executor.

LIBRARY OF CONGRESS CATALOGING-IN-PUBLICATION DATA

Gilchrist, Ellen, 1935–
    I cannot get you close enough : three novellas / by Ellen Gilchrist. — 1st ed.
      p.   cm.
    ISBN 0-316-31423-4
    I. Title.
    PS3557.I34258I18   1990
    813'.54 — dc20   90-38578

10 9 8 7 6

MV NY

Published simultaneously in Canada by Little, Brown & Company (Canada) Limited
Printed in the United States of America

For Ed

Generally speaking, all the life which the parents could have lived, but of which they thwarted themselves for artificial motives, is passed on to the children in substitute form. That is to say, the children are driven unconsciously in a direction that is intended to compensate for everything that was left unfulfilled in the lives of their parents.

CARL GUSTAV JUNG

They fuck you up, your mum and dad,
They may not mean to but they do.

PHILIP LARKIN

Contents

Winter   1

De Havilland Hand   87

A Summer in Maine   199

WINTER

1

This is a manuscript that the deceased poet and novelist Anna Hand left in a suitcase in a rented cottage in Beddiford, Maine. She left the suitcase lying on a bed, kissed her lover goodbye, then drove off in a rented car and killed herself in the November sea. She killed herself because she thought it was undignified to die of cancer in a hospital. She was so vain she couldn't bear for anyone to watch her die.

The manuscript was an unwieldy piece, half typed and half written by hand, clipped together with an old-fashioned clipboard of the kind used for theatrical scripts. The first entry was dated 1978, the last, 1984. It began —

If I am going to save Jessie, first I must understand Sheila. She is Jessie's mother. Begin at the beginning. She is mean, destructive, spoiled, dangerous, unprincipled, remorseless, the worst bitch I have ever known. Sheila Jane MacNiece, Hand, Stuart, Rothschild. My father's partner's only child, my brother Daniel's nemesis and ex-wife, my youngest and most beautiful niece's mother.

If I am going to save Jessie I must know how this woman does the things she does. How she gets people in her power, how someone who isn't even beautiful can get men to love her and do her will, men and women, she isn't particular about that, although I don't think she's a lesbian. I don't think she's anything at all where sex is concerned. She told me once years ago on a drunken night that she had never had an orgasm, that Daniel never made her come, that she couldn't come, that it was her fault that she could never come. It won't do it, she said. It just won't do it no matter what we do. It's okay, I told her. Everyone doesn't have to do that. Maybe that's what she is looking for in her madness and her silliness and her buying sprees. That time she bought all that goddamn silly shit with mirrors on it. Everything in the house was covered with those goddamn little mirrors — lamps, her dresses, the walls, ashtrays. There was a new store in Charlotte called 20th Century and she kept buying all those mirrors there. Daniel said she charged forty thousand dollars' worth of furniture that year until even her daddy wouldn't pay the bills. Poor Sheila, she was lame at birth, she had to have those operations, maybe that's what spoiled her, ruined her disposition. Oh, God, don't let Jessie inherit that darkness, that tightness, that tightmouthed hatred and despair. Oh, God damn God for ever getting us mixed up with her to begin with, but we wouldn't have Jessie if we hadn't, so it doesn't matter. Anything was worth it for Jessie. We have Jessie and nothing must take her away from us.

Now, I must remember everything. I must write until I know. I must write down everything I can remember back to the first day she walked into our house carrying her ballet shoe in her hand and threw it into Helen's fishbowl. I must follow every move she ever made in my presence or that I was told about. I must remember everything. If I write down everything that happened in the order that it happened without going off on tangents I will begin to see the pattern. If I can see the pattern I can save Jessie. I must save Jessie. I must do it because maybe no one else can. Sheila is the single most power-mad human being, male or female, that I have ever known. She has already destroyed my baby brother. Next it will be Jessie. She will suck the life blood from her. She will attach that child to her like I have seen her do a dozen people and when she gets through the only way they can live is off her whims. She is capable of anything. She might give Jessie to some director in exchange for a role. She might do anything. God knows if we can undo the damage she's already done, but Jess is only ten years old. If we can get her now we can save her. If we can keep Sheila from taking her to England. Well, I'll testify to anything. I told Daniel I would testify to anything, even under oath.

Meanwhile, I will write it down. The truth. Every single true thing any of us knows about Sheila. Names, dates, places, conversations. I'll go over and see Mrs. MacNiece. I'll take Mr. MacNiece out to lunch and let him paw me. I'll find the wedding pictures. I'll talk to her doctors, find the records. There will be a record and when we see it spread out before us we will know which way to go, know where to begin. Jessie is my heart, my dearest, most precious little child. Slow down, Anna. Begin at the beginning.

It must have been 1955. I was playing paper dolls with Helen. We were making Girl Scout uniforms for the Wonder Woman dolls and Daddy came into the room and said that Mr. MacNiece was bringing his little girl over to play and to be nice to her because Mr. MacNiece was the gravy train we were going to get on and ride.

"Oh, James," my mother said. "Don't tell the children something like that. She's a nice little girl, just Daniel's age. You children can take care of her so we can visit with her parents." Then she was there and she walked into the room and threw her shoe into Helen's goldfish bowl. "I hate fish," she said. "They're so nasty. They go to the bathroom in their cage." Then Daniel was brought in to meet her. He was all dressed up in his new Sunday School clothes and she must have thought he was all right because she took him off outside and started bossing him around. And continued to do so for the next thirty years.

A spoiled only child, a rotten spoiled bitch. She did terrible things and we watched them happen. She can't love anyone because her father didn't love her. He can't love anything but money, and she can only love things she cannot have.

Phelan was always onto Sheila. If there was one person Sheila hated more than she hated me, it was Phelan. More about this later.

I keep thinking she is running drugs. Nothing else could account for the house in Switzerland she had for a while and the jewelry. For ignoring Jessie for months on end. Once we didn't hear from her for sixteen months. Jessie didn't know where she was for sixteen months. What else do we need? Maybe she had gone somewhere for help. When the letters came they were from Zurich. And they were soft, soft. Daniel copied them and mailed them to me

to see what I thought they meant. It means she's coming
for her, I said, and I was right.

When she showed up that time she looked like a recover-
ing addict. So soft, so sweet, so vague. I must make a chart
of dates and try to figure out where she was and when. No,
I'll go to England and see what I can find out. I'll call Mic
and get her to help. Someone will know, someone will have
seen her around. We have to find out what she has been
doing over there. And then what? Tell Jessie? Say, Well,
sweetie, your mother is running dope from Marseilles to
Paris and we're lucky, she isn't dead yet. Yeah, well she had
to have money for her clothes, you know, her lifestyle your
granddaddy got her accustomed to and now won't support
anymore.

I ran into a friend of Robert's at a party near Covent
Garden who said he knew her. When was that? Last June?
He said he had met her at a house party in Scotland, a
hunting party. There were drugs everywhere, he told me.
Bloody drugs coming out of the walls. We were in a small
apartment on the third floor of a building overlooking Covent Garden and he said, "Oh, I ran into your sister-in-law
up in Scotland. She's a strange piece of work, isn't she?"
"Yes," I said. "She is. I have been wondering where she is."
"Well, don't go looking for that one," he said. "You
wouldn't be glad you found her."

We cannot allow her to get her hands on Jessie, ever
again.

When we were growing up the MacNieces lived in a white
brick house on the ninth tee of the Charlotte Driving Club.
There was a butler and a houseboy and two gardeners, Wid-

dle and Wee, and they pushed us on the bicycles. Sometimes I would actually let them push me because it seemed so impossible that Sheila let them push her. What a tight world. I don't think I ever saw Sheila once in her life when she wasn't perfectly turned out, dressed and manicured and coiffed. How could she do drugs and stay that neat? They liked to dress her in pink and baby blue and pale yellow. She would come over to our house dressed like that and follow Helen and me around. Stand by the bed while we put our makeup on. "I can't wear it yet," she said. "I look better with just my own skin. Momma says people look like white trash with stuff on their eyes. They look cheap." I remember Helen almost choked on that. Helen couldn't stand Sheila. Well, no one could. I don't think anyone ever really liked her in her life. Except Daniel or whatever man she was concentrating on at the moment. Man or woman, whomever she had decided to capture.

Then how did she do it? They envied her, I suppose. She had those cars and those clothes and all that money to spend. She could have people out to that cold tight white brick house and Wee and Widdle would push them on bikes or, later, wash their cars. Clean their golf clubs, something Niall had done out there one time. But I never heard anyone say they liked her. They said they had to go meet her somewhere or had to go to a party she was having but it wasn't even fascination. It was more like fear. The main thing she inspires in me is fear. When she was five she could make me feel uneasy. As if something bad might happen at any minute.

Trembling on the brink of what? She would point her little operated-on foot and Daniel would bow his head. Maybe he hated her. Maybe what he really wanted to do was kill her. Or maybe he just wanted to conquer her. Any other girl in town would have died for him. They all loved him and plenty of them still do. But he would be out at Sheila's house waiting for her to finish getting dressed. He took her to dances, he escorted her to parties. He was her beau. He belonged to her whenever she wanted him to. Maybe all he really wanted was to make her love him back.

They kept on living in that white brick house on the ninth tee. That same white brick house on the ninth tee, but meanwhile Mr. MacNiece was getting rich as Croesus. He bought up all that land in Mecklenburg County right before they built the airport. He told Daddy to buy some, but Daddy was saving money for our education and was afraid to risk it. That was the beginning of Mr. MacNiece's real money. Then he took the profits from that and bought a television station which no one thought would catch on and then he bought the Charlotte paper and the rest is history, as they say.

Still they stayed in that white house. "We could have a bigger house if we wanted one," Sheila told Momma. We had gone out to spend the afternoon, Helen and Daniel and Momma and I. I've forgotten why. I've forgotten a world where people just went over to visit because someone asked them to. "We could buy one in town closer to everything or have an architect build us one. But we don't want to. We will stay right here in our own house where we are as comfortable as we can be." She raised her hand and Traylor the butler came out onto the patio carrying a tray with a silver coffeepot and little silver containers in the shape of elephants to hold the sugar and cream. There were Belgian cookies and strawberries in a cut-glass bowl. Sheila poured the coffee and held out a cup to mother. She was fourteen years old. Her eyes were as cold as the winter sea.

So two months before the custody trial I went to England to see what I could find out about Sheila. The trial was set for August 20. I had other reasons to go to Europe. My British publisher wanted to publish a selection of my stories and I wanted to help him make the selections. Also, I hadn't been in Scandinavia for a while and I thought I might go to Stockholm and meet my translators. So I could work and see my friends and try to find out what Sheila had been up to in Europe. I was looking for a miracle, I suppose. Someone to walk up to me and say, I bought some dope from Sheila, or, Sheila shot a waitress because the tea was cold.

I arrived in London on a Monday afternoon, wandered around, made phone calls, slept off my jet lag. On Tuesday morning I went out in a taxi to find the place where Sheila lived. It was a ground-floor flat with a walled garden. A note attached to the door instructed delivery people to leave packages with the landlady. I descended the four steps to the yard, walked primly around a hedge and ascended four steps to a red door with a pot of pansies beside an exotic-looking doormat. I knocked, and a woman my mother's age opened the door. "I'm looking for Mrs. Rothschild," I said. "She may be calling herself MacNiece now. She's my sister-in-law. She didn't know I was coming. I just got here."

"She's off on holiday," the woman said. "Would you care to leave a message then?"

"Do you know where she's gone? How long she's gone

for? It's important that I find her. I won't be here long, in London. I need to talk to her."

"She wouldn't want me telling her whereabouts, you know."

"I will pay you." I paused, watched her, went on. "I have to find her. I'll pay whatever you think it's worth to tell me where she's gone."

The woman opened the door wider, straightened up, looked me in the eye. "I'll take a note," she said. "You can leave word for her."

"I'm sorry. That was the wrong thing to say. I didn't mean to bribe you. I have to find her, that's all. It's the welfare of a child. I'm the child's aunt. She deserted the child and now she wants it back and I'm over here to spy on her. If you'll let me come in and talk to you I could make you understand. I'm an American writer. My British publishers are Faber and Faber. I'm very respectable, as writers go. If you could tell me where she's gone. I really am her sister-in-law. What name is she using now, by the way? Both were in the directory."

"She calls herself MacNiece. You come on in. I'll see what I can do." She opened the door wider. A face came out from the soft gray hair. She had black button eyes, a wide brow, the sort of pale lustrous skin the British are famous for.

"I appreciate this," I said. "I guess you can see I'm frantic."

"You come on in. I'll hear you out." She led the way into a small cozy room with red upholstered sofas and Indian shawls draped over tables. I told her the story and she listened without interrupting. Then she opened a drawer in a desk and took out a package of American cigarettes and held them out. Viceroys, cigarette of my squandered youth. I hadn't smoked in years but I took the cigarette and the light she offered. She lit mine and then her own and sat down opposite me on a sofa. "I'm Mrs. Archer," she began. "My friends call me Amalie. I'll tell you what I know. She's no favorite of mine, your sister-in-law, that's for certain. Hardly has a word for anyone except to complain about something. Never stops for a soul. She sent a boy packing a while ago who came to wash the windows. Devil's time I had getting him to come back." Amalie inhaled and blew the smoke up into a shaft of light. "I wouldn't want her getting hold of a child of mine. I've seen her kind before, women who go all cold, dry up and hate the world."

"She didn't go cold." I inhaled and added my stream of smoke to Amalie's. They mingled in midair, a microcosm, the birth of clouds. "Sheila was born cold, came out cold from the womb. Well, she's done all the damage she's going to do to my family. It's going to stop."

"Would you care for sherry then? I've got a bottle of amontilado my brother picked up. I've been saving it. No good to drink alone."

"Sure," I said. "I'd love it. That would be fine." So we opened the sherry and poured it into small red glasses and began to talk. Then we went next door to Sheila's flat to look around. There was not much there. It was musty, depressing, bare. It was impossible to imagine Sheila in such a place. "She went off a fortnight ago," Amalie explained. "Had a party one night and the next day they all left. I've cleaned it up since then. She hires a cleaning lady when she's here but she won't trust her with a key."

"I can't imagine why not. There's nothing here."

"There were more things a while back. They were taken off. She's not here as often as she was, back last summer." I got up and walked around the rooms again. Whatever else this flat meant, it meant Sheila was broke. If she was broke, that explained why she needed Jessie. If she had Jessie, her father would have to give her money. He would never let Jessie live like this. Suddenly I wanted to be outside. I wanted to protect Sheila from this flat. If Sheila lived in a place like this, then we might all be in danger. Danger? How had I come to perceive the world as full of danger? The world is full of beauty and possibility and crazy dazzling people. I stopped at the back door and turned to Amalie. "Let's sit in the garden and finish the sherry," I said. "I never get to talk to real Londoners. I always end up talking to reporters."

"Well, we can't drink it all," she said. "We'd be in hospital if we drank the bottle."

So I spent the afternoon in a walled garden drinking sherry with Amalie Archer, who had been in the Royal British Air Force during the war and received medals from the Queen. The medals were duly produced and duly marveled over, along with pictures of her dead husband, who was killed in North Africa in the same war, and snapshots of her last trip to Bath. She had friends, Amalie assured me, and a brother in Oxford who came down for holidays. "Have to have your friends," she concluded. "Take your sister-in-law. She stays alone for weeks sometimes. Barely leaves her door."

"What does she do inside?"

"I wouldn't know, love. Sends out for groceries or the

papers. Then suddenly will leave like this and not come back for a fortnight."

"Does she have another house somewhere? In the country perhaps."

"Not that I know of. There, there's a jack — that redbird has been in this garden for twenty years. Him or his progeny. See that post, that's his post. Never fails to cheer me up to see him take his seat."

"Do you put out seed for him, for the birds around here?"

"Sometimes I do. She didn't like them being here. Said they stained the yard with their droppings. So I quit since she asked me to. They can come and get it at my place. Still, he likes to sit there."

"That's our Sheila. She always has hated animals. She hates fish. Imagine hating fish."

Amalie shook her head. "I wouldn't be worrying about a court giving a little girl to her. You can't get her to look you in the eye. If you look at her she looks away."

"She can be charming when she wants something. I've seen her get her way from people you thought would never fall for her, and yet they do. When she wants somebody she goes after them. Pity, flattery, charm, whatever it takes. She can fake it when she needs to."

"Well good luck to you." Amalie raised her glass. "I'll keep my eye out here for anything that might help you."

"You're helping now. You're helping by trusting me."

"Don't forget to have them send the books around. The ones you wrote. I'll tell you what I think of them when I get through."

"Oh, don't do that," I answered. Then I laughed out

loud. "Oh, please don't do that to me." The sun was moving down the sky behind a bank of scattered clouds. The redbird deserted his post for a tree. Amalie and I carried the glasses inside and closed up the flat and walked out onto the street. I was slightly drunk and reasonably amazed to have had such a good time. Good old universe. I squeezed Amalie's hand and walked off down the street in the direction of Queen's Square, where I hoped to find a taxi. I knew she was watching me and I sauntered as lightly as possible, wanting to give her every last bit of whatever it was she had found in me to like.

I flew to Stockholm the next day to see my Swedish publisher. When I returned to London I went back to Sheila's flat and found it vacated. "She came three days ago, with a man from Germany I've seen before," Amalie informed me. "She got it out of me you'd been here and she said she was going to the States. She said to tell you hello."

"Was she angry with you for letting me in?"

"No. I think not. She was showing off for the man, if you want my opinion. Being very cordial to me, she was. I helped her pack up her things and she paid me very well. Also, she left the rent for the rest of the month. You aren't looking for a place, are you?"

I considered it. "Is the phone still connected, in her name?"

"No, they came and took that out the day she left."

"I have a place, thank you. Let's have tea," I added. "Sometime soon. It was nice talking with you last week. A good memory."

"We'll do that then." She smiled and I saw the girl she must have been, in a war with Germany, with hair that wasn't gray and those eyes. "Did you wear a cap?" I asked. "A hat. With your uniform in the war?" "Oh, did I ever," she laughed. She squeezed my hand. "Did I ever wear my brave chapeau."

So I had found Sheila's lair but no Sheila. Sheila had flown the coop, gone home to start her court proceedings. Still, I had that afternoon in a walled garden with a British heroine and I remembered it. Every time I have seen a bird sitting on a post I have thought of Amalie, her brave life and her eye on the redbird in the garden. Maybe that's why Daniel fell in love with Sheila, to watch her. Because she seemed a different species. A beplumed helpless starving little bird. Skinny little bones and thin white skin covered with dimity and lace and figured silk, rings on her fingers, Capezio sandals on her toes, sashes and Peter Pan collars and cashmere and tweed and in the summer off-the-shoulder blouses and that red-and-yellow sundress with the tie on one shoulder and the other shoulder bare. Perhaps it was the plumage that fascinated him. That a human being was willing to devote her entire life to getting dressed. Perhaps that was her fascination. Or perhaps it was the face that stared out from underneath the hairdos and rose on its neck above the finery. That face in the middle of that perfection. That unsmiling unhappy pleasureless little perfection of a face. (Which later became beautiful in Jessie.)

Maybe Sheila was the last victim of the Victorians. Their very last devotee and victim.

*   *   *

Anyway, my brother Daniel loved her. "She's got him," I told Phelan, one summer when he was visiting. "She's got him just where she wants him."

We were sitting on the porch watching them. Daniel was shooting baskets. Sheila was sitting in a wicker chair in that red-and-yellow dress, watching him shoot. She never said, that's wonderful, never clapped, never applauded. She just sat there in that sundress with a tie on one shoulder and the other shoulder bare and watched. He had been shooting for half an hour without pausing or seeming to come up for breath, only glancing her way if a shot went in or one went seriously awry.

"How could she have anyone?" Phelan said. "I can smell her from here. There's a smell they have, the real bitches. Like the smell of something about to die or give you leprosy. Pussy smell. Uncle Dudley said he smelled it once on a whore in Memphis and that once you smell it you can never forget it."

I guess I blushed. Phelan Manning was the only boy in the world who would talk like that to a girl from Charlotte. He pretended not to notice my blushes and went right on. Got up and put his foot on the porch rail. Phelan and I were in college. I guess Daniel and Sheila were about fourteen. Maybe it was the summer I ran away and married Walker.

Phelan went on. "Uncle Dudley was sucking a whore's cunt on the table in Matamoros while we watched. Then he gave her a hundred dollars for letting him do it. He said it was to teach us not to be afraid of anything. He said the thing to fear is not doing anything you want to do before you die."

"I don't want to hear about it," I said. "I've heard all I can stand about that trip to Mexico. That's all you've talked about all summer." It was true. His Uncle Dudley and his cousin Charles Dunbar had taken them parrot hunting. A Mexican general who owns orange groves had them down to shoot the parrots that eat the oranges. The parrots come in flocks up out of the swamps and eat all the oranges and ruin the harvest and they shoot them from the roll-back top of Mercedes touring cars. Driving around in groups of three. One to drive, one to shoot, one to load. Driving around in between the orange trees shooting parrots as fast as they can shoot. On the way to the orange groves they had stopped in Matamoros to fuck whores, and Phelan's uncle had been bitten by a dog in the street and wouldn't even get the rabies shots. "He's still alive," Phelan kept saying, when he told the Mexican stories that summer. "I guess he just can't die."

"Anyway," Phelan concluded. "That's who this little girl reminds me of."

"Of what? The whore or your Uncle Dudley?"

"Of the way that smelled. Maybe it's for sale, maybe that's what I'm smelling. We ought to get Daniel away from that before he gets any older. They get their hooks in you and every time you see them you want to lay them down. You can't forget the first one."

I sighed. This was going to go on all summer. If I hung out with Phelan, I had to hear about his sexual conquests. Phelan was ahead of his time in the sexual revolution. He had leaped over his pale generation in the South. "Okay, Phelan," I said. "Who got their hooks in you? Who was the first girl you did it to?"

"I guess I can tell." He leaned down across his propped-up knee, seemed to contemplate a pressing moral dilemma. "She doesn't live here anymore so you will never meet her."

"You aren't supposed to tell even if they live in Alaska,"

I answered. I got up from my chair, moved closer to him. He turned and faced me, that wonderful soft look on his face. It was before I ran away and married Walker or I would have known what all that meant. I didn't know. We didn't know anything back then. We talked about it but we didn't know. Anyway, I never fell in love with Phelan. We were too right for each other, distant cousins, such good friends. It would have been too easy and neither of us wanted anything to be easy.

"I want to go to the library and get some books out," I said. "I want to have something to read this weekend."

"Let's go then." He took my arm. Strange, it is here now, the touch of his hand upon my arm, those clear black eyes, that lovely perfect nose. Crystal has that nose, his sister in New Orleans. That nose alone would get a family a long way if they didn't breed it out with Mexican whores.

We walked down across the yard toward the basketball hoop where Daniel was still shooting baskets. He was shooting free throws now, overhand. Phelan stopped beside Sheila's yard chair and said something. He ran his hand across her bare shoulder.

"Don't do that," she said. "Please don't touch me."

"Forgive me, Your Royal Highness. Please forgive."

"I won't," she answered, and Daniel stopped shooting free throws and came and stood beside her.

"Leave her alone, Phelan," he said. "Don't tease her. She just got back from the hospital yesterday."

"I wasn't teasing her. I wanted to see if she was real."

"That isn't funny, Phelan. Apologize." Daniel was trembling. He was really getting mad and Phelan outweighed him by twenty pounds. Sheila didn't change the expression on her face. That bored, impenetrable look. Her legs were in pale cream stockings. I had not noticed them. If there were bandages or scars, no one would ever see them. "Come on, Phelan," I said. "Don't start a fight. Momma'll punish me if Daniel starts fighting." "Okay," he said. "I'm sorry, Sheila. It's just that you looked so cool." He patted the high white wicker back of the yard chair. "See you around," he added. Sheila turned her head away. Daniel bounced the ball very hard against the driveway. Hit, hit, hit. Where is that from?

We got into Phelan's grandmother's car, a dusty blue Buick, and drove off down Sherman Street. We had just had the typical encounter, interchange, unforgettable moment, with Sheila when she was growing up. What happened, we might well be asking ourselves at such a moment. Was that our fault?

The next fall they did the very last operation. She was as tall as they expected her to be now, five-four, as Daniel kept saying when he talked about it. So they took her to Chapel Hill to a great ankle man and he turned her foot the last quarter of an inch and tucked it away inside the cast for the winter, and she was, at last, perfect.

2

There was a photograph of her in the Chapel Hill newspaper the day she was released. She was sitting in a hospital wheelchair in a soft green-and-white flowered dress. The doctor stood above her with his hands holding the back of the chair. A great triumphant pleased smile was on his face. Her second husband was a surgeon. First there was Daniel, to conquer us, then a surgeon, to conquer medicine, then a Rothschild to conquer Europe. In between, the theater, to conquer the common man. Why would I take pleasure in the end of that, be happy to find her clothes in a dumpy musty flat in London? I am the one who is diseased to take such pleasure in the end of her triumphs. God knows, I had my own. Is one kind of ambition really that much different from another? All trying to stick our heads up above the crowd and keep them there and our children standing on our shoulders and theirs on their shoulders. Who am I kidding? If I take pleasure in Sheila's fall then I am as bad as she is and the prevailing emotion she arouses in me is not fear after all, but jealousy. Maybe I wanted to live in the white brick house and be the only child and have the piano teacher come to the house instead of walking six blocks carrying my sheet music every Saturday. Maybe I wanted to look like that, that weak and defenseless, and have men in my power instead of always fighting with me. Leaving me. Her men didn't leave her, didn't die or go back to their wives. Maybe life imitates art and Sheila is the stuff art is about, the absolute self-created, self-encircling thing. I am an observer. Nothing escapes me. Watch, watch, watch, bitch, bitch, bitch.

I want to meditate on that photograph, my memory of it. Sheila sitting there with that satisfied look on her face and the surgeon satisfied too. No, he may be satisfied but she is not quite pleased, one hand over the other hand, a shadow on her face, something petulant and not quite pleased. That's the effect she had on men. She brought out something in them that made them want to prove their mettle, made them feel off-balance somehow, as if only in her eyes would victory seem sweet. I am getting lost. I must resist the urge to go off on tangents. But she is so impossible to understand. The tangential data may be more useful than the plot. I want to see the core, the atomic number, be able to map her.

It may be simple. The absolute simplicity of the Oedipus complex. A little girl loves her father. Whatever happens there is all that can ever happen. We are doomed to repeat that first terrible encounter. Sheila comes into the world one morning and her foot is bent. Outside in the hall her father hears the doctors talking. "Should we tell her first and then him?" "No, tell him and let him tell her." "Get them together in a room. Neither one of them looks like they will take it very well." "It isn't that bad. Only the smallest deformity." "Unless she can't walk."

*   *   *

Later, the operations would be successful and he would be free to love her. But Ed MacNiece wasn't into love. Besides, by the time of the operations his mind was busy elsewhere. He owned the television station and the land beside the reservoir. He had plenty of things to give Sheila that he thought were more valuable than love.

I woke this morning thinking of the year the Pear Blossom Festival was ruined by snow. Five days before the debutantes put on their white dresses and walked around the municipal auditorium on their father's arms. Between the banked arrangements of pear blossoms. The high point of Charlotte social life. The one day of her life when Sheila might have expected to have her father to herself, if not all day, then certainly from the time the march began until he turned her over to society and she made her much-rehearsed deep gorgeous bow. This was when we still had the debutante ball in the auditorium before someone decided it was a public building and we had to move the ball out to the driving club. Had to build a recreation room big enough to hold it.

After the walk there would be the dance, that would be another three or four or five minutes when Sheila would have Big Ed all to herself. Then disaster struck. A week before the ball the pear blossoms of North Carolina were buried underneath two feet of the latest recorded snowfall in our history. A thick wet blanket that began falling before dawn one morning and continued falling until late the next day. Two days of snow in the last week of March. Omens and signs, Armageddon. We are deep in Bible country here no matter how much Hume and maybe even Leibniz or Spinoza a few of us might read.

So there we were with snow on the pear blossoms, an avalanche. I was home and Sheila came over to Mother's at noon to help cut out things for a luncheon Helen was having for some of the debs. Daniel was walking around worrying about the snow ruining things for Sheila. I guess it was spring break because Niall was there. And it must have been Saturday because Daddy was there. He was making poached eggs for whoever had been sleeping late and lecturing to us about helping in the kitchen. "Alice and Daytime can't do everything. You won't have servants when you grow up. We are living in a socialistic country and the government is ruining all the Negroes. Get up and help with the toast, Sister."

"It will be the ugliest coming-out they ever had," Sheila said. "It will be terrible."

"I'll make you some flowers," Daniel put in. "They can make them out of paper. Who cares? No one cares about the flowers."

"The flowers have to be there. It's the tradition. Without pear blossoms it could be anywhere. I could be making my debut in New Orleans like Doulin Lancaster. It will ruin everything."

"Well, this snow won't stick long," Daddy said. "Let me make you a poached egg, Sheila. You're too thin. Skin and bones. I never saw such a bunch of scrawny spoiled kids in my life. Bring me that plate over here, Anna. Let's put that in the dishwasher so Alice won't have to do it." Sheila got up and handed the dirty plate to him. Carried it very gingerly over to him and handed it to him to rinse. Then she looked at me with that look that said, It's your fault, Anna.

This is your fault and there are too many people in this room and that's your fault too. She walked back over to her place at the table and picked up the half-finished glass of milk and handed it to me and then she left. Left the room and then the house and got into her car and drove away. Drove down the snow-covered driveway with Daniel standing at the living-room window watching her leave.

"She doesn't know how to drive in snow," I said. "She's crazy to go out on those streets."

"She doesn't have anyplace else to go," he answered. "She doesn't have much to do." He looked at me, very solemn. He pities her, I thought. He's taking care of her, that's it. We all take care of him but there is no one left over for him to care for. So he has Sheila, in her endless casts, waiting to be pitied and cared for and loved. I crossed the room to him and put my arm around his waist. Already he towered over me, darling Daniel, the youngest of us and the sweetest. He inherited our grandfather's way with animals. They came to him. Horses, dogs, birds, cats. He had owned a parrot once that would sit on his shoulder and kiss him on the nose. It was Sheila's fault that the parrot got away. But that was before the unseasonable snow of 1964 ruined the Pear Blossom Ball. That was when they were fourteen.

Our cousins were visiting for someone's graduation or wedding. Phelan and Crystal Manning were here. Crystal and Sheila hated each other. They were as different as they could be. And yet, if you looked at them in those years, you might think they were sisters, the same hair, the same eyes, the same meticulous attention to detail, their perfect clothes and nails and polished shoes and arch dramatic poses. I have always thought Daniel had a secret crush on Crystal too.

Anyway, we were on the second floor and LeLe Arnold was lounging around on my bed saying goddamn and fuck to shock Sheila and the McLaurin boys were in Daniel's room with Niall. Then Daniel came walking out into the hallway that was the stair landing. Ours was an old Victorian house built in 1885. The rooms went off in angles from large central halls. The second floor had five bedrooms that we children shared. There were extra beds everywhere for company and two sleeping porches for the hot months. One porch was off my room and one off Niall's. Daniel came walking out onto the second-floor hall with the parrot, Milliken, on his shoulder and Sheila left my room where she was trying not to make LeLe mad. If you made LeLe mad you really had to hear some cussing. So Daniel came to rescue Sheila with Milliken on his shoulder and he walked all around the hall talking to the bird.

"Say 'Sheila,' Milliken," he said. "Say 'Daniel loves you.' " The bird made some of its arrogant incoherent threatening sounds and everyone backed away from him. Even LeLe backed away. Phelan was sitting on the back of the hall sofa eating it up. Phelan loved to see anyone doing something grand. No wonder he grew up to run around with the crowned heads of Europe.

So Daniel had Phelan to show off for as well as trying to make Sheila forget that LeLe was saying fuck every other word. Sheila might leave at any minute if she didn't like what was going on. That was another thing that must have intrigued Daniel. There he would be, trying to protect her and bring her into the warm circle of humanity, and at the slightest provocation she would bolt and run. Go off cold and alone to wherever she nested in that white brick house.

The piano bench or the gold velvet–upholstered seat she sat on to apply makeup in the pristine white and gold and green dressing room that opened out onto the leaf-strewn unused pool. Who would go over there to go swimming? LeLe once said. Those people are a thousand years old.

"Let's take Milliken outside," Phelan said. "It's spring and he needs a breath of fresh air."

"We could take him on the porch," Niall put in. Poor little Niall, he worshipped Phelan. He would lick his boots, clean his shoes, say anything Phelan wanted him to say. Anything he could imagine Phelan might want to hear, Niall would say it. Later Phelan would take him lion hunting in South Africa and bring him home with a blood disease it took years to cure, but I guess Niall thought a tropical disease was a small price to pay for flying to Africa with Phelan.

So, with Niall leading the way, Daniel walked through my room and out onto the sleeping porch with Milliken on his shoulder cawing and making his ugly parrot talk. Phelan was still sitting on the wooden back of that frail Victorian sofa. The sofa was beside the stairs, with a phone on a table beside it. From there you could see through an octagonal room out onto the sleeping porch and the oak trees that sheltered it. They were the oldest oak trees in town. Our house was on the site of the first settlement in Charlotte when Charlotte was only a trading post and a Confederate magazine. So Daniel kept on walking through the doors and out onto the porch. During the spring an oak branch had broken out a whole section of rusty screen. A section ten feet long and five feet wide was gone and Milliken lifted off from Daniel's shoulder and flew up into the oak tree.

It was spring and Milliken was free for the first time in many years. Daniel had owned him for four years and he was already a full-grown parrot when he came home from the pet store already talking indecipherable English and demanding crackers.

Now he sat in the oak tree and preened his feathers. "Let's get him," Phelan said, and began to climb out on the oak limb. Daniel grabbed his shoulder. "Don't go out there. Don't scare him. He'll come back if everyone is quiet." We were all on the porch now. Sheila, LeLe, our neighbors Hoyt and Davis McLaurin, Niall, Helen, Little Louise. In a minute Momma came up the stairs with Alice right beside her and then the porch was full.

"You better get him," Momma said. "Hold out your hand, Daniel, and he'll come to you." We had all seen Daniel do that a thousand times, inside the house or his room. Daniel walked to the edge of the broken screen. We all moved in. "Get back," he said. "He isn't going to come with you all here."

"Come back in my room," I said, "let's all go in my room and leave Daniel alone."

"You stay," Daniel said to Phelan. "Stay here." So the rest of us moved back into the room, but Hoyt and Davis had already run down the stairs with Helen and Louise behind them. They went down the stairs and out the door and into the yard to look at the situation from underneath the tree. "Let's climb up," I heard Hoyt say. "Let's surround him." Hoyt was fifteen and Davis was fourteen. They were pretty wild, a lot wilder than you would think, since they were quiet. Their mother was a beauty queen from Texas and let them do anything they liked as long as they didn't bother her.

So there is this contingent underneath the tree and Alice is on the porch saying, "The cats will get it. The cats will get it. The cats got that parakeet Miss Saybrook had. They tore it all to pieces."

Then Milliken spread his wings and flew up above our oak tree and across the backyard in a wobbly heavy flight and landed in the silver maple in the Baileys' yard. The contingent below our tree ran over to the Baileys' yard and Phelan and Daniel started down the stairs. Sheila walked behind them with an ecstatic look on her face. "There it goes," she said. "It's gone." Sure enough, Milliken had left the Baileys' yard and was across Sherman Street and into the magnolia on the lawn of the First Presbyterian Church.

We spent the rest of the day underneath the magnolia trying to get Milliken down and the fire department came and then Milliken flew deep into the neighborhood behind the church and that was the last we ever saw of him. Daniel stayed out until twelve that night with Phelan and Niall and Hoyt and Davis. Searching and calling and pleading, but we never saw the parrot again.

It was four years later when we had the snow on Sheila's debut. Snow ruined the pear blossoms and the auditorium had to be filled with gladioli, which always looks like a funeral, and Sheila's dress was too big and had to be sewed onto her thin little body and her father was late. He was in the middle of the negotiations that consolidated his television empire. He barely got to the auditorium on time. He came tearing in at the last minute, still tying his tie, and marched her down to the presentation platform and stayed for the first dance, then the chauffeur came and whisked him away to catch a plane back to Washington. Daniel said it turned out to be the worst night of his life. Sheila was sick and cried all the way home. Then she started the allergic attacks that lasted for weeks and ended up with the MacNieces' sending her off to Switzerland where she met the people who later would ruin her for good. No, she was ruined at birth, maimed and compromised and sent out to make do in a world where her own father didn't love her. "Leave these sad designs to him that hath more cause to be a mourner." The bard. Well, we will all have cause if she gets hold of Jessie again. If only Sheila was talented. If only she could get a part in a movie in India or somewhere where you can't take children.

The case of Sheila MacNiece versus Daniel Hand for the soul of Jessica Larkin Hand, skin like snow biscuits, velvet, alabaster, marble. Eyes as blue as the skies of Delphi, bluer than that, bluer than blue. If I had given birth to a child that lovely, I would count the whole world no loss.

Addendum: Why do men love bitches? I asked Phelan that once. We were down at the seashore, lounging around on blankets in the dunes, the surf pounding not thirty feet away, seabirds diving, no boats in sight. We were out on one of the barrier islands, happy as we could be, having sailed there in Phelan's father's ketch.

"Because they are never boring," he answered. "Boredom's the enemy, Anna, not good or evil. Just plain old staying interested. And one thing about bitches — if you can ever lay them down that hot sweet stuff will happen, there's more to love than tenderness. It has to seem like surrender, there has to be a chase."

"Is that why you hunt?"

"To escape it? No, I hunt because I like to be alone and because it's ancient and I understand it. Men worry me who don't believe they're killers. Our species kills for a living. It always has."

"Is Sheila a killer?"

"No, she's a victim and a worrywart. I don't like her *at all*, Anna. Never have."

"I know that." I leaned back on the pillow of sand beneath the blanket. Phelan was stretched out beside me, his body so fine and warm, and I guess I could have loved him if I knew how to love. If any of us knew anything about love, which for many generations we have not. What's love got to do with the Hands and Mannings and MacNieces and McLaurins and Arnolds and Clarks and Scotts? Power is all any of us know, all we have known since we arrived on these shores. If anybody in these clans knew anything about love or really valued it, they have long since been left behind and forgotten. You have to make up your mind as a tribe. You either have individuals or you have couples. You can't have it both ways no matter how long and hard the preachers and therapists and headshrinkers dream and imagine and rave.

Sick or not, it was at the debutante ball among the gladioli that Sheila met Darley Mahew and decided to have him for a beau instead of Daniel. First she danced with her father, then she danced with Daniel, then she was introduced to Darley, who had just come down for the weekend to do some fortune hunting. There she is, someone must have said to him, that skinny little tight-faced one, she's the richest girl in town if this television thing continues to catch on. So he danced with her several times and told her about Germany, where he had spent the summer, and asked if he could come to call. He was at the white brick house the next day at noon and after that he was there every afternoon. It was his introductions that got Sheila mixed up with the wrong crowd in Zurich.

On the day she left for Switzerland Sheila called up Daniel at the university and told him she was in love with Darley instead, that Darley was coming overseas to be with her. So Daniel finished the semester, then packed a small bag and went out west to be a hippie. He was gone six months, during which time Darley Mahew turned out to have feet of clay and Sheila left him with his trashy European friends and came back to Charlotte. Meanwhile Daniel had discovered LSD and married Summer Wagoner and impregnated her, although none of us, including Daniel, would know about that baby for fifteen years.

Summer Wagoner came to visit us in Charlotte and stayed a week and ran away and Sheila came home with her allergies temporarily cured and let Daniel screw her in her room beside the pool, and somewhere down inside Sheila's womb, somewhere far away from words and flights to Europe and LSD and, hopefully, safe from the chlorine in the pool and the Estée Lauder bath salts Sheila used so lavishly, Daniel's sperm found Sheila's egg and Jessie was conceived. Bud and bloom and go to seed. Branch out and blossom.

Then Daddy and Big Ed's lawyers got Daniel an annulment from the lost Summer Wagoner and Daniel and Sheila were married in the MacNieces' living room by the Presbyterian minister in exchange for a new roof for the Sunday School building. Jessie was born seven months later, three months after Olivia de Havilland Hand made her entrance into the light in Tahlequah, Oklahoma. Fifteen years later I would receive my letter from Olivia. *Dear Aunt Anna, you do not know me but I think I am your niece. I think you are the sister of my father. If it's not too much trouble could you write back to me and tell me if your brother was married to Summer Wagoner of Tahlequah, Oklahoma, in the Cherokee Nation. Yours most sincerely, et cetera, et cetera, et cetera.*

So there I was in London with my business transacted and nothing to do since Sheila had flown the coop. To hell with Sheila, I decided. I need a break from the sad designs. I walked around the rest of the day looking into shop windows and exploring the area around Queen's Square. I bought flowers for my jacket and ate an omelet in a pub and then went back to the hotel and made reservations to fly home to New York. I was staying at Durrant's, a small hotel where once I heard the poet, May Sarton, holding court in the lobby. She was describing a storm that came from the sea and swept across her New England farm and everyone within earshot had dropped their chores and come streaming in to listen. I use that incident to cheer myself on when I become disheartened at the audacity of trying to be a writer in a world of video and hype.

Daniel called that night from Charlotte. "What time is it there?" I asked.

"Two-thirty. Listen, she's filed a suit to change the custody. She's got some lawyer in Washington and he's hooked up with her daddy's lawyers in Charlotte. Joe Weil and those guys. It's going to be rough."

"What does she want?"

"Custody during the school year until Jessie is eighteen."

"Oh, shit."

"Well, Bardee says there's a chance she might get it. Unless we can get Jessie to talk to the judge and tell him she wants to stay with me."

"Will she?"

"I don't know."

"Ask her."

"Not yet. I don't want to mess her up until school is out."

"What's she doing? How is she?"

"She's a normal little girl. Her friends come over and she goes to school. She rides and plays the piano. I took them to the fair last week."

"I'm on my way home. I'll come there."

"There's nothing you can do. Look, did you find anything out?"

"No, except that she probably needs money. She was living in an awful flat so, if it's dope, it's got her, not the other way around."

"I'm sorry about that."

"So am I. Do you want me to come there?"

"Not yet. Go on back to New York. I know you have work of your own to do."

"I hope so. I hope I still know how to do it."

"You know."

"I hope so. We will see."

So I gave up on Sheila for a while and flew to Frankfurt and met Arthur at the Frankfurt Book Fair. Arthur is my publisher, also my editor, also my ally and my friend. The Europeans were crazy about me that year. I had gotten dark enough for them again and so I came home feeling smart and valuable. Arthur flew home with me and we drank martinis over Greenland and talked about the future.

"You have to think before you write, Anna," he said to me above the snowbanks. "I want to find something for you, a great story or theme. I think you go off too fast after anything you get interested in. You need to get it all planned out, then do the writing."

"Well, bullshit, Arthur," I replied. We were on our third martinis, sunk deep down in the seats, compadres of the first order after a successful trip. "I was a goddamn poet when you got me into fiction writing. I'm a poet, goddammit. One more book and I'm going back to poetry."

"You always say that."

"I do not."

"What else do you want? The world loves you, isn't that enough?"

"I never wanted the world to love me. I wanted to be a poet. Right now I want to find out what my goddamn sister-in-law has been up to. She's trying to take my niece away. She's a bitch, a terrible bitch. Don't get me thinking about it."

"Well, don't start writing about that."

"Arthur, you want to write a book, write your own goddamn book. Don't start telling me what to write."

"Well, I'll tell you one thing, Anna. Another book like *Falling Away* and you're going to start losing fans. The next one has to be better."

"I've got a lot of things on my mind. I can't spend my life glued to a typewriter. If you didn't pay me I would never write another word. I'm sick of it. Sick of the mess around publication."

"You always say that."

"I know it. I mean it, that's why. If you could see Jessie, if you knew her. She's the prettiest little girl I've ever seen in my life. She's so precious. Daniel was like that, her daddy, just precious and beautiful and sweet. She's my treasure, Arthur, I'm sorry, I can't think about literature right now. You want another martini?''

"They're bringing champagne, let's wait for that.''

"We're too old to drink like this. It's disgusting.''

"You're right.'' He lifted his glass and we giggled. Once we had been the bad boys of a certain segment of American publishing. Now we were mainstream and colleges couldn't get enough of me. Even my mother's bridge club was reading me. We drank our drinks. The stewardess served dinner. We went to sleep.

We arrived in New York City at nine in the morning. We came in to JFK and collected my baggage. Arthur was traveling with a hanging bag, a feat I admire extravagantly. We shared a taxi into town and I got off at my apartment and went inside, meaning to sleep all day. I threw my bags down on the floor, took off my clothes and climbed into my bed. Just before I fell asleep I picked up the phone and called my answering service. I had hardly been back in the city three hours and already I had to make sure I was part of the scene. "Miss Adair's been calling for three days,'' the operator said. "She wants you to go to a play tonight. Some important person wants to meet you. Miss Adair said to call her morning, noon, or night as soon as you come in. She said it was urgent. She said for me to ring every hour to see if you were home.''

"What did she say?''

"It's a play you told her to get tickets to. The costume designer's here and he wants to meet you. You better call her. She's called a dozen times.''

"I'm going to sleep. Don't ring this phone. Tell her I'll

call when I wake up." I snuggled down into the sheets thinking of Celestine pacing around her apartment waiting for me to call. Celestine Adair. Divine Celestine, the last of the great artist lovers. She had loved and known them all, helped them all. She loved me too and she had plans for me. At a more practical level she owned the movie rights to several of my books. So far she had never managed to figure out a way to make a film out of my plotless, language-burdened novels but she never stopped trying. I giggled, still half drunk from the flight. Welcome home, I told myself and fell asleep.

I woke at three in the afternoon, feeling rested, glad to be in my own bed. I snuggled deep down into my own sheets, my own blankets, my own pillows, one of which was so old it had actually been on my bed in my mother's house in Charlotte, a small down pillow from a bed I had shared with my sister Helen. I arranged it behind my head and reached out an arm and picked up the phone and called Celestine.

"What are you up to now?" I asked when she answered the phone. "I just got off the plane. What are all these messages?"

"Adrian's here, darling. Adrian Moss, who did the costumes for me all those years at Spoletto. You have to meet him. He's dying to know you. He's such a fan. We have tickets to *Nine.* Can you go?"

"If I can get my hair done. I flew in with Arthur. I think we got drunk on the plane."

"Bad girl."

"Well, I couldn't find out anything — about Sheila, I mean."

"Adrian's only here for one more day. Then he's off to Japan to do costumes for that Mike Nichols thing. Please come. Have you had any sleep?"

"Some. All right. What time?"

"Come by here at six-thirty and we'll have dinner first. Oh, I'm so glad you're back. I have so much to tell you. Shall I send a driver for you? Say six-fifteen?"

"That would help. I'll meet him in the lobby." I hung up and got out of bed, thinking about Celestine. She lived in a world so far away from anything I had known. A world of agents and museum boards, the people who make things possible for artists. Celestine made things happen. Broadway plays had been born in her living room. Movies created at her dinner table. She had conceived the idea for *Playhouse 90* on a trip to Rome. There was no resisting her and no reason to resist. If Sheila was at one end of a spectrum, Celestine was at the other. I got into the shower and began to wash my hair. Let Sheila lay for the night, I decided. Go out and get sucked into one of Celestine's scenarios. I had heard her talk of Adrian for years. The two of them had run around Italy with Coco and Schapparelli and had lived in Venice at the Gritti Palace. Fuck Sheila, I decided. Here I am, where I always dreamed of being. I have cast my lot with the gypsies and I have never regretted it either.

I fell in love with Adrian. Not love love where you take off your clothes and lie down and start to devour each other. Love where your eyes meet and your souls dance and you love every word each other says. He had read all my books and wanted to make the costumes for all the characters in all the movies Celestine would probably never find a way to make except in her head.

Adrian was the perfect artist and the perfect Englishman. He had won three Academy Awards on this side of the Atlantic and everything there was to win in Italy and England. He met me at the door quoting from my books and we nestled down into a corner sofa and talked for hours.

"What were you doing in London?" he asked at last. "Celestine said you were setting a novel there."

"Oh, no. I was looking for my sister-in-law."

"Have you lost her then?"

"I wish we could lose her, down a dark black hole. She's this terrible bitch who's ruined my brother's life. She's trying to take his child away. She's a terrible mother, a terrible person, and she's been gone for several years. Now she's back in the States trying to get the child. This gorgeous child, oh, Adrian, we're afraid she'll try to make the child into a film star. I don't know what I was trying to do over there to tell the truth. I wanted to get the goods on her. Something we could use in the custody suit."

"What is her name?"

"Sheila Hand. She married a young Rothschild for a while. Peter, the youngest one. It didn't last long. Why do you ask?"

He looked quizzical. "I think I must have met her, last year at a hunting party in Scotland. Oh, it couldn't be the one."

"What couldn't?" I sat up, put my glass down. He was shaking his head.

"Is she a small blond woman, very tailored? Wears dark green and black. She had on an enormous ring with several rubies."

"And a small face and almost no makeup and her hair very perfect and in a pageboy and nothing anyone could ever do would ever please her, that's Sheila. Where did you see her?"

"Oh, this is too much. She was with a crowd of Turks. They were off to Istanbul to some political meeting. It might be the one."

"Was she unpleasant?"

"That's the word."

"Adrian, listen, I hate this woman. Tell me everything you remember. My God, this is too much."

"It was all about politics. They were some sort of communists. The man she was with was a Cypriot. David Marchman, our host for the weekend, had invited them. It was some business thing but they showed up with four extra people and there wasn't room for everyone. It was a hunting party. We were after grouse. Anyway, they only stayed one night and everyone was quite relieved when they left. I got the impression she was in love with the Cypriot. They were on their way to Istanbul. Yes, I'm sure they were. That was several years ago. Over a year ago."

"Can you find out any of their names? The ones she was with? Could you ask the man you were visiting?"

"I'll call tomorrow morning if you like. If I can find him. No one ever knows where David is. He goes all over. I'm spending the spring and summer here. Did Celestine tell you? As soon as we're back from Japan. The rest of the film will be shot here. In New York City."

"This is too much. This is too lucky." I snuggled down into the sofa. "Oh God, Adrian. This is wonderful. If she was with communists that's all we'd need for Charlotte. A communist would definitely do the trick."

*   *   *

I called Daniel that night and told him the news. "I think we have a lead," I told him. "If it pans out we might not even have to have a trial."

"What is it?"

"She's been hanging out with communists. You know how nuts Big Ed is on that subject. If it's true we can get him to call her off. I'll have to get some proof though. He won't take our word for this."

"Can I help? What can I do to help you?"

"Nothing. Just take care of Jessie. Is she there?"

"She's right here. You want to talk to her?"

"Of course I do. Put her on." Jessie came to the phone and spoke to me. Her beautiful little voice like a violin, like a song, like a bell.

"Aunt Anna, when are you coming down here? When will you come see us? We have a new pony. She's a palomino. Dad says you like them best. We might name her Anna. We might name her for you."

"I'll come when I can. I just got home from Europe. I have to write my book now. I have so much work to do."

"You could come down here and work. We'd be quiet and let you do it here."

"I'll be there soon. As soon as I can get away."

When I hung up, I was sad again. I walked around the rooms of my apartment. What was I doing so far away from all the people I love? What was I doing so cold and lonely and alone?

Adrian called just as I was feeling sorry for myself and said he had failed to find David Marchman but that he would keep trying. "When I come back to New York we must be friends," he said. "We must have lunch once a week and go to movies. I spend afternoons seeing movies, do you do that too?"

"Not yet," I answered, "but I'm ready to learn."

During the next month I finished a draft of a book. It was the best writing experience of my life. Long mornings alone with the phone off the hook and New York City outside my windows going about its business, paying me no mind. I needed to write that winter, needed a world where dragons could be slain. It was going to be the worst book I had ever written, but the writing of it was an exotic thing. I knew all along the book would not be good but I was in a strange mood and went on writing.

Adrian returned from Japan and took me out to dinner. He had found David Marchman and David was making inquiries about Sheila. What Adrian reported was not encouraging. Sheila had pretty much ruined herself with reputable people in and around the London theater world. David Marchman remembered the Turks but couldn't recall their names. It turned out it had been Sheila he had invited up to Scotland and she had brought the others along. I reported all this to Daniel and probably drove him mad with worry. Meanwhile, Jessie turned eleven and was taking ballet lessons from our old ballet teacher in Charlotte. Miss Caroline Prince, who had taught Helen and me and all our friends and Sheila and maybe the Virgin Mary. If I heard Caroline's name I immediately sat up straight and pulled in my stomach and tucked my chin.

"How is Jessie doing as a dancer?" I asked, when I called to check on her progress.

"She is exquisite," Miss Caroline answered. "This child shall not be wasted, Anna, as you were. Her music is a gift. You must come and see her dance, you must hear her play. Have you heard her play?"

"I heard it last time I was home. It's amazing, isn't it? The things she composes."

"She dances as well as she plays. Like a spirit she moves, like a dream. When will you come home?"

"I don't know. I'm writing a book. I have to finish it first. You know how that is. I'm so happy you are there to teach her, Caroline. So happy to think of her with you."

"Oh, my darling. I am not the teacher now. I only oversee. Lily is the teacher now. My precious Lily. You must come and meet her. You must see the child dance her dance of jonquils in her yellow tutu. Yes, you must come soon. The air is wrong for you up there. It will ruin your complexion. Why does it matter where you are to write?"

"It doesn't." I laughed. "But I have to stay away from my family or I get too excited. They take up all my brain if I stay in Charlotte. So it's quieter here."

"Come at Christmas and see the recital."

"I'll try," I told her. "And I'll be home to live before too long. Not to Charlotte, perhaps, but near there, in the mountains. We'll see each other soon. I'll try to come at Christmas. I'd love to see the recital. Imagine the recital still going on."

"Stay warm, my darling," she ordered and hung up. I imagined her, her hands raised to begin the music, bringing high civilization and high art to Charlotte.

In many ways Adrian Moss reminded me of Caroline. He demanded a certain level of civilization every minute of the day. I could not imagine him taking off his shoes until it was time for bed or refusing to save a drowning man or being late for dinner. Adrian was a godsend that year but he was not an Englishman after all. For all his British manners and British ways it turned out he was Polish and even his name was an assumed one. His real name was Tadeusz Rozwadowski and he was the last surviving male of a line that included statesmen and generals and a famous writer of aphorisms. When he was fourteen years old he had walked out of Poland to escape the invading Russian army. With his twelve-year-old sister, Dubravka, and sixty gold coins wrapped in a leather purse around his waist, he had walked for five days and nights and arrived finally at an American air force base on the German border. He and his sister both spoke enough English to make themselves understood.

"My father has sent me," Adrian said to the first American soldier that he met. "I am to go to the land of freedom. Would you please assist me in any way you can."

The Americans kept them for a while, then turned them over to the International Red Cross, which sent them to England, to relatives outside of London. A cousin worked for a designer and with her help Adrian had found his way into the world of haute couture, then into costume design. He might have been a general in another world. Instead he had taken what was offered and spun it into gold. It was a hero's tale, and when I heard the story it changed him in my eyes.

"And where is Dubravka now?" I asked.

"She is married and the mother of two sons. She lives in London. She is more in contact with Poland than I am. She is also sad more than I."

"For your country?"

"She writes to them. Our parents are dead but we have kinsmen still alive and friends she remembers. She writes many letters and goes to marches in Hyde Park. She thinks she can change history. Well, perhaps she can. I am more resigned. When she gets stirred up I remember how brave she was when we left our mother. How straight and uncomplaining she was and how she walked holding my hand and never asked questions. We were in woods five days and nights. Sleeping on the forest floor like Hansel and Gretel. I kept trying to wipe off her face and brush leaves from her sweater. I wanted her to be clean when we arrived in the free countries so they would be kind to us."

"Adrian," I said. "Would you mind if I fell in love with you?"

Man attains enlightenment only in flashes. If I hadn't liked him so much perhaps I would have fallen in love with him. He would have welcomed it, I think. There were moments when we almost came near enough to admit that we desired each other, but something held me back. I think now it was a lack of courage. I was too old by then to plunge myself into a world where I would have to meet Dubravka, to be involved with the lost intellectuals of Eastern Europe. For all his gaiety and art, all the brilliance of his costumes, all his exuberance and life, the other thing was always there, waiting to cross his face at the strangest moments, a Poland he could not return to, parents he had not seen grow old and die. A stillness would come over him and I would think, He is truly disinherited. What could I offer this man to make up for that?

*   *   *

It made the problems my mother conveyed to me by phone from Charlotte seem like celluloid illusions. Little Putty didn't get into Tri-Delt or DeDe was still throwing up in Memphis or Young James was stuffing cocaine up his nose at the University of Virginia and don't send him a cent of money no matter what he says it's for. These may have seemed like huge problems in Charlotte but they were still the free choices of free men. At any moment our children could change their minds, decide to be ambitious and useful. They could repent, go to law school, study biology, resolve to save the environment, get married, have babies, settle down.

Adrian became my new best friend. He would drop by in the afternoons for tea or a drink. He disdained coffee and laughed at me for drinking it. He said it would stain my brain cells and make them weak. He said it would lead me to wear black. He wore the most beautiful colors of any man I had ever known. I remember a pair of khaki slacks and a khaki-and-white tweed sweater he would wear with a windbreaker lined with dark fir green. It sounds ordinary but there was a way the dark green lining lit up his blue eyes and the white in the tweed reflected the white in his hair. I don't think any of this was studied. I think colors made sense to him the way words do to me. We went sometimes in the afternoons to see revivals of movies he had done and he would complain about how the prints had faded and the colors bled from his costumes. Anyway, we liked each other and he fell into the habit of staying at my apartment when we had been out late to dinner or a play. We would walk in the mornings to museums or sit at a café on Madison Avenue and admire the costumes young people wear. Adrian would laugh with delight at a scarf tied around a young girl's forehead or the way a boy had laced his shoes with colored laces.

He pursued the matter of Sheila diligently but no one could remember the names of the Turks. He called David Marchman a dozen times, usually in the early morning from my phone.

"Try to find someone who remembers," he kept asking. "It's bloody important to these people. Little girl about to be taken off to bloody Cyprus or Turkey. Well, thank you. Keep trying, David. Anyone you can think to ask."

"Nothing?" I asked, when he had hung up.

"Everyone who was there agrees they were communists. She was going to marry one of them. That's what she said. They were going to Istanbul to live. David has friends all over. He's an environmentalist, you know. Has a house full of computers he runs for Greenpeace. Toting up evidence from around the world. He's quite a nice fellow. You must meet him someday."

"Let's have breakfast and walk in the park," I said. I liked having him there, in his dressing gown, talking to London at seven in the morning, water boiling on the stove, the sun lighting up the tops of the buildings, a new day, a new world.

Meanwhile, Sheila was proceeding with her suit. A lawyer called me demanding a deposition but I put him off by saying I was on my way to Europe. Then Daniel called with more news.

"She's demanding to see Jessie," he said. "She's in New York, Sister, did you know that?"

"No, where is she staying?"

"At the Pierre, so if it's drugs she's ahead this month."

"Then let her come and visit. What difference does it make?"

"Because Jessie doesn't want to see her. She's still mad at her for going off without telling us."

"Well, you can't keep her out of Charlotte. It's her home. Isn't she coming to see her mother and father?"

"I don't think so. I don't think she's talking to her father."

"Daniel. Calm down. It's okay. What can I do to help you?"

"I think I'll bring Jessie up there this weekend. She can see Sheila at your place. It might be easier for her if you're there."

"Sure. Come on up. Whenever you like."

"How about Friday night and she can see Sheila on Saturday."

"Sure. It's fine. I'd like it."

"I'll call you back. Let me make some reservations."

In thirty minutes the phone rang again. It was Jessie.

"Aunt Anna."

"Yes, my angel, my darling. You're coming up, aren't you?"

"On Friday. On flight 6778 on Delta Airlines. Are you glad?"

"Oh, yes. We'll go to a concert Sunday. The philharmonic is playing Beethoven's Second. Do you still like it?"

"I'd love to go. Listen, can we buy some clothes like we did last time?"

"Of course. At Bloomingdale's. Oh, yes, I would love to go shopping with you."

"Well, Dad wants to talk to you. Here he is."

*   *   *

Then Daniel got on the phone. "Sheila's coming to your place Saturday morning at ten. I told her she couldn't take Jessie off alone and she agreed. I think she'll try to kidnap her, Anna."

"No, she won't. We'll be there."

"Did you get the flight number?"

"Yes. Do you want me to come out to the airport?"

"No. It's too much trouble. Just check the weather if it's bad. We might be delayed."

"Come on then. I'm glad you're coming."

Friday afternoon was gloomy and wet. It was seven o'clock before the taxi pulled up in front of my building. Looking down from the fifth-floor window I saw them get out. Jessie in a red raincoat with a yellow umbrella. Looking wonderful even from the fifth floor in the rain. I walked across the room and opened the door and stood watching the elevator. Then she was there and I held her in my arms. Eleven years old and already almost as tall as I am. Long arms, long legs, long waist, milky white skin, skin like alabaster, like marble, eyes as blue as the sky. The most wonderful of all my nieces, the most beautiful and perfect. I stood in the entrance hall and held her in my arms. She shimmered and trembled and was Jessie. It was like holding a waterfall. As though your arms were full of light, and of course they were.

"You angel," I said. "You gorgeous child. Listen, it's only seven-fifteen. Bloomingdale's is open for three more hours. Let's go."

"Oh, can we?" she said. I had been joking but all of a sudden I decided it was not a joke. I turned to Daniel. "Jessie and I are going to Bloomingdale's. Drop that bag. Let's go shopping. Then we'll get something to eat.''

"Let me go to the bathroom." He laughed his old childhood Daniel laugh. "Fix me a drink for the road." I went into the kitchen and got out some ice and made him a Scotch and water in a road glass. God bless my baby brother. He was still the sweetest man in the world. He knew this was a night to be lived through. If I said, Let's drop everything and go to Bloomingdale's, he knew it was the thing to do.

By eight o'clock we were walking in the huge glass doors of the store. The crowd of shoppers was thinning but plenty of people were still there. There were two hours to shop. "Where do you want to start?" I asked Jessie. "Your wish is my command."

"I want to look at some boots," she said. "Remember that time we came here and you got me those red boots?" She had been eight years old and we had gone to Bloomingdale's to find her some rain boots.

"Sure I do, honey," I said. "Who could forget a day like that."

So we started in the shoe department and bought a pair of knee-high leather boots and a shoulder bag to match. Then we bought a pair of aqua high top tennis shoes and four pairs of colored socks.

"An hour left to go," I said. "Where do you want to go next?"

"I don't know," she said. "Let's just wander around and see what all is here. Is that okay with you, Dad?" He was following us, carrying the packages.

"Good idea," I said. "Besides, we can come back tomorrow afternoon and finish up. Let's case the joint. Let's get on the escalator and ride."

We rode an escalator that went up over the jewelry department, then rode back down and looked at the makeup and perfume. Then we rode up two floors to the girls' department and Jessie tried on a fir green blazer piped in white and a Black Watch plaid skirt and several sweaters. At a quarter to ten we went back downstairs and stopped at the candy counter. We bought white chocolate squares and wandered out onto the street, holding our packages and eating candy.

"Let's go to the Stage Deli," Daniel said. "Remember when Dad's stockbroker took us there when we were about her age?"

"Buddy Friedman," I answered. "Daddy used to say, Buddy is my Jew. They would laugh and hold their stomachs when he said it and I would die of embarrassment. His son was killed in Vietnam. His only child."

We rode in a taxi to the Stage Deli and had pastrami sandwiches and potato salad and Jessie drank hot chocolate and kept her chair very close to mine.

"What time is my mother coming tomorrow?" she asked.

"At ten. I'm glad, honey. It isn't good to never see your mother."

"She went off and didn't tell me. Grandmother Elise says she will never forgive her for that and neither should I."

"Never forgiving someone only hurts you," I said. Daniel shook his head at me, so I let it go at that. I pulled Jessie closer. I kept one arm around her while I ate.

*　　*　　*

When we got home she wanted to sleep with me and of course I let her. I slept fitfully, feeling her beside me. I would wake and reach out and touch her, touch her gown, then touch her hair. She is a miracle, I kept thinking. Nothing must ever harm her.

So I'll perjure myself if I have to. Or pay someone else to do it or whatever I have to do. Spy or gossip or lie. That's that.

About five I got out of bed and went into the kitchen and called Adrian. He answered sleepily, "Hello, hello. Adrian Moss here. Hello."

"Adrian, forgive me for calling you so early. You have to do something for me, something important."

"Of course. What do you need?"

"I need you to come over here this morning, about ten-thirty. Sheila is coming here at ten to see her little girl, my niece. My brother brought her yesterday. He really does drink quite a bit, Adrian. It's possible she might get the child. I want you to drop by very casually. Say you have to return an umbrella, no, a book. Say you brought back a book. Then she will have to confront you, whether she remembers meeting you or not. You can confront her, question her. Will you do this for me?"

"Of course. At half past ten then?"

"Yes."

"I'll be there. Are you all right, Anna?"

"I will be when this child is safe." I hung up then and went into the small kitchen and began to cook.

By nine-thirty Daniel and Jessie and I were dressed and waiting. At ten we sat down in the living room and talked about Bloomingdale's. We talked about the Black Watch plaid skirt and the blazer, about how great it would look with the boots, about whether she should have one turtleneck sweater to go with it, or two. "Two," I said. "A white one and a dark blue and a dark slip. I never will forget my first navy blue petticoat. Helen and I both had one but Helen hadn't lost her baby fat and it stuck on her waist. It was stuck on her waist like a ship aground on an island. Dearest Helen, how is she, Jessie?"

"She's okay. But DeDe is throwing up, she's anorexic, isn't she, Dad? No one can get her to stop."

"She needs to be in therapy. Daniel, please tell Helen to get her some help. You can't solve these things alone anymore." Then the doorbell rang. It was twenty minutes after ten and I went to the door and Sheila was there. She was wearing a black designer suit and very smart black shoes and black hose and silver jewelry. Her hair was short and curled around her face and she seemed prettier than I remembered. She walked past me into the apartment and ignored Daniel and turned to her child. Jessie did not get up from the chair.

"I know you're mad at me," Sheila began. "But you don't know what I've been through." Jessie looked away.

"Look at me," Sheila said. "Come over here and sit with me." She pulled Jessie up from the chair and led her over to the sofa and seated herself beside her. She held Jessie's hand. Then she began to talk about herself. About her career, about plays she was being "considered" for, about her famous titled friends, about a letter she got from the governor of Virginia, about people who had said wonderful things about her. "Don't you want to come stay in London with me?'' she said. ''Don't you want to be with me for a few years now?''

''She isn't going to live with you in London.'' Daniel got up and walked closer to the sofa. ''You aren't going to go live with her, Jessie. Don't you worry about that.''

''Let her talk, Dad,'' Jessie said. ''Please let her talk.'' She looked up at him. She was trying so hard but she didn't know what to do. How does a child litigate between her parents?

''You could come stay with me and go to Switzerland to school next year,'' Sheila was saying. ''You love Switzerland and we could get you into a school there. They have the best schools in the world. You can meet princes there, the people who run the world. I want you to know the big world now. And I want you near me. It's embarrassing for me to tell people you are over here.''

''She isn't going to school in Switzerland,'' Daniel said. ''She's a cheerleader. She's on the soccer team. She's a normal girl, Sheila. She's going to stay that way. Why are you starting this? Why start this after all these years?''

''Two years.''

''Two and a half. You left in July.''

''Oh, please don't fight about it.'' Jessie turned to her mother. ''I missed you so much. I wanted to see you.'' She was beginning to cry but Sheila didn't notice. Sheila was still looking at Daniel.

''For God's sake,'' I said. ''Goddammit, Sheila, why did you come here and start all this? Don't cry over her, Jessie. She isn't worth it. Not after what she did to you.''

''I have done nothing to anyone, Anna,'' Sheila began. The doorbell was ringing. Two short polite rings. Then another. I got up and went to the door and let Adrian in. "Oh, hello," I said, in a stage voice. "Come on in. Nice of you to drop by. My brother's here. Come and meet my brother." I took Adrian's coat and led him into the living room. Daniel was standing by the sofa glaring at Sheila. Jessie had settled into the flowered cushions. Sheila started to turn on the charm, then stopped herself. She blanched. She turned absolutely white.

"This is Adrian Moss," I began. "A friend from England. My sister-in-law, Sheila Hand, Adrian. My brother Daniel. My niece Jessie." The men shook hands. Adrian smiled at Sheila, then sat down beside her in a chair.

"Haven't we met?" he said. "Didn't we meet last winter at Baden-Baden? No, it was at David Marchman's. In Scotland at a shooting party. You were there with a Mr. Tegea, weren't you? Off to some political do?"

"Zeno Makarios," she said. "His name is Zeno. He happens to be a very important man. He's the Castro of the Mediterranean. Everyone in the Mediterranean knows him. But I wasn't with him. He was fund-raising."

"Zeno Makarios. Of course. I'm so bad about names anymore. I used to remember everyone. Well, it's amazing to run into you again. So you are Anna's sister-in-law?"

"I used to be. Daniel and I aren't married now. Don't be embarrassed. I mean, we're here. What are you doing in New York? How do you know Anna?"

"We met through friends. I worship her, don't I, darling?" He turned to me. It was a terrible charade. I wouldn't have believed a moment of it if I had been Sheila and Sheila is suspicious of the truth itself. What did she think of this?

We didn't stop, however. We went bravely on, Adrian and I, with our nutty little drama.

"Adrian keeps things here," I said. "He came to bring me back a book. Can I get you tea, Adrian? A fresh croissant? Please let me fix you one."

"Oh, lovely," he answered. "Delightful. She is always feeding me," he said to Sheila. "I beg her on my knees to marry me but she will not even answer. So you are over here to visit with the little girl?"

"I don't live with her," Jessie said. "I live with Dad. We came up here to stay with Aunt Anna because Momma wants to see me. We went shopping last night. We went to Bloomingdale's. We're going back as soon as she leaves."

"I'll go with you," Sheila said. "I'll take you shopping."

"I don't know." Jessie looked at her hands. "Aunt Anna's going to take me. I guess we'll just go."

"You don't want me along?"

"I guess you could. If you want to." Jessie was still looking down. I moved into the room. Sheila stood up.

"Well, that's it," she said. "You've turned the child against me, Daniel. You and your family. I could have guessed that would happen. I couldn't help it that I left, Jessie. They were driving me crazy. Now they're after you." She glared at the child. I had forgotten how Sheila operates. How fierce and stupid she can be. So stupid she will work against her own interests. Without the protection of her father who will protect her? Answer, no one, not even herself.

Sheila was glaring at Daniel now. "You and your family will pay for turning this child against me," she said. "You're a drunk, Daniel, and everyone knows you're a drunk. I have a dozen people who will testify that you're a drunk. You will be away from these crazy people, Jessie, and you will thank me for it when it happens. You'll be glad." She reached down and tried to kiss her but Jessie pulled away. She reached for Jessie again. I charged into the middle of it. "You bitch," I said. "You goddamn stupid bitch." I shoved Sheila out of my way and sat down on the sofa and took Jessie in my arms. Sheila walked to the door. Daniel was walking with her. Jessie was sobbing in my arms.

When she was gone Adrian sat down on the chair by the sofa. "She's right," he said, "he was called Zeno. Why did she tell me?"

"Because she doesn't know how to protect herself," I said.

"Speed," Adrian said. "Dextroamphetamine. I can always spot it." Daniel came back into the room.

"You can trust Adrian," I said to Daniel. "Talk to him. I've got to take care of Jessie." I led her into my bedroom and we lay down upon the bed and I held her and let her cry. When she fell asleep I went back into the living room. "I have to go back to Europe," I said. "I have to finish this."

"You don't need to go to Europe," Daniel said. "It's my problem. I'll go. Or I'll send a detective."

"No, you have to take her back to Charlotte and keep things normal. I can go. I don't mind. I know what to do now. I have a name."

"I can't let you go to Europe by yourself again. You're a woman, Anna. You shouldn't travel alone. I'll send Niall with you."

"I will go," Adrian put in. "Do you want me along?"

"You have to finish the film. And Daniel has to take care of Jessie and I don't want Niall. It's better if I go alone. I'll let you pay for it, Daniel. If that makes you feel better."

"It will."

"Find some sherry," Adrian said. "There's a bottle here somewhere that I bought last week. Let's have a glass of sherry."

In the afternoon we went back to Bloomingdale's and bought the blazer and two skirts and a turtleneck sweater and a hat and gloves and a muff and a short beige coat and new pajamas and a robe. We bought a silk scarf for them to take to my mother. Then we went to the Russian Tea Room and had dinner.

On Sunday we went to the concert. The music was flawless, as human life decidedly is not, and Jessie and I cried during the second movement. Afterward they packed up and I rode out to the airport with them in a limousine and put them on the plane. Then I went home and called the International desk of American Airlines and made my plans to return to Europe.

To spur me on, in case I needed spurring, Daniel called Monday afternoon from Charlotte with more bad news. "She's here," he said. "Sheila's in Charlotte. She's out at her mother's. Donna Morrow called this morning and said she was looking for a house."

"Why would she buy a house? Her father owns half of north Charlotte. Why doesn't she move into one of his empty apartment complexes he cut down all the oak trees to build?"

"She wants to be in this neighborhood. Donna called at breakfast to ask if I care if she sells her one."

"What did you say?"

"I thanked her for calling."

"Good old Donna, the last honest real estate dealer. Well, Sheila's back in Charlotte. Shit."

"What am I going to do about it?"

"Nothing. You can't do anything. Get Jessie to a shrink. That's my best advice, which I know you will not take. I don't know. I don't know what to tell you to do."

"It isn't your problem. I just wanted to fill you in."

"It is my problem. Mine as much as yours. I'm leaving for London on Wednesday. I'll come there as soon as I get back. Just hold the fort until then. Has she worn the plaid skirts and the turtleneck?"

"She wore them to school today. Thank you, Sister, thanks for doing this for me."

"It's for myself. Okay, I'm hanging up."

"Love you, Sister."

"Love you too."

I hung up and stood by the window looking down on the roofs of East Seventy-second Street. Well, Sheila was in Charlotte and that was that. Fuck Sheila coming home to fuck Jessie up and fuck the meanness of unloved rich girls with scrawny hearts and tiny fucked-up spirits and where are my assassins when I need them. I was in a terrible mood and went off to meet Adrian for lunch to talk about it. "She's so shrewd," I said. "Why are mean people so goddamn shrewd and obvious and dangerous?"

"Evil is always arrogant. It believes it is right. Heisenberg taught us that."

"I have always watched this with Sheila. It fascinates me. You can see what she is up to and you still can't stop her. It makes perfect sense, you see. She goes home to Charlotte, makes up with her folks, sets up housekeeping, starts going to church, does some good works with Big Ed's money. Then she starts inviting Jessie over for chats, then to spend the night, then weekends, then trips. How will Daniel say no? If necessary she can have an operation on her foot, just for old times sake, or get sick. Make Jessie feel guilty, make Jessie cry, pull out her old operated-on foot, stumble and fall, real or symbolically. Let Jessie help her. Take Jessie shopping, buy Jessie clothes, buy Jessie a new horse, buy Jessie a fur coat, give Jessie some jewelry. Get Jessie to testify in court that she likes her mother as much as she does her father. Take Jessie off, fuck Jessie up, break Daniel's heart, break my heart."

"Do have some more wine," Adrian said. "It does set you off, doesn't it."

Two days later I left for London.

3

I got on the plane and flew to London. Mic met me at Heathrow. She is my British agent, a beautiful and deeply intelligent woman. We had a drink and then several more and talked about our love lives or lack of them and then had to eat sandwiches in the pub because we had let all the decent restaurants close. I slept most of the next day, then went to my British publishers to see my editor, then slept the second day also. On the third day I rang up David Marchman and made an appointment to see him. What a glorious man he turned out to be. An officer of Lloyds of London and a champion of the environment unexcelled in enthusiasm. You left him reeling with figures and dire warnings and urgencies. He belongs to and supports every environmental organization in the world, whales, porpoises, trees, rivers, lakes, air, land and sea. He has spent a fortune and gone to work to make another one to lend to his causes. A tall man with curly blond hair and big violet eyes, excitement coming out of every pore. He put Zeno's name through his computers and came out with a printout of innuendos and vague assessments. Nothing very damning, a sort of international floater. As I read down the list of Zeno Makarios's activities I kept thinking I couldn't have invented

a better companion for Sheila. A joiner who never did anything for the organizations he joined, an actor, in other
words. A perfect Sheila counterpart. The one thing that did
stand out, that would surely be useful, especially in North
Carolina, was that Zeno was a member of AKEL, the communist party of Cyprus. That would do it. I could have just
taken the computer printout David handed me and flown
on back home.

"Drove me crazy not being able to remember his name,"
David was saying. "When Adrian rang up with it the whole
thing came back, you know. The old AKEL, even the other
communists stay shy of them. Well, you'll be able to track
him down now. Just fly to Istanbul and check with the embassy there. Your sister-in-law couldn't have entered the
country without there being a record. They're very careful
about all that. I say, are you at all interested in mammals?
I got the most astonishing piece of mail this morning from
a lab in Australia. Can't wait to show it to someone." He
produced a photograph of the interior of a porpoise's brain,
taken with an underwater infrared camera. It was very fuzzy
but he seemed to think it was fascinating. I nibbled the plate
of cookies he had served with the tea and we went over the
photograph with a magnifying glass for the better part of an
hour. I decided not to fall in love with him, after all. I decided there was a good chance he took notes while he made
love. "I can make you a copy of this to take back to the
States," he said. "Wouldn't surprise me if they don't have
one there yet."

"Oh, yes," I said. "That would be great." He disappeared
and returned with a copy of the photograph in a manila
envelope. Then he asked if I would like to go out to lunch
with some people from Greenpeace.

"I think I'd better get on," I said. "I want to finish this. I want to get some tickets and go on to Istanbul."

"Of course," he said. He handed me the envelope. "Good luck with this," he added. "You wouldn't want a child mixed up with any of these chaps."

At nine the next morning I was on a plane to Istanbul with five thousand dollars' worth of bribe money in different currencies. Turkish lira and gold coins and British pounds and American dollars. Mic had taken me to her bank and had them supply me with what I needed. Then she took me to the plane.

"Sure you don't want me to go with you?" she said. "I don't like you going off to Turkey alone. Have you been there?"

"No."

"It's pretty horrid. I should have brought you a tin of crackers to stick in your bag. You may not be able to eat the food."

"I can stand it for a few days."

"Call if you need me. If you get sick."

"That's optimistic."

"Turkey is not a tourist country, Anna. It is another place, another time."

She was right about that. Nothing can prepare an American for their first sight of Istanbul. The poverty, the filth, the maimed and crippled beggars. I went first to the embassy to see if they had a record of Sheila's having been there.

It was a holiday. The only person I could find to talk to was a native clerk who shuffled some papers and said there was no way to find a record that long ago. Such things couldn't go through him. I reached in my pocket and brought out a sheaf of lira. "I guess it's a lot of trouble to find old records," I said. "How much do you think it costs to look for papers, lists of persons who come in and out?" He scratched his head, took half the handful of lira, then disappeared into an anteroom. I waited, watching the sunlight filter down through the dirty cut-glass windows onto the furniture and floors. Dust was everywhere. If this was an American embassy, I wanted my tax money back. In half an hour the clerk reappeared.

"Is there an officer here?" I asked. "Is there an American official in the building?"

"Not now," the clerk said. "It will be two hundred dollars. Then we can find the record maybe."

"Maybe?"

"They are looking for it. The girl is looking." She appeared behind him. A young woman with glasses, also a native. She had a white envelope in her hand. I reached down into my purse and took out two hundred dollars and handed it over.

"You can read," the man said. "But cannot take this from here. This is confidential information. We are going to do this for you because she is your sister." He took the envelope from the girl and walked around the counter and closed the door to the hall. "It is a holiday. Religious festival. We are going to leave soon."

I took the envelope. "I need a pencil and some paper," I said. "I need to copy this."

"No," he said. "Don't make copies. Only read, please." He took the money and stood very near to me while I opened the envelope and took out a sheet of paper and read.

Sheila had come into the country in 1979 and left ten months later on British World Airlines bound for Switzerland. Three months before she ended up in Amalie Archer's flat in London and seven months before she started trying to get Jessie away from Daniel. Later I learned that she had checked into a spa near Lake Lucerne as soon as she arrived in Switzerland. I could understand that. One day in Istanbul and I was ready for a cure. There is really no describing it.

She had listed her address in Istanbul as 15 Mutlu Sokak, meaning Luck Street, in the Bursa district of the city. The embassy directed me to a stand where English-speaking drivers could be obtained for extra lira and I hired a car with one such driver and directed him to take me to Mutlu Sokak. We drove down littered streets past beggars and street vendors and hollow-eyed children. We drove for forty minutes at a snail's pace and then for forty more and came at last to a building on a corner with apartments above a plumber's shop and a small market. I had told the driver I would pay him eight hundred lira if he found the place I wanted. Now I offered him eight hundred more. "The embassy knows you are with me. They are keeping much money for me to give you when I return safely. The money I have with me is for buying information. You must help me get this information. Do you understand this? Will you help me?"

"Yes, gladly," he said. Then he laughed. "Who do you wish me to kill?"

We laughed together and my unease lifted. I decided he had decided not to rob me. We got out of the car and went together into the plumbing shop. Two men were standing beside a counter. An old man and a younger one. "Does the family of Makarios live here?" I asked, and the driver translated. The men looked at each other. Finally, the older one answered.

"What do you want with them?"

"I wish to find an American, who was here. A small blond American. I will pay much lira for news of her. To know where she has gone."

"Does she owe you money?"

"No, her mother wishes to find her."

The men looked at each other. "How much lira?" the younger one said in English.

"Very much," I said. "If you tell me anything about her. Five hundred thousand."

"Seven hundred," the young man said.

"Yes," said the father. "Seven hundred."

"Done," said I. Some children were playing outside the door. Three small dark girls and a taller boy. They were pulling a wagon. A fifth child was in the wagon. A very small thin boy with blond hair. His hair was uncombed and his clothes were rags. He was staring blandly at me. He was like a rag doll, a strange little creature. Perhaps hydrocephalic. Perhaps an albino. No, it was not albino hair. It was blond hair. Sheila. Sheila's son? My God, that thing is Jessie's brother. I looked at the baby, then looked away. I was trying to hide my excitement but the men had seen it. "It is her baby," they said. "She left it here." They looked right at me. The interpreter interpreted. "The grandmother cares for it," he added. I reached into my bag to bring out lira. I was trembling.

"Tell me," I said. "Tell them to tell me everything they know. They can have all the lira I have. A lot of lira."

The men spoke for a few minutes, then the younger man

went to the back of the shop and up the stairs. The children stood in the doorway. The blond child in the wagon had not moved or changed his expression. His head hung down on his neck. It was out of kilter, out of sync. My breath was short. I turned to the driver.

"There will be two million lira for you if you help me and get me safely back to the embassy," I said. "Two million lira to stand by me."

"You are safe," he answered. "You are not in danger here."

None of this is true, I told myself. This is some terrible coincidence. This child could come from anywhere. I am dreaming this is true, wishing this is true. No one from Charlotte could be mixed up with this child. I'm a grown woman. I write books. I fly on airplanes. I believe in man, I love my fellowman. It's too easy. It could not be true. Why would I want something horrible to be true? Bad karma, for me, for Jessie, for Daniel. Pity, Anna, please pity these people, please love this child.

A woman came down the stairs and walked toward us. An old woman of sixty or seventy. She swept past me and picked up the child and held him in her arms. He lay his head down into the hollow of her shoulder. He wrapped his arms around her neck. My breath came back. The woman stood before me. She began to talk very excitedly, directing her remarks to the interpreter.

"She says the child belongs to her," he said. "She says you have no right to come here. That you must not speak to the child. She says your friend deserted the child and now it belongs to her. She says the child belongs to her son, Zeno. She is the child's grandmother. She wants you to leave now. She says we must leave the neighborhood."

I held out my hands in a gesture of conciliation. "Tell her the child is nothing to me. Say I am not a friend of the mother's. I seek information to save another child the woman deserted. Say this is not the first child this woman has abandoned."

The interpreter talked to the woman. She was stroking the little boy, her hand went up and down the child's head and spine, the old hand caressed the child and the child lay limp against her body. She listened and nodded her head. I held out a bundle of lira and she looked at it but made no move to touch it.

"Tell her it is for the child, to help with the child. Tell her to take the money, that we will never come and bother her again. Tell her I am going away and forget the name of this street."

The interpreter talked to the woman. The men listened. The grandmother nodded and the interpreter handed the lira to her. I reached in my purse and took out the gold coins. There were ten of them. I gave one each to the men and the rest to the woman. "I wish all the information you have about this woman when she was here," I said, and the interpreter repeated it for them. "If anyone remembers anything about her come to my hotel, the Hotel Ambassador, and I will give them more gold coins for information. *Many lira.*"

The woman continued to stroke the child. She put the coins and bills in a pocket of her apron. The men moved back, they watched her. Finally, she spoke to the interpreter. "She wants you to leave now," he said. "It would be best for us to leave." I nodded and smiled at the woman. I put everything I knew of kindness into that smile, everything I knew of understanding. She only looked at me and continued to stroke the child. He lifted his head and looked into her face. He raised his hands and put them into the hollows of her cheeks. He moved his face very close to hers. I thought of all I did not know and could not bear to know. I was ashamed of being there. I wanted to give them the rest of the money but I was ashamed of that too. The woman held the child. The men began to talk among themselves. I got into the taxi, in the front seat beside the driver, and we drove away. I could not look out the windows on our ride back to the hotel. I took off my glasses so I could not see the edges. I was ashamed of everything, the poverty and terror of the world. I should have let Niall come with me, I decided. I should not have come to this place alone. If someone had been with me there would be a witness. I could go back to the hotel and talk it over.

When I got to my room I spent an hour trying to call Daniel but never succeeded in getting a call through. Finally I fell asleep propped up on the pillows of the bed. I dreamed I was in a prison break. We had taken the building. Daniel and Niall and James and I. My brothers and I and a building full of men in prison uniforms. Some of them were men I had known, friends and lovers. At first it seemed a grand thing to do, to take the tall gray buildings and hold them with guns. Then Niall began to shoot our prisoners, then Daniel shot someone. Don't shoot anyone, I kept saying. Don't use the guns. We were on a subway. The prison was a subway. Soon the doors would open and the guards would come and take us to the courts.

When I woke the phone was ringing. It was Daniel. The operator had finally gotten the call through. "What's going on?" he said. "You shouldn't be in Turkey all alone. I'm coming there. Mother will take care of Jessie. I'm coming tonight.''

"What time is it there?''

"It's twelve noon. I'm at the office. I'll find mother and get on a plane. What are you doing?''

"I found out where she's been, Daniel. I just need proof of what happened here. Don't come. It's all right. If I need you I'll call you back. Give me a day. Call me tomorrow night, noon there.''

"What did you find?''

"She had a baby and left it here. I thought at first it was deformed. Now I'm not sure. Maybe it was only dirty.''

"Jesus Christ.''

"Don't leave Jessie in that town with her and don't drink until I get there. If you want to help me, promise you won't drink.''

"What's that got to do with it?''

"At this point, everything. Will you promise?''

"I'm not drinking any more than I always do. You're nuts on that subject. Jessie's got a recital tonight, by the way. I'll tell her you called.''

"Send her some flowers for me. Not an arrangement. Roses or lilies, will you do that? Call Bobbie and tell him I said cut flowers and tell him what they're for. Not an arrangement.''

"Are you okay?''

"I'm fine. Call me tomorrow. I'm hanging up.'' We said goodbye and I hung up. I regretted telling him not to come but if I had to wait for him it might take me days to get out of this godforsaken city.

*   *   *

I ate alone in the hotel dining room that night. There were other Americans at a table in the corner and I wanted to speak to them but I could not. I have a terrible shyness around strangers in foreign countries. My life has been so complicated. I always feel I'll end up answering questions about my life. I loved a man once who could talk to anyone, anywhere, strike up conversations on planes or boats, and I grew lonely for him, wishing he were there.

If Francis had been with me he would have gone over to that table and introduced himself and told our problems to those people. They would have gone to work to help us solve them, delighted, as people always are, to lose themselves in someone else's stories.

After dinner I went up to bed and turned off the lights and fell asleep. Sometime in the night the phone rang and I picked it up and heard a man's voice. "Is this Mrs. Hand?" the voice asked. "Yes? Do not leave the hotel. Someone has information for you. If you stay there. If you do not leave." Then he hung up.

When I woke in the morning I thought I must have been dreaming again and I called the concierge to see if there had been a call for me in the middle of the night. He seemed to think it was a question that did not deserve an answer.

I dressed and paced around the room and read everything I had with me. A book of Annie Dilliard's I had read a dozen times and an old *Time* magazine and all my airplane ticket receipts. I wanted to call Daniel back or Adrian or Celestine or Mic or anyone at all, just to talk, just to be in touch with some reality outside the life of Istanbul, but I was afraid to tie up the phone line. So I waited. I made notes on a yellow legal pad and read every word of the *Time* magazine, including the masthead and the ads. Then I lay down on the bed and pretended to be meditating.

At one o'clock the phone rang. "A boy is waiting for you," the concierge said. "He said to come to the lobby." I ran out of the room, forgetting my pocketbook, then went back in and got it, and ran down the stairs, too excited to wait for an elevator.

He was standing by the desk. A boy about sixteen years old, in a white shirt and black pants. "I come from Mutlu Sokak Street," he said. "My father has papers that you want. Papers of your sister. How much will you pay for them?"

"How much does he want?"

"Two million lira. You give me the money and I will bring the papers here."

"No. I have to see the papers first."

"Okay then," he said. "No deal."

"Oh, no, I'll give you some. But not all until I have them." He leaned back against the desk. The clerks were listening.

"No, you have to give me all."

"I can't do that. How do I know there are papers?" I held out fifty or sixty dollars and the lira that I had in my purse. "Here, take this. Then bring me the papers and you can have the rest." He took the money, looked it over, put it into his pocket, then shook his head. "I don't think my father will like this. I will see." He turned away. The clerks behind the desk pretended to be busy. Then he was gone.

"He may come back," one of the clerks said. "You should wait for him."

*   *   *

It was two more days before he returned. I bought all the English magazines in town and sat in my room drinking Cokes and reading them. Wandering out every now and then into the city. It did not get any better. I could not learn to love it.

Late in the morning of the third day the boy reappeared. The concierge called me and I went down to the lobby with all the money I had left stuffed in the pockets of a linen jacket. The boy was waiting, with a small packet of letters in his hand. They were tied together with package string.

"Two million lira," he said. He held them out.

"I already paid you part of it."

"Two million. I have to make another trip in taxicab."

I gave up. I reached in my pocket and brought out the lira and counted them out. I handed them to him. He folded the notes into his wallet. "My father said not to come to our house again," he said. "It would be bad luck to come to Mutlu Sokak Street." Then he bowed to me and handed me the letters. A lovely ancient impressionistic bow. Then he turned and left the lobby.

I carried the letters up to my room and opened them and began to read. They were dated June and July, 1979. The stamps had never been canceled. The first one was to Big Ed.

Dear Daddy,
I have gotten into an awful jam. Please send someone to get me as soon as you can. I am pregnant. I am at 15 Mutlu Sokak Street in Istanbul. I am almost dead now. I don't know if I will be alive when you get this. Hurry, Daddy. Please hurry and come and get me.
                    Sheila

The second letter was dated two months later.

Dear Daddy,
I guess you didn't get my letter. It's too late now anyway. I am going to have a baby by this man who
raped me and there is nothing anyone can do. You
couldn't even find me if you get this and I don't guess
you'll get it either. I cut my leg in a hundred places. I
fell in a glass hole in the street. If you get this send
someone to Istanbul to 15 Mutlu Sokak. Daddy, this
is the worst place in the world. The windows are
rusted shut. I don't know what anyone is saying. They
used to speak English to me but they don't anymore.
My leg is very bad and now it hurts my back to move.
It is my own fault I am here. I should never have gone
away and left you. If you ever get this you will know
I loved you. You will never get it.
Your daughter,

Sheila

The third letter was to a friend in London, the director of a
theater on Queen's Square.

Dear Shannon,
Sick people everywhere, maimed and broken,
sightless, broken lights, broken doors. Now I am
maimed too. If you get this call my father in Charlotte,
North Carolina. His name is Ed MacNiece, he owns
the TV stations, anyone can find him there. He will
give you a reward to call him and tell him where I am.
Two weeks later: I can't even find a way to mail a
letter. I am pregnant and I have been injured. I
stepped through a glass tile in the sidewalk and cut

my leg, a terrible gash on the knee and lacerations everywhere. A glass brick like the ones they use to let light into buildings, only this one was cracked and I stepped on it and fell in up to my knee. Someone carried me to the hospital. They poured alcohol on my knee and then they poured Mercurochrome. When I woke up Zeno was there and took me back to his mother's. Maybe the drugs they gave me will kill the baby. I want to kill the baby. When the baby comes I will kill it, I will strangle it to death. I told his mother I would kill the baby. I never speak to anyone here.

The next week I went back to have the bandages changed and they picked the pieces of gauze off — it hurt so much — then they poured alcohol on it again. It was like having the skin burned off. Please call my father, Ed MacNiece, in Charlotte, North Carolina, if you get this.

Sheila

The rest wasn't easy but it was possible. There was a record of the child's birth at the headquarters of the Greek Orthodox Church and an official at the embassy remembered helping her leave the country. There had been some holdup because she had lost her passport. I wrote down the names of everyone I had talked to and the child's name, they had named him Georgios. Also, I interviewed several people about the activities of the communist party of Cyprus. Anorthotikon Komma Ergazomenou Laou, a political Mafia, shady even by Turkish standards. There was a chance the custody suit might end up in court and I wanted as much documentation as possible. I was talking to Daniel every day on the phone, sometimes twice a day. He was determined to come over and bring me home but I kept him at bay. "I can finish this," I told him. "You take care of Jessie. Where is Sheila now?"

"She bought a house. I guess Ed got it for her."

"I'll be home. I'll be there Wednesday."

Daniel met me at the airport and swept me up into a great Daniel bear hug and took me to his house. We settled down into huge overstuffed chairs that his last girlfriend, a decorator, had piled into his living room, great sofas and chairs that looked like gigantic animals waiting to devour anyone who came near. "We'll go to the lawyers tomorrow," Daniel said. "Tom's waiting to file suit. We'll fix it so Sheila can't take her out of town."

"Is Jessie seeing her?"

"Yes."

"What does she say about it?"

"She doesn't say a thing. She just goes over there for a while and then she calls me and I go and bring her home."

"We don't need lawyers, honey. We need to go to Big Ed and get him to call her off. You can get Tom to change the visitation rights later but let's handle Sheila through her daddy."

"I'm not sure he can control Sheila anymore. She's pretty crazy now. She acts completely nuts."

"Of course he can control her. She's still his heir, or hopes she is. The only reason she wants Jessie is to get money out of him."

"No, Sister, you don't have that right. She loves Jessie. She really wants her to live with her." He hung his big head.

He was sitting with his hands on his knees, on the edge of one of those dreadful chairs, and I thought of the long years Sheila has plagued his life and made him believe things. I don't know why I always end up thinking of Daniel as a victim. He has broken a thousand hearts. But he never lied to a woman or made promises he didn't keep. All he wanted was a woman who doesn't exist. A woman like our mother, like the image she imposed on all my brothers. Infinitely kind, infinitely sweet, infinitely forgiving and demanding. They don't make them like that anymore, et cetera.

"Daniel, Sheila doesn't love Jessie. She deserted Jessie, have you forgotten that? But she loves money. She loves money the way you love pussy. Do you still love pussy as much as you used to?"

"I don't know. It's a hell of a lot of trouble." He sat up, squared his beautiful fine shoulders, gave me a cheerful, hopeful grin. "Okay, let's go to Big Ed. I hate to tip our hand if he won't help, but what the hell. You may be right. We have to take Dad though. I can't go accost Big Ed without telling Dad first. They still have joint investments."

"Let's go, then. Big Ed can't afford to have this in his newspapers. His daddy was a bootlegger down in Union County. He can't stand to be embarrassed."

"Jesus." Daniel pushed one of his fists into the other. "How'd we come to this? Asking a man to hurt his own daughter. Goddamn, Anna."

"Let's go get Daddy. Let's get it over."

We went over to our mother's house and found Daddy watching a baseball game in the library, straddling a straight-backed chair, wearing a baseball cap. He looked better than I had seen him in months. He is always happy during baseball season, although he thinks the coaches are crazy, the calls bad, and the managers crooked.

"Anna went to Europe and found out Sheila has been running around with communists," Daniel began. "So we're going over and talk to Ed and get him to stop Sheila from filing this suit to get Jessie. Who's winning?"

"The A's are ahead. Four to two." Daddy turned off the set, removed the hat, got up from the chair, turned to face us. He looked like himself again, old powermonger ready to whip a room into shape.

"What's this? What have you been up to, Anna?"

"I haven't been up to anything. I went over there to find out what Sheila's been up to. I thought she was dealing drugs but it's worse than that. I don't even know how to tell you, it's so nuts. She ran off with a Turkish communist and had a baby and left the baby in Turkey. Two years ago. Dad, she's really crazy. She can't be allowed around Jessie. She definitely can't be allowed to take Jessie off alone."

"Is all this true, son?"

"Anna says it is. Anna wouldn't say it if it wasn't true, would you, Sister?"

"Of course not." I was getting furious. No one in the world can make me as mad as our father. All he has ever done is make me mad and give me pats on the shoulder. He hugs the boys and gives the girls pats on the shoulders. He makes all of us mad. Still, compared to Big Ed MacNiece, he's a saint. "Listen, Daddy, I just went all the way to goddamn Istanbul, Turkey. On my own money. I can't believe you'd say that. I don't spread rumors. When did I ever say anything about anyone that wasn't true? I went over there to find out what Sheila has been up to and I found out.

We're going to Big Ed and tell him what we found. Do you want to go along or not?"

"Anna." Daniel had my arm. "Save it for Ed. You want to go with us, Dad? We don't need you to. I just thought I ought to tell you before we went over there." Mother came in from her greenhouse, her hands full of roses, yellow and pink and red. She had on gardening gloves. "Oh, Anna," she said. "My darling, when did you get in?" She put the roses down upon a table covered with magazines and came over and embraced me. She is still as tall as I am although once she was taller. Her soft hair, her wonderful perfume, her garden gloves. They don't make them like that anymore, et cetera, although Daniel and Louise look exactly like her. And Jessie is also off that tall blond English tree.

I told her the story. Unlike Daddy she didn't flinch or disbelieve it. She is tougher than he is, I decided. If I told her we were going to have Sheila killed she would take it better than Daddy would. Only they didn't kill them when they went bad, did they? They had them lobotomized or zapped with electroshock or sent to live in the attic.

"Are you going over there with them?" she asked Daddy. "Well, I'll send Elise these roses then." She took them into the kitchen to wrap them up. "Poor Elise," she said over her shoulder. "She's had such a sad life. I wish there was some way to keep her from knowing."

Then Daddy called Big Ed and told him we were coming to talk to him about Sheila and the three of us went off, carrying seven hybrid roses and a jar of homemade pickle relish. Three pink Tropicanas, two Fantasias, and two yellow Freulich's Gold. The pickle relish came from the church bazaar. I'm not certain what it contained.

*   *   *

We drove up in the driveway of the white brick house and
Weedle took the car and we went inside and Elise sat us
down in the living room and took our orders for drinks.
"Let me handle this," Daddy said, when Elise left the room.
"Sister, you try to keep your mouth shut and let me handle
it." He sat on the edge of a white damask sofa and Daniel
took a seat to his right and I sank back into a black leather
armchair. Elise reappeared with a tray, a Scotch and water
for Daniel, a glass of tomato juice for Daddy, and a Diet
Coke for me. I wasn't going to drink in the morning even
if this was the place to do it. There was a small glass of
sherry left on the tray and Elise took it in her pudgy hand
and went over to the piano bench and sat down and began
to sip it. Then Big Ed came in. I had the feeling he had been
waiting in the wings, hovering somewhere. He had on a pair
of tight khaki-colored slacks with suspenders and no tie. A
strange-looking man. If I didn't know better I'd think he
was an alcoholic. So pasty and sick-looking, like a man with
a bad liver. Still, there was something there and women had
been known to like him. He had even left Elise once, gotten
a Mexican divorce, and gone off and married his secretary
for a year. When he came back to the white house there
was a wedding ceremony at the Methodist Church. Daniel
and Sheila went to it and a coin merchant who turns Daddy
and Big Ed's cash accounts into gold and the minister and
the minister's wife. What did they do? I asked Daniel when
I heard about the ceremony. They got married, he said. The
minister's wife was crying and Sheila started laughing and
couldn't stop. Was Jessie there? I wondered now. Did they
take Jessie to her grandparents' wedding?

"Okay," Big Ed said. "Shoot. Go ahead." He was still standing. "Go on. Get it out."

"Anna's been in Europe spying on Sheila," Daddy said. "I'm sorry about this, Ed. I didn't know it had come to this."

"Sit down," Ed said. "Elise, go get us some cheese and crackers. And bring some water." She got up from the piano bench. She is so pitiful she doesn't even call up pity. She is the closest thing to a true servant I have ever seen in my life, a born subject. All day long she waits on him or knits her terrible ugly afghans or cooks or bakes. When she talks she stops dead still in the middle of sentences. She stopped now. "You want ice in it?" Long pause. "I don't know if we have any cheese. We might not have it."

"No ice. Just bring some crackers then. Go on." He dismissed her and took a seat in a wing-back chair and laid his hands down on the arms. Daddy sat across from him and Daniel sat back down. I think they had forgotten me.

"Sheila's been over in Turkey with a bunch of communists, Ed. Anna thinks she lived with some communist over there."

"She had a child and left it with the grandmother," I added. "I didn't make this up, Ed. It's all true. We don't care what Sheila did or didn't do. But we care about saving Jessie. You have to tell her to stop trying to get Jessie. I know she's your daughter but you have to see . . ."

"What does this have to do with you, Anna?" Ed said. "Go write your dirty books. Daniel, you don't talk for yourself anymore? That's it?"

"I talk for myself, Ed. Anna's the one that went over there so I thought you'd want to hear it from her. I wanted to call Tom Watkins and do this in the courts. Anna's the one who wanted to keep it out of your newspapers." Daniel stood up. His face was getting red. He is Momma's spoiled baby boy and he is not for sale. He might have a business in Chapter Eleven but he wasn't taking any shit off of anybody on this or any other day.

"Calm down, son," Daddy said. Elise reappeared with a tray of crackers and cheese and set it down on a table and began to count napkins, bent over like a Russian peasant.

"What's the proof of this?" Ed demanded. "I'm supposed to take Anna's word for some cock-and-bull story about Sheila?"

"I think Anna saw the people," Daddy put in. Daniel had finished his drink and handed the glass to Elise for a refill.

"Could I have a drink too," I said, "if you're going."

"Okay, Anna," Ed said. "What's your proof of this communist story?"

"I haven't been well, Ed," I began, slipping into my old Charlotte behavior patterns. Charm and beg for mercy, then disembowel. "I went to Europe because I was upset about Sheila getting hold of Jessie again. She comes into her life and then she disappears. I wasn't spying on Sheila, Ed. I didn't want to find out all of this. But we had to know what she was doing. Daddy said you'd stopped giving her money and she had that place in Switzerland and I had to make sure she wasn't running drugs."

"Drugs," Big Ed said. "You're the one to talk. Daniel stays drunk half the time and I've never seen you turn down a drink. Sheila's got her faults but she doesn't take any drugs."

"She wouldn't take them when she had the operations," Elise put in. It was the only time she spoke all morning except to take drink orders. "She never liked to take pills."

"I didn't say she took them. I was afraid she was selling them."

"You still running around with queers?" Big Ed asked me. "Is it some bunch of queers you got all this crap from?"

"I think Anna has proof of the business about the little boy." This from Daddy. "We didn't come over here to upset you, Ed. Some of mine haven't turned out too good either, you know that, but now we all have Jessie to consider. To tell the truth we pretty much think Sheila's crazy."

"Well, what in the name of God am I supposed to do about it?" Ed walked across the room to the sideboard and poured himself a drink from a decanter. "What do you people expect me to do?" He knows all this, I decided. He knew it all before we told him. So does Elise. This is not news to them.

"Tell Sheila she can't take Jessie anywhere," Daddy said. "We're glad she comes to see her. Glad she'll be around so the little girl can know her mother. She just can't take her off. Do you think Sheila ought to be allowed to go off with Jessie? Take her out of the country?"

"No." Ed drank off his drink. "But Daniel raising her is not much better. She ought to come over here and live with Elise and me. We can keep an eye on her. She's already getting a reputation. Showing her ass all over the country club while Daniel plays golf all day. I don't like the way she's being raised."

"So you were going to get her from Sheila?" This from Daniel. He was standing now. "Well, goddamn you, you old crook. It's only out of the goodness of my heart I ever let you see her. I did it to keep peace because you and Dad started together. So you thought Sheila could get her and then you'd take over. Well, I'll tell you something, Ed. She's all I have. She's my little girl, and nobody is going to raise her but me."

"I'm sorry about all this, Ed," Daddy said. "Just as sorry as I can be."

"You ought to be sorry. If Daniel wasn't such a goof-off he and Sheila might have made it. He married her and then he went off fucking every woman he saw. You did this to yourself, Daniel. You did it by letting your dick lead you around instead of your head. I would have taken you into my business if you'd acted right. You'd be a rich man now instead of owing everybody in town. Well, I've had enough of all of you." He stood by the sideboard, old mangy lion cornered and his teeth gone. Where had I seen that before? It was Sheila, standing in my living room in her black suit, raging and threatening and pretending to have power. This wasn't power, it wasn't even evil. It was the old reptilian brain, old reptile dumbness. Evil is always dumb. How had I forgotten that? Dumb is the animal Ed represents. Big dumb cat with fur on its face. Hoarder, hitter, biter, hater of fish. Of course Sheila grew up to hate anything that lives in water. Anything that lives period, I guess. I stood across the room looking at Ed standing by the sideboard with his thin stringy hair and his back beginning to bend from a lifetime of perceiving enemies and protecting himself from the human race and I knew that no power on earth would ever put Jessie in their power. Jessie's own glory and light, which she had inherited from Daniel, would keep her safe.

Daddy moved toward Ed, feeling sorry for him now. "Go on outside," Dad said. "Wait for me in the car."

Ed pushed Daddy aside and went for Daniel again. "I'll tell you something else, Daniel. No matter what Sheila has done, it's not a patch to what I hear about you. You get something straight before you leave here. You start acting like a man. You settle down and stop carousing or I'm going after that little girl myself and when I want her you won't be sending your big sister off to Europe to spy on me." Ed was on Daniel now, his fingers digging into his arm. "I mean it. You settle down and take raising this little girl seriously. She's all Elise and I have. I don't want to hear about her associating with your lowlife girlfriends. Do you hear me?"

"They aren't lowlife, Ed. The main one I go with is Dobbins Hobart's daughter. She works for Merrill Lynch."

"Well, just remember what I told you." We all began to move toward the door. Elise scurried before us and opened it. She won't even call and tell Sheila, I decided. She'll let him do it.

Later that day I went out to Daniel's and picked up Jessie and we drove out to Summerwood and caught the horses and went riding. We rode all the way to the back of the property, past the Deadening to the pond. Jessie moved ahead of me on the old mare, Bess. Her back was as strong and supple as a birch, her neck so long and sweet rising from her spine, her little riding hat pulled down around her ears. Our Jessie, the divine end of all the mess and confusion of the genes. In any world she would be the daughter I would wish for. Now I had helped steal her from her mother. Any act creates both good and evil and comes from both. I watched as Jessie guided the mare down the path into the meadow. I watched her hands on the reins.

When it was settled I went back to New York City to live among strangers for several more years. At that time it was not possible for me to live among my kin. I do not mind suffering in my own life. I believe life is supposed to be tragic, why else would we need whiskey or need God? But things which are bearable in my life are unbearable to me in the lives of my family. I cannot bear to watch them suffer. It is a flaw of character to think I am so above them. As if I say, see, I can suffer, being tragic and brave, but you are too dumb and weak to suffer. Here, let me bear that for you. Let me haul all those crosses. I would rather carry them than worry about you not being able to. Of course it's proprietory to think like that, but I'll defend myself to this extent. I am the oldest daughter. As I once wrote, cause and effect, for whatever percent believe in that.

DE HAVILLAND
HAND

1

The creation and first sixteen years of life of Olivia de Havilland Hand, only child of Daniel DeBardeleben Hand and Summer Deer Wagoner, of Tahlequah, Oklahoma.

First there had to be a revolution and there was one. In nineteen hundred and sixty-one the young people of the United States of America looked at their parents and said, Oh, no, I cannot bear to be like that. The girls looked at their mothers in their girdles and brassieres, with their diet pills and sad martinis and permanents and hair sprays and painted fingernails and terrible frightened worried smiles and they said, There's got to be more to life than this. This is not for me. Then the boys looked at their fathers dreaming of cars and killings in the stock market and terrified of being embarrassed or poor, poor fathers with their tight collars and tight belts and ironed shirts and old suits, with their hair cut off like monks, and the boys said, I don't care how much he beats me, I won't look that way. Then the boys and girls turned on the brand-new television sets and saw images of a new president and a new time that was dawning and they said, Let's get out of here, something new has got to happen, something's got to give.

*   *   *

Then the earth moved a fraction of an inch to the left or right of its orbit and the music began to change. Singers sang of changing times, feeling good, trying new things. People began to dance sexy Negro dances. Poets appeared in Iowa and Minnesota, in Boston and New York City, in Mississippi and San Francisco and L.A. Smile faces were sewn onto the rear ends of blue jeans. Girls started burning the brassieres. Boys quit going to the boring brutal barbers. Small bags of marijuana began to circulate. Then the children stopped going to school, or else they smoked marijuana, and then they went to school. Let them bore us now, the children chuckled to themselves. Just let them try.

By nineteen sixty-six the revolution was in full swing and taking up the front pages of every newspaper in the United States. News of it had even reached Charlotte, North Carolina.

Daniel Hand was having a hard time in school anyway. Even without marijuana he kept going to sleep reading *The Pearl* and *The Lottery*. What a bunch of nuts, he would think. Why would anybody act that way? Daniel liked to read comic books or books about football or, better yet, nothing at all. He liked to do life, not read about it. Then he broke his collarbone in the first game of his last season in high school and a week later his girlfriend got sent to Switzerland to school and as soon as she was there she wrote and told him she was in love with a boy from Winston-Salem. That was it as far as Daniel was concerned. He tied his arm up in his purple sling and went down to the record store to find out where to buy some marijuana. A month later he was out in California with the hippies.

*   *   *

A year before, in Tahlequah, Oklahoma, Summer Deer Wagoner, who was two years older than Daniel, had become bored with her brothers and sisters and trying to be a Cherokee Indian in the modern world. She was bored with living in a tiny house with seven other people on the outskirts of Tahlequah. Summer Deer had known about marijuana all along. It grew wild in the Ozark Mountains and bootleggers had been harvesting it and selling it to Mexicans for as long as anyone could remember. Then some white kids at universities around the area began to smoke it and some of the more ambitious ones began to drive out to Colorado and California to sell it to richer kids at richer schools. The year Summer Deer was eighteen she was invited along on such a trip. She told her brothers and sisters goodbye and headed west in an old Buick with four of her friends. By the time Daniel arrived in Berkeley she was settled in and was well known for her common sense and her unbelievably long and beautiful black hair. She was also much admired for her promise as a poet. "The White Man Is No Man's Friend" was a poem she had written that had been printed up as a flyer and tacked to a thousand telephone poles in the area.

> *The white man is no man's friend,*
> *Even his own woman*
> *Even his own child*
> *So sorrowful, like a river*
> *Without water*

That was the whole poem. It was the only poem Summer Deer had written. The sight of it tacked up on telephone poles was very strange to her. Sometimes it made her happy to see it tacked up beside notices of meetings to stop the war or pleas to outlaw prefrontal lobotomies. Mostly, however, it made her afraid to write another poem for fear it would not be as good as the first one.

On the day Summer Deer met Daniel she was sitting on the lawn in front of Sproul Hall on the Berkeley campus. She was sitting cross-legged on a blanket breathing in the morning air and cultivating her reputation for reticence and silence. Occasionally she would reach down into a bag from the baker's and take a bite of the cinnamon roll she had bought for breakfast. Then she would go back into her stillness. Daniel did not know of Summer Deer's reputation for enjoying solitude. He thought she looked like she was lonely. He was lonely. He had been in Berkeley for three days without finding anyone to talk to for more than an hour at a time. He stopped his bicycle to admire her long black hair. Then she smiled at him. She was wearing shorts and a khaki T-shirt that said *KISS* in long drips of red paint. Underneath the letters her breasts moved and rearranged the word. Daniel returned her smile. He was a gorgeous young man with curly dark blond hair and eyes as blue as the sky. Summer Deer liked the way his hair lay against his forehead in ringlets, plastered down by the sweat he had worked up riding the bicycle to the campus from his rented room twenty blocks away. She smiled through her solitude. She smiled again.

"Hello," he said. "I'm Daniel Hand from North Carolina. I just got here. I'm looking for friends."

"You want to smoke a joint?" she asked. She lifted her head and smiled at him again. One breast moved into the angle of the *K*, the other moved into an *S*. Her hair fell across her shoulder.

"Sure," he said. "You got anything? I've got lots of money if you want to buy anything."

Six hours later they were in her room near the campus smoking Arkansas Razorbud marijuana and making love on a pallet of hand-loomed blankets. By midnight they were eating pizza and telling each other the stories of their lives. By the fall equinox they were married in a ceremony in Golden Gate Park attended by fourteen of their friends and several hundred other people they barely knew. In January, on a night when the moon was full and they weren't even stoned, they made Olivia. Neither of them had dropped acid for a week. Fog was blowing down the street and beginning to lift. The moon rode high in the January sky. Four miles away the great whales rolled against each other in the ocean. All around them the children of the revolution slept in their lumpy rented beds and sleeping bags and bedrolls. In the living room of their tiny apartment four guests from New Orleans were curled up on the floor. In the midst of that Daniel rose from his sleep and took Summer Deer into his arms and they made Olivia. Or, to be exact, Daniel contributed his sperm and the next day Summer Deer's egg began to fall. It was at ten o'clock the next morning when Olivia was actually made. Summer Deer was walking home from the market where she had gone to buy vegetables and eggs for lunch. She stopped beside a tree and put the basket down, feeling the sharp quirky pain of ovulation, and she remembered that she had forgotten to use the sponges in the night. What the hell, she told herself. She couldn't get pregnant. She had been screwing nonstop for two years and she wasn't pregnant yet. He was so sweet last night, she was thinking. He looked like a movie star doing the dishes with that yellow hair. If I go to India with the Peace Corps he'll come along. I know he will. Jesus, he's got the most money of any boy I ever shacked up with. Where does he get all that money? He doesn't even sell dope. I ought to send a picture of him to Tahlequah. They won't believe I'm shacked up with someone so good-looking.

She picked up the basket and walked on. The sun was out in full force now. The sidewalks were full of people, wearing T-shirts and sandals, wearing headbands, passing out pamphlets against the government, against the war, giving away flowers and joints and poems. It was the New World and she was here to share it.

The money was coming from Daniel's mother. No matter how many times Daniel's father told her not to, she wired Daniel money when he called. She believed him when he said he didn't have a place to sleep or enough to eat. She could not believe he would smoke or swallow or inject drugs because it was impossible for her to imagine anyone doing something she would not do. Finally, her husband found out about the money she was sending Daniel and closed her bank account. When Daniel realized the jig was up where money was concerned, he suggested to Summer Deer that they should go and visit his family in Charlotte.

"I'm really worried about all that acid we've been doing," he said. "I think we ought to stop dropping acid. People are getting too weird."

"How can we get to Charlotte? We don't even have a car."

"They'll send us money to fly. I called my father this morning. He wants to meet you. They all want to meet you. I wish you'd go. My sister Anna's there. You'll really like her. She's a lot like you. She's real liberated."

"They might not like me. I don't know about going to see a lot of society people. They don't have any society where I come from. In Tahlequah everyone is the same."

"I thought you said you were a princess or something."

"I am, because my grandfather was a chief. But I'm just a farm girl really. I grew up in the country." She stood before him with her chin up. No matter how strange he made her feel she never let it show. Still, she was falling more in love with him all the time. It was making her weak. She was falling in love with the orderly side of his nature. He cleaned up the apartment. He made a budget and stuck to it. He made up the bed and shaved and combed his hair. He brushed his teeth. He was like a movie star. He was so polite to people. People came over all the time to talk to him and tell him things. She was lucky to have him. There wasn't a girl in Berkeley who wasn't waiting to take him away from her.

"We love each other, don't we?" Daniel said. "That's all that matters." Then he pulled her into his arms and the chemistry took over.

"Okay, I'll go," she said. "If you really want to go, I'll go with you. How cold is it there?"

"It's cold this time of year but there'll be clothes there you can wear. Or Dad will buy you some. He really wants us to come home. He said not to worry about money. We could have all the money we needed if we'd come on home."

Then Daniel called his father and his father called a travel agent and the tickets were ordered. Daniel put on his shoes and walked down to the American Airlines ticket office on Telegraph Avenue and picked up the tickets. When he got back to the apartment Summer Deer was waiting for him, sitting on the floor on her prayer rug, dressed in a pair of cutoff blue jeans so old they were as soft as velvet. On top of the jeans she wore a black T-shirt that said *DEATH SUCKS* in drips of white paint. It had been made by the same T-shirt artist who made the shirt she was wearing the day Daniel met her. As long as Daniel lived, whenever he thought of Summer Deer he would think of her breasts moving around beneath the mottoes and innuendos and warnings on those T-shirts. *REGRET NOTHING* in green on green. *LIVE NOW* in orange on pink. *LONG SLOW LOVE* in blue on lavender.

"I got the tickets," he said. "The plane leaves at twelve tomorrow."

"Let's smoke a joint," she said. "Then we'll go eat."

They went up on the roof and smoked a joint and then wandered down to a coffee shop and had fruit and rolls for lunch. It would be their last lunch as part of the revolution. They sat on a little balcony watching the cloud formations as they ate. Clouds were all over the sky when they ordered their meal. By the time they finished a huge hole had appeared in the center and the sun was breaking through. Lines of blue and pink and mauve and violet and gold appeared along the edges, like ancient paintings of the skies where the gods live. Daniel's mother had a painting like that over the sideboard in the dining room. Daniel was so stoned he decided that he and Summer Deer could just step through the clouds and end up in his mother's dining room. "How wonderful to see you," Mrs. Hand would say. "Won't you please come in."

"We're going to North Carolina to see his folks," Summer Deer told a friend who stopped by the table. "Won't that be a kick?"

"You better wear a different shirt." The friend laughed. He was older than Summer Deer and Daniel.

"He thinks they aren't going to notice I'm Indian." Summer Deer laughed with the friend. "He says they're going to love me."

"They might," the friend said. "But you ought to wear a different shirt." He was a nice man, who had once been a history teacher in a girl's school in Virginia. He only meant to be helpful about the shirt but the damage was done. Now Summer Deer would definitely wear the shirt on the plane.

The Hand family was waiting at the airport. Mr. and Mrs. Hand and Daniel's older siblings, Anna and Helen, and Helen's husband, Spencer Abadie, and James and Niall. Daniel's baby sister, Louise, held her mother's hand. Always on the lookout for a threat to her domain, she was the only one who didn't smile at Summer Deer when Summer Deer moved toward them. Louise had the heart of a sergeant of arms of the Daughters of the American Revolution. She could tell at a glance this wasn't going to work. While the rest of the Hand family cooed and smiled and was gracious, Louise inspected Summer Deer's unshaved legs and T-shirt and leather vest and knew disaster could not be far away.

"Do you have luggage, son?" Mr. Hand said.

"Yeah. We have a lot of bags. We came to stay. I told you that we would."

"We're so glad," Mrs. Hand said. "We are so happy to have you here."

Summer Deer was quiet on the ride into town. Daniel kept his arm around her and the Hand family kept trying to bring her into their conversations but she pulled deeper and deeper into herself. They were in two cars. The car she was in was a Buick. Mr. Hand was driving. They turned off into a neighborhood and began to drive past bigger and bigger houses. Finally, they pulled up a driveway past gardens of wisteria and azaleas. Above the azaleas were tall delicate dogwood trees. In this season they were black leafless sculptures. Behind the gardens was a three-story Victorian house painted gray. There was a tower and porches around three sides. It was a rich house. The richest house that Summer Deer had ever been invited to. The car stopped. Daniel got out and picked up a basketball that was lying beneath an azalea bush and began to shoot the ball through a basketball hoop attached to a garage. "Look at this, Summer," he said. "My old basketball. I haven't seen it in so long."

Ten days later Summer Deer was on her way back home, hitchhiking across the country with sixty dollars in her pocket and enough rage to keep her heart from breaking. She thought she was lucky she hadn't killed anyone in Charlotte, North Carolina. The main thing she thought about was how much she had wanted to kill several people.

She caught a ride with a truck as far as Nashville, then took a Greyhound bus to Memphis. In Memphis she stopped for a few days to visit some old friends from the Ozarks. A black musician and two poets from Fayetteville, Arkansas. Summer Deer had not felt well since she left North Carolina. All the way across the country she had been sick at her stomach. She couldn't even light a cigarette without wanting to throw up. She suspected she might be pregnant but she couldn't believe it. How could such a thing happen to her? One of the poets was a scrawny little judge's daughter who had worked at a hospital when she was young. "I think you're knocked up," the poet said. "You better go and get a test."

"I'll get one when I get home," Summer Deer said. "I can get one free at the clinic." She lay her head back down on the pillow and thought about how terrible she felt. I wish I had killed some of them, she thought. I wish I'd killed his mother and maybe Helen.

That night, in an effort to cheer Summer Deer up, they went to a dilapidated movie house near the Memphis State campus to see some old movies. The first movie came on, a film starring Olivia de Havilland in a story about a woman locked up in an insane asylum. Summer Deer began to cry in the movie. She cried so hard the black musician had to take her out to the lobby and get her a drink of water. He held her in his arms. Behind them the popcorn machine popped happily away. "Go on and cry," he said. "Shed your tears."

"I guess I'm pregnant," she said. "I guess I'm really fucked."

"We thought you were," he said. "We thought you must be."

"I'll name it Olivia de Havilland," she said. "Since it's driving me crazy."

"How come you have to have it?"

"I might not. I might get fixed when I get home. There's a doctor there that will do it." She leaned into the black man's arms. His name was Willy Bugle. Six years later, when Olivia was five years old, he would make a big splash on Broadway in a musical from New Orleans. For now, though, he was only a trumpet player trying to make a living and he held Summer Deer in his arms and let her cry.

Summer Deer didn't get it fixed. She didn't even go to a doctor until she was five months pregnant. She stayed around Memphis for a few more days and went to hear the poets read their poetry in a bar and went to hear Willy play his trumpet with a band. Then she took the rest of her money and caught a bus to Tahlequah. She was so tired when she got home she slept for several days. By the time she woke up she was feeling better. Spring was coming to the Indian nation. An early spring with cold sharp rains and warm spells in the middle of the days. The rivers were filling up. I can get rid of this baby any time I want to, Summer Deer decided. All I need to do is get on a horse and ride.

"This guy's rich?" her married sister, May, asked. "Really rich?"

"Yeah, he's got all kinds of dough."

"Go on and have it then," her sister said. "You're half-way there. When you get it you can sue him for some money. You can make him send you money to take care of it."

"I might do it," Summer Deer said. "Or else I might go riding."

"You can get child care from the government, too," May said. "You could be rolling in dough."

Summer Deer thought it over. May was right. She was halfway to having the baby already. Besides, it might be a nice good-looking kid. A big blond boy, or a girl, either one. "I might take the money from the government," she said. "But I won't tell him about it. I don't want his money enough to have to talk to him." She held out the letter she had gotten from Daniel the day before. It was a letter that said his father had arranged for him to get an annulment of the marriage. "Since you won't even answer my letters," the letter said. "And since it doesn't count since we were stoned."

It was beautiful in Tahlequah that spring. Forsythia bloomed, then redbuds, then mystical white dogwoods, then wildflowers everywhere. Summer Deer went out at night with her friends and drank beer and smoked and talked about her life in California. The baby in her womb wasn't any trouble. She was so young she barely knew it was there. Her breasts grew round and full, her thighs widened, her face became as beautiful as a dogwood blossom. "You look great," her friends all told her. "You can get money from the government when it comes. You can get enough to stay at home."

"Yeah. It's okay," she answered. "It's nothing having a kid. See if Judie has a joint on him. Let's get stoned. You ought to feel it move around when I get stoned. Yeah, I'm happy with it. There's nothing to it. I don't even go to the doctor. You don't need a doctor to have a baby. My sister's going to deliver it. Yeah, it's a piece of cake."

It was a piece of cake until the end. Then, in September, Summer Deer traded in her life for the baby's. It was true what she had told her friends. She had only gone to the doctor twice. Once to make sure she was pregnant and once for a checkup. The second time the doctor was tired. He'd been up all night with a difficult delivery. He was short with Summer Deer and she decided he was a snob. She was always on the lookout for snobs. She didn't go back after that and she didn't pay the bill. She did remember the date he said the baby was due. Five days before the date she began to get impatient. She had been a good sport about the pregnancy and now she was sick of it. She wanted to get back to real life. She wanted to put on some tight jeans and go dancing. She wanted to find a boyfriend and get laid. So she began to walk. For six days she walked the hills around the house. She walked all morning and half the afternoons, up and down the hills, down to the road and back. On the sixth day her back began to hurt. All day her back drove her crazy. That night she went to bed. Her mother and grandmother and Mary Lily stood by. They called the midwife and the midwife came. The pains would begin, then they would stop. Another day went by. On the second night the midwife called a second midwife. The second midwife was very old. She knew what was wrong. The baby was upside down. She reached up inside of Summer Deer and turned the baby with her hands. Summer Deer began to scream, then she began to bleed. "We should call the doctor," Mary Lily said. "I'll call him now."

"No," the midwife said. "Give her time. It will happen now."

"Get the doctor," Summer Deer screamed. "Get some dope. Get him to bring some dope." Mary Lily went to the phone and called the hospital in Tahlequah. "I called them," she said, coming back to the bed. "They're on their way."

"We don't need them," the midwives said. "It takes its time. It's coming now."

"I want some dope," Summer Deer screamed. "Get some dope for me." A terrible pain went through her body and then another and another. Olivia moved down into the birth canal, down the small tortured pathway to the light. There were sirens in the distance now. "They're coming," Mary Lily said. "They're on their way."

Olivia's head emerged, then her shoulders, then her arms. Summer Deer stopped screaming. She was leaving now. She was leaving it for good and she regretted that. She regretted bright blue skies and rain and jazz and sun and lysergic acid and cigarettes and beer and sandals and flowers and food. She regretted rivers and trees and stars and full moons rising behind white translucent clouds on warm nights in the Ozarks. She hated leaving fucking. She had loved to fuck. She hated leaving Olivia crying in her sister's arms. It had been a good pregnancy. Up until the end it had seemed like a good thing to do.

The family gathered around the bed. Little Sun and Crow Wagoner, grandparents of the newborn child, May Frost, the married sister, Roper, the oldest son, Creek, the youngest, Mary Lily, the old maid. It was late September. The trees were gold and rust and silver and red. Maples, walnuts, sweetgum, birch and sycamore, sumac and cedar. Round bales of hay were in the fields. Small yellow flowers covered the pastures. Huge crows made their deliberate journeys from the tall white birch trees to the taller pines.

The Wagoners gathered around the bed.

"Her name will be Olivia," Mary Lily said. "Summer wrote it on a piece of paper."

"We should tell the father," Crow said. "The father should know."

"We tell no one," Little Sun said. "The child is ours. Mary Lily will care for her." He took the child from his wife's arms and handed her to his youngest daughter. "Here, Mary Lily. She is yours. She is entrusted to you."

2

The house where Olivia was born stood on five acres of land beside a creek that ran down to join the Illinois River. The land belonged to the Cherokee nation but the house was the Wagoners' and no one could make them leave as long as they wished to stay. Two miles down a gravel road was a highway. Three miles farther was the town of Tahlequah. As Olivia grew she was allowed to travel farther and farther from the house. First she could go to the edge of their property. Then she could go to the Hawkkiller place, then all the way to the highway. She would rein in her pony beside the last fencepost and watch the cars come down the winding highway going into town. She could not understand what kept them on the road. She thought it must be the Holy Spirit, but the priest said no, the Holy Spirit was too busy for cars. Cars were guided by Saint Christopher.

When she was six years old she began to walk the two miles to the highway. There a dilapidated school bus picked her up and took her to the Roman Catholic school.

"I don't want to go," she told Mary Lily. "It's boring there. You can't take off your shoes."

"You have to go," Mary Lily said. "It's the law."

"Don't tell them you have me. Say I'm gone. The bus smells bad. It smells like poison gas. We have to sit, sit, sit. I won't go anymore. I won't go there."

"Never have I seen a child talk so much," Little Sun put in. He was sitting on a straight chair watching them. "Talk, talk, talk, like a magpie. Talk all day."

"Like a jaybird," Crow agreed.

"Like a dove," Mary Lily added. "Always calling."

"Why do I have to go?" Olivia said. "I won't go after this. No more after today."

"We'll find the goats this afternoon," Mary Lily bribed. "They've been eating up the yard." She swooped the child up in her arms and tried to kiss her. "Getting so big," she said. "Too big for me to carry."

"I won't go," Olivia said. She laid her hands against Mary Lily's cheeks, a move guaranteed to get her anything she wanted. "I will stay with you and help you beat the goats."

Wild goats lived in the woods behind the Wagoners' house. They came in at night and ate the gardens and the low branches of the trees. There were also blue curved-horn sheep in a corral and three hens and a rooster. There were five fox terriers, several cats, a bee box with no bees, nine bronze turkeys in a pen, a pet deer, and four apple trees. Olivia's bedroom window looked out upon the apple trees. As long as she lived the sight of blossoming apple trees could make Olivia lonesome for the hard brown soil of Cherokee County and the timeless days when she was smelling and hearing and watching everything and was earnest and terribly momentous and sweet and hot and brave.

*   *   *

When she was six she learned to read. The nun who taught first grade at Saint Alphonsus was good at reading out loud. She made Olivia hungry for books. "I want books to read," Olivia told Mary Lily. The next weekend there was a bookshelf in her room and Mary Lily set to work going to yard sales to fill it up with books. A Girl Scout Handbook appeared, a copy of *The White Cliffs of Dover, The Best Loved Poems of the American People,* a set of five Nancy Drew murder mysteries, *The Cat in the Hat, The Cat in the Hat Comes Back, Do You Know What I'm Going to Do Next Saturday?,* a book of Cherokee history, three Bibles — the New Catholic Bible, the King James Version of the Bible, and an illustrated children's Bible. Also, a complete set of *Compton's Pictured Encyclopedia.*

One of the main reasons Olivia hated going to school was that it kept her from staying home to look at her books. Especially if it rained. On rainy days she loved to stay in bed with her books all around her and read them to herself and tell herself stories. In Volume B of the encyclopedia there was a story of a family of bears getting ready for their hibernation. She read it over and over again. Sometimes she would take the story into her grandfather's room and snuggle up beside him and beg him to tell her stories of real bears when the Cherokee hunted them. "The head of the bear was a great treasure in the old days," he would begin. "The father of my father owned three such heads. He earned the first head when he was only sixteen. He went out all alone in spring to trap his bear."

"How can I make her go to school if you fill her head with stories?" Mary Lily complained. "No wonder she pretends to be sick all the time."

"I'm sick now," Olivia would say and clutch her stomach and begin to groan. "I threw up all night long." Then her grandfather would laugh out loud and Mary Lily would go to work and leave them there.

3

When she was nine years old Olivia asked Mary Lily for a photograph of her father. She already had a photograph of her mother, a five by seven school yearbook picture taken when her mother was seventeen. "Now I must see a picture of my father," she said. "You must get me one."

"There isn't one," Mary Lily said. "There is no such thing."

"Then write to England."

"What makes you think he is in England?"

"I think so. I'm pretty sure that's where he must be. We had it in school. It's where those white cliffs are in that poem."

"He might not be in England."

"I think that's where he is. He will be coming to get me before too long. I need to know what he looks like."

That night Mary Lily discussed the conversation with her father. "Tell her what we know," he said. "Yes. Tell her."

"No," Mary Lily answered.

"If she wishes to know what he looks like, tell her what we know."

"We don't know. We never saw him. Well, there is a

photograph in the box of Summer Deer's things. Some photographs.''

"Then give them to her." Little Sun put his hand on his daughter's arm. "She wants it. She has a right to it. Let her see it."

"In a while," Mary Lily said. "After a while." When she left the room Little Sun worried about her. She was too fat for men so she had given all her love to the little girl. It was too much love for one child. The child is not like us, Little Sun told himself. She will leave us someday and then where will my daughter be. He folded his hands. There was no use to borrow trouble. Trouble would always come. In the meantime he would keep his own counsel and wait and see.

Mary Lily walked around for two days looking like she might cry. She even stayed in bed one day running a fever. The third day was Saturday. She took Olivia into her grandfather's room and opened the safe and took out the shoebox with Summer Deer's things. There were letters and a marriage certificate and an envelope with photographs. Seven snapshots made one day in Chinatown. Olivia looked at the photographs a long time. She kept returning to one of Daniel and Summer Deer together. Daniel had his arm around Summer Deer. Behind them was the great arch of the entrance to Chinatown. In the photograph Daniel was wearing cutoff blue jeans and a blue shirt. His long skinny legs stuck out beneath the jeans. A big grin was on his face. He had his arm around Summer Deer's shoulders. She was wearing white shorts and a stretched white T-shirt. She was wearing her mysterious look.

"It is very warm there, isn't it?" Olivia asked.

"It is California," Mary Lily explained.

"Is that where he is?"

"No. He's in North Carolina."

"Oh."

"Well, that's enough of that for now. Let's go out in the yard and feed the deer. I saw him peeking over the fence this morning. He's hoping you'll come and see him. He is far away from his people. If we don't pet him he might die."

"I want to keep this picture," Olivia said, holding up the one of Daniel and Summer Deer together.

"All right. Keep it then." Mary Lily gathered up the rest of the things and put them away in the shoebox and put the lid on it. Then she tied the string back around it and put it back in the unlocked safe and shut the door. Nothing was ever locked in the Wagoners' house. There was nothing they owned they thought was valuable enough to need to be secured.

The safe was always there, in her grandfather's room, and it was always open, but it was several years before Olivia decided to look at the photographs again. It was the fall she was eleven. One Saturday morning she was alone in the house. The other members of the family were in the woods gathering pecans for Thanksgiving cakes. Olivia had gone out with them early, then come back to the house. She was pulling off her sweater as she passed her grandfather's room. One arm was still in the sleeve as she came to the door. The house was very still. The smell of blackberry jelly they had made the day before was everywhere. Olivia stood in the doorway of her grandfather's room and looked at the emptiness of the bed and the chair and the space beside the window. She pulled the other arm out of her sweater and went into the room. She went over to the closet and opened the door and sat down beside the safe. She opened the safe door and took out the shoebox with her mother's things. She carried it very carefully over to the space beside the bed, below the window, where sunlight was shining on a braided rug. She put the box very carefully down upon the rug and untied the string and removed the top. She looked at the photographs for a while, setting them up around her. Then she took the papers out, one by one, and began to read.

The first paper was an elaborate marriage license with flowers all around the edges in gold and pink and blue and red. The other papers were letters.

Dear Summer,

I am sending this to Jimmy because I called him at Elsie's and he said maybe he knew someone that knew where you were. We are married in case you forgot. Please just let me know you're okay. My mom says to tell you she liked you a lot.

Love, Daniel

Dear Summer,

My dad called the Indian reservation in Oklahoma where you said you were from but they never heard of you. If Jimmy gets this to you please call me up right away. It's important.

Love, Daniel

Dear Summer,

I have gotten this girl in trouble and we have to get married pretty quick. She is the daughter of my dad's business partner. I guess you can see I have to talk to you as soon as possible. I know damn well you are getting these letters. This is mean as shit not to call me. My dad's lawyer says he can go on and get me an annulment, have the marriage declared illegal, since we were stoned. I guess I'll do that.

Love, Daniel

When she had finished all the letters Olivia folded them carefully back into their envelopes and put them in the box and put the top back on and put the box away. She kept one picture, a picture of Daniel standing beside a grove of eucalyptus trees on the Berkeley campus. Daniel, she said to herself. His name is Daniel. Daniel of North Carolina.

The sisters at the Catholic school sent out a letter to the parents saying the children should be taken to visit a public library and given a library card, so Mary Lily drove Olivia into town and introduced her to the library. It was an old Carnegie library that rose like a temple between frame buildings on either side. Olivia thought she was entering heaven to go through such wide painted doors and come into a room with so many books on shelves so high. "Can I come every Saturday?" she asked the librarian. "Is it all right to come here all the time?"

"There is a bookmobile that goes to your neighborhood," the librarian said, looking at the address on the card. "It goes to the Hitchcock store on Highway Sixty-two every Saturday at ten. Haven't you seen it there?"

"I don't know what it is," Olivia said. She looked at Mary Lily, but Mary Lily just shook her head.

"It's a bus filled with books that comes around. If you

take your card you can check out books without coming into town. You can tell them which books to bring and they will have them the next Saturday. If they're in."

"Can we go?" Olivia asked, turning to take Mary Lily's hands. "Can we go to the bus?"

"Of course you can," Mary Lily said. "We'll go next Saturday."

So Olivia's world expanded beyond Dr. Seuss and the *Compton's Pictured Encyclopedia.* Every Saturday morning she would ride a pony down the gravel road to Highway 62, tie him to the fencepost, and walk down the highway to the store. If there was plenty of money that week her aunt would give her fifty cents to buy candy at the store. She would go to the bookmobile first, climbing up into the little airless space between the books, staying all morning choosing the ones she wanted. Then she would present her card and check out four books and only then would she go to the store for her candy. Then, carrying the candy and the books in her backpack, she would hike back to the gravel road and climb on her pony and ride back to her house. "Here she comes with her books," Mary Lily would say. "I wonder what she got this week."

"See how she rides," the grandfather would say. "She rides without stirrups like an Indian should."

"She is not an Indian," Crow said. "She is a cuckoo bird."

4

"This is North Carolina," Olivia said. "This is where my father is." She was sitting on the floor, playing with a puzzle map of the United States. Mary Lily was sitting at the dining room table in a straight-backed chair. It was late in the afternoon and Mary Lily was tired. It was the year she worked at the canning factory. She had on her uniform shirt and a long black shapeless skirt. Her hair was pulled back in a bun. She had imitation jade earrings in her ears. Except for the earrings there was no adornment of Mary Lily anywhere. The work at the factory was loud and unpleasant. It was the worst job Mary Lily had ever had. When she was through for the day she came home to Olivia, to watch her do homework or read her things out of the newspaper or take her to yard sales. Mary Lily loved yard sales. She would scan the newspapers for yard sales as far away as Springdale, Arkansas, or Muskogee or Broken Arrow. Olivia would poke around among the used books while Mary Lily looked for pieces of clothing and toys and utensils for the kitchen. The puzzle map of the United States was one of Mary Lily's prize finds. She had bought it for twenty-five cents because it had a piece missing. Nebraska was missing, so Mary Lily had cut a small Nebraska from a map and glued it to a piece of cardboard.

"Where's Nebraska?" she said now. "You haven't lost it, have you?"

"How do you get to North Carolina?" Olivia said. "Could we go there in a car?"

"When you are sixteen years old we might go. Your father has another life now. He might not remember all these old things."

"I am twelve years old. He will want to know where I am. I think he is thinking about me."

"What would you say to him if you saw him?"

"I would show him my horse. I would take him to our baseball games. I bet he'd like to come to them."

"I don't see Nebraska anywhere. I think you lost Nebraska."

"No, I didn't. It's right here." Olivia put North Carolina back into its slot below Virginia and searched in the box for Nebraska. "Here it is," she said. She held up the blue Nebraska. "It's right here."

Mary Lily reached down and touched her hair.

Girls' baseball games in Tahlequah were wild events. They played on a field by the swimming pool and parents came and cheered and yelled and whistled. Olivia was a great but erratic hitter. She would swing at anything and pitchers tried to walk her at crucial points in tight games. Once or twice she had even managed to hit pitchouts and drive runners in. She was also a fast runner. Once she had hit the ball she would sprint around the bases, never looking to see where the ball was. This was Olivia's Achilles' heel in baseball, however, and she had made some devastating outs by overrunning the bases. When she was up at bat the coach would tell the girls coaching at the bases to slow her down if necessary.

Mary Lily and her married sister, May, were very proud of Olivia's baseball prowess and never missed a game. May would bring her children and they would sit in the stands eating homemade fudge and yell and scream and cheer.

Still, the ball games often made Olivia sad. If she had made a good play or hit a home run she longed for a father to slap her on the back and say well done. She watched other girls going off with their fathers after games and thought, He didn't see that and I might never be able to do it again. "Cut it out of the paper," she told Mary Lily, whenever there was a mention in the *Tahlequah Bugle* of the scores of the games. "Someone might want to see it someday."

An English teacher inadvertently led Olivia to find her father. The English teacher was young. It was her first year teaching high school and she was very eager and worked hard to find new things for the students to read. She was teaching Olivia's class out of an anthology that included a story by Olivia's aunt, Anna Hand. A story about a young girl whose mother was a drunk. The teacher was worried that the story might be too sophisticated for sophomores in high school but she was wrong. The students understood the story better than she did. There was hardly a boy or girl in the class whose life had not been touched by alcoholism.

Olivia read the story several times. Then she looked in the back to find the biography of the author. "Anna Hand," the biography said. "Born in 1942, in Charlotte, North Carolina. The oldest of six children, Ms. Hand's stories often deal with the trials and tribulations of family life."

The next day Olivia waited after class to talk to her teacher. "This lady has the same name as I do," she said. "I would like to write to her. How do you write to a writer?"

"Let's see," the teacher said. "There should be a copyright acknowledgment in the back. Oh, here it is. See, this is the name of her publisher. We can go to the library and find out the address and write her there. I'm so glad you want to write the author. That's wonderful. I used to do that sometimes."

"She's kin to me," Olivia said. "She has to be. She will know how to find my dad."

5

As soon as she had the address of the publisher Olivia went to the public library and took out all of Anna Hand's books. She took them home and read them as fast as she could, skipping from one book to the other. Then she sat down and wrote the first of the letters that would lead to her becoming a liar and cheat. All she needed was a box of stationery, a pen, and a few blank report cards from Tahlequah High.

Dear Mrs. Hand,

I think I am your niece. If you have a brother named Daniel. My mother was named Summer Deer Wagoner and she was married to Daniel Hand in 1967 in California. I have their marriage certificate. I have read all your books they have in our library and I think they are wonderful. I am enclosing a photograph of myself. If you have a brother Daniel tell him I am writing to him too. Here is my address if you would like to write me back. Please write back to me.

Yours most sincerely,

Olivia D. H. Hand

P.S. It is hard for me to write this letter. I am afraid it might startle you like a snake in the grass. I am not a snake in the grass. I am a very nice girl. I am fifteen. I'm a cheerleader and I make straight A's. I think you would be proud to be related to me.

Dear Mr. Hand,

I hope this won't come as too big a surprise to you. I think you are my father. If you were married to Summer Deer Wagoner. If you are the Daniel Hand on the marriage certificate to my mother then you are my father. If so, I am dying to see you and know you.

My mother died when I was born and my grandfather said I could write to you when I was sixteen years old. I am fifteen and I can't wait any longer. I am enclosing a photograph of myself and a copy of my grades for the last six weeks so you can see I am not someone you would be ashamed to know. I don't want anything from you. I just want you to know I'm here and maybe sometime in the future let me see you.

> Yours most truly,
> Olivia De Havilland
> Hand, age 15
> Birth date, September
> 21, 1968

Dear Aunt Anna,

I can't believe you wrote back to me. I came home from school and the letter was propped up on the salt and pepper shakers waiting for me on the table. I almost fainted I was so excited. I can't believe you are my aunt. I told my English teacher today and she said she can't believe it either. Listen, I'll have to write to you again and tell you everything I am thinking about. But for now I want you to know that I got the letter and I love it so much.

I am sorry it is cold there and you are having a hard time living in the city. I think it would be hard for me too. I was in Kansas City once and I have been in Tulsa many times. It is not good to have that much noise morning, noon and night. Maybe you should go to the Metropolitan Museum of Art and look at the paintings. I have this book about a girl who went there to live when she ran away from home. They didn't find her for months. To tell the truth everything I know about New York I know from books. I bet it's not as bad as you think. You ought to see Tahlequah. Talk about dead. You could die of boredom here in the winter. But it's always beautiful here the rest of the year.

I'll write more later.

> Love,
> Your Niece, Olivia

Dear Father,

I cannot tell you how much it meant to me to hear from you. If there is any way you could come here to see me sometime it would mean a great deal to me. Here are my newest grades. Glad you liked the other ones.

> Love,
> Olivia

Dear Aunt Anna,

I'm sorry it won't work out for me to come up there and visit you but I think you are right. It will be better if you come here and see me and see what my life is like. It might give you something to write about. We have a museum with the history of our people in it. Of course, it is only half my history. I guess you could call me a halfbreed, couldn't you? Well, it turned out all right for Cher, didn't it? So I guess it can turn out all right for me. Especially with you writing to me.

I love you,
Your Niece, Olivia

Dear Aunt Anna,

It's sooooo boring on a Sunday afternoon in Tahlequah. It's boring all the time but especially on Sunday. We went to Kansas City on a bus to see the art museum. There was a show there from Washington, D.C. I was thinking of you constantly while I was there. I kept thinking I bet she would like this or that. There was a picture called *The Girl in the Red Hat*. I kept thinking this means more than just that. It was about something you could never forget once you saw the expression on the girl's face. She is waiting for something, I told myself. Something is going to happen.

We are going to study the pictures in class next week and talk about them. We didn't get home until twelve last night and Aunt Mary Lily had to come down to the school to get me. I didn't get to sleep until two. I guess going to the city Friday and Saturday makes Sunday especially bad for me.

Have you talked to Dad lately? I have written to him twice but he only wrote me back once. I guess he's pretty busy this time of year with his business and everything. I guess Christmas is about to come to New York City, isn't it? Don't take that for a hint to mean I want a present. You have already given me the greatest present of my life by writing to me. Your loving (not so bored now) niece.

Olivia

Dear Father,

Of course I understand why you can't come now. I bet it's really hard running a business in this day and age. Don't worry about me. I am doing fine as you can see from my grade report. I guess you could say I am a book worm. Well, I guess that runs in the Hand family. Anyway, I love having you write to me and I'll be here when you get time to come and see me.

Your loving daughter,
Olivia

P.S. Here is my new school picture. It's pretty silly. I always end up clowning around when they take them. Could you send me one of you if you have one and if you have time?

Those were the letters that were mailed. There were other letters that were not mailed, letters Olivia knew better than to mail but could not throw away. She kept them in the bottom of her cedar chest, underneath the hand-loomed blankets that had come down to her from her mother.

Dear Father,

My friend, Bobby Tree, and his father took me deer hunting yesterday. I wonder if you hunt deer there. I had a rifle of my own to take with me. A Winchester that belonged to my uncle when he was my age. He was my uncle that was killed on a motorcycle. I am a good shot and can hit five bottles in a row when my grandfather sets them up on a post for me.

I got the first deer. I guess you can't imagine me killing a deer, especially without a license. We don't pay much attention to licenses here. It's our land, all the land we have left after you kept North Carolina. I guess you know the whole state of North Carolina belonged to the Cherokee nation until they were sent out on the Trail of Tears. Half of them died on that. The ones that lived are here. Well, back to the hunt, I was in a blind with Bobby. It was a bad blind because his father had taken the best one. They really wanted the deer. They wanted it to eat. You don't know anything about that if you are rich and live in a city. I'm not saying there is anything wrong with that. Look, I was drinking beer with them last night and I'm in a pretty strange mood for me today.

The deer I shot was an old buck with beautiful antlers. They are going to clean the antlers for me and Grandfather will mount them for my room. I am putting off what happened when we cut into the deer. It felt like it wasn't dead yet, the stomach and blood got all over our hands and the entrails, the intestines, spilled out. I didn't care. It was no different than killing a bird or anything you need to eat. It is a kinder death than getting old as the hills like my grandfather and barely able to hear and no one pays any attention to you anymore. Father, I would like to be there with you when you get old and help you if you need it but if you keep treating me like this then you will be alone when you are old and I won't know you.

The deer lay on the colored leaves, green and red and orange and yellow, all wet on the forest floor, and silver clouds moved across the sky and the sun could not be seen. It was very still and no birds sang. They had flown from death. The deer I killed lay on the forest floor and we cut it open and mutilated it. I was Cherokee then and no kin to you and I thought of you and hated you. I hated Aunt Anna too for writing to me and getting my hopes up but never coming to see me. She said one time she would send me a ticket to New York City to visit her but she broke her promise. She said she was sick. She said she would make up for it by coming here but she hasn't done it.

The meat is in the freezer now. Part of it is in the freezer behind Mr. Tree's trailer and part of it is downtown in a freezer for Grandmother and Granddaddy and Aunt Mary Lily and me. The blood was everywhere. It was on my boots and on the leaves of the forest floor. I was the killer and the bringer of food to people. I could stay here and marry Bobby and never see you. I could give up my hopes of education and go on and forget your bad blood inside of me. I could go on and be a Cherokee but your bad blood won't let me.

I think I'll go sleep in the woods alone tonight. I might spend the night where the deer fell and build a small fire or maybe not have a fire to warm me. There isn't a thing out there that can hurt me. The things that hurt me are people. I am very young to know so much about the world but I have only had old people around me all my life so what do you expect me to do?

Your daughter, Olivia

Dear Father,

I have fallen in love with a boy but not really in love. Only I think about him all the time now. I think he must look like you did when you were young. Because he is strong and can ride better than anyone in Oklahoma his age and can calf rope better than the men. He lives in a trailer with his dad because his mom is dead and there isn't a woman to take care of them and make them a home. The trailer is in a trailer park two blocks from our school and is nice like a neighborhood. It has been there since the Second World War. They call it Jones Park. I was over there the other night and helped them cook hamburgers for supper and then we sat around and talked about everything. I told them about North Carolina and that you are coming to see me soon. Aunt Anna said she would come soon. She wrote to me five times this year but I have told you that. Now I have to go. I was going to tell you my dream but I will not. This is silly. Well, you will never see it anyway.

Dear Aunt Anna,

I think I am in love with a boy. The boy I have been going with. He took me to Kayo's room on Running Deer and we went in and lay down on the bed and I almost let him do anything to me, then I remembered my mother and how she ended up. I don't think I'll ever be able to let anyone do that to me. Stick it in and maybe kill me. I don't have anyone to talk to. If I told Aunt Mary Lily this she'd kill me. I am so different from the girls here. None of them read anything but the paper or movie magazines and the rich girls are snotty to me. I liked the books you sent me. Especially the one about Mahatma Gandhi. I have read it twice and am reading it again. I also like *The Little Prince,* although I guess that's a children's book. I have seen the desert. We drove to New Mexico to see some friends of my aunt's. They live on the side of a red mountain. In the afternoons it was so beautiful, everything would turn purple. This purple light was on everything. Anything that was white was turned purple. The man we were visiting is a painter. He and his wife asked us to come back but we never have. Maybe you would like to go there with me someday.

Say hello to Dad for me and tell him I'm waiting to get to know him. I am still making all A's. Well, I won't mail this. It's too mixed up. It's stupid but I liked writing it.

Dear Dad,

This morning I went riding at dawn. It was drizzling rain by the time I had gone two miles. The hills behind me were full of mist. It is beginning to be spring here, my favorite time of year. I need to see you so much. My heart is bursting with the things I want to say to you. I am a very nice girl and everyone loves me. I have brown hair. I don't look much like an Indian. I would never embarrass you. I know I will never mail this letter so I can go on and tell you my dream.

We were in a canoe together, on a wide river like the Arkansas below Lee Creek. We were together in the canoe and I was all dressed up in my new green suit Aunt Mary Lily bought me. I had on high-heeled shoes and a beautiful white blouse with lace down the front. I looked so nice and you were taking me to meet my cousins and water was all around us. Finally, we came to a curve in the river and I slid out of the boat and got into the water and I was pulling the boat along. I still had my shoes on. Somehow they did not fall off into the water when I swam. I was sorry I had gotten all messed up but in a way I didn't care, because I looked behind me and there you were, smiling at me as if it didn't matter that I was all wet. We were going somewhere together, maybe to visit my mother's grave, but I doubt that. I think we were just riding along in the canoe, watching the trees. Birch trees were all around us, yellow and green and white, and the light came down between the branches and you were smiling at me.

When I woke up I was weeping. I was crying like a baby from that dream. Please come to see me or let me come there. Is that too much to ask?

6

It was Mary Lily who supplied Olivia with the report-card forms on which she was creating the straight-A student the Hands were becoming interested in. Anna Hand thought she had finally found a child who had inherited her genes for language. Daniel Hand thought he had miraculously fathered a child who was smart in school. He couldn't help being excited by the prospect of a child who did well in school. Daniel had been kicked out of three preparatory schools and had never even been able to finish the University of North Carolina. He never finished college because he was spoiled and indulged and drank too much but he thought it was because he was dumb. With the marvelous intuition of the young, Olivia had found the perfect way to make the Hand family think they needed her.

Mary Lily didn't mind giving Olivia the first handful of report-card forms. Olivia was with her at the office of the high school, where Mary Lily had a Saturday job cleaning the offices. The forms were sitting on a shelf with many others. "Can I have these?" Olivia asked. "I'll just take a few."

"Okay," Mary Lily said. "Just a few."

*   *   *

By the time Olivia needed more forms Mary Lily had caught on to what she was up to. Olivia talked so much that sooner or later she told everyone around her everything she knew. "I need some more report-card forms," she said one afternoon. She and Mary Lily were sitting at the kitchen table eating a sack of doughnuts Mary Lily had picked up on her way home from work. "Will you get me some on Saturday?"

"No. I won't do it anymore."

"He's a rich man. If he thinks I'm worth it, he'll send me to college."

"No. We won't do it anymore. We won't take things."

"They're only pieces of paper. They aren't worth anything. It isn't stealing."

"It's stealing. It's a sin."

"Rich people steal things all the time. They stole North Carolina from the Cherokee. I only need two more. Two or three. That's all."

"No. I won't do it."

"Then I'll do it. I'll go in Saturday and help you clean. I'll take them. Then you won't have to tell the priest."

"No. I won't do it."

"Please, Aunt Mary Lily. It's so important. It's my future. All you have to do is take me with you."

"I don't know. I don't think it's good." Mary Lily stuffed the remainder of a doughnut in her mouth, thinking of the trouble it could make. She could lose her job, Olivia could get caught, she would have to tell the priest. She chewed the doughnut. Olivia watched her with pleading eyes. Mary Lily began to change her mind, persuaded by the sugar and the loss of North Carolina, not to mention North America. "I'll let you go with me," she said. "But only take one. One or two. You're going to get in trouble doing this."

"No, I'm not. I just want them to send us some money."

So, the following Saturday Olivia went with Mary Lily to the office and took a handful of report-card forms and began to think about the computer. I could change the grades on the computer, she decided. They would never know the difference. They have so much to do they probably wouldn't even know I did it. They couldn't prove it even if they found out. I make good grades. All I'm changing is the math. By the time they find out I'll be in North Carolina being rich.

Olivia kept the blank forms in a cedar chest with the un-mailed letters. It was a chest Mary Lily had bought at a fair when Olivia was a baby. It opened on brass piano hinges and had a brass pole to hold the top open. The outside had been sanded and shellacked but the inside was unfinished and smelled like the woods in winter, when snow is on the ground and the creek is frozen to a trickle. Mary Lily kept Summer Deer's possessions in the chest. Three quilts, a brown leather vest with silver fittings and fringe (the vest had hung down to the tops of Summer Deer's boots when she wore it with no shirt and no brassiere in the heat of summer in San Francisco), a small red velvet box that contained three pieces of jewelry. A small gold watch Summer Deer had bought at a pawn shop in Tahlequah, a golden chain with glass beads, and a thick gold wedding ring with writing inside. *DH to SW, 1967,* then a peace sign. Olivia would put on the necklace and the watch and the ring and look at herself in the mirror, then take them off and put them back in the box and replace them underneath the quilts.

There were other things in the chest. A black dancing dress, a pair of ballet shoes, a cheerleader sweater with a dark red T intersected by a warbonnet, a notebook from a biology class, and a history textbook with five names on the first page.

7

It was several weeks before Mary Lily had time to go to confession and talk to the priest about the report-card forms. "She took some more of them," Mary Lily said. "I'm sure she did."

"She shouldn't have left Saint Alphonsus. I wish you had been able to stand firm."

"I couldn't help it. She doesn't listen. She says she can't go to college if she didn't change. She wants to go to college. It's all she thinks about."

"Is she still seeing that boy?"

"He's a good boy. She doesn't love him. She doesn't love anyone but herself. She's like her mother was. Like our father, cold."

"You are doing a good job, Mary Lily. You're doing what you can."

"I'll make her put them back. I'll do it tomorrow."

"Good. You're a good woman."

"Do I have a penance?"

"Oh, yes, five Hail Marys and ten Our Fathers. Bless you, my child. Good child." He slid the window shut and listened to her shuffling around pulling herself together. Shook his head. *The things they thought of as sin. They should have been in Chicago. Father, forgive us. Dear people, such dear people, I do not deserve to be here with these dear people. I don't deserve this easy job.*

Mary Lily went home full of resolve. She called Olivia into the kitchen and told her she had to give back the grade-report forms. "Tomorrow I will put them back where they belong. Then it's over."

"I'm not doing anything wrong," Olivia said. "I'm just making sure I can go to college."

"You could go to college. There's a college here. Anybody can go to Northeastern. You get loans. You can go."

"I want to go to another school, somewhere I've never been."

"What did you do with them?"

"I put them away. There were hundreds in the box. They'll never miss a few."

"It's stealing."

"No, it's what I have to do." Olivia stood in front of Mary Lily and looked her in the eye. "I want to go up there and see them. I want to know who I am."

"They don't want to know you. If they wanted to they would have come to see you. Just because they write to you doesn't mean they want you up there."

"They will come. Wait and see." Olivia left the kitchen and walked out across the backyard and into the barn. She took a bridle from a peg and climbed the fence to the corral where two old mares were standing flank to flank against the fence. "Come on," she said. "You, Chaney, it won't hurt you to get some exercise." She slipped the bridle on the mare's head and carefully adjusted the bit in its teeth. Then she led the horse into the yard and pulled herself up onto its back. "Okay, I know your teeth hurt. I won't use it if you don't make me. Come on, let's go to Baron Ford. You know the way." She led the horse, half by the bridle and half by its mane, out of the yard and down the gravel road in the opposite direction of the highway. The gravel turned to dirt, then led back across a meadow to Baron Ford Ranch where Olivia had worked as a groom one summer. As soon as the mare sensed the direction, she shivered with excitement and began to run. Olivia moved her heels down under the mare's body and lay down against her neck and forgot lost fathers and Mary Lily's sad disapproving face. "Let's go," she whispered to Chaney. "You are a yearling. Take me to the king."

Of course, she wasn't going to a king, although Baron Ford Ranch was as close to a palace as anything in northeast Oklahoma, two thousand acres of pastureland and woods, with a forty-room mansion and an absentee landlord and air-conditioned stables for the horses. It employed two full-time grooms and five stable boys and the weekend services of a landscape architect and a forest ranger. One of the stable boys was a young man named Bobby Tree, whose ancestors were Assiniboin hunters and Italian immigrants. In another world he might have been a baseball player or a rugby star but he had grown up in a trailer park in Tahlequah, Oklahoma, so he had learned to calf rope and barrel race instead. Bobby was so good with horses that the grown men at Baron Ford deferred to him. The chief groom, Kayo, was his uncle. He let Bobby have the run of the place just for the pleasure of watching him grow up. If there was such a thing as a prince in a world this poor, Bobby Tree was a prince. He had things just about the way he wanted them.

Except for being in love with Olivia Hand. No one had things the way they wanted them with her. She walked around Tahlequah High School as if she owned the place. Bobby had seen her first when she was a freshman and he was a senior and he had been in love with her ever since. He had been in an upstairs window of the school and seen her get out of her aunt's car and come walking up the sidewalk to the front door, walking as if she was twenty years old, as if nobody was even around, as if she didn't care if anyone liked her or not. She always looked to Bobby as if she was thinking about something else. Even when he managed to get introduced to her, even when he took her to a rodeo and won three events with her watching, even when he managed finally after seven months to get her onto a bed and make her come, after all of that she still acted as if she didn't care if he called her up or not. All she ever talked about was whether or not she would get pregnant and how he had to pay for the abortion. With every girl in Tahlequah in love with him he had had to go and fall for this snooty little kid, Olivia. "All she talks about is her rich relatives in North Carolina," he said to Kayo. "I get sick of hearing it."

"Maybe you aren't doing it right," Kayo said. "If it don't make her want you."

"It isn't that. She just goes off and forgets it. She's calling the shots on me, that's how it is. She always says she's studying. Then she comes over here."

"Well, that's women," Kayo had answered. "Stick to horses is my advice."

Bobby Tree was sitting on a fence talking to Kayo when Olivia came riding up. "Here she comes," Kayo said. "Hold on to your heart."

"Hello, princess," Bobby said. "Long time no see." She reined the horse up to the fence.

"I started to jump her but I was afraid to do it. She's got bad teeth. You can't even use the rein."

"You ought to shoot her," Kayo said. "Or turn her out. She's too old to ride."

"She likes me to ride her as long as I stay away from her teeth."

"Well, come on," Bobby said. "I'll get you a real horse."

"Can I leave her here? You got anything in this pasture?"

"Nothing that would do her any harm. You want to see Solomon go through his paces?"

"No, I just want to ride. There're two hours of daylight. You want to ride with me?"

"If Kayo says I can. Can we take off, boss?"

"Sure, go on. But get the horses back by dark." Olivia dismounted and took the saddle and bridle off Chaney and she and Bobby walked toward the stables.

"So what you been doing?" Bobby said. "I been missing you."

"I've been taking care of my future. I'm trying to get my dad to come and see me."

"That's still going on? Well, he'll show up. I know he will. You want to ride the Arabians? They need a workout."

"Sure. Let's do it." They walked down the open space between the stalls and found the Arabians and began to saddle them, calling to each other from stall to stall.

"He'll come see you. He'll go crazy when he sees how nice you are."

"Yeah, he might. I don't even care anymore. I just want to make sure he pays for my college." She tightened the cinch on the saddle and led the Arabian out of the stall. He was prancing, getting itchy. She could hear Bobby behind her. Now they would go riding. Now they would ride. "Don't talk about it," she said. "Let's get out of here."

"Where do you want to go?" he asked. "You want to go to the place on the river?" He was beside her now, shoving open the gate. She moved in front of him, keeping a short rein on the gelding, as the horse was jittery from being kept in a stall. "Sure," she said. "Let's go. I've been missing you too." She allowed the horse to prance, then gave him his rein and let him run. The great muscles stretched out beneath her thighs.

Kayo watched them from the office door. "Hot stuff," he said to his assistant. "Shit, I'd give anything to be that age again."

Olivia led the way for a while, back across the meadow and down into a pasture of winter wheat. Bobby was behind her, reining in, letting her get in front of him. When she stopped at the far side of the field he turned his horse loose and rode to her side. "You lead now," she said. "I don't know the turns of the path." He moved out in front of her and led his horse to the entrance to the woods. A bridle path opened before them, a path Bobby had groomed the week before. He had spent five days cutting the low branches and digging roots and making a manicured path that the owner of Baron Ford would probably never even see. The whole time he was working Bobby had thought of Olivia riding there. "I cleared this," he called back over his shoulder, and she nodded her head but didn't seem to hear. "I cleared this goddamn path," he called again. "I worked my ass off. Say you think it looks great."

"It looks great," she called back. "I knew you did it. It looks like you."

He stopped beneath an oak tree. "What do you mean, it looks like me? What's that supposed to mean?"

"It looks nice, like you did it right." She moved nearer to him. The flanks of their horses touched. He leaned out of the saddle and kissed her on the mouth. "There're some things I want to do to you," he said. "Goddamn, I think about you all the time. Do you know that?"

"I know. Okay," she added. "Let's go do it then. If I get knocked up you have to pay for the abortion."

"If you get knocked up I will."

They rode through the woods until the path came out at the bottom of a hill that led upward to where a modern house stood on a rise overlooking the river. It wasn't the main house. It was a river house so the owner of Baron Ford could see the sunset on the river in case he ever came to Tahlequah and got tired of staying in the main house. Bobby had made himself a key from one Kayo had lent him when he helped out cutting bushes on the lawn. He had it on a key ring in his pocket.

They rode around to the river side and tied the horses to a hitching post near the boat dock. Then they walked up the steps to the house.

"You'll get fired if they catch us," Olivia said.

"They won't catch us. Kayo knows where we've gone. He won't let me get in trouble."

"Does he know we do it?"

"He knows I'm in love with you." He kept on walking, not looking at her as he spoke.

"Why are you in love with me? I don't give you anything you need."

"Yes, you do. You give me everything."

"I don't give you anything. I'm just selfish. I only think about myself."

"You're fine. You're the one I want. The only one I want." They were at the top of the stairs now, on a wide wooden patio that looked down across acres of deserted land and a winding fork of the Illinois River. The patio was furnished with wooden settees with yellow cushions. Bobby picked up a cushion from a settee and shook the leaves from it and put it back down upon the wooden stand. He wasn't sure where to start. You never knew what to do with Olivia. You never knew where you stood. She might say one thing and do another. She might change her mind. I could pick her up and break her in two, he thought. I could fuck her anytime I wanted to, but she's not scared of me. Well, she doesn't need to be. She's got the pussy and she calls the shots, just like Kayo said. As long as they have the pussy they get to tell us what to do. He hung his head, looked down at the river, waited to see if she'd make a move.

"How come he never comes down here anymore?" she asked. "Why does this just sit here?"

"He's in Chicago doing business. He's a nice guy. He can ride like a son-of-a-bitch when he has time. You ought to see him ride. He's a good guy. He's going to start a polo team. He's sending us some polo ponies."

"Well, I'd live here if it was mine. I'd have a helicopter and come here and spend the night."

"You want to go inside?"

"Not yet. I think I'll stay out here." She walked over to a railing, inspected some moss that was growing up in a groove on a railing board. Bobby walked to her, touched her arm, the skin of her arm made his throat tight, made him tremble. "Oh, baby," he said. "I think about you all the time." She turned around to him then and let him take her into his arms. "Uh huh," she said. "Oh, yes. Yes indeed."

He took her hand, led her toward the door. They went into the high-ceilinged glass-walled room and moved across the fine blue rugs and found a bedroom and a bed and sat down upon the edge and Bobby began to undo her blouse. Olivia didn't care about any of it now. Didn't care if he wore a rubber. Didn't care if they got caught. Didn't give a damn about a thing in the world but having him inside her and keeping him there.

"Take your clothes off," she said.

"You take them off."

"Okay. I will." Then they made love on the blue silk coverlet of the bed and on the floor and on a straight-backed desk chair. They made love with awkwardness and seriousness and hot young murderous desire. They made love until the sun had left the sky and the blue and lavender lights of evening had completely faded and the moon was riding eastward through the clouds.

"When was your period?" he said. "Are we in trouble?"

"No. It's okay. If I didn't think it was okay I wouldn't have done it. I'm not crazy, you know."

"You ought to go to Planned Parenthood. I've had enough of this. This is Russian roulette. I don't want you getting pregnant. I don't want some doctor cutting on you."

"Okay." She lay back against the blue linen sheets. Stretched her hands across the fine damask-covered down pillows, moved her legs against his own.

"Okay what? Okay, you'll go?"

"Yeah, I'll go."

"When will you go?"

"I'll go tomorrow. I've been meaning to."

"You want me to go with you?"

"No. It's okay. Frieda will go with me. She used to work there. She had a job there last year."

"You're sure?"

"Yeah. I'm sure." She sat up and began to put her clothes back on. He sat across the room from her, smoking a cigarette. His legs were trembling. She always did that to him. She was the strangest girl he had ever known. She never called him up. Sometimes she wouldn't even talk to him when he called. She acted as if she was twenty-five years old. When she wanted him she came and got him.

Olivia watched him. She loved it when he trembled. He was beautiful, sitting in the dark room, smoking and looking at her. He's so pretty, she was thinking. I can't help wanting to do it with him. I can't help it because he's so good-looking and so tough and he never makes mistakes with the horses.

Outside, the Arabians were neighing, stamping their hooves. They had been making unhappy noises for half an hour but Olivia and Bobby hadn't heard them.

"They want to go," Bobby said.

"Yeah, they're tired of being tied up. We'd better go."

"Yeah, I guess we had."

They walked down together to where the horses were tied. The moon was moving through a line of cirrus clouds. The moon was very full. "It's a perfect night," Bobby said. "Everything's always perfect with you."

"You just think that. I didn't make the moon."

"Maybe you did. I might not know it was there if you weren't here. I might be playing cards or something, shooting pool."

"You shouldn't waste so much time. You ought to go back to school."

"I don't like school. I don't like to be inside." He was close beside her. Their arms touched as they walked. Nothing they said mattered now. Now words didn't matter. For a while words could not harm or part them. The smell of the river was in the air, moonlight and river and honeysuckle and pine trees, night smells and sounds and the beautiful Arabian horses, stamping and waiting to be ridden.

They untied the horses and walked them to the path, then mounted and rode through the woods. The trees cast elaborate shadows on the ground. The horses were subdued by the moonlight, cautious and quiet, remembering panthers and coyotes and bears. Olivia and Bobby were quiet also. They came to the pasture and galloped the rest of the way to the stables. Then Bobby unsaddled the horses and led them into their stalls.

"Horses shouldn't be penned up," Olivia said. "If I was rich I'd buy this place and turn all the horses loose."

"No one knows what they would do if they get rich. I had a friend who married a rich girl in Tulsa. He went crazy being rich."

"Who was that?"

"A guy I played ball with in high school. He married Ellie Baumgarten. They own a lot of land in Tulsa."

"I don't need to get rich. I just want to get out of here and get somewhere where something's happening."

"Things happen here. Things happened tonight."

"Yeah, I know. I better not get knocked up, that's all I can say."

"You're going to go to Planned Parenthood, aren't you? You said you would."

"I'm going tomorrow. Or Monday. I'll call Frieda and go on Monday."

An hour later Bobby delivered Olivia to her door. They had left Chaney in a pasture and he had driven her home. "You going to be in trouble?" he asked.

"Not if I was with you. They think you're the hottest thing since sliced bread. Well, it was great." She took his arm and they walked toward the steps to the kitchen. "I'll come over and get Chaney this weekend. I might come tomorrow."

"I'll take care of her. I'll put her in a barn."

"Well, it's been great. Thanks for letting me ride the Arabian."

"I hope those guys come see you. Your dad and your aunt and all of them. Shit, I can't imagine they don't want to know you. You're the greatest."

"Well, you think so anyway."

"Olivia." It was Mary Lily standing in the door in her bathrobe. "You and Bobby come on in here. It's ten o'clock at night."

"I got to go," Bobby said, and backed down the path. "Hi, Mary Lily. Thanks for letting her go riding. She's a hotshot. She's a pistol."

"Hi, Bobby," Mary Lily said, and held open the door. Olivia climbed the wooden stairs and went on in. "I rode an Arabian," she said to her aunt. "They're really something. Listen, they're going to get some polo ponies. Mr. Shibuta's starting a polo team.''

"What have you and Bobby been doing all this time?" Mary Lily folded her hands into her nightgown, searched Olivia's face.

"Nothing. We went riding. Then we had to groom the horses. Well, I'm dead. I'm going to bed. I'm about to fall asleep standing here."

8

The next day was Saturday. Olivia woke up thinking about Bobby. She pulled her knees up to her stomach and rubbed her hips with her hands. She was getting horny again just thinking about it. I guess I'll go back over there today and get Chaney, she decided. I guess we might as well make a weekend of it. I couldn't get pregnant four days after I stopped bleeding. I don't care if I do. If I do we'll go to Tulsa and get an abortion. He's making plenty of money. We could do it.

She wriggled deeper down into the covers, thinking of sitting across his lap on the chair, doing it. That was great, she decided, that was the greatest of all. Well, I'm getting up. Goddamn, I'm starving.

She got out of bed, pulled on a flannel bathrobe and a pair of socks, and padded into the kitchen to find something to eat. She stuck two pieces of bread into the toaster and began to cut an orange. The phone was ringing. That's him, she decided. He probably woke up horny too."

It was a woman's voice on the phone, a voice Olivia had never heard. "Olivia," the voice said. "Is that you?"

"It's me. Who's this?"

"I'm your Aunt Anna. The one you've been writing to.

146

I want to come and see you tomorrow. I can't wait another day. Will that be all right? Could someone meet me in Tulsa? Is Tulsa near there?"

"Oh, yes," Olivia said. "We'll come. I can't believe it's you."

"I should have come months ago. I made a reservation on a plane for tomorrow. Is your grandmother there? Is there someone I should talk to? Oh, my darling child, I'm dying to meet you."

"Oh, God. Wait a minute. I don't believe this. You're coming here?"

"As fast as I can get there if you'll let me. There isn't anything to worry about. We'll love each other. I don't care who you are, what you look like. I am coming there so we can know each other. If you'll let me."

"Of course I will. We can come to Tulsa. We go up there all the time. We can come whenever you want us to."

"Tomorrow afternoon. Look, is there someone else I need to talk to? Is your aunt there? I guess I ought to ask her, don't you think so?" The voice was so sweet, so kind, so gentle. There was nothing to fear from it and Olivia wasn't fearful. The voice was right. There was nothing to fear.

Then Mary Lily got on the phone and took down the details and later that day Olivia drove into town and bought a dress to wear to meet the plane, a thin white cotton dress with lavender and green flowers.

"It costs too much," Mary Lily said. "You don't need that dress to meet her."

"Yes I do. And I want you to get dressed up too. We have to make a good impression."

"I don't have anything to wear but my own clothes."

"You've got that gray suit you had for when the arch-bishop came."

"I don't know if it still fits me."

"Please wear it. Please do this for me." Olivia moved in close. Put her hands on her aunt's face. That had never failed to get her her way and it did not fail now. Mary Lily found her gray suit and Olivia shook it out and inspected it and the next morning, after neither of them had had a bit of sleep, they got dressed and drove to Tulsa and waited for the plane.

Then Olivia's father's sister Anna got off the plane and took Olivia in her arms and hugged Mary Lily and began to talk very fast, being so charming, so vastly, endlessly charming, that even Mary Lily began to soften up and unbend. Every time Mary Lily would stiffen up and get scared, Olivia's Aunt Anna would pour on the charm. The charm she ex-uded was real. She was terribly glad to be there. She was charmed and excited and thrilled to be in Tulsa, Oklahoma, claiming her niece.

"I want to know everything," she said. "I want to know everything I've missed."

"There's not much to know," Olivia said. "I wrote you all about myself."

"I should have come months ago. I should have come the day I got a letter."

Then the three of them got into Mary Lily's old Pontiac and started driving back to Tahlequah. They were sitting together in the front seat. Every now and then Anna's hand would reach for Olivia's hand and touch it. She's here, Olivia thought. My famous aunt. But she's old, a lot older than I thought she would be. She's as old as Kayo. I wonder how old she is. I better not ask.

"I can't believe I'm here," Anna said. "I can't believe it took me so long to come."

"Is my dad coming? Is he coming too?"

"I don't know, honey. If he doesn't I'll take you there. Will you go with me to Charlotte?" Mary Lily speeded up at that, began to drive the Pontiac at breakneck speed down the two-lane highway leading from Tulsa to the Indian nation.

The next day Olivia stayed home from school and took Anna driving around the country. She took her to downtown Tahlequah to see the Indian museum and out to the replica of the Indian village and to the Methodist camp on the river and drove her around the outskirts of Baron Ford Ranch. "They're going to have a polo team," she said. "This friend of mine is going to be on it. I guess he'll be the star."

"Is he your boyfriend?"

"No. I don't want any boyfriends. I just want to go to college and get out of here. Do you think my dad is coming down and meet me? Or not?"

"He'll come. He's just afraid, Olivia. Men aren't as brave as women are. Haven't you noticed that?"

"The men I know are brave. The ones I know aren't afraid to see their own kids."

"He'll come," Anna said. "And when he does I hope he'll beg you to forgive him."

"I don't want him to beg me for anything. I'm not mad at him. I'm just tired of waiting." They were standing beside a creekbed near the ranch. Olivia bent over and picked up a flat smooth rock. She held it out in the palm of her hand. Anna watched her in a kind of wonder. Everything she did seemed charged with meaning, purpose, intent. She was a strange girl, half child, half woman, half mystery, half light. Water and light, Anna knew. Starcarbon, that's all we are. Olivia broke the spell. She sailed the rock out across the creekbed and scared a crow up from its perch on a tree.

The waiting wasn't over either. It was February before Daniel invited Olivia to visit North Carolina. It was an awkward, unsettling meeting and Olivia was relieved when it was over. Then, as soon as she was home, she began to dream of going to North Carolina to live. She wrote to Anna of her plans and called her several times to talk for hours in hushed hopeful terms. Anna was her support in her dealings with the Hands. Then, in November, without saying goodbye to anyone, in secret and with great haste, Anna took her own life. Knowing it would harm other people and Olivia among them, she died as she had lived, alone and in her own way, without giving a damn who liked it or what happened next.

When she learned of Anna's death, Olivia got on a plane and flew to Charlotte and stayed several weeks. In their grief the Hands grabbed hold of her and thought they loved her. Whether they needed her or not, now they would not let her go. When she returned to Tahlequah it had been decided she would come to Charlotte and go to school with Jessie.

It was a terrible decision, a stupid destructive thing to do. To take her away from a place which had nurtured and protected her and transplant her to a world that would never really accept her and which she would never understand or be able to love.

Still, there was no stopping her once the Hands told her she could come. She was tired of Tahlequah. She wanted some excitement and she wanted to be rich.

There was one problem. Now a transcript of her grades would be sent to Charlotte.

9

"I have to fix those grades," Olivia told Bobby, as soon as it was settled that she was going to Charlotte to live. "I have to do it before they send my records. Will you help me?"

"What do we have to do?"

"We have to change the computer."

"Goddamn, Olivia. We could go to jail for that."

"For changing some grades on a high-school computer? There's nothing to it. Anyone could break into Tahlequah High. They don't even have a guard at night."

"Why don't you just tell them the truth?"

"Are you kidding? Well, if you won't help I'll do it myself."

"I didn't say I wouldn't help. Why can't you do it when your aunt goes in to work? You told me once you were going to do that."

"She won't let me. She doesn't want me to leave here."

"Neither do I. That's another thing. Why should I help you leave me?"

"Well, will you? Will you or not?"

"Okay, I will."

*   *   *

The following night they went over to the high school and jimmied a window and climbed in and Bobby held the flashlight while Olivia keyed into the computer and changed her grades. At first she made all the grades into A's, then she thought better of it and changed a few math grades to B's. When she had figured out a transcript that satisfied most of the lies she had told the Hands, she turned off the computer and she and Bobby locked the window behind them and went out through the gym door.

"Piece of cake," she said, when they were back in the car. "I won't forget you did this, Bobby. When you want a favor you can come to me."

"Next time ask me something hard," he said. "Like what I'm supposed to do with this thing in my trousers."

"I know what to do with that," she said. "But you better have a rubber."

Then it was time for her to leave. On a Saturday in the early morning Bobby came to tell her goodbye. It was so early mist was still on the ground. Silver half-frozen water closed in around the house, covered the swing beneath the oak, muffled every sound. Olivia stood in the doorway looking out on the mist and waiting. When Bobby drove up she ran down the stairs and got into the car and gave him a crazy jerky kiss.

"How you doing?" he asked.

"I'm okay. Let's get out of here."

"Where you want to go?"

"I don't care. Go to the lake. I wouldn't mind going to the lake."

They drove across the Arkansas line to Lake Wedington and sat in the car and watched the mist settle onto the water and kept on watching until it lifted.

"Well, I guess this is it," Bobby said.

"Yeah. I guess so. I'll be coming back to see everyone." She sat with her hands on her legs, desiring him, but fighting it. *I guess I'd get knocked up,* she decided. *That would be about my luck. I'd be knocked up in North Carolina where I don't know how to get an abortion.*

A wind was blowing the leaves of the oaks, the scarce yellow leaves of the walnuts. A few leaves had blown onto the surface of the lake and floated there.

"You won't come back," he said.

"Yes, I will." The wind was picking up, blowing the fog and the leaves across the water.

"I'll write to you."

"Good. I want you to." He reached for her but she wouldn't let him kiss her. It was over. She was leaving now. Leaving the woods and the lake and Bobby and the smell of saddles and Camel cigarettes. *It will be real clean where I am going,* she thought. *The cars will be clean and smell like Aunt Anna and her perfume. I'm going to get me some of that perfume. I guess you have to go to New York City to get it.*

"We're going to Switzerland in the summer," she said, unfolding her hands, spreading them out on her knees. "They all go there all the time. To Europe and Paris and Switzerland."

"Ray Faubus went with his band," Bobby said. "He said the food was terrible. He said he couldn't get anything to eat he liked." He paused. "Well, I guess you'll be in better places than Ray was." He pulled out a pack of cigarettes, rolled down the window, lit one. The wind was really blowing now, bending the branches. Bobby started the motor and drove back to town.

10

The first month she was in Charlotte Olivia was too busy to think about Tahlequah. Her mind raced through the days, cataloging people, trying to find out who to be. At the private school where she was enrolled she pretended to be a brainy eccentric who couldn't settle down. At home she pretended to be a loving sister to Jessie, an awestruck grandchild to her grandparents, an interested listener to her aunts and uncles and cousins and their friends. For a couple of weeks it was a pretty convincing performance and almost convinced Olivia herself. Then the blackbirds in her head started singing. Bullshit, bullshit, they came singing. What is all this bullshit? What are these people talking about? Who do they think they are? I can't stand these boring bullshit dinners. I wish they would stop asking me how I feel. I wish Dad would let us go somewhere at night. I wish they had a polo team.

Bobby had written her that Mr. Shibuta, the owner, had come back to Baron Ford to live and was building a new barn for his polo ponies. He had hired the whole Tahlequah football team to come out to the place and learn to play polo against him so he could practice. A rival team was starting over in Arkansas and everyone in Tahlequah was looking forward to the summer when the teams could play against each other. "I guess I'll be the star," Bobby wrote. "It's easy as shit if you know how to barrel race. All you got to do is swing a club at a ball and not fall off. What a deal. He's giving me a raise just to fool around with him while he practices. We might go down to New Orleans this summer and play some teams down there. Well, I miss you, baby. I sure could use some loving."

By the time a month had gone by Olivia had taken to spending as much time as she could in the country, at the Hands' country place. At least out in the country she could think. At least out there no one was around to ask her how she was feeling all the time. At least out there she didn't have to think about how lost she was in all her science classes and in math.

Olivia stood by a tall black fence, watching her father's horses. There were mares with colts in a pasture. In another were yearlings and a two-year-old her father had said was her own. "He was born on Shakespeare's birthday," Daniel said. "You should like that since you are our scholar. Born down in the woods. You can have him. He's all yours."

"Can I break him?" Olivia had asked.

"Sure, if you want to. No, on second thought, of course you can't break a horse. It's too dangerous. We'll get some-one to do it."

"I know how. There's nothing to it. It just takes time."

"Well, go ahead then. Do it if you want to. I'll come out and help."

That conversation had been a week ago. Now Olivia stood by the fence watching the two-year-old and thinking over all her lies. Well, maybe she could break him. Maybe she'd get killed and it would save her the trouble of going to jail, or wherever they were going to send her when they found out about the grades.

If I could figure out the math it would be all right, she decided. But I can't try harder than I already am. What else could I do? I could kill myself. Or I could get a lawyer and make them keep me. They can't just kick me out. It would be too embarrassing for them. I could go on and tell Dad the truth but I can't. He's too nervous. I can't tell him anything.

She climbed down from the fence and walked toward the two-year-old, watching him as she walked, feeling in her pocket for the sugar he had come to expect.

"Come on, Sugar," she said out loud. "Come and get your sugar, Sugar." He raised his head and looked at her, shook his neck, opened his nostrils. He could smell it. He trotted toward her. "You beauty," she said. "You gorgeous boy. Come to de Havilland Hand, your master." She crooned to him, hiding the sugar behind her back. Then held it out for him to eat.

"I'm here now," she told him. "I might as well enjoy it while I can." It was true. She was there, right where she had dreamed of being. Being petted and indulged, going to the finest school in town where the girls talked continually of things she didn't understand and people and places she had never known. In this world there was more of everything than anyone could use, more clothes, more houses, more money, more horses than anyone could ride. She was here and everyone liked her and was amused by her and at any moment it could end.

She pulled the colt's neck toward her own, rubbing his

backbone so he would be accustomed to weight when she moved her body onto his. I really will break him, she decided. The black boys will help me. It will make up for never getting laid. Jesus, there's no one here to do it with. I wouldn't do it with any of these dumb boys for any amount of money. There's always King. He might not always be in love with Jessie. They might break up. He likes me too. I've seen him look at me.

"Olivia." It was Jessie, calling from the fence. "What are you doing? Dad wants us to go to town with him. Come on in. Dad's waiting for you."

Olivia allowed the horse to go. Turned her back to him and faced her sister, stuck her hands in her pockets and waited.

"Don't turn your back on him," Jessie called, scrambling over the fence. "He's wild as anything. Olivia, come on. You might get hurt." Jessie was hurrying toward her, long blond hair blowing in the wind. "They kept me there until five o'clock. I'm so dumb. I'll never figure out algebra as long as I live. I don't care anyway. Get out of here, Sugar." She clapped her hands in the air to spook him and continued walking toward Olivia. "Mrs. Guest loves you. All she can talk about is you. She said I ought to let you go to school for both of us, since you like it so much. Well, Dad's waiting on us. He wants to go to town to see something at the bank. Some art show one of his girlfriends did. I don't know which one." Olivia watched her sister. What a baby, she was thinking. What babies they are, every one of them. "I'm coming," she said. "I'm going to break this colt in the summer. As soon as I can."

"You can't do it this summer. We're going to Switzerland to live on the lake. Don't you remember? You said you'd go. You're going, aren't you? I'm not going if you don't."

"Switzerland," Olivia said. "Oh, sure, Switzerland. I'd forgotten about that."

They walked across the pasture to the house their great-grandfather had built when the place was a working farm. This land belonged to the Cherokee before it belonged to the Hands, Olivia was thinking. White people stole North Carolina from the Cherokee, then sent them off to die. They can't throw me away. I have more right to be here than they do.

Daniel stood in the doorway watching them. His child by Sheila he had fought so hard to keep, and this strange powerful girl he had left in the womb of Summer Deer so long ago in California. He had them both now, one by the defection of her mother through death and the other by her mother's stupidity and evil. They were his, his reasons to get up every morning and go out and face the assholes of the world. "Come on," he said. "We've got to get to town. Come on in and wash your faces and hands and don't start changing clothes because we have to go."

They climbed into the Mitsubishi and headed into town. It was Daniel's hunting truck and was filled with guns and shells and orange vests and camping paraphernalia.

"Where are we going?" Olivia asked.

"To the bank to see Doreen's paintings. She's got a show and I promised her I'd bring you."

"Doreen's the one with the long hair?"

"Yes."

"She's a buyer for Montaldo's," Jessie put in. "That's where she gets all those clothes."

"We're going to the lake first," Daniel said. "I want to show you something."

"It's the turkeys," Jessie said. "He always shows us the turkeys."

"Well, you need to look at something besides yourself." Daniel shifted into low gear and began to drive across a field toward the scrub woods on the back of the property. He had been cultivating wild turkeys for six years now and the flocks were everywhere. He drove slowly down across the pasture and stopped and got out to open the gate. Olivia jumped down from the other side to close it for him. She climbed back in and they drove farther down into the scrub and stopped beside a lake surrounded by cottonwood trees. A beautiful still lake fed by springs that joined an aquifer that led all the way to the mountains. No one had ever cultivated this part of the property or used it for a thing until Daniel decided to raise turkeys on it. Not to eat and not even to hunt really but because he was growing older and was tired of flying around the world getting drunk with people he barely knew and spending money he had to fuck with assholes to replace.

"Here," he said, and pulled two pair of army surplus binoculars out of a knapsack. "Get these adjusted so you'll be ready when we see them. They're used to the truck. But don't talk. They spook if they hear voices." He handed a pair of binoculars to each girl and waited while they adjusted the lens.

"What time is Doreen's show?" Jessie asked. "We'll be late."

"Hush up, honey," he said. "I'm taking care of that." He began to drive the truck across a narrow dam in the middle of the lake. The truck was so wide and the dam so narrow that the wheels were almost in the water on both sides as they inched their way across. They arrived on the other side and Daniel put the truck into low gear and pulled up a hill and came to a stop beneath a cottonwood. "Look there," he said. "There they are." He reached up and turned Olivia's glasses in the direction of the turkeys. There were about thirty of them, fat and beautifully colored, their amazingly small heads bobbing back and forth on their stringy necks. They were eating seeds, moving as a wave across a narrow stretch of field to the east of the lake.

"That's the fescue," Daniel said. "They love it."

Olivia watched them move, two and three as one, a family, she thought, they are a family, as I dreamed we would be. Behind the binoculars she felt her eyes fill with tears. Tears began to fall down her face onto her blouse and vest and hands. Terrible motherless, fatherless tears. "Oh, please," Jessie said. "Don't cry. There's no reason to cry."

"It's just so beautiful," Olivia said. "Everything is so beautiful here."

The next morning Daniel called his sister Helen and told her about the crying incident and asked what he should do. "She started crying for no reason," he said. "We were looking at the turkeys. I took them out to see the turkeys. There wasn't a thing to cry about."

"Did you drive across that low water dam?"

"Of course. What's that got to do with a little girl bursting into tears while she's looking at a flock of turkeys."

"Because it's dangerous and you shouldn't have driven over there with those girls in the truck. I've driven with you, Daniel, remember that. It might have scared her and she was too embarrassed to say so."

"Look, Helen, she wasn't crying about driving across the dam. She's the bravest kid I ever saw in my life. She rides the horses bareback."

"Well, we need to get her into therapy. She's had too many shocks too fast, Daniel. Anna dying and Daddy driving them home. Coming here to live. It's very traumatic to change schools in the middle of the year. I don't think Lynley's recovered yet from when we did that to him. I told you not to do that. How's she doing in school?"

"She's doing fine. They're having some trouble getting her records from that place in Oklahoma. Aside from that they're all crazy about her."

"I'll come over this afternoon and see about it, talk to her. Will you be at home?"

"Sure. Come after five. We'll be there."

"I'll see you then."

"Thanks, Sister." Daniel hung up the phone and began to straighten the pencils and miniature tractors on his desk. Good, Helen would come over. Helen would sort it out. Women crying. He shook his head, lined five pencils up in a row and took a miniature DC-8 and pushed them into a neat stack and carried them over and set them up beside a desk calendar his mother had given him for Christmas. Then he called his salesmen in and went to work.

11

Back at Tahlequah High School a ninth-grade music-appreciation teacher named Mrs. Walker was pondering a problem. She had taught Olivia music appreciation and had directed her in the chorus of a play. Like everyone else at Tahlequah High, Mrs. Walker had been delighted when she heard the girl was going to North Carolina to live with her father. The problem Mrs. Walker was pondering had to do with a piece of paper she had noticed on the new secretary's desk. It was a copy of Olivia's transcript. Mrs. Walker had glanced at it out of curiosity and noticed that Olivia was credited with an A in music appreciation. Mrs. Walker almost never gave A's. She was very stingy with A's as she had received her degree from Indiana University and had very high standards where Music was concerned. She was certain she had not given Olivia an A.

There were A's in almost everything. There were not many straight-A students at Tahlequah High. The only straight-A student Mrs. Walker could think of was a Jewish boy whose father was a lawyer. Mrs. Walker walked around thinking about the transcript for several days. She was not a person to rush into things. Finally, she sought out the freshman-sophomore mathematics teacher during a break and asked him some questions.

"Do you remember Olivia Hand when she was here? The girl who went to North Carolina at the beginning of the term?"

"Sure. Nice kid."

"Was she a good student for you?"

"Good enough. Average. I don't know if she learned anything. I don't think I teach ninety percent of them a damn thing they will remember."

"She didn't make A's?"

"Oh, God, no. She barely passed."

"Well, thank you."

"Why do you ask?"

"Nothing. No reason. I was just thinking about her the other day. She was in that production of *The Music Man* we did. Did you see it?"

"I'm afraid not. We don't go out at night much. I'm sorry."

"No reason to be." Mrs. Walker put her tray on the revolving dumbwaiter, shook her head. Her aunt works in the office, she remembered. Oh, I hate to get involved with this. I hate to start something like this. It might not be true.

The transcript was lying on the secretary's desk because the school in Charlotte had written to Tahlequah High asking for a copy. "We think there might be some mistake in the mathematics grades," the letter had said. "Could we also have any test scores for Olivia? We want to make certain that we have her in the right class. Thanks so much for taking the time to do this."

The principal handed the letter to his new secretary to take care of. The letter annoyed him. The letter was exactly the sort of thing he expected to get from a fancy private school in North Carolina. Arch, apologetic, asking him to waste his time on some bullshit detail. Why didn't they give the little girl a test themselves if they wanted to know which mathematics class she belonged in? They had plenty of money and time and extra office help. Not to mention the implied assumption that being from Tahlequah High she was deficient in basic skills no matter how good her grades had been. "Take care of this when you get time," he told the secretary. "It's low priority."

"What?"

"Put it on the bottom of a pile."

"Oh. Okay."

So the letter from North Carolina lay on the bottom of a stack of unanswered mail and the transcript sat on the desk beside some stationery order blanks. The secretary filed her nails and talked to her sister on the phone about the sister's recurrent bouts of cystitis. It was spring and the golf courses had just dried off from the winter snows. The principal had been a champion college golfer and he wasn't interested in unanswered mail. He was out at the Tahlequah Country Club every afternoon playing golf with the pro and getting ready for a tour he planned to make in June.

If Mrs. Walker hadn't walked by and noticed Olivia's transcript, it might have lain on the desk for years.

12

The students at Saint Andrew's Episcopal School were filing out into the parking lot and climbing into their cars. They were getting ready to enjoy their only real freedom of the day. All the way home from school to their houses no one would be trying to civilize them or watching them to see if they were drinking or taking dope or getting pregnant. All they had to do for the next hour was get into their cars and turn on their radios and talk to one another. It was freedom, or, at least, it felt like freedom. It could pass for freedom. They climbed into their cars and threw their books and satchels on the floor and began to drive out of the parking lot, waving and calling to each other in the most heartfelt and democratic camaraderie of the day. There's Larkin Sykes in her daddy's BMW, they were thinking. Look at old Travis in that Jeep, that's cool. I wish I had something to drive besides this beat-up Honda. I wish they'd let me have the Buick. I wish I could win a lottery.

Along the boulevards and neighborhoods near the school, the Bradford pear trees were in bloom. Even the most corrupted mind among the children was not immune to that much beauty on a bright spring day. Five weeks to go, they were thinking. Five more weeks and summer's here.

Jessie and Olivia were among the envied ones. They threw their book satchels into the back of an Oldsmobile convertible and Jessie got behind the wheel. The convertible was old but it was in good repair and had been painted the year before. A convertible of any kind was better than a sedan or a family car. A convertible was right up there with a Jeep. Not that Jessie and Olivia were thinking they were lucky or envied. Olivia was thinking about her forged grades and Jessie was thinking about how sick she was of having Olivia live with her. I don't care, Jessie told herself. It's too much. Every day there she is, asking me questions. I don't know what she wants with me. I can't even go off with my friends unless I take her along and she keeps asking about King. I don't believe Dad did this to me. It's Aunt Anna's fault. If she hadn't died none of this would have happened and we'd be like we used to be.

"You ready to go?" Jessie said. "You got everything?"

"Yeah. Go on. How'd you do on the English test? Did you do all right?"

"I don't know. I didn't have time to finish all the questions. She never gives us time." Jessie drove out of the parking lot. "I talked to Dad at noon. He said to come straight home because Aunt Helen was coming over to talk to us."

"What about? What do they want to talk about?"

"Oh, nothing. He always gets her to talk to me if he's worried about anything. Maybe he wants her to take us shopping."

"I don't need anyone to pick out my clothes. I can pick out my own stuff." Olivia sat back. Maybe it was nothing.

"Well, anyway, we have to go straight home." Jessie speeded up, moved onto a boulevard of blooming pear trees and potted flowers. There had been a Flower Festival the week before and the street department had planted thousands of forced blooms along the streets, tulips and lilies and daffodils.

Jessie drove the convertible down the boulevard of flowers. Olivia slumped down in the seat beside her. "I have a lot of homework to do," she said. "How long is this going to take with Aunt Helen?"

"How do I know? All I know is he called and said he wanted us to come straight home. He got me out of a study period. Why were you crying yesterday?" Jessie stopped for a stoplight.

"I don't know. It just seems hard somehow. I don't know what to do to make him like me."

"He's Dad. That's how he is. He doesn't make over people."

"Does your mom make over you?"

"No. She doesn't either." Jessie shifted into low gear and took off, going as fast as she dared. She went down a ramp and out onto a freeway. "I might get a letter from King today. That's all I care about. I don't want my parents to make over me. I want to get married and have a life of my own."

"You got a letter a few days ago."

"He's trying to fix it so we can be together this summer. We can't live on phone calls and letters."

"Maybe I need a boyfriend."

"You've got that great-looking boy in Oklahoma. He was the best-looking boy I saw out there. But I guess you want someone in Charlotte, don't you?"

"I don't know what I want. I'm really not thinking about boys right now."

"Coleman Toon's got a crush on you. Dad would like it if you went out with him. You ought to go out with someone, Olivia. You can't just study all the time. I go out, even if I'm in love with King."

"I have to study. This school's a lot harder than the one I went to. I don't know if I can even pass some of this stuff."

"Well, I can't help you with that. Look, Olivia, I'm sorry we've been so mean to each other lately. I don't know what's going wrong. It makes the house so cold. Let's try to be nicer to each other, okay?" She turned her head. She smiled. She was determined to try, or to pretend to try. She didn't know why she felt such confused feelings toward Olivia, or why she kept having such bad dreams at night, dreams in which Olivia pushed her off of cliffs or wouldn't help her from the water.

"We ought to do something together," Olivia said. "Let's go out to the farm and ride tomorrow. Let's go spend the whole day. You want to do that?"

"I don't know. I don't like to mess around with Dad's horses unless he's there. They don't get ridden enough. You can't tell what they'll do."

"You don't like to ride, do you?"

"I got hurt a couple of years ago. An Appaloosa threw me. I can't stand to even think about it."

"Why'd he throw you?"

"I don't know. Maybe I lost attention. Dad almost beat him to death. It was the worst thing. One of his girlfriends was there. The one who's a model. She ran after him and dragged him away to make him stop beating the horse. Well, I guess I shouldn't tell you that."

"Where I'm from everything happens. I've seen men beat up other men on the street. Well, I guess you don't want to go riding then, do you?"

"I'll go. If we take Spook to saddle the horses."

"I'll saddle them and I'll ride yours until he settles down. We can go back to that lake and have a picnic or something. That lake's so beautiful. It's got a mystery to it."

"Aunt Anna loved the lake. She used to swim there in March when she was young. She had to be the first person to swim every spring. Aunt Helen said she'd disappear and they would always know that's where she'd gone. We have to be friends, Olivia. She wanted it so much. Remember what she wrote to us." She reached over and touched her sister's hand. She raised her eyes and met her sister's serious, hopeful smile.

"I'll take care of the horses," Olivia said. "I won't let you get thrown again. You have to see how they're feeling. They have moods, like people, like the weather."

When they got home, their aunt Helen was waiting in the library, dressed up in a Chanel suit with matching jewelry, planning on catching a plane at seven to fly to Boston. The last thing she wanted to do was come over to Daniel's and sit around trying to counsel his crazy daughters. Still, the Hands came when they were called. No matter what they were doing they had to help out if one of their siblings called.

"You look nice," Jessie said, coming into the library, throwing her book satchel on a leather sofa. "Why are you so dressed up?"

"I'm on my way to Boston to work on Anna's papers. Hi, Olivia, how are you doing? How are things at school?"

Olivia stayed several feet away, still wearing her book bag on her shoulder.

"I'm doing okay. I need to study though. I've got hours of work to do. Do you mind if I go upstairs and do it?" She was backing into the hall.

"Well, your father asked me to stop by and see if there is anything either of you need. Do you need anything? Do you have everything you need?"

"I'm fine. I haven't worn all the clothes we got last month. I need to write a history paper though, so if you'll excuse me." She had made it to the archway leading to the stairs. "It's nice to see you though," she added. "Have a good time in Boston."

"Oh, it will all be work," Helen began, but Olivia was gone up the stairs. "Well," she said to Jessie. "Is she always that nervous?"

"I don't think she likes it here," Jessie said. "I think it was a mistake of Daddy to bring her here. She had a good life at her own home. She can't even get a boyfriend here."

"Why is that?"

"I don't know. She doesn't know how to act. She acts too smart-alecky around boys. She does around girls too. My friends don't like to come over if she's here."

"Oh, my. I'm so sorry to hear all that. Is there anything I can do? Have you told your father?"

"No. And don't you. She's my sister, Aunt Helen. I have to learn to love her. There are two hands on every person. That's what Aunt Anna said. She said — well, never mind about that. I'll find a way to get along with her. I have to, don't I?"

"Anna didn't always get things right, Jessie. She had a

lot of romantic ideas about things." Helen hung her head. Even from the grave Anna's power over her was great. Anna had been the oldest and the most controlled. Anna didn't get mad the way that Helen did. Didn't get jealous and feel sorry for herself. She was perfect, Helen thought despairingly. She would never have said bad things about me. "Oh, God," Helen added, out loud. "I didn't mean to say that, Jessie. But Anna's gone and we're left with all of this. So what is it Olivia does that irritates you?"

"I don't know. She's just so changeable. She'll be real sweet for a few days and drive me crazy following me around and trying to get me to play the piano or something. Then she'll change and I think she's mad at me. I don't know how to act around her."

"You're an only child. You never had to put up with it. Well, I think it's good to be an only child. Camilla is an only child, my best friend I play tennis with, and she's a doll. Maybe I can have Olivia over to stay with us some weekend and give you a break."

"When will you be back?"

"I don't know. It depends on how long it takes to sort the papers. Do you have any idea why she was crying yesterday? At the farm?"

"No. She might be homesick. Maybe she wants to go back home. We're okay, Aunt Helen. It was nice of you to come over, but it's fine. We're going riding Saturday and try to be better friends. I'll really try. I really will."

"All right then. I'll go on so I won't miss my plane. Tell your father I was here." Helen took Jessie's face in her hands and gave her a kiss. "Take care of yourself first of all, honey. Don't let this disrupt your life. And call me if you need me. You're the important one to us. Not this girl."

"She stays home every night and studies and Dad gets mad if I want to go out. That's the main thing I'm mad about."

"Tell him."

"I already did."

"Okay. Well, I'm leaving." Helen was almost to the door. She stopped in the hallway and hugged Jessie again. "I love you, darling. You're our darling, darling girl."

"Thanks for coming by," Jessie said. "It was really nice of you."

Helen went down the flagstone path to her car and got into it and drove off waving. Jessie watched until she was out of sight. Upstairs a window slammed shut. There she goes, Jessie thought. Locking herself up to study. When he comes home she'll be up there working like a dog and he'll think I ought to too. Well, I'm not studying in the afternoon. I've been in school all day. Okay, I'll look at them. I'll just look at the history, nothing else. She marched back into the library and spread her books out on a table. Then she turned on the television to watch the Oprah Winfrey show.

It was a show about homosexuals trying different ways to get babies. There were people in the audience on their feet screaming at each other. On the stage were three homosexual couples who had found ways to adopt babies or have them. The homosexual men had adopted two orphaned street children. The women had used artificial insemination. At least they wanted to have a baby, Jessie thought. At least they love their little kids. I'll be like that. If I ever have a kid I'll love it to death. I'll take care of it myself, not some maid. "We want to raise her to love herself and love the world," one of the women was saying. "She is our flower. We try to teach her to respect all living things."

"What's going to happen when she goes to school?" an irate woman in the audience screamed out. "What's she going to tell her friends?"

13

Saturday morning was beautiful and cool. Outside the windows of Daniel's house the sun moved up the sky through a bank of clouds, robins sang, the sky was very blue. When he had been a rich man Daniel had commissioned a great architect to build him a house in which to raise his child. Make it peaceful, he told the man, so when she wakes up she'll be glad she is alive. Then Daniel went off to Europe for the summer and left the architect with two acres of land in the middle of the best residential area in Charlotte. When he returned the house was almost done. A long rectangle of stone and glass with a staircase leading to bedrooms that looked out upon a line of apple trees. Daniel had paid the bill and moved in and started letting his girlfriends fill the place with furniture. It was eclectic, to say the least, but it was peaceful. Jessie felt the peace around her now, waking in the peach-colored sheets girlfriend number twenty-seven had bought for her one year. She moved her legs onto the floor and went over to the window and thought about Olivia. I will love her no matter what she does, Jessie thought. I will stop thinking she is in my way.

Across the hall Olivia woke up thinking about the country, of catching a horse and saddling it, swinging up into a saddle, riding like the wind to find a river. Only here it is a lake, she remembered, and all I'm going to have between my legs is an English saddle. She giggled and got back into bed and made herself come with her fingers. Oh, baby, she was saying, oh, baby, you make me feel so good.

"You can't go out there alone," Daniel said at breakfast. He was poaching eggs, cooking bacon in the microwave, making a terrible mess. "Eat this, Olivia. Both of you are thin as a rail. Go on, sit down and eat some breakfast if you're going to the farm."

"I can catch the horses," Olivia said. "I'll take the Jeep."

"No, you're not going alone. I'll round up Spook and send him with you. I'd go myself but the goddamn Japs are in town and I have to talk to them."

"We don't need Spook." Olivia nibbled at the eggs.

"Well, you're going to have him. He's been wanting to get out there anyway. He was raised out there." Spook was the handyman at Daniel's tractor company. Daniel had moved him into town when his wife died and he resented it. He wanted to go back out and live on the land.

"There's no point in arguing about it," Jessie put in. "If he wants to send Spook, he will. He always makes me take Spook out there."

Daniel made a phone call and in fifteen minutes Spook drove up in his pickup. His real name was Marcellus Biggs but his cousins called him Spook because his hair was so light. He was sixty-seven years old but he hadn't told his age in so long he had almost forgotten the exact age himself. He and Daniel loved each other. They were a matched pair for haughtiness and snobbery and always getting their way.

Spook was glad of a chance to go to the country. Since Daniel had moved him into town he had almost worn himself out getting laid. He had nightmares of horny young women following him through corridors. He wasn't getting any fishing done and hardly any thinking.

"Do I have to let her drive?" he asked Daniel, indicating Jessie. There was no question of him getting in a car with Olivia at the wheel. He had taken one look at her and decided he didn't trust her. "I don't like the look of her," he had told several people at the tractor company. Word of that had reached Daniel, who had it out with him while he watched him sweep the showroom floor.

"I ride with both of them," Daniel said now. "So can you."

Half an hour later they were headed for the country, Spook in the back seat of the convertible and Jessie driving.

"Who you going to ride?" he asked. "Them horses haven't been ridden all winter. I'd take the palominos if I was you. Don't go fooling with that red horse."

"I can ride anything," Olivia said. "I used to rodeo in Oklahoma."

"I don't care what you used to do. You ain't riding anything but palominos today."

"We'll ride the palominos," Jessie said. "That's okay."

"You better believe it's okay. Daniel told me to catch the palominos." Jessie speeded up and all further conversation was lost in the wind.

"This little mare's the sweetest horse on the farm," Spook said, leading the horse around and handing the reins to Jessie. "I was here when she was born. We bred her mother to the palomino Mr. Jody Kelley used to keep at stud on Monte Cristo. Hard to believe everybody's gone to town."

"We're not in town now," Jessie said. "We're here." She swung herself up into the saddle. It felt grand. Olivia was right. All they needed was to get out in the country and get some exercise. It would be all right. They would be sisters now and friends. She would stop thinking Olivia liked King. She would have the milk of human kindness where Olivia was concerned. And maybe, by the time she got home that afternoon, a letter would be there from him. It would say, I love you, Jessie. I will love you till I die. Love, King.

Olivia was mounted on a gelding. She was sitting very still, hardly touching the reins.

"How do you do that?" Jessie asked. "God, that looks so good."

"Do what?"

"Do it without the reins."

"I use my knees. I keep my weight where he's going. Didn't they teach you that?"

"I think so. I used to get thrown a lot. I wasn't good at it, was I, Spook?"

"Sometime you was. When you wanted to be."

"He knows I can be trusted," Olivia went on. "You make them trust you. Then you're safe."

"Well, go on if you're going," Spook said. "Enough of all this talk. I'm going fishing."

They rode to the back of the farm, past the deserted cabins and the deserted store, far back onto the land where their ancestors had created a life they could not imagine. Their father and aunts and uncles could remember the farm filled with meaning and life. To the girls it was only a place of ghosts and stories, on its way back to wilderness.

They crossed a gravel road into the oldest cleared part of the land, walking the horses through the rough parts and finding paths no one had used all winter. "The meadow's back here," Jessie said. "The one that joins Dunleith. You ever been back here?"

"Yeah. The first time I came to visit. Don't you remember?"

"It's so ancient back here. I'm so glad we came." Jessie paused at the edge of the meadow, reached down into her jacket pocket, took out some cookies in a plastic sack. "You want a cookie?" She held one out and Olivia took it from her. They stuffed the cookies in their mouths and chewed them up. The sun was almost to its zenith now. It had turned into a perfect cloudless day.

"Did you ever bring King here?" Olivia asked.

"No."

"We could bring him here if he comes to visit."

"I might go there this summer. He won't come here."

"Why not? His grandmother's here, isn't she. Isn't that old lady we met his grandmother? I thought that's what they said."

"Miss Clarice Manning, and she's not an old lady. She was a great beauty. She's grandmother's best friend."

"Anyway, I guess he has to come see her, doesn't he?"

"He's my boyfriend, Olivia. Look, you want to ride to the lake or not?"

"Sure. I was just waiting for you. You don't have to get mad just because I said I wished he'd come and visit. I don't want your boyfriend. I've got plenty of boys if I want them." Olivia led her horse away from Jessie, sighted down across the meadow to the lake. Fuck them all, she was thinking. I can't stand all this stupid crap they get into. She can't even ride a goddamn horse. She's scared to death to ride a tired old mare. Olivia lifted her head, caught a smell of wild grass, fecund, hot, the meadow and the earth. She rose up in the saddle and began to ride. She left so fast that Jessie was startled. She finished her cookie and wrapped the package back up and stuck it in her pocket. I can ride too, she thought. Anybody can ride a horse fast if that's all they want to do. She moved her knees, urged the old mare on and began to ride down across the meadow. I will bring King here, she was thinking, but I won't bring her too. I don't have to take her everywhere I go. Oh, God, he's so beautiful and sweet, he's so manly, he has such a kind face. I love him so much. No one will ever know how I feel about him.

She was off in daydream. She and King together on a beach with dark skies and a storm coming. The mare galloped on. It was Jessie's old problem with horses, daydreaming as she rode. She drove cars the same way, a foot on the gas pedal and her mind a million miles away. King turned to her now. The wild surf was pounding at his back. His white shirt was blowing in the wind. I love you until I die, King said. I cannot live without you. Will you be my wife?

The mare galloped on through real-life North Carolina. A real-life rabbit darted out in front of her hooves and she spooked and reared. Jessie jerked the reins. The mare reared again and turned. Jessie pulled her feet from the stirrups and began to fall. Her years of gymnastics stood her in good stead and she rolled as she fell. Rolled her neck down into her chest, her legs into her waist. The mare shivered, terrified, then galloped back toward the road.

*   *   *

When Olivia realized Jessie was no longer behind her, she turned around and began to ride back across the meadow, calling her sister's name. She caught sight of Jessie's jacket in the tall grass, then Jessie, with her face between her arms, stretched out flat upon the ground. She dismounted and tied her horse to a tree and ran back and knelt beside her sister. "Oh, God, oh, be all right. Oh, Jessie, please wake up. For God's sake don't die on me."

The mare made straight for home. Skirting paths and flying across the gravel road barely missing a pickup truck. She stopped once to shiver and tremble, then galloped straight back to the farm. Spook was on his way to the pond with a six-pack in one hand and his fishing pole in the other. When he heard the horse coming he dropped them and went on a run for the Jeep. He had been on the farm when Clara Abadie had broken her neck in a riding accident and, although that was forty years ago, he remembered it as if it were yesterday. The riderless horse coming galloping back and the days that followed. He jumped in the Jeep and began to drive back across the pastures. At the road he stopped a passing car and asked them to call Daniel. Then he drove the Jeep as far as possible into the deadening, then he started running.

Olivia was sitting on the ground by Jessie, who was beginning to come around. "I'm okay," she kept saying. "I'm okay now."

"Please don't move. You don't know if you broke anything."

"I didn't break anything. I'm okay. We have to find the mare. She might kill somebody on the road. Dad's going to have a fit. I never fell off in the ring. I never fell off a single time in the ring."

"Maybe the saddle wasn't right. I don't think Spook knows what he's doing with the horses. I had to tighten my girth. He thinks he's so smart. He's just an old man."

"It wasn't Spook's fault. I wasn't concentrating. I always have accidents. It's always me."

"Oh, Jessie." Olivia reached out and very tentatively put her hands around her sister's waist. It was the first time they had ever really hugged each other, except once, many months ago, when Jessie had come to the airport to take Olivia to Anna's wake. Now, awkwardly, sitting on the dry prickly grass, Olivia reached for her sister, felt the small bones of Jessie's ribs. For a moment she was so near it seemed light-years had blown away between them. "I take my sister to the lake at dawn. To search for the great liveoak tree at Mandeville. To stand naked in its arms and know spider and moss and oak and vine." Where had she read that? What was she remembering?

"Go find the mare," Jessie said. "You go try to catch her. I can walk back now."

"No. To hell with the mare. I'm not leaving you."

"We have to catch her. She might get out on the road." Jessie stood up. Her hip was hurting but her legs moved. "I was thinking of the seashore," she said, shaking her head, embarrassed, giggling. "I was thinking of the ocean, then I was flying through the air."

"It isn't funny," Olivia said. "Nothing about this is funny to me."

*   *   *

Spook came in sight, running toward them in his overalls, mad as hell and winded and ready to fix some blame. "What the hell you doing way back here? You know you not supposed to go on this side of the road. When Daniel gets here I hope he wears you out. You okay, Jessie? You going to make it?"

"We have to catch the mare," Jessie said. "She ran off somewhere."

"She ran home. How you think I know where you're at?" He stood before them, breathing hard, hands on his hips. "I guess I'll have my heart attack any minute. I sent a man on the road to call your daddy and the doctor. You shut up, both of you, and walk with me. Jeep's across the road behind the fence. How'd you get across that fence? That's what I'd like to know."

"We went through the gate," Olivia answered. "So stop yelling at me. I don't let people yell at me. Nobody told me not to ride back here. Dad told me to ride anyplace I wanted to on our land."

"Our land," Spook muttered, pulling the girls along beside him. "Move in here and take up everything you like."

"Let go of me," Olivia said. "I'm riding the horse back home."

Daniel arrived soon after they got back to the house. The message had been relayed to the country club where he had taken the Japanese to eat lunch and see the golf course.

"What happened?" he asked, striding into the house. Spook was in the kitchen eating a sandwich. Jessie was on the couch talking to King Mallison, Junior, long distance on the phone. Olivia was reading a book.

"They went back across the road to the old place. You told them to stay out of there. I heard you say it." Spook looked up from his sandwich and motioned toward the girls. "It's a wonder nobody's dead. That pasture's full of rabbit holes. I was here when Clara Abadie got knocked off by a tree branch and broke her neck. I seen what happened to all of them. Old Mr. Abadie never did get over that. You told them to stay on this side. I know you did. I wouldn't have come out here if I'd thought they could go anyplace they liked."

"It's my fault for thinking it up," Olivia said. "I thought it up."

"I have to go. Dad's here," Jessie said into the phone. She put the receiver down into its cradle and pulled the quilt up around her legs. Daniel went straight to her.

"You got knocked out?"

"No. I was just scared."

"Yes, you were," Olivia said. "You were out cold."

"No, I wasn't. I was lying there but I could hear."

"Let me see." Daniel knelt beside the couch. He took Jessie's head in his hands, began to feel for bumps. Olivia watched him in a sort of wonder of jealousy. He had not even spoken to her. Had not acknowledged she was in the room.

"I caused all this," she said. "I know Jessie doesn't like to ride. I know it's dangerous for her."

"It isn't dangerous for me. The horse spooked. But it wasn't the horse's fault, Dad. Don't blame the horse. Don't blame anyone but me."

"They was back across the road on the deadening," Spook repeated. "They said you said they could ride back there but I heard you tell them not to go across the road.

You want me to make you a sandwich? I guess you had to interrupt your lunch, didn't you?"

"I ought to take you to the hospital," Daniel said. "I think a doctor ought to look at you."

"I'm okay, Dad. I'm perfectly okay." She put her hand over his. She looked into his eyes, so exactly like her own. She seemed so perfect to him, so beautiful and fragile, so impenetrable a mystery. Olivia got up and came and knelt beside them on the floor. She added her hand to her father's hand.

"She's okay, Dad," Olivia said. "We're both okay."

"You want a sandwich or not?" Spook asked again. "I'll be glad to make you one."

14

That same Saturday Mrs. Walker finally told her husband what she was worrying about. "They have so few chances to escape," she said. "To get a real education anywhere. I was so happy for her when I heard she was going up there. Her father's a wealthy man."

"That doesn't have anything to do with your job, Marion. If you think the grades have been changed, you need to go to the principal. You're an accessory if you don't."

"Okay."

"Okay, what?"

"I'll call him then. Or maybe I'll go over there and talk to him."

"It's your duty, Marion. You can't ignore this. What did the transcript say?"

"It was all A's. Except for a couple of B's in math. She couldn't have all A's. There's only one boy in school with all A's. His daddy is a lawyer and they own that department store on the square."

"Marion."

"Yes."

"Go do your duty."

*   *   *

Mrs. Walker put on a dress and went over to the principal's house and told him what she suspected. Then the two of them went to the school and keyed into the computer and looked at the grades. They pulled up Olivia's junior high school grades and test scores. Then they called the registrar.

On Monday morning the principal called the headmaster of Saint Andrew's Episcopal School in Charlotte and he called Daniel and at three that afternoon Daniel was sitting in the headmaster's office waiting for Olivia. They had sent someone to get her out of gym class.

"This is serious, sweetie," Daniel said, when she came in the door, still dressed in shorts and a sweatshirt. "We've got a problem here. Do you know what it is?" The transcripts were spread out on the desk. Olivia took one look at them and collapsed into a chair. "I wanted to come here," she said. "I wanted to come so much." She dissolved in tears, folded into a paroxysm of tears. Daniel and the headmaster looked at each other. Then the headmaster called for help. "Get Lila in here," he yelled to his secretary. "Go get the counselor and tell her to get in here right now."

"I'll take her home," Daniel said. "Come on, Olivia. We'll go home. You can talk to me then."

"It doesn't matter," Olivia sobbed. "I might as well kill myself. Now I'll never go to college or have anything, anything at all. I can't have anything."

"Oh, my God," the headmaster began. "This was badly handled. Olivia, we shouldn't have called you in like this, with both of us here. I should have done something else. This was badly planned."

"You better believe it was," the school counselor said.

She had arrived and was on her knees by the sobbing child. "What a crazy thing to do, bringing her in here and springing this on her like that. My God, Morgan, you know better than this. You should have called me. Goddamn, you make my work so hard. You make it impossible." The headmaster hung his head. He and the counselor had been fucking each other on Tuesday and Thursday afternoons and sometimes on Sundays for seven months now. He was so much in love with her he was crazy. He had never loved a woman the way he loved this bossy brown-haired psychologist from Greensboro. Now he had bungled this matter of the half-Indian Hand girl and she might never give him another piece of ass.

"Lila, I'm so sorry," he said. "You're right. Take her to your office. We'll talk without her. Olivia, just one thing. Are you saying what we suspect is true?"

"Morgan, this is not the time," the counselor said. "Shut up, for God's sake." She pulled Olivia up and started with her toward the door.

"I'm sorry, Dad," Olivia said. "I guess you'll hate me now. I guess I'll never have anything, will I?" She started sobbing again and Lila led her off into an adjacent room. Daniel stood up. "I better go with them."

"No, give Lila time to calm her down. Well, I guess that's it, then. I don't think we have to go into an investigation here."

"What are you going to do?" Daniel lowered his chin, did the mental equivalent of taking his hat in his hands, got wary, thoughtful, shrewd, weighed the public scandal, weighed Olivia's chances of following his sister Anna to a suicide's grave, wondered what Morgan needed, wanted, had to have. "I hope you won't kick her out, Morgan.

We've been associated with this school for years. Sending money, sending kids. You can't just kick her out, can you?"

"I might have to." Morgan sat back in his chair, imagining the room filling up with the tormented parents he had counseled in the last six years, more tormented every year and more of them. "I have to run a school, Daniel. We have to have rules and principles. What if it gets out? That we condoned this kind of cheating. Lawlessness. This is lawlessness. Breaking and entering in Tahlequah. Forgery. I'm sorry. I know it's your daughter but I have a responsibility to the school."

"You want to ruin her life without giving her a chance? Goddamn, Morgan, she's only a kid. I've only had her a few months. She's a good little girl."

"We know she is, Daniel. We all like her. But there may be criminal charges. I can't even talk to that guy down in Oklahoma. He sounds like some kind of mad dog."

"There must be some probation she could get on." Daniel had been kicked out of three prep schools. They had always let him be on probation first. Surely this fairy had heard of probation. Daniel was getting mad now. He was too spoiled to be much good at hiding his temper. "So what are you telling me, Morgan? You're kicking her out for sure then?"

"No. I have to think about it. She has to have some counseling, Daniel. No matter what happens here. You can't take this lightly."

Daniel stood up again. Began to walk around the room. "I'm not taking it lightly. Where did that woman take her? I need to see her."

"Will you come back and talk to me tomorrow? After we sleep on this? After we all have time to think? I might have to consult the board."

Daniel stopped pacing. He gathered up his store of balance, became his most courteous self. "Of course, Morgan. I'm sorry if I seem upset. She's just a little girl. I don't know those folks who raised her. I'm doing all I can. All I know how to do."

"Let's go find your daughter," Morgan said, coming around the desk, taking Daniel's arm. "You can take her home."

The next morning Daniel rounded up his brother, Niall, and they went back to the high school to try again. Niall was the most civilized person the Hands had thrown up for three generations. He was a throwback to the old teacher and classics scholar who had given the family its proper names. Niall spoke four Romance languages and Greek and corresponded with Sanskrit scholars. He had met the Dalai Lama. Also, he traveled with Phelan Manning. He had hunted with Phelan all over the world. How does Niall justify Phelan to the Dalai Lama? Anna had always been asking. Tell me that. He just goes along, Daniel always answered. He doesn't carry a gun.

This morning Niall was in his backyard fertilizing his roses when Daniel came over and rounded him up. "Calm down," Niall said. "It will be all right. We'll fix it."

"She's just a little kid. She was on the make, so what? We would have been in the same situation. Goddamn, Niall, that goddamn little fairy preacher. She was crying her little heart out. We had to get Momma over last night and Ben Torrey came by and gave her some tranquilizers. I gave that goddamn school two grand last year for their building fund."

"Maybe it wasn't enough."

"Well, shit, what a thing to say."

"How much is left in Grandmother's education trust?"

"I don't know. Louise raped it a couple of years ago. You know about that. She got Momma to give her all that money to go to England."

"How much is left?"

"Forty thousand, give or take a grand."

"Well, let's go by and get Momma to give us a check big enough to get this headmaster in a good mood."

"A bribe?" Daniel watched Niall spreading fertilizer on the straw beneath a rosebush. Niall never ceased to amaze Daniel. One month he was holed up reading books and voting for black candidates for mayor and the next month he wanted to bribe an Episcopal priest.

"He's an Episcopal minister."

"Well, he's still got a school to run." Niall put the sack of fertilizer back into a lard can and stood up and wiped his hands on his apron. Then he removed the apron and took his brother's arm and walked into the house.

"I like your little dark-eyed girl, little brother. I can see the Asian in her. She will flower someday and make all this worthwhile. How I envy you those daughters. I was thinking of them the other day, for hours I thought of you over there with your riches."

"You wouldn't think so if you'd been at my house last night. She was crying and Jessie started crying. Then Ben gave them tranquilizers. House full of kids on tranquilizers. That's what I'm down to. What do you mean, Asian? Goddamn, Niall, you get the nuttiest ideas."

"American Indians came from Asia across the Bering Strait. I love the darkness in her, the brooding. I was so thrilled when I met her on the street one day last month.

She was out walking and I saw her from a distance. I don't think she recognized me at first. To think, we have this young creature in our midst, with so much history in her face."

"Are you going over there with me?"

"Would you like me to put on a suit?"

"Well, you can take off that old shirt. You want to go by Momma's and see if she wants to give us a check?"

"You call her while I change clothes. Tell her we're coming."

The two men, Niall now dressed in a plaid shirt and khaki jacket like the ones his mother had bought for him down through the years, Daniel as always dressed to the nines in the finest slacks and sweaters his girlfriends could pick out at the best stores in Charlotte, went over and found their mother in her rose garden pruning her Frau Karl Druschkis and directing two men who were making her a bed for pink azaleas. There was nothing in the world that pleased Mrs. Hand more than the sight of good-looking men appearing in her yard at nine o'clock on a spring morning. She had been a belle and she was a belle and she needed courting. "My darlings," she said. "Oh, Niall, Daniel is having such a bad time."

"We need some money, Momma," Niall said. "We need some money from Grandmother's trust."

"What for?" she asked.

"To give the school," Niall continued. "We have to get the little girl out of trouble."

"Of course," Mrs. Hand said. She pulled off her gardening gloves, looking down, thinking that she was tired of handing checks to her children. "How much do you need?"

*   *   *

At ten-thirty they presented themselves at the high school. The school counselor was waiting in the anteroom and escorted them into the headmaster's office. She was in a good mood this morning, wearing a dark silk dress with a string of pearls and a lot of Chanel 19. She and the headmaster had been at it for hours last night after they made up. He had gotten home so late it was sure to ruin his marriage. This time his wife could not pretend he had been working late. Even his dumb old wife would catch on now.

"Mr. Hand and his brother," the counselor said, looking her lover in the eye, wetting her lips with her tongue. "I'll wait out here, Morgan, in case you need me. I'll tell Jennette to hold your calls."

"We don't want to fool around with this," Daniel said, when she had left the room and closed the door. "We want to put it on the table. Mother gave us a check for ten thousand dollars. We want you to know how much we value this school. How much we thank you for all the help you've been to our family over the years."

"The little girl deserves another chance," Niall put in. "We ask for your compassion, Morgan. You know you can count on us. It won't happen again. She won't embarrass you. We're asking a favor. We don't know what would happen to her if you kicked her out. It needs to be covered up, Morgan."

"I don't know how far I can go. They know about it at the school in Oklahoma. It isn't only me." Daniel put the check on the desk.

"Will you call them? Will you ask them to let it lay?"

"I can keep her here." The headmaster picked up the check. It was for the school. He could add it to the scholarship fund. Half for the scholarship fund, half for the new gym. He held it in his hand. He was goddamned if he would be ashamed of taking it. Money does God's work. Money is food and clothes and teachers' salaries. "She'll have to have a math tutor, Daniel. And some therapy. We'll help you find someone. And I can't guarantee they'll keep it off her records out there. The principal's an irritable guy. I talked to him again this morning. He's fairly intractable, I think."

"But you'll keep her here? She can stay in school." Daniel reached over and squeezed his brother's arm. "You won't kick her out."

"We like Olivia, Daniel. She's a bright child. No one wants to kick her out. She has to have some counseling however. For her sake as well as ours. I didn't realize she'd lost her mother at birth. If you'd told me that when you enrolled her, I would have suggested counseling then. Well, better late than never." The headmaster stood up, feeling the long stretch in his loins that great sex always left him with. The wonderful itch that fresh money for the scholarship fund always gave him. Tell me there isn't a God, he told himself. Tell me it just happened that Carole decided to spend a few more days with her mother just when I needed time with Lila.

He smiled his beatific pulpit smile and came around the desk and walked Daniel and Niall to the door. Lila was waiting by the water cooler. He laid his hand on her shoulder. "Go get Olivia and bring her here," he said. "Get her out of class if necessary. Let's put her mind at rest."

Daniel and Niall got back in the car and started driving toward Niall's house. "Do you have to go to work right now?" Niall asked.

"I guess so. If I still have a business. I guess it's still there."

"I thought maybe we could ride out to the country and go swimming in the lake. Don't you think we should celebrate this morning's work?"

"What for? We paid that fairy ten thousand dollars and now I've got to start paying some shrink to fuck up her head. Remember what happened to Louise when she went to that shrink? She turned into a nut."

"Yes. She left us, didn't she. Well, she seems happy. She's working on some film in England now. A documentary about Stonehenge." Niall reached over and put his hand on his brother's knee. "Take the morning off, Daniel. Stop worrying. Things work out. We could go swimming. We could be back by three."

"I can't." Daniel stopped the car in front of Niall's house. "I've got those Japs in town. I got to get down there and talk to them."

"Let's see each other more often. Let's take time to know each other."

"If I can. If I ever get some time." Niall got out then and stood on the sidewalk by his tulip beds watching his baby brother drive off down the street. Daniel's huge freckled hands gripped the wheel of the car. His face was pointed toward the east.

Thank you, God, Olivia was saying to herself. If you're there thanks and if you're not thanks anyway. Now I'll have to work my ass off. I'll have to have a tutor and I have to go to counseling. I guess I'll have to talk to Lila all the time. I saw her looking my dad over. No wonder she's so nice to me with such a good-looking unmarried guy for my father.

I guess she thinks she'll be coming over to see me at my house.

After they got through talking to me this morning I went back to history class and Mrs. Braxton was talking about the Korean war. She was saying they promised they'd get the troops home for Christmas and all I could think about was that Christmas when Bobby and I went out to the old Methodist camp and built a fire by the creek and sat around and smoked a joint. Then we got the idea to go down the river in the snow. We got one of the canoes from the camp and went all the way down to the island where the crows nest in winter. I don't guess I'll ever smoke dope again or get laid by anybody I like, but that's okay. I guess that's my childhood I have to leave behind.

Yeah, I won't ever be that way again. All cocky and stretched out and fine like it was that day I lay back in the canoe and heard those crows and felt the small soft snow falling on us. Oh, baby, baby, he used to say. I bet all my life I'll be a sucker for anyone who calls me baby.

A
SUMMER
IN
MAINE

1

TRACELEEN So it was summer and Miss Crystal had decided we should all go up to Maine and get to know that part of the country. She borrowed this very large house which is actually an estate. She borrowed it from Mrs. Noel Chatevin, who is a friend of ours and lives around the corner from us in her room. She never leaves that room although once she was a great actress and was in plays in Paris, France, and London, England, and Madrid, Spain. She is very old now but she is still beautiful and has skin so pale you can see right through it. She is very strong-willed, more strong-willed than Miss Crystal even and she is very interesting to talk to. I get sent over there to take her flan and angel cakes and things Miss Crystal cuts out of magazines. They have a large collection of things from magazines. Miss Noel started it and now Miss Crystal is in it too. INTO EACH LIFE SOME RAIN MUST FALL, it says over the door to Miss Noel's room. "Raindrops keep falling on my head" is a song she plays over and over on a little crystal music box she keeps beside her bed.

NOEL Noel was alone in her room. Holding the letter from Helen Abadie begging to see Anna's letters. Please let

us have them, Helen had written. You can't be that selfish.
Don't you want to help preserve her memory? She wrote to
you all her life. Why won't you give them to us? Why won't
you talk to me?

It was eight o'clock in the morning and the terrible letter
had come and then the roofers and plumbers and electri-
cians had appeared at the door. The ones the lawyers sent
to fix the things that were broken by the storm.

"The hurricane," she told the repairmen, calling down
from the window when they appeared. "Well, come on in.
Marissa will let you in."

"They said to replace the windows," the good-looking
boy from the glass company called up. "Is that all right?"

"Come on in. Come on in." She pulled her head back in
the window and padded over to the door that led to the
stairs. She called down the stairs to the Spanish maid: "Let
them in. It's all right. They want to fix the broken things.
Hombres a trabajar. Let them in."

So now the roofers were crawling all over the roof and the
glass people were changing the windows and the electri-
cians were everywhere and she was going to be forced to
go downstairs. She put on the raincoat she kept for such
emergencies, a pink raincoat she had bought one spring in
Paris, and slipped on her bedroom slippers and took the
dogs and went downstairs and holed up in the unused living
room. She sat down upon a velvet loveseat facing the fireplace, the spaniels all around her.

" 'Now every third thought is of my death,' " she began,
playing to the spaniels. "What am I doing in this aging
body? Where is the spark that kept me warm? I won't let
Helen get the letters. Anna was nuts to leave the things to

Helen. Back to the family, back to the killers. I'll send Lydia to get them. I will send Crystal and Lydia. Yes, that's it. Lydia will bring them to me. Lydia won't tell Helen where they are."

Noel opened the drawer of the table beside the loveseat, took out the chess set, began to lay the players out. A classic problem. The old queen cornered with her knights gone. A bishop left and two pawns. Noel lifted a knight and held him in her hands. How many years since Julius died? Nine? Ten? A moment in time. Darling, damned Julius, who said no ships were coming in. Who said tomorrow would not be better, who said goodbye and meant it. Was that all in the letters? Yes, it must be. What had he wanted that the world did not give him? Gorgeous Julius in his velvet breeches, doing *Hamlet* at the RSC, doing anything he wanted to. You could have stayed around to console me, Noel thought. You could have finished out the play.

But of course the letters were not about darling, damned Julius Key or anything else of much import or weight. They were simply a packet of letters Anna Hand had written to one of her greatest and most flattering admirers. You are so wonderful, Noel would write to Anna. There is no one like you, no one can touch you, divine Anna, Anna of light. Write to me, please. I haven't heard from you in so long.

Then sooner or later Anna would stop whatever she was doing and sit down and write back to Noel and tell her everything that was happening in her blossoming career. As Anna's career moved toward its zenith, Noel's moved into darkness, sickness, despair. Send poems, Noel would write. Here they are, Anna would reply, and mail off first drafts of things she supposed were poems. So an illusion was created, an illusion of meaning, life, action, art. It was not the last illusion these letters would generate. Anna's sister Helen, living in sin with a poet in Boston, dreamed they would bind him to her. She believed he would be so greedy to edit Anna's letters that he would never tire of her, never send her home to her husband and children, never notice she was aging, never long for younger arms.

The maid came in and found Noel crying and tried to get her to return to her room.

"Not until they leave. Not until they get off my roof."

"I will get your pills. You must take them. I think you forgot to take them today."

"It was too late to save him," Noel said. "He was dead. There was nothing I could do, Marissa. You know there was nothing I could do. I did everything I could."

"Of course you did. I will get your pills for you. Let me get your pills."

"In a rose bedroom facing east. So long ago. He did it to punish me. He did it because I failed him."

"They shouldn't send those men here so early in the morning. Now they make you leave your room."

"I have to get the letters. I'll get Lydia to help me. Lydia will go and Crystal. They'll bring them to me, won't they? Don't you think they will?"

"Of course they will. You sit still and I will go and get the pills for you." The maid covered Noel's legs with an afghan, put a pillow behind her head, ran up the stairs for the bottles of lithium and Valium and the blue cut-glass Venetian tumbler Mrs. Chatevin always used to take her pills.

"Lydia will get them," Noel was saying. "Lydia won't let Helen find them and put them in a book."

CRYSTAL   So now Noel has it all figured out that we are going to go up to her house and spend the summer. I can't believe I said I'd go and invited all these people. Now I can't back out. Traceleen is planning on it and her niece Andria and King has invited Daniel and his girls.

Maybe Alan will come. Maybe he'll give me a piece of ass for a change if he comes up there. Maybe he's impotent or he thinks I'm too old. I'm not old. He's just a gold digger and a social climber but he's the best thing I've got.

I'd try to make my marriage work but what's the use. I married Manny for his money and now I have to pay. Well, I can't help it. I have to raise my children and do the best I can. Life isn't perfect.

Maybe we'll have fun up there. Lydia's coming and she's always fun. We're never bored when we're together. Well, the main thing is I'm going to please Noel. She is so sweet and brilliant. The sweetest woman I've ever known. She has been all over the world and now she's old and in that room. It's all loss. Sooner or later it's always loss. So go on up to Maine and see what happens. If Jessie comes I guess that will seal King's fate. Well, he could do a lot worse. He could fall in love with someone we don't know. Some girl from any kind of family.

It might be great up there. I might meet someone. Who knows, a fisherman or a simple country man who only wants to fuck and doesn't want anything from me. I'm tired of people wanting things from me, taking things from me, never giving me anything in return.

LYDIA The minute I got the letter I knew I should have thrown it away, but no, I got on the phone and called New Orleans and got sucked in. As much as I hate to travel, I have agreed to fly halfway across the United States on an airplane and then drive the other half with Crystal and her children. I end up doing anything those people want me to. Leave my psychiatrist and my rational friends and go on down to the land of twenty-four-hour azalea bushes. Not to mention gardenias, cape jasmine, night-blooming jasmine, honeysuckle, golden raintrees. You name it. If it smells like sex, it grows there. Once I went down there for a year and all I did was paint butterflies and flowers, ladies leaning against tombs, black jazz musicians. Well, the paintings of the musicians were pretty good. Actually all the paintings were pretty good. Actually I can't stay away. Garden of Eden. It's all so hot and surprising.

My psychiatrist was worried about my going. "Where exactly are you going?" he asked, getting his hooded look.

"To an estate a friend owns. There are some papers she wants me to bring to her. She's going to pay my expenses if I'll go and get them. I guess they're about Anna."

"Wait a minute. I'm getting confused. What does Anna have to do with this?"

"She was Noel's friend. They corresponded for years. God, it's impossible to believe she's dead."

"She's the one who had melanoma?"

"She killed herself. She wouldn't let them treat her."

"Do you know any normal people, Lydia? People who are married to each other and come home at night? I know you think they're boring."

"They are boring. There's a studio in the place in Maine. It has everything I need to paint. So I'll be working. I won't just be wasting time. Why don't you want me to go? You never want me to have any fun."

"I don't care if you go. I just want you to understand what you're doing. You're still in the family dynamic with these people, Lydia. You're still letting yourself be treated like a child. This woman, Noel, wants to pay your expenses. This is not the independence you've been striving for."

"I'm tired of striving for independence. Daniel's coming from North Carolina. I've been in love with him for years. He's so gorgeous. I can't believe he won't get interested in me."

"Then go on. It's fine with me."

"I'm going. I told them I was going and I can't back out now."

TRACELEEN   So one morning in March, right after Mardi Gras, Miss Crystal says to me, "Traceleen, I have an adventure planned. Mrs. Chatevin wants us to go up to Maine and stay at her house all summer. You could take your niece Andria and let her earn money for college. If I go, will you go?"

"What is it like?" I asked, getting cautious. I have traveled with Miss Crystal before and I have learned to ask questions before I agree to go. Once she took me to an island off the coast of Belize and that is the most uncomfortable I have ever been in my life. There was an outdoor toilet and the worst food I have ever tasted. But back to Maine.

"It's this house Noel bought years ago when she was a hit on Broadway. It's very old and has about twenty rooms and there is a caretaker there. It's on the Atlantic Ocean. Think how good it would be for the children."

"I'll think it over."

"It's on a peninsula. The Atlantic Ocean, think of that. We'll be cool and breathing pine trees while the people of New Orleans swelter. If you don't like it you can leave. Will you go and try it?"

"Let me talk to Andria. If she wants to go I might."

"Noel really wants us to go. She's got it all planned out."

"She doesn't have anything else to think about." It's the truth. Miss Noel lives through other people now. She is always thinking about the ones like Miss Crystal who are her favorites. When she wants them to do something she is very good at talking them into it. Sometimes she calls here very early in the morning wanting Miss Crystal for something and Miss Crystal throws on her clothes and goes right over. They are extremely close friends.

About a week after Miss Crystal first mentioned Maine to me she mentioned it again. "Let's go over and talk to Noel," she suggested. "She'll tell you about it better than I can."

"All right," I said. "As soon as I finish this kitchen. I can't stand this refrigerator another day."

"Come on now," she insisted, "when we get back I'll help you with it." Then the two of us walked around the corner to pay a call on Miss Noel and get more details.

She was sitting up in her bed with frilly pillows all around her and books and papers and all the mess of her projects on tables by the windows. Many paintings were propped against the walls and there were glass jars with cookies and several opened boxes of candy on the tables. Miss Noel herself is very thin. She keeps the candy and cookies for her visitors.

"It would be wonderful to get out of the swamp for the

summer," she began. "Traceleen, you owe it to your niece
to let her see the world. Did she say she might go?"

"She was all for it. I'm the one who can't decide. What
is there to do up there for black people?"

"The same things there are for white people. Rest and
think, see the ocean, sleep in the ocean air. Don't you think
Crystal needs a change, after what you've been through
with King?"

She was referring to problems we have had with King
and taking drugs. We had had him back in school and off
of them for several months when this idea of Maine came
up. But Miss Noel was right. It had been a terrible year and
Miss Crystal hadn't left home even to go skiing or sail their
sailboat in the British Virgin Islands or do a thing but worry,
worry, worry. I have no children myself and lately I have
begun to think I was lucky not to. The things they do to
your heart.

"Go on up there," Miss Noel insisted. "Have an adventure. See the world."

"I'm seeing the world right now," I answered.

"Go to Maine," Miss Noel said again. "You'll be glad you
did."

"If Traceleen will go, I will," Miss Crystal put in. "You
can hire all the help you need, Traceleen. And if you don't
like it you can leave."

"Let me think it over," I said. "Give me another week."

Of course in the end I agreed and we began to make our
plans. Here is who all was going once the plans were laid.
Myself and my niece Andria, to keep the house and let Andria earn money for LSU. Miss Crystal and her son, King,

age nineteen. Crystal Anne, age nine. Plus our visitors, the list of which was growing with every phone call.

King said he would only go if he could invite Mr. Daniel Hand of Charlotte, North Carolina, and his daughters, Jessica and Olivia. Then Miss Crystal found out Mr. Manny would not be able to join us because he was on some big case involving millions of dollars, so Miss Crystal invited Miss Lydia, her best friend from Seattle who is a painter and an actress on television. Miss Lydia has never married and lives alone in a cottage by a rain forest and devotes herself to art. She is deathly afraid of airplanes because she is so sensitive to the internal workings of things. Still, she manages to come to New Orleans several times a year to visit and sell her paintings at shows Miss Crystal and Miss Noel arrange. Miss Lydia is also a very close friend of Miss Noel's and lived in her house one year while she was painting the flowers of New Orleans and the debutantes and the graves. It was Miss Noel who talked Miss Lydia into flying down to join our expedition. She told her an artist has to know the exact moment when they must agree to take their life in their hands.

So Miss Lydia came and joined us. She arrived in the middle of the afternoon with all her bags and paintings. She still travels like they did when they were hippies, with her clothes rolled up in little sets in a canvas bag and her paintings underneath her arm. She takes them off the frames and rolls them up and brings them to show Miss Crystal and Miss Noel every time she comes from California. Both Miss Crystal and Miss Noel have collected quite a few of Miss Lydia's paintings. I think Miss Lydia's paintings are more wonderful than any I have ever seen and I can never understand why she wants to waste her time being a television actress.

"I am only listening to country music all summer," she declared as she came into the hall, with King behind her carrying her things. Miss Crystal had had to go to Crystal Anne's graduation at Saint James and couldn't meet the plane, so King had gone in her place. "I have given up on the real world. Let's go to Maine, wherever that turns out to be."

"Oh, Lydia, you look so wonderful," Miss Crystal said. It is always the first thing she says to any of her friends. Of course Miss Crystal is blind as a bat without her glasses, which she never wears, so all she sees of her friends is the colors they are wearing and their smiles. Occasionally, she will look up at me when she is at her desk doing bills or wearing her glasses in the kitchen to see a recipe. Then she will move in real close and really look at me as though she had never seen me before, and begin to comment on the color of my eyes or my earrings, the same ones I have worn every day since my auntee died down in Boutte and willed them to me. Amethysts set in eighteen-karat gold that were given to her by a Mrs. LaDoux Provostee of Ascension Parish. I had my ears pierced to receive them when I was twenty-five years old and I have worn them ever since. Anyway, Miss Crystal goes on about how wonderful Miss Lydia looks and I put on some coffee and get out some home-made chocolate walnut cookies and they settle down at the breakfast-room table to talk.

"I am only listening to country music and only painting people I admire and only acting in plays written by geniuses. I have had it with the culture," Miss Lydia says. "I am in love with a program called *Austin City Limits*. Chet Atkins is my ideal now. When he puts that guitar down close to his dick and begins to play, I almost faint. I am into older men." Miss Lydia lets the shoulder bag she is carrying drop onto the floor and holds out her arms to Crystal Anne, who is dancing around in her red tutu wearing a tiara. She falls into Miss Lydia's lap and begins to study her beads.

"Noel said you could paint in her studio in Maine," Crystal said. "She said everything you need is there."

"I'm going to paint a series of heroes," Miss Lydia declares. "I'm going to paint Barbara Jordan and Cesar Chavez and men and women who have served their people. Oh, God, Crystal. I saw a wolf last week down in Northern California. Oh, God, you wouldn't believe it. It had this intelligent haunting gaze. I almost died."

"Maybe they'll have some up in Maine," I said. "They might have them there. Where is this Maine anyway?"

Then we got out the maps and looked them over and planned what roads we would go on and then Miss Crystal and Miss Lydia went over to spend the afternoon with Miss Noel and get the keys to the mansion and last-minute advice about what to do if the electricity went out. It was the twenty-third of May. In the morning we would leave.

After I left work that afternoon I went by my sister's house to see if Andria was ready to leave. She is my oldest niece and the apple of my eye. She has always made the finest grades and worked to prepare herself for the future. She had just finished high school at the New Orleans Center for the Creative Arts, and was planning on going to Louisiana State University in Baton Rouge in the fall. She was going to study with a poet there who is on a radio program everyone around here listens to. This poet from Russia or somewhere who came once to Andria's school and talked with them. So Andria was saving money for LSU and was delighted when Miss Crystal offered her six hundred dollars a month and room and board to come along to help out in Maine. It would be so nice for me to have her company at this time in her life. They grow up so fast, the young ones that we love. Before long all we have are memories and they are gone out to the world.

"You ready to go?" I said. I had found her in the living room, watching television and polishing her toenails. "You got your things packed?"

"I'm almost ready." She looked up, finished a toenail, then put the nail-polish brush back into the bottle. I looked around the room. It was so dark and crowded. Such a musty old place to have a pearl like Andria sitting in the middle of it, polishing her nails. I won't comment on my sister Mandana and the life she lives. Who are we to judge?

"Miss Lydia's arrived and they want to leave by noon tomorrow. We are going to start off slow and drive to Montgomery, Alabama, and stop to see a Shakespearean play at a theater there. Then the next day we can begin to really drive."

"How long is this going to take?"

"About six days the way they have it mapped now. They want the trip to be educational for everyone."

"Is King going?" Andria screwed the cap down on the fingernail polish and got up from the sofa. She was wearing a pair of very tight blue jeans cut off so short you could see her underpants and a little tight halter top. I guess they all wear that now but I cannot get used to it. Still, if someone has to go around half naked it might as well be Andria. Her body is like a beautiful tall young tree. I delight in her until my heart could break. All her life she has been the same lovely little pale chocolate tree, growing taller and taller without ever getting awkward or whining. She is of mixed blood. Her father was a sailor from Norway that my sister met in the French Quarter, never heard from again.

"Is King going for sure?" She pulled down the top to cover her little nipples and kicked the television set off with the very tip of her painted toe. Then she moved over nearer to me and gave me a little hug.

"Of course he's going. Miss Crystal is paying him the same as she's paying you because he is supposed to do the heavy work and be the lifeguard when people go out to the sea."

"Good," she said. "I'm glad he's going. I like him a lot. He's always good to me."

"You will like everyone that's going along," I said. "Come on, let me see what you are packing. It might be cold up there, honey. You can't just take summer clothes."

"I got everything packed," she said. "I got everything you told me to bring." Then we went into her room and she let me look at what she had packed and I suggested a few other things and she put them in. Then she put on a skirt and we went down to the K&B drugstore and bought her some shampoo and deodorant and powder and a new toothbrush and some other things I thought she might need. If I had any second thoughts about taking her off for three months with only a bunch of white people, I put them aside because of the chance it would give her for an education.

We left at noon the next day. We were in two cars, preparing to go all the way up the United States from New Orleans,

Louisiana, to Maine. Here is who was in the cars. Andria and myself and Crystal Anne and King in one, with King driving. That was the Peugeot. Then Miss Crystal and Miss Lydia in the station wagon with the luggage and supplies. It is the baby blue station wagon Mr. Phelan bought for us in Texas when the oil bust caused all the Mercedes Benz cars to go on sale. It is a very comfortable automobile and the prettiest blue I have ever seen, inside and out.

It was a beautiful hot day when we left New Orleans, the sun beating down out of a blue sky and reflecting on the Bonnet Carré spillway and the lake. We headed east toward Mobile, then turned and drove up the state of Alabama to Montgomery. We were taking a route that would lead us to Atlanta, Georgia, and Greenville, South Carolina, then over to Lynchburg and Alexandria, Virginia, and Washington, D.C., after which we could just drive up the Eastern Seaboard all the way to our destination.

I can't tell you everything that happened on the trip but some of it is worth writing down. Like the play we saw in Montgomery, Alabama, the first night. *The Midsummer Night's Dream* with this Robin fellow sprinkling lily juice on everyone to make them fall in love. The costumes were so lovely and the way the stage was decorated. Everyone was quite set up afterward and had to talk for hours and couldn't sleep.

Another thing was the plane ride over the city of Atlanta. Miss Crystal's old roommate from college, Miss Alexandra DeMent, lives there now and is married to a man so rich he buys her airplanes and she flies across the ocean by herself and into Canada and is in races. She took us up in a little one-engine plane called *The Debutante* and we looked down

on Atlanta, Georgia, going out to lunch. It is hard to believe
there are that many people in the world, much less only in
Atlanta. First Miss Crystal and Crystal Anne and I went up
and flew around, then we came down and Miss Alexandra
took the others up. Afterward, we spent the night at Miss
Alexandra's house and had a very interesting Chinese dinner of artichoke and cold fish and sliced fruit. No wonder
Miss Alexandra stays so thin, I told Miss Crystal. Eating such
exotic food and flying around in airplanes all day.

"Oh, she does many other things," Miss Crystal answered. "She collects money for charities and teaches other
women how to fly. She flies in the Powder Puff Derby and
each year almost wins. As soon as she gets the right plane
she is going to win."

"I hope she does," I answered. "She is the epitome of
what a rich lady should turn out to be and looks so dashing
in her slacks and scarves."

"I'm going to be a pilot," Andria put in. "The minute I
get a chance I'm learning how."

"Me, too," Crystal Anne says. "Flying is the thing for
me."

"You've got to let me have lessons," King added. "I don't
care what it costs. I'll pay for them myself."

Later that night King and Andria went off for a long walk
alone in Miss Alexandra's neighborhood and I stayed up
half the night worrying about them. That was two nights
my sleep was interrupted and we had barely begun our trip.
Well, who ever said travel would be easy? No one did.

The next day I got Andria off and questioned her about her
talk with King. "I don't want any hanky-panky going on

with him," I said to her. "I can't have you spoiling my summer that way."

"It's not your summer," Andria said. "And it's not your life. Don't start bossing me around, Auntee Traceleen, or I'll quit and hitchhike home." She thought she had me where she wanted me. They know just how to do that at that age. They get you in a position where you can be embarrassed if you make a fuss and then they go and do whatever they want to do. Most grown people fall for that, but I do not. I have spent too many years counseling young people at the church to be fooled by anything they say.

"You will not have to hitchhike," I told her. Just as cold as I could be. "I will put you on a bus myself."

The next day I insisted that Miss Crystal change the personnel in the cars around and let Andria drive in the station wagon part of the time with Miss Lydia. Not that Miss Lydia is a perfect influence on the young but at least I didn't have King and Andria in the front seat of the Peugeot day after day looking at each other's legs.

2

TRACELEEN Five days later we arrived in Maine. It was not a disappointment although it was not as beautiful as I had expected it to be either. Here is how it looked as we crossed the New Hampshire state line at Dover and began to drive along the coast. Huge pine trees everywhere, and, as the afternoon wore on, the beginning of these funny-looking cloud formations. Mackerel clouds, I found out later they are called, like the scales on a fish. When you see those clouds in the daytime you know there will be a beautiful sunset later on. There was one that day. We had to stop the cars several times to get out and look, sunlight reflecting off all sides of these little scales of clouds. I couldn't help thinking this was fisherman's country, although the seafood up here was all going to be new to me.

Besides the giant pine trees and the sunset, there was also this very clean smell to the air and along the way small white houses with no decoration or porches to speak of. No flowers growing and the cars were very plain. The only bumper sticker I saw was one that said DO NOT CUT THE PINES. It was on a Volvo driven by an old man.

"I thought it would be prettier," Crystal Anne said. "Miss Noel said it would be pretty."

218

"It will be better when we get there, I guess," Andria chimed in. Then we came around a curve and began to drive along the sea. It must have been six or seven o'clock by then. The sea was not much better. No surf at all and the beaches were small and gray. To tell the truth the ocean looked mean up here in Maine, gray and uninviting. Of course we are used to Gulf Shores, Alabama, with its big wide beaches full of people in the summer and everyone having a party.

Then it was night and Andria spelled King at the wheel and the rest of us took a nap while we waited to get to our destination. I woke up once and saw a sign that said, "Cranberries for Sale." Aside from that, it was mostly white houses and pine trees. Welcome to Maine, I was thinking. How on earth did we decide to come all the way up here? We must have lost our heads or been under some sort of spell.

It was cold by the time we arrived at the house. Miss Noel had warned us that the nights were cold but I don't think we took her seriously enough. The little skimpy sweaters I had brought for myself and Andria were not going to be any protection against this wind.

The night watchman was standing on the porch of the house waiting for us when we got there. He had only one light on in the house and hadn't even bothered to start a fire, although we had called to tell him we were coming. He shuffled down the stairs and let us in and showed us where the bedrooms were. We collected all the blankets we could find and divided them up and then fell out on the beds. We were just completely worn out. Seven days and six nights it had taken us to travel the United States. Along the way we had seen a Shakespearean play and driven a thousand seven hundred and sixty-four miles and been to the Smithsonian Museum and the Lincoln Memorial and the Washington Memorial and the Vietnam Veterans Memorial Wall, where I cried my heart out over my cousin, Taylor Brown, and for all the mothers and wives and fatherless children. We had seen Philadelphia, PA, and New York City, New York, and the Plymouth Rock Plantation and been to Boston Harbor. Just to name a few of the sights we took in, not to mention sleeping in five different motel and hotel rooms and eating at twenty or thirty different restaurants. We were worn out and full of enough educational sights to last several years. I decided I had made the right decision to bring Andria along no matter what happened next. We had seen half the United States already and here we were, having our first night's sleep in Miss Noel's mansion on the ocean near Tennant's Harbor, Maine.

In the morning Miss Crystal and I got up and made some oatmeal and coffee and scrambled eggs. We were scurrying around the kitchen in our bathrobes and socks trying to decide what to do to get warm. The night watchman was nowhere to be found and we didn't know how to start a fire in the old-timey kitchen stove so we just turned on the electric oven and let it help out while we cooked.

The family started to filter in. King came in and took over building a fire. "Don't burn us down," Miss Crystal said, so I took her arm and frowned. We have made a pact that whenever she starts saying things to King that might start a fight or make him feel he is not a man I am to stop her. "The wood is right here," he said. "It wouldn't be here if it didn't go in the stove."

"Watch out for spiders," I warned. "They hide in the wood pile."

Then Andria came to stand in the door. "I'm freezing to death," she said. "I can't believe it's this cold in June."

"Eat some of this oatmeal," Miss Crystal advised. "We will have a meeting as soon as everyone gets up. It's clear there is more to living in Noel's house than we imagined. I guess it's like learning to ski."

After everyone was up and fed we got together around the kitchen table and decided to go into town and buy some long underwear. Then come home and have each person learn to use all the stoves and the fireplaces. Then we would tour the house and decide who would sleep where. The house had turned out to be much larger than we imagined, although we had seen pictures. It was three stories counting the attic and there was also an apartment over an old garage. Three living rooms and a dining room and the kitchen. Porches all around and woods going out in all directions and the ocean not half a mile away. We had been there since nine o'clock the night before and none of us had seen the ocean.

"The ocean," King said. "I just remembered we are on the ocean." Then we all got up and banked the fire in the kitchen stove and went out to look at the sea. We bundled up in whatever we could find, there were jackets and old coats in a closet under the stairs, that Crystal Anne, bless her heart, had found. She had been running all over the place finding everything while the rest of us were eating oatmeal.

We walked in a line toward the sea. King and Andria and Crystal Anne, then Miss Lydia and Miss Crystal and me.

King began to do little jumps. Then Andria would push him. Then Crystal Anne would run ahead and King would catch her and tickle her.

"I hope the young people find plenty to do," I said. "I hope we can keep them busy." I took Miss Crystal's arm as I said it. She is so sensitive about King. She is sensitive about everything, especially since she quit drinking. You can say the slightest thing to her and she will worry about it for days.

"They need to meet other young people," Miss Lydia said. "Noel said there was a place in town called The Hangout where they can go and meet people their age. We'll take them there. I want us to have an open house where they can bring people that they meet. A salon."

"I would like for Andria to meet some young people of her own race if any are up here," I said. "You must understand I am very old-fashioned about that."

"I've got a whole list of things for them to do," Miss Lydia went on. "There's a boat to take them deep-sea fishing and a sailing boat with a captain we can charter. Also, there are people who can take them back into the woods to see the old logging camps. Don't start worrying about the kids, Traceleen. We're going to keep them busy."

"As long as we keep them from drinking or having bad companions," I added. "What are Mr. Hand's daughters like that are coming from North Carolina?"

"They're just normal teenagers," Miss Crystal said. "Jessie's a sweetheart, the prettiest girl you've ever seen. But Olivia is the smart one. She came in third in some big essay or debate contest in Washington this year. She's a brain. She's part Cherokee Indian, Traceleen. That ought to be good for Andria."

"Normal teenagers," Miss Lydia said. "Full of sadness and perfection. I wish I could remember what it was like to be that age. It had a smell to it, there was something about those summers. Do you remember, Crystal, what it was like to be that age?"

"We used to get drunk," Crystal said. "Don't remind me of it, Lydia."

"Well, I think we came to the right place," I put in. "This seems like a very healthy environment."

"Oh, God, smell that," Miss Lydia added, getting a whiff of the pine trees.

Then the ocean opened up before us. So dark and cold and far out in all directions. The waves seemed stronger than they do at home, as if they were coming from far away across a cold long sea. In Gulf Shores I always think of the water going down to South America or over to the British Virgin Islands where Miss Crystal took me one Christmas to live on a boat. This water seemed to come from a darker place, although it is all the same ocean really. It had a nice smell, however. The air was so clean you might have to get used to breathing it. We quieted down when we saw the sea. The young people ran ahead and began to wade along the edge. Miss Crystal and Miss Lydia and I held back, standing at the very edge of the sand, trying to take it in.

"It's magnificent," Miss Lydia said. "We need to see this, ladies. The world is wide and full of mystery."

"Thy winds, thy wide gray skies, thy mists that roll and rise," Miss Crystal added. "I think Millay lived up here somewhere. Maybe in New Hampshire. I'll look it up."

We walked for a while, then made a place to sit and watch the children and Miss Lydia said now she understood why Miss Noel had insisted we come there and that Miss Noel was right as always, because she is a genius.

Later in the morning we all drove into town in the station wagon and bought groceries and long underwear and four inexpensive blankets. One for Andria and me. One for Miss Crystal and Crystal Anne. One for Miss Lydia. One for King.

If only things could have stayed the way they were that first morning. By the time we got back to the house and put the groceries away the phone had begun to ring. First it was Mrs. Helen Abadie from North Carolina, the sister of Daniel Hand, and her boyfriend she is not supposed to have because she is married, calling to say they may come up and spend a weekend soon. They were in Boston working on the papers of Miss Anna Hand, who was Miss Crystal's cousin that was a novel writer. Then Mr. Alan called from Virginia and said he and his tennis partner were on their way. Mr. Alan is Miss Crystal's Achilles' heel. He is this very shallow type of man who thinks he is God's gift to women. He doesn't do a thing for a living that I can see except get his name in the paper for going to all the right parties. He also gives parties, although Miss Crystal doesn't go to them. She helps him plan the menu and makes shrimp Creole for him to feed his friends and runs down to the French Quarter to buy lemon ice and Italian cookies for his desserts but only his friends his own age go to the parties.

I do not know what Miss Crystal could possibly see in him or why this thing has dragged out between them all these years. Last winter she decided to give him up for good and try to mend her marriage to Mr. Manny, but it did not work. There is something wrong between Mr. Manny and Miss Crystal, some old scar or bad chemistry. No matter how hard they try to make their marriage work it never sticks. So here we were, up in Maine, and Mr. Alan calls. Crystal Anne and King hate the sight of him, so of course he calls and says he's coming up to ruin the summer. We hadn't even assigned the rooms yet or put the groceries away.

Only a fool would think they understand the smallest thing about why people do the things they do. Only the world's biggest fool would think they know why something happens or can ever guess what will happen next. I had had such big hopes for this summer, a quiet time to teach the children about a state almost into Canada, with bear and deer and giant pine trees and swamps of cranberries growing wild. (Some of the things I found out about Maine in the *Encyclopaedia Britannica* I bought for Andria last year.) Maine is as far north as you can go and still be in the United States. Still, it wasn't far enough to keep Mr. Alan away from a free meal and a free you-know-what-else.

"Alan's coming?" King asked, when his mother got off the phone. "He's coming up here?"

"Go into town and get some more blankets," Miss Crystal said. "Here's some money. He won't stay long. He's only coming for a visit on his way to teach tennis up in Canada. He'll be gone when Jessie gets here." She looked down, pretending to be poking around in her purse for her money. King just stood there, getting his old devil-may-care attitude. "Well, I'll take Andria and we might stop by that Hangout place," he said. "Don't look like that, Mother. It's your vacation. You can have anybody up here that you want. I just came along to earn my pay." He started for the door, Andria lined up behind him. I guess she knew what was going on.

She's been around the Weisses since she was a little girl. And the Weisses don't keep anything they do a secret. "You don't care if we spend some time in town, do you?" King added, in this bitter tone.

"Of course not," Miss Crystal says. "Do you want some money? Do you need some money?"

"No," he says. "I have everything I need." Then he and Andria headed out and took the Peugeot and disappeared. I looked at Miss Lydia and shook my head. Miss Lydia returned my look. Crystal Anne came over to her mother and put her arms around her waist. She is the sweetest little girl I have ever known. She was born that way.

"Let's look at the house," Crystal said. "We are so lucky to have this great big scary house to stay in all the summer. Come on, let's go and pick out what rooms we want."

"Why is Alan coming?" Miss Lydia asked. "Crystal, why are you letting him come up here?"

"He won't stay long. He's on his way to Canada. And he's bringing Joe. Joe will give the children tennis lessons. They'll earn their keep."

"I bet they will," Miss Lydia said. "I'm sure they will."

"Come on," Crystal Anne said. "I want to see my room."

So then we decided to explore the house. On the first floor were the living rooms and dining room and kitchen and one bedroom and bath added onto a living room. I suppose someone got old or wanted to be downstairs for the winter. This is an extremely old house Miss Noel has lent us. It was built before the Civil War by a man named Mr. Walker. He was a physician and a politician and other things.

On the second floor were five bedrooms, very large with

bathrooms in between made from closets. There are no showers, only very large old-fashioned bathtubs.

On the third floor, which once was an attic, was a play-room for small children. It was very dusty and had not been used in years. It had a slanting roof and cunning little window boxes built in the windows and toy chests with old toys Miss Noel had collected at auctions and left there. It made me sad to pick up the toys and think of Miss Noel when she was young and beautiful, before she became an invalid and had to stay inside a house in New Orleans. When she could travel around the world and go to her house in Maine. Many famous people from the stage had been there to visit. Tallulah Bankhead had come one time. Miss Lydia wanted to have the bedroom where Tallulah Bankhead had stayed. She called Miss Noel several times to see if she could remember which one it was. They decided it was a front bedroom painted blue, so Miss Lydia took her blanket and moved in there.

That was one of the nicest days of my life, the first day we spent in Miss Noel's house in Maine. If only things could stay like their beginnings and not get complicated. Still, what are people for if not to have problems and untangle things when they get tangled. Andria has gotten involved with some Buddhist ideas and she says you could keep things from ever getting out of hand if you could be content to sit still. Like old people that sit all day on the swing or in a rocking chair and don't bother anything. But we come to that soon enough without wanting it our whole lives. All these things are so complicated. Just thinking about them is complicated. Much less when they are really happening all around you as they started happening during our vacation in Maine.

For some reason that summer I often thought of how the deer in Louisiana mate in the forest in the fall. How my husband Mark goes out with his cousins to shoot the deer when they are rutting. The deer get so crazy they leave their place of safety and run all over the forest putting themselves in danger. That is Nature having its way with us and why we have invented religion and civilization to calm us down. I was the only one that went to church that summer. Although I took Andria whenever I could get my hands on her. And once I took Crystal Anne.

ANDRIA   The minute King found out Alan was coming he started going crazy. I went with him because I felt sorry for him and because I was afraid he would start drinking. Aunt Traceleen doesn't know it but I used to run into him down by Tipitina's before he quit. You never saw a boy that wild or crazy. So I was prepared for the worst but all he did when he got in the car was start complaining. Men complain all the time. They're always accusing women of complaining, but you listen sometime and see who does the most.

"I'd like to know what she expects me to do," he says, stripping the gears and driving off down the rutted driveway as fast as he could go. "I went to that goddamn clinic and listened to all those old sad bastards and I quit shooting up and now she's letting Alan come up here. Goddamn Alan."

"Don't drive so fast," I say. "I'm not getting killed just because your momma made you mad."

"So I'm supposed to go into town and get him a blanket.

Let her keep him warm. She's the biggest whore in New Orleans. You know she is."

"Don't talk about your momma like that."

"I want to find that place Lydia told us about. That Hangout. I've got to find someplace to get away from her."

"Well, don't start drinking around me. I'm not getting in on you starting drinking again. You were some kind of fool when you were doing all that shit." He looked at me like I can't believe you'd say that, but then he slows down and starts acting like he has some sense. He is one good-looking boy and that's for sure. If only he would act as good as he looks.

"Are you going to start drinking?" I ask. "Say so if you are."

"No, I'm not starting drinking. I'm going to town to find where they have meetings. I haven't been to a meeting since we left New Orleans. I'm supposed to go every day. Not that she cares. She has to get up here to shack up with her boyfriend." He looked so sad then, so much like a little boy, I began to lose interest in him. I don't need any men with problems. I have problems of my own.

"Well, your girlfriend's coming, isn't she?"

"She better be. The only reason I came along is because she's coming. I would have gone to stay with Dad except for that. Mother's bad enough when she's alone but now she's got Lydia, my so-called godmother, and next it will be Alan. What a piece of shit this summer's turning into."

"Let's go and find those meetings. I might go with you to one. I'm a Co-Dependent of my mother. My counselor at school last year said I should check out those Co-Dependent meetings at the AA."

"It's not the AA. It's just AA."

"Well, let's go find it. There's nothing else to do." So we drove on into town and found The Hangout and had a Pepsi and then we went by the Episcopal Church and talked to the minister and got King set up for some AA meetings at the church. I signed up for the Co-Dependent group but I only went once. It looked like a bunch of whiners to me. Let my mother drink if she wants to. I'm out of there.

CRYSTAL   Oh, God, now King will ruin everything with Alan. I'm so sick of never being happy. I let him have Jessie come up here. I came all the way up here to let him see his girlfriend. I talked Daniel into letting her come. If Daniel wasn't in love with me he wouldn't let his daughter go out with King. I wouldn't let my daughter go out with him even if he has quit drinking. He's too much like his father. He'll never be faithful to one woman. Well, he loves Jessie now.

I'm sick of being a mother. I want my own life. I want to get laid occasionally, even if it's only Alan. Oh, it's so nice when we're together. He's so funny and so mean and he's so graceful. After that long car trip and Lydia feeling sorry for herself until I could throw up. Thank God Traceleen came along. If it wasn't for Traceleen I couldn't stand it here. She is such a divine person, anytime she's in a room things get better. Traceleen and Crystal Anne. What a pair. I guess Crystal Anne imprinted on Traceleen. I was so sick after she was born. I don't remember the first few weeks. I guess Traceleen was holding her every minute while I got well, just filling her up with that weird goodness Manny says is a form of genius. I wish he had come with us. We might make it if he'd quit working so hard all the time. We're rich enough. What else does he want?

Well, I don't care. I can take care of myself. I have plenty of friends. And Alan will be here and fucking him is worth all the trouble that it makes. If King starts drinking just because Alan's coming, then I give up on him. If he starts drinking, I'll tell Daniel not to come.

Poor Manny. If he could fuck me it might be all right. He just isn't any good. He isn't bad. He isn't impotent. He just isn't any good. Maybe it was the boys' school. Maybe they masturbated all the time. I don't know. Maybe when he fucks me he has to confront something that scares him to death. I have never been able to understand it and I've given up. I'm sorry. I'm a beautiful woman and I want a lover. I don't care how much trouble they are. I can't sleep with sexually immature men. Oh, God, why has my life turned out this way? And look at King, just like his daddy. He will have every woman in the world before it's over. He will never be able to control it. Give me the man who is not passion's slave. And I will give you somebody who can't fuck worth a damn.

3

TRACELEEN I can see I am going to have to tell this one love story at a time. I will begin with Miss Crystal herself. She is married to Mr. Manny and they are determined to stay married because of Crystal Anne and because Miss Crystal is so accustomed to Mr. Manny's money that she cannot imagine herself with a different lifestyle. Unfortunately, Miss Crystal and Mr. Manny are no longer in love with each other. The romance has gone out of their marriage.

At the time of our trip to Maine Miss Crystal had been in love with Mr. Alan off and on for several years. "I would rather have one night with him than a lifetime with any other man," she said to me one time.

Personally, from what I have seen of Mr. Alan he does not look like a great lover to me. I don't think he cares about a thing except himself. Of course, Miss Crystal's father is the same way. A very spoiled unpleasant man and extremely handsome. My auntee always told me you must watch and see how a person's parents are and from that you can tell who they will fall in love with. Well, my niece Andria's

232

father has never been heard from again, so where does that leave her where men are concerned? But back to Miss Crystal.

We had been in Maine for six days when Mr. Alan got there. He shows up with his buddy, Mr. Joe Romaine. They are on a tennis-playing tour to make money for the summer. As soon as he gets there Miss Crystal starts sleeping with him again. She has this ecstatic look and starts losing weight and wearing light colors and letting Crystal Anne and King do anything they like. Also she starts cooking. She is cooking and directing the household and planning picnics and playing tennis. They have cleared off the tennis court. She is getting a tan and dressing up in four different outfits a day. I hadn't seen Miss Crystal like that in a long time and it worried me. She starts going on like that and I think she will spin off into the other side of the universe. If only she doesn't start drinking, I was thinking, and would shudder whenever she got out a bottle of wine and opened it for the others. People are so sensitive. Sometimes they are like balls of light and hardly seem to touch the floor as they move around each other saying things. The things they say are the hardest things of all and seem to have the most weight.

By the time he's been there three days, Mr. Alan brought it down to earth. He began to pout. Miss Crystal had asked him to stay two weeks. He starts saying he doesn't know how long he and Mr. Joe Romaine can stay. They may have to go up to Canada and teach at a camp because they are so broke. Then he's on the phone a lot and acting so phony anyone could see through it, only of course Miss Crystal can't. Because she is back to being in love with him.

Andria said to me, "He's a manipulator if I ever saw one. He's manipulating her by moping around like that. He's a dope." We were folding clothes in the living room. Andria is studying psychology this summer. She is planning on having a minor in psychology at college so she can fall back on being a counselor. She is reading so much psychology she can hardly enjoy anything from figuring out what it means in psychology.

On top of everything else Mr. Alan started taking Miss Lydia for long walks along the ocean's edge. I couldn't believe she would go. It isn't like Miss Lydia to let someone break up her friendship with Miss Crystal. Especially a man like Mr. Alan who won't even say how many days he is going to stay. Mr. Romaine, on the other hand, was turning out to be a delightful guest. He was giving free tennis lessons to Crystal Anne and Andria and King and even tried to give one to me. He said he had heard from Andria about my basketball prowess when I was a girl in Boutte and he dragged me out onto the tennis court one afternoon. I caught on very quickly but I couldn't see the fun of playing tennis with the wind blowing off the ocean and blowing the balls everywhere. I had played some when I was young on the courts beside the Coca-Cola bottling plant in Boutte where there is no wind and it was quite a different game. Still, I appreciated Mr. Romaine wanting me to be in on the tennis lessons. Also I liked the way he thought he had to do something to pay us back for our hospitality. Mr. Alan, he acts like the world owes him a living from the word go.

* * *

While these entanglements are going on with the adults, Crystal Anne is building onto a treehouse she found behind the garage in an old maple tree. Andria is studying psychology books. King is fishing and waiting for Mr. Daniel Hand to get here with his daughters and I am interviewing applicants from the employment agency to find someone to do the heavy work.

4

LYDIA   Of course the reason Noel sent us up here is to get the letters Anna wrote to her. They're right there in the dining room in the blue chest. We hadn't been in Maine twenty-four hours before Noel called up to see if I had found them yet.

"They're right there," I said. "Where you said they'd be."

"Good. Bring them when you come."

"Why are you so worried about them?"

"I don't want anyone seeing them. I want you to bring them here but don't read them first."

"I don't want to read them. I'm furious with Anna for killing herself. It was a stupid cowardly act."

"Just bring them to me. You don't mind doing that, do you?"

"You want me to mail them?"

"No. I want you to bring them to me yourself."

Noel. Who could ever figure her out? My psychiatrist says she is living vicariously through all of us now that she can't live for herself. He says I should learn from that to live my own life and not expect others to create it for me. Which brings me to Alan. I suppose I have to try to justify that. I'm not perfect. I don't mind admitting I make mistakes.

I will focus on the day Alan arrived. I could see right off he and Crystal were through. He doesn't love her anymore. He got tired of waiting for her to divorce Manny and start supporting him. She stays married to Manny for Manny's money and Alan wants to marry her for her money, although she doesn't have much of her own. Besides, she's too old for Alan. He's my age.

I know all this sounds cynical, but so what? I will tell the truth, not some romantic version. Alan showed up and I was horny and as soon as he and Crystal got over their short honeymoon I got the hots for him.

That's the truth. It's wonderful to tell the truth. You can get sick from lies. You can get lies inside you like bacteria and they will kill you.

Alan arrived one afternoon, just as we were coming back from the beach. I had met him before, one terrible week in New Orleans after Francis Alter died, but we didn't like each other then. I thought he was a callow youth and I guess I will think so again. Anyway, the truth is I betrayed my friend. Alan got interested in me while Crystal was still interested in him and when he asked me, I went walking with him down by the sea.

"Come on down to the ocean with me," he said. "I want to walk and Crystal won't go."

"I have to help King with his homework," she explained. "He has a class to make up that he missed when he was in the hospital."

So Crystal stayed there and Alan and I walked down the

paving stones and on down across the lawn that turns to sand and climbed over the stone wall. When he took my arm to help me over the wall I trembled. I know it was because I hadn't been laid in so long. Everyone in Seattle is afraid to do it with anyone. I can't even want to do it. All I think about is AIDS and chlamydia and yeast infections and ascending cystitis. Something I got the last time I made love. One night with an old boyfriend I've had for years. By morning I had this nasty little cystitis and had to take antibiotics for two weeks. Is it worth it? I'm beginning to doubt it. So why did I think Crystal's snotty social-climbing tennis player boyfriend would be any better? Because fucking isn't thinking. Fucking is desire and is ancient and born of danger and fraught with danger. My subconscious got a whiff of danger and wormed its way into the light by telling me that *Alan was my astral twin.* Is there no end to superstition and insanity? What day were you born? Alan says. July twenty-fifth, I answered, and he says, So was I. Eureka! Same day, same year.

"Crystal's too fragile to make love to," he told me later. "She's ten years older than I am."

"I know," I said, perfidious. But that came later. On this first day, the day he touched me and I trembled, we just walked along beside the sea. We barely spoke. We wandered down across the sand dunes to the beach. It was overcast and gray. The surf was falling so lightly against the rocks, waiting, spinning. To remind us that the world is spinning and that we have no idea what we are doing here.

The surf touched the rocks in its insistent, sensuous way, and I walked next to Crystal's lover and thought of the poverty of my life, going out with rugby players and gallery owners and television people. At least Alan was from a good family. Or at least he knew how to pretend to be from a good family. Joe told me later he had called Alan's home in New York once and the mother answered the phone and she sounded very middle class. Anyway, Alan had gone to Princeton and had good manners and was down in New Orleans trying to make it in society. Climbing any ladder he could find. He had joined Grace Episcopal Church and was going to work in the fall for a wealthy Jewish importer. To be the liaison, he said, whatever that means.

"So you're broke until then?" I asked, trying to break the spell.

"No, I'm not broke. I just don't want to stay here on Crystal's hospitality all summer. We can go up to Canada and pick up some change and come back. It's my last summer before I settle down to the grind." He stuck his hands in his pockets, looked out at the sea. I could see him in his suit and tie, being the liaison, working in the real world. Men are amazing, aren't they? Why do I always want to fuck them? Well, I had put this one on hold by talking about money. Whatever had happened when we crossed the wall had been ruined by my asking him if he was broke.

The next morning he was waiting for me on the porch when I got up. He was dressed and sitting on the top step looking out toward the sea. It couldn't have been later than eight o'clock. "You ready to go see the ocean?" he asked. I was wearing a dressing gown, holding a coffee cup. The dressing gown was white with pale blue flowers and a small ruffle down the front and along the hem. I was barefooted. I let the gown fall open so he could see my chemise. Then I tied it back together. I set the cup down on a colonnade. "Yes," I said. "Let me get on some clothes. I'll be right back."

When I came back Crystal was with him. "We're going walking," he said. "Lydia and I are going to walk to town. Can we bring you anything?"

"It's four miles," she said. She got up, looked at me. I had on white shorts and a T-shirt. I had on tennis shoes. I had on makeup. "Well, enjoy yourselves," she added. Then she was gone. She turned and disappeared into the house. "Let's go," I said. "I need to get some exercise."

So Alan and I walked all the way down to the pier beside the bridge and we walked out on the pier and stood there, side by side with our hips touching, and talked about doing it. How we would do it, why we had a right to do it, if we should tell her we were going to do it.

Then we decided not to do it.

Until the next afternoon when Crystal took all the children into Tennant's Harbor to The Hangout. Traceleen was in the kitchen folding clothes and watching *Days of Our Lives* and Alan came into my room while I was dressing and we did it. I still can't believe I did it. It was the single dumbest thing I've ever done *in my life* and I still haven't figured out why I did it and I'm not sure I learned much from it but I did learn this. Our appetites are waiting. *Homo sapiens* will finally eat and finally get laid so McVey is right and I owe him an apology. No matter how particular I am or how picky or how much I think no one is good enough for me or how much I'm afraid of catching the tiniest little germ, when I get home I have got to find a lover. No matter how much trouble it is or how much time it takes from my work I will never again treat my body the way I treated it the year before I ended up in this nutzoid expedition to the state of Maine.

* * *

Afterward, we put our clothes back on and ignored each other. It was two days later before we met by accident in the yard and decided to go for another walk. We walked down to an old deserted gray house with swings in the yard and sat in the swings and talked about our childhoods. He didn't mention doing it and I didn't mention doing it. I began to think we didn't do it. Maybe I just think we did it.

On our way back we ran into King and Andria sitting on a rock beside the gardens with the flower clock. Andria had her knees tucked up around her breasts. King was talking and she was listening. That's the mating dance. In the mating dance the men talk and the women listen. Later, only the women talk.

"Hi there," Andria said, as we drew near. "Where have you been?"

"Nowhere," Alan said.

"Come walk back with us," I added.

"No. You go on." This from King. He hates Alan. Also, he has started liking Manny *at last*. When Crystal first married Manny, I thought King might kill Manny. He cut down all the roses in Mrs. Weiss's garden during the ceremony. The worst morning of my life. Later, he cut off the tops of the Japanese magnolias Manny planted on the lawn. Then he broke up the marriage. Now he had relented on Manny and was going to decimate Alan. Only Alan was too smart for him. *Alan Dalton*, I can't believe I let myself get taken in by him. Still, he took my arm when we climbed the wall and I started trembling. It's all touch. Be careful who you let touch you, especially if you're far away from home or by an ocean. The ocean in Maine is so powerful and cold and gray. All night, every night all summer, while we were sleeping, the ocean was tugging on us, calling us back to our senses.

"How do you think it's working out with Andria being here?" I asked Crystal, later that morning. I had found her straightening out the silver in the dining room. Just like Noel to have antique silver in a summer house. She used to shop all the time at auctions and yard sales when she spent her summers here. The house is full of gorgeous linens and antiques, things she picked up over the years.

"I think Andria is just fine," Crystal replied. She laid three embossed soup spoons on a red velvet cloth. She didn't look up.

"You aren't mad because I've been taking walks with Alan, are you?" I said. "I won't do it if you don't want me to."

"I don't care what Alan Dalton does. I'm not in charge of his life."

"I thought you still loved him."

"Well, you thought wrong. You can do anything you like with Alan." She stopped, looked straight at me, as if I hadn't been there the spring before when she was so much in love with him she was almost crazy. As if I hadn't driven around with her looking for his car outside of bars and sat for hours one night at Tyler's because she thought he was coming there. As if I hadn't lied to Manny the time we met him in Mandeville for the weekend.

"You don't love him anymore?"

"No. He's too unambitious. He's been out of law school for two and a half years and he still doesn't have a job. I'm not going to put up with any more of Alan's bullshit, Lydia. I don't know why he even came up here."

"Crystal," I began. She had gone back to sorting the silver. Not looking at me. It was dark in the room, the blinds were drawn. I wanted to open one but I went on. "Crystal, please don't start getting mad at me. I love you. I have come all the way across the United States to stay with you. I don't want anything to come between us."

"I don't care what you and Alan do. Do you understand that? When are they leaving anyway?"

"They aren't sure."

"Well, they have to be gone before Daniel gets here with his girls. There isn't going to be room for everyone."

"Don't kick them out because of me. Crystal, please talk to me." She had stopped what she was doing. She was glaring at the napkins. She was sitting cross-legged on the floor in the dark room staring down at the napkins and she was really mad at me. "I want Alan and his friend to leave by Friday morning, Lydia. That's that. Go on up to Canada with them if you want to. This is a family holiday."

"All right," I said. "Hold on. Okay." I walked across the room and began to open the shades. The second one I touched tore off the roller and came crashing down upon a table covered with bric-a-brac. A hand-painted glass lampshade clattered to the floor but did not break.

"It didn't break," I said.

"Well, goddammit," Crystal said, and got up and picked up the lampshade and put it back up on the table. Then she picked up the broken window shade and rolled it up. "Ask Traceleen to come in here and bring a ladder," she said. "We'll have to put this back up."

*   *   *

Helen Abadie called that afternoon. If Noel had told me the exact truth to begin with I would have known what to say. If Noel had said, Lydia, I want you and Crystal to go up to Maine and get Anna's letters and hide them because I don't want Helen to get them, I would have said, Sure, I understand. Those are your letters and Helen doesn't have any right to them.

Instead Noel just tells me this very mysterious thing about getting Anna's letters so I think it's another of her made-up dramas and I don't take it seriously. Then Helen Abadie calls and I answer the phone.

"I want to come up there and bring Mike to meet you," she says. "I've told him all about all of you."

"Sure," I said. "Come on up. I don't know how many rooms have decent beds. But the view is great. Come on."

"We don't need much room," Helen answered. "Just one room. Mike teaches at Harvard. You know that, don't you?"

"No," I lied. "I don't know anything about it." Of course everyone knew Helen had lost her mind and left her husband and five children to live in sin with her fellow literary executor, Mike something or other, in a shabby little apartment in Boston. She hadn't even gone back to Charlotte for her clothes. Poor old Spencer Abadie was down there running the family as best he could while his wife went crazy.

"Helen's coming Saturday," I told Crystal. "Crystal, please stop being mad at me. Nobody's perfect. Jesus Christ."

"I'm stopping being mad," she answered. "I'm stopping as fast as I can."

*   *   *

Everyone was mad at me for a while. I tied my hair back in a knot and stopped wearing makeup and tried to make up with them. I decided to start with Traceleen.

"Is Andria your sister's child?" I asked. I had found her in the breakfast room ironing Crystal Anne's clothes and watching *Ryan's Hope* on a little ten-inch TV she had brought with her from New Orleans.

"Sure is."

"The oldest child?"

"Second to oldest. She's a peach, isn't she?"

"She's a beautiful girl. I hope she's having a good time. I'm sorry there isn't more for them to do."

"There's plenty to do. She's got books she has to read."

"I guess she and King are hitting it off pretty well. I saw them the other day out for a walk."

"Well, his girlfriend's on her way." Traceleen whipped a small white cotton blouse off the ironing board and laid it on a chair. Then she took up a little blue skirt and began on that.

"Are you mad at me too?" I asked.

"Yes," she said. "I certainly am. You know better than to do the way you're doing. You know it isn't right."

"What isn't right? What are you talking about?"

"You know what I'm talking about. You know what I mean."

Traceleen was right. I had traded in my best friend for a mess of pottage. I had rented my house in Seattle for the summer and I didn't have any work waiting and nowhere to go. I had one thousand, seven hundred and fifty dollars to last for three months and now I had fouled my summer's nest. I walked down to the tennis court and found Alan. He was practicing with Joe Romaine. I watched for a while, waiting for them to take a break. King wandered down and then Andria showed up.

"Alan," I said finally. "Could I talk to you?" He laid his tennis racket against the net and came over to where I was.

"What do you need?" he asked.

"Let's go over here," I said. I led him over to a little stagnant fish pond beside the path. King was watching us. The whole time we were talking King stared at us without blinking.

"Look, Alan," I said. "I need to talk. Crystal's furious with me. She knows something's happened. Did you say anything to her?"

"No. God, no. And don't you. Look, I have to finish practicing with Joe, Lydia. Couldn't this wait?"

"She wants you to leave by Friday. Did she tell you that?"

"Joe and I are going up to Canada anyway. I don't care what Crystal does, Lydia. She invited us up here. We didn't ask to come." He bounced a tennis ball with his racket on the stone beside the pond. Bounce, bounce, bounce.

"I'm really worried about all this."

"Well, don't be. Just forget it. I have to get back to the court." He was walking away. He just turned his back and walked away. I looked at King. He was glaring now. Crystal's glare. He looks so much like her it's amazing. I don't know about the Hands and Mannings. No matter who they marry the children all come out left-handed and with those eyes.

That was the night of the Terrible Supper. Traceleen had sent to town for fried chicken from the take-out place and there was salad and bread and store-bought cake and ice cream for dessert. We ate in the dining room on gold-banded china with ancient Strasbourg silver and crystal water glasses. There was German wine in heavy leaded wineglasses. There was a thick white linen tablecloth and cloth napkins and candles on the table. Then Traceleen brought out the chicken on a silver platter. Here we were, in all this baronial splendor, eating fried chicken from a take-out place. Crystal wanted Traceleen to eat with us but she wouldn't do it. Andria ate with us but Traceleen disappeared into the kitchen. As soon as she had food on her plate Crystal Anne disappeared too. Later, when I went to the kitchen to bring out the ice cream for the cake, there they were, the two of them, sitting at the breakfast-room table eating fried chicken and watching a National Geographic special about Canadian bears.

"You should be here," I told Noel, when I called her later that night. "You could get a nurse to bring you on a plane. Hire an RN and get on a plane and come and watch. You owe it to yourself."

"What's happening?" she said.

"Traceleen won't eat at the table but Andria will. Andria's in love with King. I fucked Alan and Crystal knows it. I guess that's all for now."

"You didn't do that, oh, Lydia, say that isn't true."

"It's true. I couldn't help it. My life's a mess, Noel. I've made all the wrong choices. It's done. I've completely ruined my life. This summer is just one more example."

" 'We make the best choices we can based on the information we have available at the moment.' It's all we can do. We don't know enough. We never know enough. You didn't know enough. Don't do it again."

"What's that from? Was that in a play?"

"No, I think that's from Redmond." She giggled. Redmond was a psychiatrist she used to go to. She was in the habit of crediting him with anything she said that she didn't want to take credit for.

"Say it again."

"It means you aren't to blame. But don't do it anymore, Lydia. Apologize to Crystal. Make it up to her. *Tell The Truth.*"

"I tell the truth. I'm the only one in this little summer operation who would recognize the truth if it hit them in the face."

"Good. You be good, Lydia. Please be good." Her sweet old voice was drifting off. I supposed she had taken the night's supply of Valium and lithium and whatever else they are drugging her with these days. "I love you," I said into the receiver, hoping she would hear it.

"Love you too, darling girl," she whispered. Then she was gone.

Telling the goddamn truth. I had to wait until morning to do it. I didn't sleep all night, tossed and turned on the hard wooden bed. About four o'clock I got up and searched all over the kitchen for a Sears catalog. I had decided to order some mattresses for the beds. All that goddamn silver and crystal and gold-banded china and the beds were as lumpy as a girls' camp. I couldn't find the catalog and I remembered I was broke so I ate half a coffee cake instead. She gets fried chicken at a take-out place and makes butter pecan coffee cakes and leaves them in the refrigerator to ruin my life. Why was I mad at Traceleen? I ate the coffee cake and drank a glass of milk and went back upstairs and tried to do some Zen. Something must have worked because I slept finally from four until seven. At seven-thirty I came downstairs again. I was wearing an old chenille robe I found in a closet. Sackcloth and ashes. I found Crystal in the kitchen and dragged her out to the yard. She had on a seersucker robe that was almost as matronly as the one I was wearing. What had happened to us? Could we bear it? Would we hold up? I looked up into the great pine trees on the lawn. I could hear the sea. The beginning of wisdom, I prayed. Just a glimmer of light will do. Light at the end of the tunnel. Light coming down through the cell wall. "Crystal, listen to me. Forgive me. I slept with him. Okay, I did it. It isn't even worth talking about. I'm sorry. I'm sorry as I can be. Forgive me." I tried to take her hands but she pulled away. She walked farther down the lawn, moving toward the ocean. "I'm begging you," I said. "You're the best friend I've ever had. You have to forgive me. Please forgive me. It didn't mean a thing. What can I do?"

"You can't do anything. It's done." She wasn't looking at me. I could see her shoulders going up and down beneath her robe. I have always loved her shoulders so much. I have always wanted to paint her but she never would commission me to do it. That's it, I thought. I will paint a magnificent painting of her and give it to her for a present. Whether she forgives me or not, I will paint her and send it to her.

"Why are you looking at me that way?" she said.

"Because I want to paint you. Like that, in that robe."

"Oh, bullshit, Lydia. You won't pull that with me. I've seen you do that too many times."

"I wasn't pulling anything. I meant it. I want to paint you."

"Lydia, you fucked Alan, okay. I wouldn't have done that to you in a million years and you fucked him."

"I'm so sorry. I'm trying to say I'm sorry."

"Sorry isn't enough."

"Well, Traceleen's coming. Don't talk about it anymore. I don't want her hearing this." She was right. Here came Traceleen running down across the lawn, coming to protect, God knows what, Western Civilization.

"Miss Crystal," she was calling. "Come here, honey. Mr. Manny is calling you. He says he needs to talk to you on the phone."

So we were saved for the moment. I walked down to the sea and tried to decide what to do. I walked all the way to the water and in up to my knees, holding up my robe, not caring if all the Yankees in Maine saw me and sent the sheriffs.

Something happened to me while I fumed in the ocean. I began to want to paint. I ran back to my room and started making sketches for a painting of Crystal. I hadn't worked in so long I could barely tolerate the emotion. My work had been so dogged and uninspired for several years. Now, suddenly, worn out from no sleep and with a headache coming on, I was drawing as if I had never stopped. Sitting by a window looking out on the flat, uninspiring midday ocean, black and cold, totally uninviting grave of a sea, Anna's grave, I had a vision of Crystal as the prototype of all the southern women I had ever known, worn out from dreaming of perfect worlds, perfect lives, perfect lovers, husbands, children, friends. While the life of the world went on she stopped a moment to look down and gather strength before she went back to motion and to dreaming.

That afternoon I cleaned out the studio over the garage and the next day I began to paint.

So I decided not to leave. To hell with Crystal. It was Noel's house, not hers, and besides, Alan was supposed to leave on Tuesday so that was solved. I stretched a canvas, laid out my paints, swept the floor. On Tuesday Alan announced he was staying a few more days. I tacked a diagram to the easel, got out my computer, figured the perspective, altered the angles, began to paint the face. On Wednesday I went to the studio at dawn, stood in the corners of the room and thought about it. Turned the canvas upside down, went over my litany, "Paint as if you were dying," "Leonardo always seemed to tremble when he began to paint." "Draw, Francesco, draw, Francesco, draw and do not waste time."

After a while I left the studio and went down and helped Traceleen start breakfast. Then I walked down to the beach, past the old abandoned boathouse to a spit of rocky land called Druid's Perch. I was thinking about Crystal. It was her fault for having Alan here and introducing him to me. For telling me what a great lover he was. Fuck Crystal, I was thinking. Who does she think she is?

I walked out past a local man folding nets on the sand. He raised his eyebrows at my bathing suit. It wasn't *that* risqué. He kept on looking at me, though, which made me madder. How dare he judge me, look at me. I stuck my nose up in the air and walked around behind the largest of the rocks, thinking I would find a place to look out toward the sea.

"Lydia." It was Crystal. She was already there. With Alan by her side. So now she would think I was following them.

"Oh, Crystal," I said, stupidly. "I didn't know anyone was here."

"We came at six. We decided to watch the morning come. Alan's leaving today."

"So sorry to hear it. Well, I guess I'll be getting back to the house. I was just trying to keep that old bastard with the nets from looking at my legs."

"Stay if you want to."

I looked toward Greenland, thought of the birth of icebergs, of the paltriness of man's life on earth, after all, what was there to it? What was there to lose?

"No, because you're mad at me for fucking Alan. It didn't mean a thing, did it, Alan? It was less important than a fly, the death of a fly. I should have gone home the afternoon it happened and I didn't. Well, I've had enough. I'm definitely going now."

"Oh, God," Alan said, and got up and dove in and started swimming out as fast as he could go.

"Oh, God," I said.

"He's okay," Crystal answered. "He could swim to England if he wanted to. Well, don't leave Maine because of me. It's not my house. It's Noel's house. She invited you."

"She only got me to come to bring her some goddamn papers of Anna's. It's all about Anna, Crystal. The reason all of us are here. Some stuff Anna wrote her that she wants. Poems and letters and things."

"That isn't why she asked me. Noel is my friend." She had stood up and was putting on a blouse.

"I guess we are enemies now," I said.

"I don't know, Lydia. I really don't know." She turned those steely ice-blue eyes on me.

"Stop hating me," I said. "It's yourself you hate. It isn't

me. It's you and Alan and me. I'm a victim as much as you and so is he."

"Do you really believe that?" She shook her head. Then she started climbing back over the rocks. I followed her. Alan was still swimming away. Maybe he was going to England.

"I'm going to town and buy some clothes," she said. "I'm going to spend some money."

"I'm really leaving," I said. "I'm going to call and get a reservation."

"Then go on, I won't stop you." We strode back to the house and I went upstairs and called the airport in Rockland and got a seat on the first plane out the next day. Then I packed. This time I really did it. I wrapped my shoes in paper and put them in the bottom of my canvas bag. I folded each blouse and skirt and rolled them and stored them on top of the shoes. I went out to the studio and started to roll up the canvas of Crystal. So far it was only sketched in and the face half painted. Then I decided to leave it there. One day she would come out to the studio and see it and know what she had missed. I cleaned off a brush and mixed some lavender paint, very pale, far outside the field of blue, lavender that was almost white. I painted one fold down the center of the sketched-in robe. Then I cleaned the brush and left it there.

I went back to the house and climbed the back stairs and went down the hall to the library and got a book and took it upstairs and lay down on the bed to read. It was an old book by this Scandinavian named Pär Lagerkvist, all about an old woman who used to be the oracle in Delphi and had to screw this goat to get high and inhale these burning leaves. Then she'd have this fit and the priests would inter-

pret what she said. When it started she was this simple peasant virgin and at first she liked being waited on and having
everyone look at her in the morning when she walked to
the temple. Then she got fed up with it and started fucking
this boy who swept the leaves and so they kicked her out
and nobody would talk to her anymore. Also, she had a
baby, this deaf and dumb child, and everyone thought it
was the god's son but it was really the boy she fucked who
was the father. What else? In the end this man who had
been mean to Jesus on Jesus' way to the cross came to her
to ask his fate and she and the man and the boy walked up
to the top of the mountain and died in the snow. It was so
beautiful and sad and I was crying like crazy when Crystal
found me. I guess she thought I was crying over her. Not
that I was in the mood to take advantage of something like
that.

"This is the most beautiful, sad book," I said. "I want to
paint like this. To make people feel this way."

"Noel knew that man."

"You're kidding. I thought a woman wrote it. It feels like
a woman's work." I held it out, a small red-bound book.

"Pär is the man's name. Ask her about him. She had a
lot of copies of that book. I can't believe she never gave you
one. Well, look, are you leaving?"

"Yes. I made a reservation for tomorrow afternoon."

"Alan's leaving today."

"So what?"

"So we could make up, couldn't we? I mean, let's stop
it. I want you to stay."

I got up and walked to the window. "I started painting
so I hate to leave in the middle of that. But I'm not going
to stay here with you acting like the ice-maiden. I didn't do

anything but fuck him once. And I've said I was sorry and I am." I turned around. She was looking at me.

"Okay," she said at last. "I'm sorry too. Alan doesn't belong to me. He's just Alan. And you're you and I'm me. That's that. It's all we have to work with."

I looked down at the book. "I might paint this oracle," I said. "Not as an old woman but when she was young and starting out. I could call it 'Smoke Gets in Your Eyes.' I could call it 'The Past Was Not Any Better.' It was worse than now."

" 'Patron Saint of Horoscopes.' "

" 'Virgin Wanting to Believe in Something.' "

" 'Anything Beats Keeping House.' Lydia, I'm sorry this all happened."

"So am I. Really and truly sorry."

So it began to heal between us, not very fast at first, about as fast as nerve tissue heals, or bone.

Alan left finally on Thursday afternoon. I didn't mean to tell him goodbye but I did. After all, we're only human here, et cetera. There are no innocents. Everyone is guilty. Et cetera, et cetera.

I was standing in the ivory-painted parlor door when he told Crystal goodbye. "Don't take any wooden nickels, Alan," she said. "I'll try not to," he answered. King came out from the back hall and stood there, holding a gun case. I looked out the door to where Joe was loading the racquets in the car. Alan raised his head and looked from Crystal to King to me. And suddenly, it was as though Alan didn't really exist, as though letting him squirt his come inside of me one stupid afternoon while Traceleen was watching television hadn't made a mark on me, not really. Maybe I am finally getting cynical enough to live. Maybe I'll be able to work.

I wonder if things will ever be the same between Crystal and me. Married people get over worse insults than this. But friendship is a stranger thing than marriage. After Alan had gotten in the car and ridden off, with sweet Joe Romaine driving and waving out the window, after they had disappeared down the driveway, I said, "Crystal, let's go for a walk. I need a friend."

"All right," she answered. "Let me change my shoes. Put that gun away," she said to King. "It makes me nervous for you to carry that around." She went to him and took his arm.

"Put that gun away and go with us," I put in. "I'm supposed to be your godmother, in case you forgot. Come on, I want to work on your spiritual development. Spiritually developed men get all the women, hasn't your mother told you that?"

"Like good old spiritually developed Alan?" he answered.

"He can use the language," I said. "It's a beginning." He walked with us as far as the boathouse and then we went on by ourselves.

"This is the path I took to get the hots for your retrograde boyfriend," I began. "I want to talk this out, Crystal. I want to defend myself."

"Go ahead." She sighed and we walked fast with our hands in our pockets. We were on the sand now, skirting the water's edge.

"I think part of it is your fault for telling me what a great lover he is. The next time you get a hot young lover, don't advertise it. Keep it to yourself."

"I told you I liked to make love to Manny and you never went after him."

"He never went after me. When was he so great a lover? Before you got pregnant with Crystal Anne? Before King started the bicycle-stealing ring?"

"He was so tender and funny back then, so shy. I'm shy too, Lydia, and so are you. We've just forgotten it. I might go back to being shy."

"Go back to liking Manny." I couldn't believe I said it. It wasn't the kind of advice we gave each other.

"I can't. It's too complicated. It's complicated by the kids." We turned and walked around a runoff channel, then back down to the hard-packed sand at the water's edge. The sun was behind clouds. A breeze was coming from the shore. No black flies or mosquitoes for twelve days. Maine at its best, the natives kept assuring us.

A long time went by and we didn't talk. Then something came to me.

"You could love Manny. You could think of him as part of Crystal Anne and just go on and hold him and try to make something of it."

"How can I? He works all the time. All he thinks about is his work. I'm just a sideline. I've tried doing that, then an hour later he's at his desk, caught up in some litigation. And he doesn't do it for money, which I could understand. He likes it that way. He likes to play games and fight."

"So do you. Maybe you could go downtown and work for him."

"Maybe men and women expect too much from each other. That's what Daniel says. He says, 'Goddamn, I don't know what you girls expect from us.' "

"When's he coming?"

"Soon, I hope. Let's call him tonight, shall we?"

"Sure. I hope we do." We walked to the marina and back again. We didn't speak again of Daniel. And in the end she called him by herself.

Helen Abadie and her boyfriend arrived on Friday. She is Daniel Hand's sister. Anna's sister and, God forbid, literary executor. Anna did that for a joke, or so everybody thinks. Only Helen took it seriously. The boyfriend, Mike Carmichael, is about a ten to the tenth power, one of those Irish faces that seem to know the things the rest of us are seeking. A poet, of course, but also pretty famous for some book about the consolations of art. The sort of man who would have understood me. I took one look and wanted to show him what I was painting. That was all I wanted him for. I had had my fill of the rest of it.

"Helen says you are a painter," he said, sitting down close to me. Everything he was wearing was soft and old, brown boat shoes turned the color of dust, a khaki shirt so soft it looked like skin, old chinos. Intelligence pouring out of his dark sweet eyes. He poured some on me and I basked in it a moment, then I turned away. I turned to Helen and drew her in.

"Noel says you're making a book. What will be in it?"

"Papers, letters, poems. I'm not mad at her anymore. I think it was okay for her to die that way. She always did everything she wanted to. That was Anna. It's the price we paid to have her. I knew her so well, Lydia. I didn't know how well I knew her until I began to read the papers. Mike says we all know more than we dream we know, about each other and the whole world."

"There must be a lot to go over. It must be quite a job."

"Oh, God, you can't imagine. There are thirty boxes full of stuff."

"So why do you need things from Noel? It bothered her to get your letter, Helen. She's so compromised now, her life has become so small."

"Well, this should cheer her up, give her something to think about. I can't imagine why she won't let me read the letters that she has. I'd fly down there and read them. God knows her life was scandalous enough and certainly Anna's was an open book. What could Anna have written Noel that both of them didn't tell the world." She sniffed, it was the same old Helen. Whatever remorse I had been feeling about holding this conversation with the trunk of letters in the next room was dissolved in Helen's dopiness. How could someone be that dumb, I was thinking. How can women like that get hold of men like Mike? Scandal, what a funny old word. Imagine anyone thinking Noel's life was scandalous. Jesus Christ.

"Well, Helen, maybe Noel thinks they belong to her. Maybe she thinks her lifelong friendship with Anna doesn't belong to the world."

"We need those letters. There are several years when the only person Anna wrote to was Noel."

"I hate to denigrate what you're doing, Helen, but Anna's work can stand alone. You don't need to publish volumes of letters to plump it up."

"I've told her that," Mike said. He had a wonderful deep voice, with laughter in it.

"I want you to intervene," Helen said. "Ask Noel to reconsider."

"I don't have a pipeline to Noel. She runs her own show."

"What does she do down there in New Orleans? I've never met her, you know. I saw her once in Charlotte on the stage, at a benefit. It was right after she retired, before she got to be a recluse. Anna said I could meet her but something happened and I never got to."

"She doesn't do anything. She stays in her room. She calls me up and tells me what to paint." I smiled, thinking of the calls I had received at six o'clock in the morning from Noel. "She calls and wakes me up and tells me things she dreams up for me to paint. Once or twice I took her advice and they were very nice. Anyway, she always bought them for whatever I told her they were worth."

"She calls you up at six in the morning?"

"She never remembers the time difference."

"Let's get up some tennis," Mike said. "I'd like to try that court. I haven't played on clay in years. The yard man keeps it up?"

"We've all been working on it. We had tennis players here last week and they helped."

"Round up King and the four of us will play." He looked at Helen. "Come along, girl. I won't care if you're good or not. I don't keep you around for tennis."

"I'm good at tennis," she said. "We had lessons when we were young. I'm extremely good at follow-through. Anna always said I had a perfect follow-through."

We rounded up King and spent the afternoon playing doubles. It was hot and intense and everyone played above their abilities, drawn along by Mike's enthusiasm. No wonder Helen threw away the world. When that one comes along, you count the world no loss. So she thinks she has to give him Anna's papers to make him happy? She would probably be better off cooking and keeping house and letting him write his own poetry but it was clear she didn't think of herself as sufficient dowry. She wanted to deliver a book. I couldn't help feeling that if she knew the letters were in the house she would just go on and steal them.

I called Noel that night and asked her what to do. "I think she knows they're here," I said. "I'll bet you anything she's figured out they're here."

"Not unless she's psychic. That's just a coincidence, my darling. Well, where are they now?"

"The chest is in the dining room."

"Well, move it. Take it out to the boathouse and put it in a locker."

"It might get wet."

"No, that's all right. Is there someone there to help you carry it? Can you find old Mr. Farnsworth?"

"I'll get King. He'll take it."

"Then get him. Do it right away."

After everyone had gone to bed King and I carried the chest out to the boathouse and put it in a locker. This boathouse is entirely different from anything in our part of the country. Built up on concrete blocks way up on the sand, so that even the highest tide can barely reach it. "What good does it do to have a boathouse that far away from the water?" I asked King.

"I don't know," he said. "I guess that's the way they do it here."

We set the chest down on the steps and looked around. The boathouse was made of wonderful old planks a foot wide and two or three inches thick, all weathered now to the color of the bottom of the clouds above the sea. We carried the chest inside to an oblong room, dusty and full of spiderwebs and unused tools and lockers that held sailing gear. There was a built-in table on a wooden platform and, around it, several old captain's chairs. "I bet they played poker here," King said. "This looks like duck camp."

"Mended nets and smoked pipes is more likely," I answered. "I don't think New Englanders are into playing cards."

"Well, where do you want to put this chest?"

"See if it will fit in that big locker." We opened the largest locker and set the chest down inside and closed the top.

"What kind of papers are in there?" he asked. "You didn't finish saying."

"Letters from your mother's cousin, Anna, to Mrs. Chatevin. Your cousin Helen wants to put them in a book and Mrs. Chatevin doesn't want her to. It's all pretty juvenile, but I'm doing what I was told to do. I hate to ask you to keep this secret."

"I wouldn't want anyone reading my letters. I'm glad to help."

"A writer's letters aren't like yours or mine. They know they'll be seen by other people. Writers think every word they write is something sacred the world will want to read. Well, it's true. I've known enough of them. They may say it isn't true but it is."

"I won't tell anyone where they are," he answered. "Who would I have to tell?"

He didn't have anyone until Jessie and Olivia Hand arrived. Meanwhile, Crystal Anne had discovered the boathouse and talked Andria into helping her clean it up. I saw them out there sweeping out the sand and polishing the captain's chairs with a can of Lemon Pledge and it may have crossed my mind to worry about the trunk being there. Still, Crystal Anne was creating a new hideout or fort every day so I blew it off and forgot about it. I had enough to do making up with Crystal and painting to worry about Noel's paranoia over the things in that blue trunk.

It never crossed my mind that the young girls would read them or think they were important, much less use them to start a literary cult.

Mike and Helen stayed three days. On Saturday we went into Rockland and poked around in antique stores. We found a small bookstore near the quay and bought books. Mike found a book by the poet Seamus Heaney and read a poem out loud.

> *On the day he was to take the poison*
> *Socrates told his friends he had been writing:*
> *putting Aesop's fables into verse.*

> *And this was not because Socrates loved wisdom*
> *and advocated the examined life.*
> *The reason was that he had had a dream.*

> *Caesar, now, or Herod or Constantine*
> *or any number of Shakespearean kings*
> *bursting at the end like dams*

> *where original panoramas lie submerged*
> *which have to rise again before the death scenes —*
> *you can believe in their believing dreams.*

> *But hardly Socrates. Until, that is,*
> *he tells his friends the dream had kept recurring*
> *all his life, repeating one instruction:*

Practise the art, *which art until that moment*
he always took to mean philosophy.
Happy the man, therefore, with a natural gift

for practising the right one from the start —
poetry, say, or fishing; whose nights are
    dreamless;
whose deep-sunk panoramas rise and pass

like daylight through the rod's eye or the nib's
    eye.

When he finished the poem he was looking at me. I forgot about the junky troubled life we were living in Noel's house in the name of being on a vacation. I wanted to paint. I wanted to paint as long and hard as my eyes and hands would allow it. No matter how hard I run from it or how much I bitch when it's going badly, my work is my life. I take the world and create art from it. Ideas born of sadness or jealousy or rage, who knows what. A rage to order. Noel sitting in her bed among her toys. Crystal Anne asleep. Traceleen dreaming by a window. Crystal looking down at a book of sonnets. Sooner or later I would paint all these things because I had lived through and survived this summer. But I did not know that now. All I knew was that I was standing in a dusty book shop on a quay in Rockland, Maine, being read to by a poet. He looked at me when he finished and it was okay that Helen got to fuck him. I got to understand what he had read. I was pretty sure no one else really had. King was embarrassed. Andria was charmed, but wary. Helen was gaga. Crystal was sad. Anna, who should have been there, was dead, and the bookstore owner probably thought we all were crazy.

"Do you want to buy it?" Helen asked. "I think we ought to buy that book."

The next morning I drove Helen and Mike to the airport. "You must come and visit us sometime," Mike said. "Since you hate to travel, you should come down to Boston while you're in the area."

"I might," I answered, knowing I never would. Helen Abadie would have had a fit if I had shown up in Boston to pay a visit to her love nest. Are you going to marry her? I wanted to ask. Will he marry you, Helen? What will you do if he doesn't? But I didn't ask it. I kept my mouth shut, tried to be polite.

"You keep this," Mike said, and pressed the book of poems into my hand. We were at the airport. The desk clerk had taken their bags. "You might want to read the rest of this man's poetry. He's the best there is right now."

"Except for you," Helen put in. She took his arm. "He's the best, Lydia. Everyone knows that."

"Well, I think I'll go on. You'll be off in a few minutes. He said the plane was on the ground."

"Don't forget to talk to Noel. We need those letters. Tell her how important it is to our work."

"Sure," I said. "Thanks for the book. Come back up. Come back when Daniel comes."

"We might," Helen said. "Be sure and talk to Noel, won't you?"

5

TRACELEEN   At last Mr. Daniel Hand of Charlotte, North Carolina, was due to arrive with his daughters. King was in such a state of excitement. I don't think he had slept for three days. He would sit on the porch or in the yard swing, his big legs stretched out in front of him, and smoke cigarettes and pretend to read, or pace all over the house. No one could calm him down, not even Andria or Crystal Anne. Crystal Anne adores her big brother. When she was little, about three or four, we would dress her up and let him take her for walks. He took her with him once to deliver the Christmas wreaths he was selling for Trinity School. She was so happy he was letting her tag along. As they were starting out the door, he took her hand to lead her along and she put her little precious face down and began to lick his hand. I'll never forget that moment. Miss Crystal and I were standing in the oval doors to the dining room and Crystal Anne and King and his buddy, Matthew Levine, were in the hall and she put her little precious face down on his hand and licked it. He didn't know what to do. He was so embarrassed. "Don't lick him," Matthew said. "Give him a kick if you want him to go faster."

Andria and Crystal Anne stayed with King while he waited for the Hands to arrive, following him around. Not lecturing him about smoking. We had all made a vow not to say a word about his smoking. "In the fall," Crystal said. "We'll get him to a smoking clinic. One thing at a time. Conquering drugs and alcohol is enough for one year."

"If it was my lungs I would not wait another day," I said. I am adamant about smoking. I have seen one of my friends die of lung cancer already and another one on her way. I haven't got a good thing to say about cigarettes.

"He is madly in love with this girl," Andria told me. "He says he will die for her, but there might be a problem."

"She doesn't return his love?"

"No. She loves him too. But her father doesn't like him. He told him he had to show some ambition before he would trust him with his daughter."

"Then why is he bringing her up here?"

"Mr. Hand is in love with Crystal and will do anything for her."

"Oh, no, the last thing Miss Crystal needs is someone else in love with her. Mr. Manny is coming, I hope. Crystal Anne's been writing to him, begging him to come and visit. We have not given up on keeping this marriage alive."

"Auntee Traceleen."

"Yes."

"Stop calling Crystal Miss Crystal. It's nineteen eighty-eight. It's time for all that to stop. Call her Crystal. Or Mrs. Weiss. It embarrasses her. She told me so."

"Andria, please go on with your story of Mr. Hand and King."

"Well, that's all I know. If King does well at Tulane and

gets a degree in engineering, then Mr. Hand will let him think about marrying his daughter. Until then, he's on his honor not to touch her."

"Who told you that?"

"King did. They can come up here and visit but King can't make out with her. He had to promise Mr. Hand on his honor."

"I don't believe King told you all of that. That isn't like him to tell his personal secrets that way."

"There aren't any secrets anymore, Auntee Traceleen. Everyone tells everything to their friends."

"So he is telling you all these things and, when Jessie Hand gets here, if that doesn't work out, with him having to love her from a distance, then you will be there waiting to mend his broken heart? Is that what's happening now?"

"I'm not talking to you anymore about it." We were cleaning out the cabinets in the old-fashioned kitchen. Trying to make some sense of all the plates and cups and spoons. Miss Noel had collected enough things for three kitchens and stuffed them into one, and we were putting some things in boxes to store in the attic until we left, so we'd have room to operate. Andria went over to the other side of the kitchen and started wrapping up extra glasses as fast as she could.

"There are plenty of good black men in the world," I said, "without you wanting to complicate your life by a mixed marriage."

"I can't even talk to you," she answered. "You are living in a world that is gone and dead. That's the main thing wrong with you, Aunt Traceleen. You don't believe in the future." She finished off a box and hoisted it on her shoulder and carried it to the bottom of the kitchen stairs. Then she pulled another box off the back porch and began to fill that one up. She is the fastest worker I have ever seen. Every move she makes is just right. She can do anything she wants to do in the world. She could be a politician or a teacher or fulfill her largest ambition and work for *Time* magazine or CNN as an overseas correspondent. It will break my heart if she decides instead to be in love with a white man and fight that battle all her life. What am I supposed to do? All I can do is say what I think and keep on loving everyone I love. I can't control the world. Enough about that. It is time to tell you something about King.

You could blame it on the divorce of his parents, if you were looking for things to blame other things on. I don't think things always have to be blamed on someone. I think it all just turns out as it does and there's a plan we can't see. Miss Crystal thinks it is his genes. She says all the men in his father's family are the way he is and all the men in her family are the same. He is just so big and strong and has all this nervous energy. He's got this sandy red hair like his father. His father was a football player and has never gotten over the fact that King quit the team and became a dope addict instead. Even now that he has straightened out and begun to make something of himself, his father is very cool to him. That's part of our problem. If Mr. Hand comes up from North Carolina and is cool to him also, it will not help our situation. We will have this big grown boy on our hands with no man to counsel with him. He has alienated Mr. Manny, his stepfather, and you have seen how he treated Mr. Alan, so that leaves him with only women to talk to. I had hopes for Miss Lydia being good for him but she got sidetracked with Alan. It was looking pretty hopeless. Tincture of time, that was my main hope. If only he would settle down.

"We must begin to cook better meals," I told Miss Crystal. "I want you to go with me to the store this afternoon. I would like to make macaroni and cheese for supper and a meat loaf. We'll make all his favorite dishes. We'll feed him up."

"Oh, Traceleen, you precious angel," she said. "You think of everything."

"We could get him some chewing gum while we're there. He could chew gum when he wants to smoke."

Then Miss Crystal and I took the station wagon and went into town to buy more groceries. One thing about going grocery shopping. If you have money to pay for the food, it is a satisfying thing to do. You make a list, you drive to the store, you get the things you need, you bring them home, you put them away, you cook them.

Miss Crystal and I drove along this asphalt road that goes between these gigantic pine trees. We had the windows down and it smelled so good. I hadn't had a chance to talk to her alone in days. I was quiet for a while, enjoying the breeze and the smell of the pines and the deserted country road. I watched her every now and then, her blond hair was tied back with a pretty little brown-and-white scarf and she had on white slacks and a rumpled linen blouse. She is starting to look older the last few years. Just as pretty as she always was, but more thoughtful. Not sad, and not that the wrinkles made a dent in the loveliness of her face, but she is getting tired of having problems. I guess we all get tired finally, much as I hate to admit it. It looks like we could get smarter instead.

"If we feed him more he won't smoke so much," I said. I couldn't stay away from the topic.

"Don't say anything about it to him, Traceleen. The doctors told me not to harp on that."

"I wasn't harping on it. I just said I knew a person who died of lung cancer and I told him how they looked at the end when they couldn't get their breath."

"We can't do anything about it this summer. We have enough to do. I'll be glad when Daniel gets here with his girls. That will liven things up."

"Every time he lights up I see my friend JoAnne, lying there in Touro Infirmary breathing on that green machine and gasping to talk."

"Well, we can't do anything about it now. What do you want to cook, Traceleen? Get a notebook out of the glove compartment and let's make a list."

"I didn't mean to add to your worries." I reached in the glove compartment and pulled out all the cups and plastic spoons and straws we had collected from places we stopped on the trip. I put them in a sack that was on the floor. Then I found a pad and pencil and began to make a list. "Butter, flour, macaroni, cheddar cheese, asparagus if they have any, rump roast, ground-up pork and lamb and beef, tomato paste, onions."

"I am so tired of worrying about him," she said. "I thought when we got him home from the hospital things would be all right. Since he met Jessie he's been better. I don't know, Traceleen. I don't know what to do with him. I don't know when to help and when to leave him alone.

Everyone says I baby him too much. Do you think so?"

"I guess you do a little bit," I said. "Well, we will cook for him instead of worrying about him. We will set an example of being busy and happy and make our meals pleasant and hope for the best. He's in Tulane University for the fall. It's working out, Crystal. You wait and see."

"You called me Crystal."

"Yes. I did. That doesn't mean I'm going to keep it up. It's too much trouble to break all my habits at my age." We had come to the turn-off to the main highway into town, which saved us an embarrassing moment.

I took my half of the grocery list and went off to collect the things. I don't know how Miss Crystal can let herself suffer so much over a grown boy. I don't know how he got so mixed up to begin with. But I know the order of events, because I have been there for all of them.

First it was the bicycle-stealing ring. That happened because he didn't get into this club he wanted in. Valencia, it's called. It is this club for teenagers in New Orleans that all the children in the private schools think they have to get into or die. Miss Crystal had just married Mr. Manny and moved to New Orleans and she didn't even know they had it. Also, Mr. Manny is Jewish and that might have made a difference. This club is mostly for people that are not Jewish. What happened was Miss Crystal didn't know the club was there so she didn't have her society cousins put him in an application. Then, one day that first fall he lived in New Orleans, he came home from school and said there was this club he hadn't gotten in. Miss Crystal went crazy calling around and making sure he had passes to visit but it soured him on New Orleans. He hadn't wanted to move there to begin with. He wanted to stay in Mississippi and be on his own football team and go to the white supremacist school Miss Crystal's father had him going to.

"I brought him down here to get him away from Rankin County," she told me that day. She was in tears and King was downstairs pouting in his room. It was the first fall I worked for the Weisses and I think that has been the cause, kernel, and real beginning of all our problems with King. That one afternoon when he came home from school with that terrible expression on his face and said, "What is this Valencia? Why didn't I get in?" He was used to living in a world where he was the richest boy he knew. Now he was down here in New Orleans with a Jewish father being left out of the main club that people at Newman School have to belong to to be happy.

You can see why I want to protect Andria from a mixed marriage. "Look what happened with only an Episcopalian marrying a Jewish man," I said later to Miss Lydia. We were arguing over whether Andria should go out with white boys. Miss Lydia was taking the liberal position. I was arguing the more practical side. Andria was listening while she stirred up some diet Jell-O for her diet dessert.

"Well, it's not the churches that do it," Lydia put in. "Or the color of the skin. It's the system. Marriage sucks, Traceleen. Marriage is hard to do. I read this article by Dr. Joyce Brothers and they asked her what the main things people wrote to her complaining about were. You know what she said?"

"No. What?"

"Wait a minute. I'm trying to remember exactly how it went. Okay. She said poor people wish they were rich, rich people wish they were famous, single people wish they were married, and married people wish they were dead."

"That is one way of looking at it."

"Well, you like your husband. You don't know how unusual that is."

"He's my second, you know."

"Mark is your second husband?"

"I had a young love once."

"What happened to it?" She was all ears. Even Andria had stopped thinking about herself and was listening. They thought I was about to reveal a deep secret about myself, but I kept it in. "That's enough about me," I said. "We were talking about how a person might be happy in the world."

"They can't be," Lydia said. "Pursuing happiness is doomed. All you can do is learn to live in the present and do your work and have friends."

"I'm going to do my work," Andria said. "I'm going to have a good job and a condo and a car." She stood up and stretched her lovely long arms over her head and I couldn't help but think of African princesses with those necklaces around their necks.

Miss Lydia must have been reading my mind. "You look like a Watusi priestess planning the exodus," Miss Lydia said, "or a revolution. I want you to come to Seattle and visit me sometime. Can she come, Traceleen?"

"I might come with her," I said. I knew that surprised them. No one thinks of me as anyone who might like to travel.

Then Crystal Anne came in and said her momma had gotten a splinter in her hand taking down a storm window and we went to see about that.

*   *   *

But back to King the first year he lived in New Orleans. So we had the episode of him not getting into Valencia. Then we had this gorgeous boy in a rage on our hands. Then he quit the football team and then the baseball team and then he was into drugs and then he was stealing bicycles. It all happened so fast we could not keep up.

Now he was nineteen years old and about to go to college and back on the road he left that day he found out he wasn't in the club. We had our fingers crossed.

"You can't depend on Daniel's daughter to save him," I heard Miss Lydia say. "Don't go handing your responsibility over to a child, Crystal."

"What's that supposed to mean?"

"Don't think you can let down your guard just because Daniel Hand shows up with this girl."

"I don't see you accepting the responsibility for anything, Lydia. I don't see you in the role of my psychiatrist." They were drinking whiskey sours in the kitchen by the brick fireplace. Miss Lydia had a real whiskey sour and Miss Crystal had a virgin one. It was late one afternoon and only the three of us were in the house. "Besides," she went on, "that's how it happens. Men are civilized because women make them be. It's the way it goes."

"But it's supposed to be their mothers," Lydia went on. "Not maids and girls their own age."

"What else can I do, Lydia? Can you think of one stone I've left unturned where my son is concerned? Well, can you? I paid twenty-two thousand dollars to that hospital out of my own money just last year. Twenty-two thousand dollars, Lydia. I guess you didn't know that, did you?" She got up and made another fake whiskey sour and began to pace around the kitchen.

"Okay," Lydia kept saying. "I'm sorry. You used to be able to take criticism, Crystal. You used to listen when someone was trying to help."

"I don't call that help," Crystal answered. "I call that bullshit. You spend too much time with that psychiatrist, Lydia, and not enough time in the real world."

"Okay," Lydia kept saying. "Whatever you say. Whatever you want it to mean. It means whatever you say it means, okay?"

"I'm a good mother, Lydia. Whether you like it or not."

"I know you are. I think you are. Okay, okay, okay."

I hated to hear them argue but I was glad they were back in the groove of being friends. It might sound like arguing if you were listening, but in reality it is just the way they act together. They have this way of setting each other off. The minute they get together they heat each other up. Miss Lydia will come in off a plane ride and before she sets her bags down in the hall they are drinking coffee. (It used to be wine or vodka martinis, even in the morning. I have seen them sit down at the dining room table at ten o'clock in the morning with a martini in their hand and the jazz poet dragging himself out of bed to come and join them or the skinny poet, Mr. Lancaster, that you can hardly understand a word he says he drinks so much and is so brilliant, and there is no telling what other poets or artists coming over and beginning to talk about things that interest them. Miss Lydia getting up and going to put classical music on the record player and the sunlight pouring in the leaded-glass windows of the doors out to the balcony. Red geraniums in pots without a single yellow leaf. Their voices rising with excitement. Oh, the good old days.) Anyway, here they were in Maine and Miss Crystal down to virgin whiskey sours and Miss Lydia down on her luck so much she has to have a fling with Alan, and they have made up. Thank goodness. "You have got to paint on a grander scale." Miss Crystal is taking over the conversation. It sounds like she might have slipped a small amount of whiskey into her drink. "You can paint the human face better than anyone working in the United States, maybe the world, so go for it. The next time you get a portrait commission tell them twice the price and you'll stretch a canvas the size of Whistler's ladies at the Frick. Tell them twenty thousand dollars and they can be the subject of your masterpiece." Miss Lydia chuckles. I guess she is thinking about the secret project she has going over the garage. I had a peek at it when I went out there to take supplies but she made me swear not to look again or tell. Oh, it is going to be so fine.

"I'll do it," she's saying. "They'll go for it. The bourgeoisie. Jesus, Crystal, they're so pitiful. They dream of art. They want what I can do. Don't let me get discouraged. Don't let me forget."

Finally, Mr. Daniel Hand called at ten one morning from Tennant's Harbor and said they were on their way, tell them the directions. Fifteen minutes later they were pulling up in the driveway. They were in a convertible. Mr. Daniel in the back and the girls up front, the dark-haired one was driving. The blond one got out and King scooped her up into his arms and kissed her while everybody watched. If this was the beginning of keeping his hands off her it was a strange beginning. Mr. Daniel pretended not to notice and began unloading luggage from the trunk. They must have brought everything they owned. It took three of us to carry in the luggage.

"This is Jessie, Traceleen," King said to me, handing her over. "This is the girl I love. And this is her sister, Olivia. They're the same age."

"We had different mothers," the dark-haired one said. She was looking right at me. Ready to take on the world. "If you can wrap your mind around that one," she added. "Well, now we're here. We were going to go to Switzerland but Jessie had to see her boyfriend. We're glad we came."

"This is my niece, Andria," I answered. "She will show you around the place. And this is Crystal Anne." Andria stuck out her hand and Crystal Anne moved in close to see her long-lost cousin. "Are you really a Cherokee Indian?" she asked. "I think that is the greatest."

"Some days more than others," Olivia answered. "It depends on the positions of the planets." I was taken aback by that. I am not accustomed to young people talking like they know the world. This was a strange young girl for sure and would add spice to our summer.

Then the young people put on tennis clothes and spent the afternoon playing tennis games. Crystal Anne was so excited. She almost ran herself to death carrying Cokes and Gatorade out from the kitchen. I caught hold of her one time and hugged her to me, her little sweaty body was like trying to hold a hummingbird. "What's happening out there? Who's beating who? Who's winning the games?"

"King and Jessie are playing Andria and Olivia. It's the third set. King has to serve with his right hand because he's a pitcher and it wouldn't be fair and I'm the scorekeeper. Andria and Olivia won one set and King and Jessie won one. Now they're in the third set. It might take a tiebreaker. It's five-five. Let me go, Traceleen. I have to get back." She flew down the stairs, her hands full of Coca-Cola bottles, a bird on the wing. I'm as bad about her as Miss Crystal is about King.

That afternoon, the afternoon the Hands arrived, was as nice as it could be. Crystal and Lydia and Mr. Hand sat on yard chairs watching the tennis match. The young people played until they were exhausted. King and Jessie won in the end. Even right-handed, King could serve better than the others could. Then the young people went in to take off their wet clothes and change to go have a bonfire on the beach. And the grown people began to play. They kept coming in trying to drag me out but I wouldn't play. I am going to have my own standards about how I live in Maine and that is that. "I am the cook," I told them. "Not the tennis star. You can have the tennis court," I added, when they insisted. "I will take the kitchen."

I want to stop a minute and tell you about this kitchen. It is the most unusual one I have ever seen. The original kitchen was in a separate house so they wouldn't burn the house down when all the cooking had to be done on wood-burning stoves. This new kitchen was made out of a down-stairs bedroom and stairwell and hall. It has several different ceiling heights and a large brick fireplace with the bricks stripped down that takes up most of one wall. There is a cozy breakfast room with a big wooden table and heavy chairs and there is a little organ that children can play. Every morning someone would play some notes while breakfast was going on. Just look over and remember the organ was there and sit down and play half a song or part of a song.

But the main thing was the cabinets. One summer Miss Noel had been all alone up there and she decided to make a work of art out of her kitchen. She took all the doors off the cabinets and painted the insides beautiful colors. Blue, yellow, pink, red, orange, green, even chartreuse. A dark burgundy was in one, in another the deepest purple. When the sun was shining in the old wavy glass windows and lighting up the cabinets you knew you were cooking with art. I have been wanting to do that for my own house ever since I got home but I haven't found the time to do it.

Inside the cabinets was an assortment of dishes for breakfast and lunch. Many different kinds of glasses and cups and bowls. The nicer things were in the dining room. We used the nicer things a few times but mostly we would end up eating in the breakfast room with everyone walking around looking in the painted cabinets and picking out their special cups and glasses. I got attached to a blue drinking glass with a painted plate to match. For cereal I had a red bowl with a flower on the bottom. There were a number of things about this summer that seemed to make children of us all.

Jessie and Andria liked each other right away but the same wasn't true of Andria and Olivia. They had a standoff. To begin with, Olivia had hardly ever seen a black person in her life until she started coming to North Carolina.

"She's from Oklahoma," Miss Crystal told me. "She says there isn't a black girl her age in the whole town of Tahlequah. She just needs to warm up to Andria."

"Andria doesn't wait for any warming up. She's got that bad temper, and if she gets mad at Olivia she'll stay mad. We have enough going on around here without there being a feud among the young people."

"Don't worry," Crystal said. "Just wait. They'll like each other. They have to. Who else do they have to talk to?"

She was right. Jessie and King were paired off and Crystal Anne was Andria's slave. If Olivia wanted a friend she would have to come to Andria.

It didn't happen for three days. Then it happened in the strangest way. They got on this diet together. One morning about three days after the Hands arrived Olivia came down to the kitchen and announced she was going on a grapefruit diet.

"I can't look at myself in a bathing suit," she said. "I look so terrible I can't stand it. I'm getting the fat off my hips before I show my body on that beach again. This will do it."

"What kind of diet are you going on?" Andria shoved the plate of bacon and eggs I had prepared for her away and got up and walked around the table to where Olivia was reading a diet out of a *Seventeen* magazine.

"It's this article about diets women used to go on that aren't good for you. Listen to this. 'The grapefruit diet was popular in the fifties. Women would eat nothing but grapefruit and eggs for four days, then nothing but grapefruit and eggs and one banana for three days, then back to grapefruit and boiled eggs!' I've heard of it before. My Aunt Lily went on it once. She lost twenty pounds in two weeks."

"How much do you want to lose?" I put in.

"Only ten," she said.

"Oh, my God," Jessie said. "If you lost ten pounds you'd look like a starving orphan or a refugee. Don't go on a diet, Olivia. That's no fun. You look just fine."

"I'm going on it too," Andria said. "I bet I've gained a thousand pounds since I've been here."

"I want to go too," Crystal Anne put in. "I'm getting fat." She pinched up a tiny bit of skin from her midriff and showed it around. "Look at this fat."

"If I catch you going on a grapefruit diet I'll skin you alive," I said. I had singled out Crystal Anne because it was clear there was no reasoning with Andria and Olivia. Andria shoved her breakfast away and she and Olivia drank a glass of grapefruit juice instead. Then they borrowed the Peugeot and went into town to get what they needed for their diet. By the time they returned they were fast friends. They brought their grapefruits and extra-large eggs into the kitchen and began to make their pitiful little lunch, chattering away about things they thought. After that they were inseparable.

Crystal Anne stuck to them like glue. Everywhere they went she wanted to go there. Since Andria's main job was to keep Crystal Anne out of Miss Crystal's hair, it looked like everything was turning out fine.

Miss Crystal also brightened up after the Hands' arrival. I suppose it made her feel good to have Daniel Hand worshipping her when it was obvious Miss Lydia had a crush on him. I guess that made up for the rivalry over you-know who. Also, Mr. Manny was calling quite frequently and sent several dozen roses on their anniversary.

"This isn't your wedding anniversary," Miss Lydia said, when the roses came. "You got married in September."

"It's the anniversary of the day we met. I was visiting a friend in Cleveland, Mississippi, and Manny came there to try a case and came over to have a drink with my friend's husband. I came wandering into the kitchen in a dressing robe looking for a light for a cigarette and he walked out from behind a screen and lit it. So we fell in love."

"He said she had the prettiest hair he had ever seen in his life," Crystal Anne put in. "He said if he could have a little girl with hair like that he would never ask for another thing."

"So he got you," I said, and hugged her. What a wonderful little girl she is. I cannot believe Miss Crystal pays so little attention to her when she is such a fine smart little girl. Not that Miss Crystal is ever mean to her or lets her be neglected. She just doesn't seem to know she's there half the time.

"Are you going to call Daddy to thank him?" Crystal Anne asked.

"Yes. I'll call him now."

"Good, then I can talk to him. I miss him so much. I hate to think he's missing all this fun."

"I'll talk to him," Daniel said. "I'll tell him I need another man around this place."

So they put in the call but Mr. Manny was somewhere in Colorado conferring with his client in his million-dollar case and afterward Miss Crystal and Mr. Daniel went off for a walk and I played Monopoly with Crystal Anne. She was the banker and kept trying to sell me hotels and houses at cut rates. Also, she always puts hotels on her utilities and railroads and I never tell her not to. We have our own rules.

"You better buy another hotel," she would say, her little precious brow wrinkled over her banking operation.

"I don't have a hundred dollars," I'd reply.

"How much do you have?"

"I have twenty-two."

"Okay, then I'll sell you one for twenty-two. You want to buy one for twenty-two?"

"Sure I do, honey. Twenty-two sounds good." Then she would pick out a fine red hotel and set it down on my property and take in two tens and two ones and we would go on with our game. By the time Crystal and Daniel came back from the beach we had every house and hotel in the set on the board.

"Let me cook supper," Mr. Daniel said.

"What can you cook?" Miss Crystal asked.

"Anything you want. But I think I'll grill some steaks."

"They're in the freezer," I put in. "Get them out."

"I'll watch you cook," Crystal said. "If you're good you can stay on regular. If not, back to Traceleen and me."

"He's good," Jessie put in. She had come to stand at the door. "He always cooks for me. He makes fettucine or tomato pie, don't you, Dad?" She walked across the room and took an apron off a peg and began to help him unwrap the steaks.

"I've got to marinate them," he said. "This may take a while. Fix me a drink, sugar. We'll show these folks how to put a meal on a table." He was clearing off a space on the counter, taking over the kitchen like a four-star general. Jessie started boiling water to make the tea. Crystal Anne and I put away our Monopoly set and began to set the table. This is the sort of evening that I cherish, when no one has a thing to fight about and are working together toward a goal. King joined us and started getting out the double boiler for the asparagus. "Get that on the back burner," Mr. Daniel yelled. "Now don't go eating a lot of bread and crackers. I want hungry people when these steaks are done."

"I don't eat steak," Miss Lydia said. "But I can boil some eggs."

"You'll eat this," Mr. Daniel answered, sprinkling pepper into the marinade. "Get out of my way, little daughters. Your father is about to show his stuff."

Later that evening, after we had eaten and cleaned up our mess, Daniel and Miss Crystal and Lydia sat out on the porch for many hours, talking and listening to the short-wave radio. I went on up to bed about eleven-thirty. I don't know what happened after that.

6

LYDIA So they are here at last. Daniel and his daughters. They look like people Blake would paint. There I go again, angelizing Daniel. Well, I can't help it. That kind of physical beauty drives me mad, I'm a painter, I'm supposed to believe in beauty. Daniel is more than beautiful. He is good. That kind of grace can only come from goodness; Jessie has it too. She is the single most beautiful young girl I have ever seen in my life. Skin like alabaster or cream or snow. She has softened since I saw her last, the moxie isn't as apparent. I guess she's pulled it in for love. Women do that, go all soft and mushy when they're weaving a spell. There's a metaphor for you. All the ancient stuff is still the best, ancient paintings, language, music from when the world was young. That's why I'm a realist. I see the thrill of cubist painting and the clean thrust of the abstractionists but in the end I want the human face and form. After all, it's the highest invention of nature, the most mysterious and complex.

So I am painting Crystal and someday I'll paint Jessie. Every time I see Daniel Hand I think I have always loved this man. God, he tries so hard with those girls. Imagine having that pair to watch out for and guard. Jessie's never really had a mother. I never met Sheila but even Anna hated her and Anna didn't hate anyone. She thought people were interesting or funny. Once she said to me, ''I think I have lost every passionate response to people, Lydia, they amaze me in their diversity and need. I want to document them and give them meaning. I want to stop laughing at them but I can't because it's all so comic and so funny. Sometimes I wake from dreams and laugh at my own behavior, laugh out loud at everything I do. Listen, I think consciousness may only be a way to escape from dreaming and this idea that consciousness is a curse may be the silliest idea of all. Why are we so glad to wake? We are always glad to wake from sleep. We crave the light and the dazzling light-filled dramas of our days. It's night we hate and the caverns of our dreams. Helen used to dream she left one of her babies at the grocery store. She almost ground her teeth to powder dreaming mothering dreams. We had to take her to a psychiatrist to cure her of thinking she was making mistakes about her babies *while she slept.''*

Daniel's girls look alike. I can't put my finger on it though I might be able to paint it. Jessie is taller and blonder but there's a look they have, that goddamn Hand/Manning thing they all inherit.

Crystal Anne will have three grown girls to ape this summer. It will be good to get her away from her attachment to Traceleen. She is Traceleen's child, as everybody knows. Crystal was so sick after Crystal Anne's birth and Traceleen nursed her for the first few months of her life. She imprinted on her, they all say that, as if it were a joke. Well, you couldn't find a sweeter stronger soul to have for an imprintee. Nobility, that's the word you come back to where Traceleen is concerned. She's so Zen. She goes off fishing with

that Zen look on her face and she cooks with it and she
always tells the truth. I hope she has stopped being mad at
me. I know I'm not perfect. And I couldn't help that thing
with Alan. It was not my fault. It absolutely was not my
fault.

I dreamed the other night that King turned into Parsifal. The
afternoon before I found a copy of *The Dancing Wu Li Masters*
on top of his gun case and I thought, There is hope yet. He
made a descent into cocaine hell and Traceleen and Crystal
and Manny and Crystal Anne dragged him back into the
world. If I was one of the old painters I might paint them
lined up at the abyss dragging King back into the world. I
wish we still painted things like that.

I want to learn to paint the night sky. There was a meteor
shower the other night. Daniel and I stretched out on lawn
chairs from twelve to two-thirty scanning the skies, watching the shooting stars. "Is it complicated to love another
person, or simple?" I asked him.

"Both," he answered.

"Are you in love with Crystal?"

"No. I just want to take care of my girls. I've got more
work than I can do, Lydia. I've got creditors breathing down
my neck. If I don't get some breaks soon, I'll have to go into
bankruptcy. The bastards are after us. It's tough to run a
business now."

"You spend too much money."

"It isn't that. It's not being able to make it. Well, I've got
a few things in the pot. I've got a couple of new franchises
that may help. We'll see."

"You really have to leave tomorrow?" I was turned all
the way around on the yard chair, facing him. I had on my

purple silk harem pants and a pair of thong sandals. My best white silk blouse. It was only starlight, but he could see how great I looked if only he had looked. He wasn't looking. I couldn't believe I was lying on a yard chair beside this good-looking man and he wasn't going to make a pass at me.

"I've got to go back to Charlotte in a day or two," he said. "Take care of my girls for me, won't you? Keep an eye on them."

Two days later he left. I adore him even if he won't fall in love with me. Where did I go wrong? Why, when I was young and had it all going for me, didn't I latch on to some-one like Daniel? Because when they are young the Daniels of the world are silly and gawky. The higher the intelligence the slower the rate of maturation. Not that Daniel has ever considered himself to be intelligent. He thinks he's dumb because he doesn't like to read. Oh, well, I wish I wouldn't start idealizing Daniel Hand. He's got his faults like every-body else. You can see them writ large in both those girls. The strange mixture of bravado and shyness in Jessie. The drive and ambition and self-doubt of Olivia.

7

JESSIE   I love King because when I'm with him there isn't any need for anything else. If he's there then I'm happy and that is that. None of them understand that. They think just because he was fucked up last year that I shouldn't love him. Well, Dad was fucked up when he was young and so is everybody else. If I look at King's shoulders or when he kisses me, that is that. I think Olivia is jealous. She'd give anything to have him or anybody. She is the most boy-crazy girl I ever saw only she won't admit it. She covers it up with trying to be smarter than everyone else. Well, there's nothing I can do about it, Dad wants her to live with us and I was the one that told him to. Aunt Anna started all that. She loved me best though. I know that. Because I didn't love her because she was famous or anything like that. I just liked to go around to wherever she lived. I remember when we used to go visit her apartment in New York. We would go to Bloomingdale's and get clothes. Once I got these leather boots that were so beautiful and I got some plaid skirts and sweaters there. We went to see opera and ballet. Not like the Charlotte ballet, but where no one makes a single mistake. She would understand about King and me. She gave up anything for love. She told me that. And she didn't mind if she had to be sad in the end. How could she get cancer? How could anyone that beautiful have to die? I can't think about her drowning herself. It's all Olivia thinks about. Olivia says she is Aunt Anna's spiritual daughter. She told Andria that the other day.

Oh, never mind all that. I am here and I can see King every day. We went out the other night and sat in the car for three hours. I could hold him in my arms forever and I want to do it as much as he does. We are going to. Dad can't tell me what to do with my own body.

ANDRIA   If anybody's keeping a vow not to fuck around here I'd like to know who it is. I'm really sick of them holding on to each other all the time. It's about like high school or junior high. I'll tell you what it reminds me of. It reminds me of this play we saw in Montgomery where this fairy kept sprinkling lily juice on these people and whoever he sprinkled it on when they woke up they fell in love with the next person they saw. Two of them were sprinkling it. This guy, Puck, and this other man, the king of the fairies.

I told Olivia about it and she said, "Oh, I read that play." Which was an outright lie because a few hours later I found her with a book she got out of the library reading it. "He's really called Robin Goodfellow," she goes.

"Who is?"

"The one sprinkling the magic potion from the flower."

Why does Olivia have to lie about everything all the time? Everybody always knows she's lying. But no one says so and if you do she just faces you down.

Nobody's sprinkling that shit on me. Not this year or next. I'm going out and be somebody. If you know who you are, you don't need some guy telling you you're great and beautiful all the time. Masturbate. Do something. Give it to some dope you couldn't really like but stay away from that lily juice. Stay away from love. So I'm cynical. You have to be cynical to survive. Leon said that when he spoke to us, he said you have to be cynical to think straight. I wrote it on a piece of paper and taped it to the bathroom wall so I can see it when I take a bath.

OLIVIA   I'm sick of watching Jessie and King moon over each other. My old boyfriend Bobby was twice as much a man as King Mallison. Even if he did live in a trailer. He wasn't nobody and he never had to go to a drug hospital and have his mother pay twenty thousand dollars to get him well. I wish I was making out with him right now instead of up here with all these snotty people. If it wasn't for Andria, I'd be all alone. Andria is great. She's going to really go places in the world. She looks like this great black princess but she's as white as I am. To tell the truth, she could pass for white.

Anyway, we went into town about a hundred times looking for some boys to have over or hang out with but they're all so weird. They talk like this. "Where do you go to school?" They weren't interested. They'd get interested if I got in Harvard. I figured that out. That's about the only thing that would shut them up.

Where was I? I was leading up to us finding the letters from Aunt Anna to Mrs. Chatevin. Oh, my God. Her handwriting. I get this weird feeling every time I touch something that belonged to her, much less her handwriting. It's like the minute I do it's three years ago when I wrote to her and she wrote back to me and my whole life changed. I cannot stand for her to be dead. She cannot be dead.

So the other day we were all out in the boathouse. It's this old place sitting up on sand with lockers in it lined with tin. They are full of tools and ropes and things for when people kept sailboats there. It has a table and four chairs and dishes. We cleaned it up to use for a place to sit and talk. Andria and I cleaned it up. Anyway, we were out there and Crystal Anne was with us and she started poking around in everything. She is so curious about everything. She will sit on her haunches for ten minutes looking at anything she finds.

She is Traceleen's child. She and Traceleen are always together. She tells Traceleen everything. She never tells her mother anything. Well, she tells Andria and me things too. She's crazy about us, which makes it easy for Andria to take care of her.

Anyway we were sitting around talking and Andria and I were drinking rum Cokes. We took the rum out of the liquor cabinet in the house and brought it out to the boathouse and fixed a couple of rum Cokes. We weren't getting drunk or anything. Just fooling around. We had all these magazines and we were planning our fall wardrobes. Crystal Anne is poking around in the lockers, straightening things up.

"I want to concentrate on basics," Andria is saying. She had on this one-piece cut up on the thighs with strings for straps. Aqua. She looks so great in that suit. "Then I'll get me a big pink linen bag or something flashy in accessories. It's summer all the time down there."

"I don't know where I'll be," I was saying. "I might get into Harvard. I'm on the waiting list."

"I wouldn't plan on that," Andria goes. "I don't know why you want to stay up here. It's too damn cold. I don't know how people live up here."

All this time Crystal Anne was being so quiet, then she comes over to me. "Come look at this," she says. "This used to be in the dining room. I wondered where it was. Now it's out here." She pulled me by the hand and there inside this locker is a little blue painted chest, very old and pretty. Andria was right behind us and she reached in and took one of the leather handles and I took the other one and we lifted it out and set it on the floor.

"It's got letters in it," Crystal Anne says. "They're in some satin bags."

An hour later we were still out there looking at them. Twenty letters Aunt Anna wrote to Mrs. Chatevin. Her precious writing. No one will ever know what it meant to me to find those letters. Like no one ever dies really, do they?

"We have to put these in plastic bags and make copies of them," I said. "They are very valuable."

"I'll go tell Momma," Crystal Anne puts in.

"No," I said. "Don't tell anyone about these."

"Why not? She's Momma's cousin."

"Because there's something I have to tell you." I had some of the letters in my hand. It was very still and then I said something I didn't know until I said it. "Because she isn't dead but no one knows it but me. I have to tell you but you can't tell anyone else. Promise me." I stopped talking and they stared at me.

"She is too dead," Crystal Anne said. "I went to the funeral with my mother. They had this videotape of her on television and Miss Anna and Cousin Helen cried and cried. They all cried and got drunk. That's the first time I saw you, Olivia. Don't you remember that?"

"It wasn't a funeral. It was a memorial service because she drowned herself and they never found the body. Only she didn't die. She went to Switzerland to see this famous doctor who is curing her. I have been dreaming this and then I got a letter and I knew it was true." I'm not sure I got the letter anymore but I still think I did. How could I make up something like that? Now I tell them it's a lie but I believed it on the day I told it to Andria and Crystal Anne and sometimes I believe it still. If it's a lie that I got the letter, where did I get the idea? Everything isn't black and white in the world. One and one don't always make two.

"I don't believe that," Andria goes.

"Well, I don't care if you do or not. I'm sorry, Andria, but people like Aunt Anna don't just kill themselves. If you had known her you wouldn't say that. And don't tell anyone I told you this. I wish I hadn't told you."

"I won't tell them," Crystal Anne says.

"What did your letter say?" Andria asks.

"It said she wanted me to know she was okay. She wanted to adopt me. She loved me so much." I was crying then and Crystal Anne started patting me. She is such a sweet little girl. "We have to put these in plastic," I said. "We have to make copies of them. We have to study them."

"What for?" Andria says.

"For clues to where she is." I stopped crying and stared right at Andria. "If we study her writing we can find out how to write."

"I'd do that," Andria says. "There's a lot of money in it if you get some breaks. This poet from LSU, he drives a

Firebird and he gave five hundred dollars to the scholarship fund. It was his fee for talking to us. He said we needed it more than he did."

So then we borrowed the car and went to town and made copies of the letters and bought some plastic bags to seal them in and put them back into the chest. Andria and Crystal Anne were with me now. Andria was in it so she could find out how to be a writer and Crystal Anne was in it because she's so sweet and helpful when anybody cries or gets unhappy. She should be a nurse or a psychiatrist when she grows up. I wouldn't mind having children someday if they'd turn out to be like her.

With my luck they would turn out like Jessie. She's about the moodiest person I've ever met in my life. She had a fit when she found out I had the letters from Aunt Anna. She got so jealous it was pitiful. "You shouldn't have these, Olivia," she said. I had taken her out to the boathouse to show them to her. "They were written to Mrs. Chatevin."

"So what. She was my aunt."

"You ought to tell Aunt Helen. She's the executor." She was holding one in her hand. Just holding it as if it wasn't anything special, just a piece of paper with writing on it. Jessie's been acting funny anyway ever since we got to Maine. She doesn't even look happy with King. She's gotten so serious and her mother's been calling her from England. She always starts acting funny after her mother calls her. "You need to tell Aunt Helen about these letters," she said again. That's all it means to her to hold one of Aunt Anna's letters in her hand. As if it's nothing. Like anyone could have written it. It made me mad.

"Never mind the letters," I said. "Just forget I told you about them. You've got what you wanted, Jessie. We have to come up here for the whole summer so you can see your boyfriend and I lose out on a trip to Switzerland. So just do me one favor, okay. Keep your mouth shut about these letters. We are studying them."

She put the letters down and moved away. "What for?" she says.

"Because we want to. They're about how she wrote poems. They're writing lessons for us."

"Okay," she goes. "I won't say anything. But you should tell Aunt Helen. She's the executor."

No one will ever know what finding these letters means to me. Her spirit is in me. I live for her now that she's dead. I went out to the ocean one night when it was cool and there wasn't a moon or a single mosquito to bother me. I walked in up to my knees and thought about how close I was to her. She isn't dead because her spirit is everywhere. Her spirit is free because she left her body behind. I could walk out into the ocean and join her spirit. Drowning might hurt for a moment, but so what? It hurts to be alive and have to fight, fight, fight every minute to have people like you. I should go back home but I can't. I can't stand Tahlequah. I want to live with rich people and go to good schools. I want so much and it's so hard to get it. I love Aunt Anna's poems. They are so sad and they know about death. I know about death. I was born in death, wasn't I? I killed my mother being born. I'm lonely for my mother. I want my mother to hold me in her arms. My mother and Aunt Anna might be up there right this minute talking about me and watching me. If I had the courage I could go and join them. If I don't get in Harvard or Duke, then I'm going to do it. To hell with it. What do I have to lose?

Here's one of the poems. It's an unfinished one. In the letter with it she said she couldn't finish it because it was about being "torn in two." God, isn't that beautiful and sad?

METAPHOR

Three times he built the web across my door,
Two feet wide and intricate as glass, a thousand
thousand strands and joinings.
I admired it so I could not kill him,
though I tore the web down with the broom.

Three times I tried to board a plane
to come to you. Made it all the way to
the airport counter, the last time in the rain,
The rain, the rain, as Cummings called it.

I was going to keep notes on our meetings. Like a journal or the notes for a club but now I'm not going to. It's too important to even talk about. I can't tell you what it's like to read her letters and know she is inside of me, kin to me, made out of the same stuff as me. Of course, we're all made out of the same stuff in the end, but if someone is kin to you you might be able to read their mind even after they're dead. I don't think she's dead. She is always with me now. She tells me what to write. I wrote this poem called "Friction." It goes

Friction makes the worlds collide
Friction makes us want to fuck
Friction burns us up inside
Listen, this is no joke.

Well, that's only part of it. It goes on for ten pages. She made me write it, she held the pen.

Here is how we set up the meetings. First we lit the candles with a reading of her poems. Then we burned incense and I read some of her stories and we all prayed to be good writers who always told the truth when others were afraid to do it.

ANDRIA   They weren't just letters. There were poems and things cut out of newspapers like THE LIGHTS ARE ON FOR ANNA, made out of pieces of words cut out of advertisements. Also, THE GREATEST CREATIVITY IS THE LEAST RESENTMENT. I thought about that for a long time. I think I will write a paper for school about it next year. It only takes one break and you've got it made in the writing business. That's what this teacher Leon said when he taught at NOCCA last year. Look at him. First he was nobody. Now he's on the radio and his books sell like hotcakes.

Well, all that is the real world and this shit Olivia is into in the boathouse is not the real world. I can't even decide what we're supposed to be doing out there. I thought we were going to get in touch with the spirit of her aunt and get some inspiration for our lives or something like that. That was goofy enough. Now I don't know what we're doing. It's getting pretty boring being up here. I would like to get on home and start getting ready for school. I have saved almost two thousand dollars because Lydia gave me three hundred extra she said was to buy some good-looking clothes for school. It wasn't her money. It was money some secret source said to give me. I bet it was Mrs. Chatevin. I heard they had to put her money in some conservancy to keep her from giving it all away. She gave all her silver and china away to the antiwar effort during the Vietnam war. Well, the lives of these people are really complicated and none of them ever have sex with anyone that I can see. I been getting laid off and on since I was fifteen but now I stay on the pill and don't even do it anymore since I decided to be ambitious for my future instead. The next time I get a boyfriend he is going to be somebody and also a stud or nothing. He's going to be a man, like the captain of the basketball team at LSU or in law school or something really hot. It's all or nothing for me where men are concerned from now on.

So the first time we have one of these literary meetings we light some candles and Olivia gets out this jasmine incense we got in Tennant's Harbor last weekend and we start reading the letters and poems. Then Olivia says, "Well, I have to tell you the whole truth. Someone has to know it. It's killing me to keep this to myself."

"What?" we go. "What's it about?"

"Aunt Anna is definitely in Switzerland with this doctor she loves. He is trying this desperate cure. They take her blood out and put it in a machine and then they inject it back in and she has to sleep for many days. It's so experimental only the strongest people with the strongest genes can even try it. If it works they might win the Nobel prize for their work. She is in love with him and he is in love with her. He is this great scientist that used to treat children with cancer and there is this other doctor with them. A Chinese doctor. She wrote to me again. She couldn't bear for me to think she was dead because she knew I was depending on her to love me. It is driving me crazy to keep this secret." Then she starts crying and Crystal Anne goes over to her and starts rubbing her back with her darling little hands and patting her.

"You can't ever tell a soul," Olivia says. "This is the greatest secret of my life. Don't talk about it, even to me. Well, now you know."

"Why would they keep it a secret?" I say. "People get cured from cancer all the time. They don't have to go off to Switzerland and pretend they're dead."

"You don't understand," Olivia goes. "It's against the law to try this stuff. What they are doing is so dangerous and terrible. Only Aunt Anna would try it. If it works on her it could save other lives. You see, what she had might be hereditary. We might all get it, so she has to find a cure to save everyone who is kin to her. At any time it could break out in Jessie or in me or Aunt Helen or Aunt Louise or Dad or anybody in the Hand family."

"In me?" Crystal Anne says. "I'm your cousin."

"No, you're too far away. It can only be a niece or someone. Wait a minute, let me see." Olivia stopped crying and starts rubbing her head with her hands. "Your grandmother and my grandmother are sisters but you couldn't have this gene because it's a Hand gene. It is only passed down in people related to the Hands."

"Don't tell Crystal Anne all that stuff," I say. "If you got a letter from your aunt, let us see it." She ignored that. She got up and started pacing around and talking real fast like she does when she's lying.

"My Indian blood can probably fight off the disease. The one I'm really worried about is Jessie. She's left-handed, remember, and so was Aunt Anna."

"Let's see the letter," I said.

"The main thing to worry about is finding a cure before

anybody else gets it. That's why this has to be a secret. They would stop what Aunt Anna's doing. The government doesn't let you experiment on yourself.''

Crystal Anne is being very quiet and has come over to stand by me. All I can think is that Aunt Traceleen will kill me if I let her get any weird ideas about she's going to get a disease.

''Shut up, Olivia,'' I say. ''That's all I want to hear about you thinking you get letters from a dead lady.''

''I'm going to tell Dad,'' Crystal Anne says. ''He can ask our friend Lake who's a doctor.'' She was hanging her head. She wouldn't look at Olivia or at me.

''You don't need to ask anyone,'' Olivia said. ''You're a Connell and a Manning and a Weiss. This doesn't have anything do with you. I shouldn't have told you anyway, but you have to keep it secret.''

''We're going to get our perms tomorrow,'' I say. I was playing into Olivia's bullshit but what was I to do. If Aunt Traceleen knew I'd let Crystal Anne listen to all Olivia's shit she'd jump all over me. Aunt Traceleen doesn't float around on a cloud in my head. Aunt Traceleen is real. ''We're going to do body waves,'' I went on, pulling Crystal Anne over close to me and hugging her. ''You want to get your body wave, don't you?''

''Yes.''

''Then don't tell anybody about our secrets out here. If you tell we won't let you in our clubs anymore.''

''I should tell my dad,'' she says. ''He ought to know about this because he is a lawyer.''

''Let's clean up this mess and go up to the house,'' Olivia said. ''We can't let you come to the meetings, Crystal Anne, unless you can keep the secrets.''

"Okay," she says, but she isn't looking at us. She's look-ing at her hands. "I won't tell him then."

"There's no way you can get it," Olivia says. "The only ones in danger are the Hands."

The more I think about all this bullshit the less I believe it. I like sitting out there reading the books and studying how to write. And I like getting to read the letters and poems. It's funny to touch the writing of a real writer and see their name on the bottom of letters all about regular stuff they write their friends. But this stuff Olivia says is total bullshit. Still, it's a job. I have two thousand dollars saved already and they'll probably all give me some tips when the sum-mer's over. You don't have to give a fuck about being black if you don't want to. You just get your education and get out there and start making it and you're okay. Nobody can stop you if you make your mind up to get what you want. Take the pill, go to school, get a job. I'm pretty horny. I'll admit that. But I can take care of that until the guy I want comes along. Let the rest of them do whatever they want. I'm like a tiger walking along through the forest minding my own business. That's how I see it. I walk along. I stop to drink. I hunt and eat. At night I sleep.

CRYSTAL ANNE   First they lit the candles and then they got some incense they bought in town and smoked up the whole boathouse and then Olivia read all the stuff in the stocking bags and Andria read this love stuff out of the books Olivia's aunt wrote. She is supposed to be dead but she isn't dead. She is in Europe or England and Olivia is going to see her soon. But then after we did it twice Olivia goes, Well, we need to get in touch with her spirit so we will do the Ouija board and talk to her. Then Andria said if she isn't dead how come we need to talk to her spirit, we could call her on the phone, and I said, If that's true you ought to tell your daddy because it is his sister and he has a right to know.

"No one gets to know," Olivia said. I was about to choke to death on this incense. It is called jasmine and we got it at that T-shirt store with glass prisms in the window at the pier at Tennant's Harbor.

I'm sick of reading those old books about love, love, love all the time. I want to read some of the *National Geographic World* magazines Traceleen and I ordered last year when Bobbie Green was selling magazine subscriptions. Dad loves them. He couldn't believe it took Traceleen and me to tell him about some magazines that are so good for children. Well, I am in the ninety-ninth percentile of readers in the United States now anyway. I am reading at the ninth-grade level but Dad says don't brag about it and make anyone feel bad. Some people are just better at reading than others and have more books around to practice on. I have always had all the books I want. Dad takes me down to Maple Street and Miss Faust lets me get all the ones I want and tells me ones to buy. So anyway, I'm sick of always reading these same books every time we have a meeting. Olivia also read some of her poems but they are sadder than her dead aunt's are. I wish we could finish our beach coats instead.

Wednesday night we had our fourth meeting and I told Olivia I wasn't staying if they burned all that jasmine incense again so we burned candles instead. Olivia read some nicer stuff this time. Some stories her aunt wrote that have children in them. Most of the children she writes about are not too happy with their homes or else they fight with their brothers and sisters. I only have King and he is so much older we couldn't have fights. I guess I am just an only child. Olivia and Jessie are too but now they have each other. I think it would be so great to have a lot of children in one house like the Carloses that live down the block. I go there a lot when I'm home. They don't even notice if several other people stay for dinner. They just move over and pour another glass of tea. I might have a lot of children when I grow up. If I ever get married. I don't think I want to live too far away from Mom and Dad.

So Olivia got out the Ouija board again and we sat around this table and tried to get her aunt to make the little piece move. I was so scared I couldn't sleep. I wish Olivia would say whether her aunt is dead or not.

When you go outside and stand on the sand looking up at the stars and it's so dark and there aren't any lights to remind you of human beings to protect you, it is very spooky to do that and then talk to some dead person that might be in the ocean or something.

Traceleen is asking me all kinds of questions about what are we doing in the boathouse and Andria made me swear not to tell her. I don't like to keep secrets from people. It made me feel bad to tell Traceleen we weren't doing anything when we are doing all that stuff at our meetings.

I wrote to Dad and told him about the club. I don't know if I'll mail it or not. I never keep secrets from Dad. I can tell him anything. But I promised them I wouldn't tell, didn't I?

8

TRACELEEN   The main love affair of the end of June was between King and Jessie. King had promised Daniel not to lay a hand on her and we were watching that.

Absurd, that's all Miss Lydia would say. She thought they should give Jessie some birth control pills and let nature have its way. Miss Lydia is always wanting to give birth control pills to someone but it turns out she does not take them herself. She depends on the rhythm method of birth control because she does not like to take any substances that interfere with her natural system. She says she wouldn't take an aspirin unless she had a broken leg.

"Then why are you so hot to give hormones to Jessie?" Miss Crystal asked. We were having a conversation one morning at breakfast. The young girls were all within earshot.

"Because I am a grown woman who understands the workings of my body, Crystal. I know how to watch my temperature and use sponges and I know when I ovulate. A young girl can't be expected to give that the attention it takes."

"I wouldn't trust taking my temperature to keep me from

getting pregnant. My God, Lydia, that would scare me to death."

"The French have been using rhythm for generations and you don't see them being overpopulated. It's a matter of being fastidious." The girls were all ears now. When she noticed that, Lydia raised her voice. "I have made my stand. Anyone who wants information or help with birth control can come to me." She got up from the table and took her plate and rinsed it at the sink.

"The best thing is an IUD," Miss Crystal said. "No, the best thing is tubal ligation."

"Don't let anybody do it to you is the best thing," Olivia said. "It doesn't take a genius to know that." Then Daniel and King wandered in and started wanting someone to feed them and the conversation went off into the other room.

So we were all involved in the love affair and forgot about Andria and Olivia. Crystal Anne had fallen completely under their spell. First it was Andria she copied, then it was Olivia. Olivia has her hair cut real short in a very fashionable way, and Crystal Anne began begging to have hers cut too.

"Why would you go and cut off all your gorgeous hair?" I asked. "Your daddy would have a fit if we cut your hair."

"It's my hair," she said. "I'm tired of looking like some little girl. I want a hairstyle."

Nine years old, and now she wants to be in style. Here is Olivia, who is only a young girl from an Indian reservation, and she is the fashion expert in Maine. She talked Andria into letting her straighten her hair with permanent wave solution and then Andria used the leftover part to put curls in the bangs of Olivia's hairstyle. Andria has enough ideas of her own from being raised in New Orleans. Pretty soon the table in the kitchen was littered with fashion magazines they bought in Rockford. *Mademoiselle, Cosmopolitan, Elle, Seventeen,* the Spiegel catalog. They have set up a sewing club in a little sewing room they found upstairs. It has yellow-and-white wallpaper and all the furniture is painted ivory. There is an old-fashioned table with a Singer sewing machine. Miss Noel's daughter, Andine, lived here once for several months while she got over a nervous breakdown caused by being in the retail clothing business in New York City. To heal herself she set up the sewing room and made clothes for poor children. Some of the designs for her things are still on the wall. They are just lovely with animals appliquéd on them or cars and trucks. There is a design for a pair of overalls with a red truck on the bib that is the cutest thing I've ever seen. Any child would want a pair of those. "What happened to Andine?" I asked. "Where is she now?"

"She married a doctor and moved to Minneapolis. Noel misses her so much." Miss Crystal and I were up in the sewing room with the girls. They had invited us up to see what they were doing.

"Does she keep in touch?" I asked.

"She talks to her on the phone."

"We're going to make orange-and-yellow beach coats," Olivia said. "We're copying them out of *Vogue.*"

"Look at the material," Andria put in. "Isn't that wild?"

"It's perfect," Miss Crystal said. "It's what I dreamed would happen if we came up here. When I was young we always had projects in the summers. One summer we copied a dress that Audrey Hepburn wore in a movie. She was this chauffeur's daughter that goes to Paris. We made the dress for my cousin Baby Gwen to wear to be sweetheart of K.A.

It was a sheath of grosgrain silk with a huge peplum of darker silk, like this." She took a piece of material from a chair and tied it around her waist. "You can't imagine what a gorgeous dress we made. LeLe and myself and Baby Gwen and Saint John. Now he's a gynecologist. We listened to *Aida* and made that fabulous dress."

"What color was it?" Olivia asked.

"It was ivory grosgrain silk. The skirt was a shade of gray. We didn't know what color to make it because the movie was black and white." She held out her arms. The girls drew near. Then they showed us the patterns they had bought for beach robes and caftans. We spread the material they had purchased out on the table and began to pin on a pattern. Then we began to sew. The afternoon wore on into evening. It was six o'clock when we stopped work and went to the kitchen to begin dinner. Jessie and King were coming in from a fishing trip. They had caught some halibut and King was filleting it at the sink.

Andria got out the corn muffin pans and I began to beat up cornbread dough. Jessie made ice tea. Olivia cut up salad. Mr. Daniel drifted in and made toddies for himself and Miss Lydia and a diet Coke for Miss Crystal and we ate in the kitchen on an assortment of plates and saucers.

Afterward we went out into the yard and watched the stars for a while and talked about how nice it was to be on the water without mosquitos and no-see-ums exacting a price for the night.

It was so nice but it was all a front. Miss Crystal and Miss Lydia and I thought we had those teenage girls right where we wanted them, living in the safety of the past. But we were mistaken. The sewing club and the permanent waves and the interest in fashion were all a front. The whole time they were sewing beach coats all Olivia and Andria were really thinking about was the secret cult they had started to study the works of Anna Hand and make copies of her letters. They were trying to find clues to where she had gone. They did not believe she had committed suicide. They believed she had gone off somewhere to try some desperate cure. Olivia had told Andria and Crystal Anne she had a letter from Ms. Hand after she died telling her she wasn't dead. Then the letter mysteriously disappeared. She made it up to make herself important because she was so jealous of her sister having a love affair with King, then she began to believe it. By the time we found out and stopped it, Olivia believed every word she had said.

"I never believed it," Crystal Anne said, "I only wanted to get a permanent wave. I only wanted to make my beach coat and have a hairstyle."

They had made Xerox copies of the letters on one of their trips to town. I found one months later when I was cleaning out a box of Crystal Anne's games. She had drawn some Barbie clothes on the reverse side. On one side was this ball dress for Barbie colored in silver and bronze and gold crayons with a little tiara to match and long white gloves and a bottle of Perfume Pretty cologne.

On the other side, the Xerox side, was this terrible sad letter Anna Hand had written to Miss Noel.

Dear Noel,

Do not feel guilty. DO NOT FEEL GUILTY. It is not your fault that he killed himself. I don't care what you said to him. We all say horrible things to each other every day of our lives. And THINK WORSE THINGS.

But we don't kill ourselves because of it. If he killed himself it's because he couldn't take the heat of his notoriety, fame, whatever we call this two-edged sword. Please stop telling people that you killed him. They will start believing it.

Love from here,
Anna

OLIVIA   Last night I woke up in the middle of the night and thought Aunt Anna was out on the beach waiting for me. I put on some shorts and sandals and went out there, there was a full moon, so beautiful, so much light. I walked as fast as I could down to the water's edge and let it climb up to my thighs and then I saw her floating above me like a cloud, in a white dress, and she said, Write, Olivia. You will write great poems. Don't drown yourself. I want you to stay alive and finish my work.

Then I went to the boathouse as fast as I could and lit candles and started writing everything. I wrote about ten poems before it was dawn. It was so wonderful and then I ate all the cookies left in the sack and walked back down to where I had seen her but it was only the beach at dawn. One more thing. Even when she was floating above me telling me to write poems, at the same time I thought she was in the water waiting to eat me up or drag me under.

9

TRACELEEN   Then it was August and Lydia's birthday. We made a cake and had a party in the backyard. We covered a picnic table with a pink linen cloth and had the party just as the sun was going down in the mackerel clouds. The children had worked for days making a stage play. They hung Japanese lanterns from the trees and built a stage and brought out an upholstered chair from the parlor for a place of honor for Lydia. As soon as we had all gathered in the yard the show began. Crystal Anne started it off. She danced a beautiful dance to a piece of music called *Liebesträume* while Olivia read a poem she had written to go with it.

> *The music swings and sings and swirls*
> *And seems to fill the room*
> *While we wait unknowingly*
> *Of what may be our doom*
>
> *Will someone come to fill my arms?*
> *Will he love and heal me?*
> *Will I walk alone forever?*
> *Undaunted, cold and free?*

It was a very beautiful poem and everyone was astounded that Olivia had made it match the music so perfectly. Crystal Anne had on this seafoam green tutu they had made for her in the sewing room. It was hard to imagine anything they could have next that would rival that.

Then Andria came out and read a poem about what it is like to be half black and half white. It made chills run down my spine to hear her read it. Next she sang a song she had written while Jessie accompanied her on the guitar. Andria's song was called "Ice Angels on My Wings."

Get them ice angels off my wings
I got rid of my daddy
I got rid of you
I got rid of my math teacher too
All the men that haunt me
I don't let them haunt me
But the ghosts keep hanging on

Get those ice angels off my wings
Melt them in the light of day
Melt them like Antarctica
Melt them like the Arctic Sea
Leave my gossamer alone
Let me fly away and flee.

Oh, get the icy ghosts of men
Melted off my silver wings
Let me fly to find my destiny,
How the bell that calls me rings.

All those men who haunt me. I don't let them haunt me
But the ghosts keep hanging on.

That got a big round of applause. After that night I noticed everyone treated Andria differently. Even Lydia warmed up and began to take a real interest in her.

After Andria's performance Crystal Anne danced again, this time in a yellow outfit. Then King read a scroll dedicated to Lydia about what a good friend she was to young people and understood them. I took that to mean she had taken Jessie to Planned Parenthood behind our backs.

Next Jessie sang some folk songs accompanying herself on the guitar. She looked beautiful in a peasant skirt and white off-the-shoulder blouse. Still, even Jessie could not compete with Andria and her song about ice angels on her wings. Of course, Andria had spent the summer devoting herself to literature while Jessie devoted herself to love.

Later that night Mr. Manny called and said he was coming up. He was very upset about a letter he had gotten from Crystal Anne. He was sending it to Miss Crystal on a Fax machine first thing in the morning and he was coming up as soon as he could get away.

"What have you been writing to your daddy?" we asked her, when we told her he was coming. "What did you say to upset him?"

"I told him he should come up here. Now he's coming."

"He thinks you're sad. Are you sad, Crystal Anne?" This from Miss Crystal.

"I am sort of. I'm tired of being here. I want to go home."

"I thought you were having so much fun, with your show and everything and all your clubs."

"It's time for people to go home." She went to her mother and put her hands on her mother's knees and looked up at her with that very honest look that melts anyone's heart when a child will do it. "Are we going to have a broken home?" she asks. "I don't want to have a broken home." Then she began to cry. She pulled away and went to stand in the shelter of the refrigerator door and began to sob. It scared Miss Crystal and me to death. We had never seen Crystal Anne that way. She has never cried, even when she was a small child. She rises above her tears.

"There won't be a broken home," Miss Crystal says. "We are only on a summer vacation to broaden our horizons. Stop crying, Crystal Anne. Stop being so dramatic. I want you to go and take a bath and wash that makeup off your face. Your daddy might want a broken home when he sees what you've done to your hair."

Crystal Anne cried harder at that, putting her hands to the side of her hairstyle. Miss Crystal relented. "He'll love your hair," she said. "He likes modern art."

I interfered at that point. I picked Crystal Anne up in my arms and took her off to have a bath. "Your hairstyle is very nice," I told her. "At least you didn't dye part of it blue."

10

TRACELEEN The next morning Miss Crystal and I
drove into Rockland and waited for the letters to come out
on the Fax machine. I hated for the woman at the copying
place to see our personal mail but I suppose she reads so
many things each day that she has lost interest in the details.
There were five letters. Four Mr. Manny received early in
the summer and one he had gotten that week. Except for
the last one I didn't think they were that upsetting and only
went to show that Crystal Anne had inherited her father's
brain and is very advanced for her age.

Dear Daddy,
   I want you to come up here immediately. I want
to show you this ocean and I'm sooo lonely for you.
It is not good to work work work all the time. Alan
is here with his friend Joe and they are giving us les-
sons. I hit five perfect serves in a row today. Joe says
I could get on the pro circuit if I wanted to. I wish I
could go back to camp. It's hard to swim in this ocean.
This ocean is dark and cold. It isn't like Moorhead or
Sea Island or even Gulf Shores. I guess it is good for
us to see the world.
   We stopped on the way up and saw Plymouth

Rock. Momma said when you were a little boy you sat on it. Is that true? You couldn't sit on it now. There's a fence around it. Momma said you were real little then. How little were you?

Your loving daughter,
Crystal Anne

Dear Daddy,

I dreamed last night you were putting me to bed. You said, I want to be sure she has a nice bed with a good pillow. You pulled the covers up around my chin and kissed me and then you left the light on for me. You said, I am leaving this light on, don't be afraid. It is the first time I have ever dreamed a dream with you in it.

Please write back.

Your loving daughter,
Crystal Anne

Dearest Dad,

Mom said you might come up in a week or so. I hope you are. I'm dying of lonesomeness for you. You're the only father I have. And I could use some discipline.

My lessons are over now as Joe and Alan left, but Andria has been playing with me. She and Traceleen hired some people to clean the kitchen. Andria doesn't like to work. She only likes to nurse me and go to school. Well, that's civil rights. I'm glad they got it. Traceleen said you were one of the main ones that worked on it. She said you were a guard at McCormick School when they let children of all races go there. Good for you. I am proud to be your daughter.

Love and love again,
Crystal Anne

Dear Dad,

It is storming today. A northwester. There are advisories on the radio. Get the boats to port, they say. It is storming outside right now as I write this. Someday I will read this and remember it was storming like crazy when I was in Noel's mansion in Maine. I will not have forgotten it because I captured it on paper.

The rain comes down in waves and the wind blows it like the sea. You could drink the rain if you needed a drink but not the sea. If you are in a lifeboat and you drink seawater you will only want more and more. The more you drink the more you want. It will kill you finally. Many sailors have died that way. Dana, my friend that comes over to play with me, her father was at sea for many years. He told me about drinking seawater. He said everything in life can be that way if you let it. The more you drink the more you want.

Love from Maine,
C.A.

Those were the letters that weren't too bad. Then we read the one that set Mr. Manny off and made him come to Maine.

Dear Dad,

Something terrible is going on. Olivia says she is going to drown herself if she doesn't get into Harvard. That's one thing she said when they were drinking rum Cokes. The next day she said she didn't mean it. She is always saying Momma's cousin Anna isn't dead. Then sometimes she is dead and we have to talk to her on the Ouija board. They made me swear not to tell Traceleen or Momma, but they didn't say not to write you. So I am writing you. I think you ought to come up here and take us home.

> Love and love again,
> Your daughter,
> Crystal Anne

P.S. Could I get the kind of cancer Ms. Hand got even if I'm only related to Grandmother? Olivia says all the Hands will get it. Three out of five will get it. The whole family may have to go up to Duke University to get tested. I hope I don't get it. It eats up your bones and your chest. Well, don't worry about that for now. Love again. C.A.W.

As soon as we read that Miss Crystal and I went home and marched straight down to the boathouse. There is Crystal Anne and Olivia and Andria and King and Jessie all lying in the sun. Miss Crystal starts asking questions.

"Okay," she says. "What is this about a Ouija board and Anna being alive? Olivia, is this some of your doing?"

"You told," she says, and glowers at Crystal Anne. "You big baby. You told your mother."

"No, I didn't," Crystal Anne says. "I only wrote to Daddy and I told him not to tell."

Then they all began to tell different lies and parts of the truth and accuse each other of things. Except for Crystal Anne, who was so glad to get it off her chest she told us everything. Then Miss Crystal and I went into the boathouse and got the letters and all the copies we could find and the Ouija board and the incense and took it to the house. Olivia follows us demanding we give the letters to her. "They are mine," she says. "She was my aunt that came and found me and messed up my life getting me to live with Dad. I guess I at least get to have some souvenirs."

"I'm going to call your daddy," Crystal says. "This is scary, Olivia. I don't know what to think. You don't really believe Anna is alive, do you? Tell me you made that up."

"She might be alive," Olivia began, but when Miss Crystal reached for the phone to call Daniel she decided to change her mind. "Well, I know she isn't really alive but I had to keep their interest up or they wouldn't come to the meetings."

"I think I should call your father anyway," Miss Crystal said, but Miss Lydia was into it by then and talked her out of it. "Let it alone," Miss Lydia advised. "It's over now. Olivia knows that Anna's dead. You know that, don't you, honey?"

"She's dead if you mean her body," Olivia says. "But her spirit isn't dead. Her spirit is in every word she wrote. You ought to know that, Lydia. If you don't, nothing you paint will ever be worth a damn." Can you believe a young girl would speak to a grown woman like that? Girls didn't talk like that where I came from. But that was long ago and far away and we are in the new world now.

The next day Mr. Manny arrived. He came driving up in this little beige car he rented at the airport. He was looking very tired, wearing his rumpled-up beige suit. Of course he put on this big smile and acted like all was well with the world and he didn't have a care. Crystal Anne came tearing up from the beach and threw herself into his arms. Then Miss Crystal came out and they started being so polite.

"I'm glad you're here, honey," she said. "I guess you're tired. I bet you want to get out of that suit. Well, come on in and see the house. King, come here and speak to Manny. Manny's here."

They followed him into the house and into the kitchen. "Traceleen, what are we doing way up here?" he asked me. "Is there a glass of water in this house?"

"Seeing the world," I answered and got out the ice and put it into one of the best blue tumblers and filled it with water and handed it to him.

"Well, I'm sick of everybody being gone. The dogs are lonely and the house is full of dust."

"Didn't Grace come? She's supposed to be there Wednesdays and Fridays."

"She leaves the curtains closed. The place looks like a morgue. Tell her to open up the curtains, can't you?" He was smiling and putting on his old joking mood, his little daughter hanging on his arm. So here he is and he hasn't seen his wife in two and a half months but all he does is joke with me about the house in New Orleans. What goes on between people when they get this deep into a troubled marriage? Here he is, and he should be saying, What is going on here, Crystal? Are we married or not? But I could see the chances of him saying it were slim. She was watching him, like you'd watch an actor perform a play, only he wasn't an actor, he was deep into a world very far away from the one where he was raised. My auntee worked for his family for many years and it is like another country from the one where the Mannings and their connections do and say exactly what they please all day every day. In the Weiss family everything is very secret and no one dares to do a thing they aren't supposed to do. That is why they have collected all that money Miss Crystal spends any way she likes and throws away. She pays me more money than any housekeeper ever made in uptown New Orleans and any time she thinks about it she gives me another raise.

"Open them up yourself," Miss Crystal says. "Manny, even you can figure out how to open up the drapes." She turns away. She might have been hoping he would start something and now she has given up.

"I'm making lamb and soufflé for dinner," I declare. "Why don't you go show your daddy his room, Crystal Anne. And all your forts you have everywhere." Then they went off to the upstairs and I began to get out the things I needed to prepare for supper. In a little while Crystal Anne came down and said her mother and father wanted to be alone. I called Andria and told her to take Crystal Anne to the beach.

MANNY   I said (as carefully as I could phrase it, not blaming anyone, just stating the facts), I said, Crystal, the child has gotten the idea in her head that she is going to get some genetically caused cancer. Have you explained to her that we are not going to get cancer? I want us to sit down with her and explain to her that she has four healthy grand-parents, not to mention hybrid vigor.

Could I have phrased it any more carefully than that? She immediately took umbrage and began to berate me for thinking she is a bad mother. *I am a wonderful mother.* She must have said it a dozen times. Then, when I tried to put my arm around her, she ran off to the other side of the room and started screaming at me about not making love to her.

How can I make love to her when she is never there? How can I make love to her when I know damn well she is unfaithful to me? How can a man forgive that? I have to leave her. I have to let her leave. But then Crystal Anne would be left at the mercy of these people. I don't need a psychiatrist to tell me what to do. I need the strength and wisdom to ride this out. This is my marriage. I have to live with it.

CRYSTAL   I said, "Manny, the trouble with us is we're not in love. If we were in love we wouldn't fuck like this. We'd fuck differently. We'd fuck the minute we see each other, not after we have six hours of talk. We don't love each other. That's the problem."

"I love you."

"No, you don't. You love going down to the law firm and pleasing your goddamn daddy. I don't know why you married me. I don't know why you wanted me and I don't know why you quit fucking me. That's why I run around on you. Because you quit fucking me. What do you expect me to do? Sit around and never get laid? Have you forgotten who I am?"

He sat on the bed and took it in. He didn't say, Crystal, that's the best I know how to fuck. I don't have some great sexual stuff to give. He didn't even say, Crystal, I'll learn how to make you come. I'll eat your pussy. I'll touch you with my hands. All he did was sit on the bed with his head on his hands and think. That's what he's good for in the world, to make money and to think, and I love that. I LOVE THE FACT THAT HE CAN THINK. I loved him for that and I married him for it and it was a terrible mistake. I thought I could fix the fucking part. I thought he'd learn how. I'd never known a man who wasn't good in bed. I didn't know about it. I thought somehow it wasn't true.

"What do you want to do?" he asked. "I'll do anything you want."

"Will you fuck me now? Will you take off your clothes and your goddamn armor and have a drink of brandy or whatever it takes and stick your dick in me and keep it hard until I come? Will you do that?"

"I don't know," he said. "I don't know if I can."

So he took off his clothes and fucked me for about thirty seconds and then he lay on his back and looked up at the ceiling. I wanted to commit suicide. How in the name of God did a woman like me end up with a man like him?

And you want to know the worst thing of all. The very worst and strangest thing of all. I love the man. I honest to God really love the man and there have been times when it was all okay. Every now and then out of the clear blue sky the man can fuck me. Because of that I lay there beside him with my body and mind totally anxious and mad and evil and unsatisfied and wasted and I said to myself, Well, I'll masturbate later. Then I got up and got dressed and we went downstairs into the kitchen and I made a tomato sandwich and we started having a terrible fight right in front of Traceleen, and Crystal Anne heard us.

What am I supposed to do, I'd like to know? I know life isn't easy for anyone and it certainly isn't perfect but at least you ought to get to eat and fuck. Even rich people should get to eat and fuck.

I want Crystal Anne to grow up and love a man and fuck him. I want King and Jessie to fuck all up and down the coast of Maine. They're doing it. I know they are. At least someone around here is getting laid.

TRACELEEN   Several hours went by while Miss Crystal and Mr. Manny stayed upstairs. What was there to do but make a pie? We had been out to an orchard the day before and picked some Jonathan apples and I cut them up in pieces and made the crust from scratch and added plenty of brown sugar and cinnamon and stuck two pies in the oven. Mrs. Chatevin has pie pans up here that are large enough for meat pies and I used them. They had barely come out of the oven and were sitting on the cooling rack when Miss Crystal comes down to the kitchen and goes and stands by the breakfast-room table looking out around the side of the stained-glass picture. I knew she could smell the pies. If she wanted a piece of pie I guess she would ask for one. I went on with cleaning up. I didn't say a word or ask a question but I knew one thing. Nothing good was going on. If a woman and a man have made up and put their souls and bodies together there is a glow on them that spreads out all around. There was no glow on Miss Crystal. Only this look of what next and how many hours until I die.

In a little while Mr. Manny follows her into the kitchen. He compliments the pies, then gets a piece of bread and butter and goes and stands beside her near the window. I go out onto the back porch where the washer is and start folding up some clothes. "You didn't even come up here for me," I hear her say, "It took Crystal Anne writing you to get you to fly up here. You call that love, Manny. What am I anyway? Some girl at Mount Holyoke you write to when you're afraid the boys won't think you have a dick? Is that who I am? The token girlfriend so the guys at Andover think you're normal?"

"Is this what that psychiatrist tells you? That guy I gave twelve thousand dollars to last year?"

"It isn't your fault, Manny. It's not your fault they sent you off to school when you were twelve. But I can't suffer all my life from it. It wasn't me. I didn't sacrifice my life to get in Harvard. That's one thing Gravis told me. He said it was probably the boarding school that ruined you."

"You had your tennis player. Wasn't he enough?"

"I didn't have Alan Dalton. Lydia's got a thing with Alan, not me."

"Do you really think I'm that big a fool?"

"What are you accusing me of now?"

"I don't care what you do, Crystal. I've lost count of all your boyfriends. But I care about my daughter. I want my daughter home. I'm taking her this afternoon. I've had enough of this craziness your family gets into. This crazy girl of Daniel's and this cult stuff. Thinking she's got cancer. I can't believe you didn't watch them any closer than that."

"You won't take her anywhere. She's mine, Manny. I almost died having her. She's my daughter and you'll never take her from me."

I could see them through the open door between the back porch and the kitchen, standing so close to the window and the stained-glass picture. I thought, Glass will start to break. What am I doing in this Godless place? Why did I come up? Why don't they go on and get a divorce and stop all this terrible hate and using up their lives for no good reason? I must have begun to cry. I felt tears on my cheeks at the thought of how nothing turns out right. No matter how hard we try or how many miles we go it is fight, fight, fight to stay alive and so little love. I walked down the back steps so I wouldn't hear any more. I thought, I will go and find Andria and take her for a walk. These white people can solve their own problems. I must make sure my niece is still on the right track and hasn't been caught up in this disease of never loving a thing but ourselves. A butterfly was on the flat green leaf of the rhododendron plant beside the back steps. Not one, but many butterflies, a dozen or so very small white butterflies with yellow specks or a cast to their wings. How wonderful they were. How wonderful the sunlight and the plants and all the things that God has made to grow but all we do is talk and fight. I had no more lifted my eyes from the butterflies than I saw a spider's web stretched across the broom that leaned against the stone wall that bordered the old rose garden. A web of such lacy and delicate patterns. I turned and saw Andria coming up the front lawn with Crystal Anne beside her. They were talking and laughing about something. The young are all we have and we should worship them because they still have moments that are not sullied with the darkness of remorse and adultery and hate.

I stood in the backyard breathing very hard, feeling my heart pound in my chest and my blood pressure rise. Trying to beat it down. I get lonely too and scared. I sat down on the stone wall and tried to pray and thought of the sea with its beaches.

In a moment voices began to come out from the kitchen again. This time they were yelling. "You put that goddamn IUD up there. You stuck that wire up in your body to kill my babies. That's why. I'm not giving you any more babies of mine to kill with a wire."

"You're out of your mind. I had Crystal Anne at the risk of my life. I had her and then I decided to stay alive if you don't mind. Kit told me not to ever have another one. He said I was lucky to be alive."

"You killed my babies with a copper wire," he yelled back.

"If you had fucked me I wouldn't have needed other men," she said. "You did it, Manny. You did it to yourself. I did what I had to to survive. Don't come near me. Don't you dare hit me. If you hit me, I'll call the police."

Then I heard something smash. She must have thrown something at him. I got up and moved toward the steps. I don't know what I thought I was going to do. Then the back door opened and here came Crystal Anne running out with Andria behind her. "Hold on, baby," I yelled but she only looked at me and ran straight down the lawn toward the water. Andria stopped. "She heard them yelling at each other," Andria said. "You want me to go after her?"

"I'll go," I said. "She is my baby. I'll see to her." I began to run down the way that she had gone. Behind me I heard Manny and Crystal coming out the back door and stopping to talk to Andria.

I ran to the bottom of the yard and climbed the wall and started toward the sea. Crystal Anne was not on the beach. She was not in the boathouse or by the rocks. I headed back toward the house and met Mr. Manny coming the other way. "Did you find her?" he asked.

"No. I thought she must have gone back to the house."

"She heard us arguing. It's too hard, Traceleen. It's all too hard. Well, where do you think she's gone?"

"I couldn't say."

Five hours later we still hadn't found her. When the sun went down she was still nowhere to be seen. We had combed the beach and torn the house apart. King was running everywhere and Jessie and Mr. Manny would not leave the water's edge. Olivia and myself and Lydia and Miss Crystal and Andria were going up and down the road asking at houses and seeking her in town. My heart was in my throat and my blood pressure was cooking about two hundred. I knew she was not dead or harmed. I knew she was not drowned or kidnapped or taken by Gypsies. She had run away. But where had she gone and how long would she stay? Was there any other way to raise a bunch of children? Is there something we have lost sight of, some secret of being happy, or has it always been this way? So it was in the oldest times told of in the Bible, brother against brother, men wanting many wives, prodigal sons and so forth. But you never read of little girls running away because their fathers yelled at their mothers for having an IUD. Still, I guess that would come under the heading of spilling your seed on a woman's stomach.

When the sun went down and still no sign of her, Mr. Manny called the cops. A Sergeant Mossbacher and Lieutenant Madison appeared at our door. Lieutenant Madison was a woman with short brown hair cut in a modern style. She was very quiet and kept pursing up her lips and looking like she thought there was more to this than we were telling. Sergeant Mossbacher was more the old-fashioned type and kept shaking his head. "They go off that way," he said. "There's a spate of it each summer."

"You want it on the radio and TV?" Lieutenant Madison asked. "If so we'll need a picture." The phone was ringing behind us. We were on the front steps. "There's your phone," she added. "They usually call in when it gets dark."

It was Crystal Anne. I was the first one to the phone and there was her lovely little voice, sounding very old and far away. "Where's Dad?" she said. "Tell him to come here."

"You tell me where you are before I say another word," I answered. "I have combed the town for you. Oh, honey, how could you do us all this way?"

"I'm at Dana's," she said. "We went out on her dad's boat. We went out to the island."

Then Mr. Manny grabbed the phone and started listening very hard and talking in small sentences and saying, yes, no, yes. Miss Crystal grabbed his arm. Her hands were all around the sleeves of his thick white shirt. It is just like Mr. Manny that he hadn't bothered to change out of his suit pants to spend the afternoon searching for his daughter on the beach. He has the least vanity of any man I have ever known and should have had a different career, been a scientist or rocket engineer or inventor. His whole part of the house is filled with models of inventions or telescopes or binoculars or things like that. Once he set up a hydroponic garden on the back porch and grew experimental vegetables until King discovered it and put in marijuana plants.

Back to Crystal Anne. Mr. Manny was still talking to her. "Don't leave there. Stay right there," he kept saying. "Let me speak to Dana's father."

"I'd like to paint a woman in uniform sometime," Miss Lydia was saying to Lieutenant Madison. "I'm painting a series of heroes from everyday life. If you get time before I leave, would you spend an hour posing for some sketches?"

Then Mr. Manny hung up the phone and he and King drove over to Dana's house and picked up Crystal Anne and brought her back. The police stayed until she got there to see that she was all right and make her promise not to do it anymore. I went in and got our supper started. We had fried chicken Andria picked up at the Quik Stop place and salad and mint jelly I had meant to put on the lamb and French bread. We all went into the dining room and gathered around the table. We lit candles Olivia found somewhere and sat down like normal people in a normal life and began to eat. Mr. Manny began to tell jokes and then told us all about what was going on in New Orleans since we left. They have had another scandal about the Superdome and the teachers are threatening to strike in the fall.

"I want you to come on home," he said at last. "How long are you all planning to stay up here?"

"I thought we'd stay till the middle of August," Miss Crystal said. "Does that suit all of you?"

"I don't want the summer to ever end," Jessie said. She and King were being very quiet lately. She looked at Crystal now. "This is the best summer of my life."

"Well, I have to get ready for school," Olivia put in. She has had disappointing news from both Harvard and Duke and has decided to stay home and go to the University of North Carolina in Charlotte with her sister. "I have to go to Oklahoma and see my aunt before school starts. And my grandparents. I guess they think I've deserted them."

"I have to get home too," Andria put in. "I got to make sure all my loans came through. I don't trust Momma to take care of my mail." She looked my way. I felt sorry for her at that moment. She is the only one who has to borrow money. Then I thought better of it. Adversity is the fire that makes us strong. So my auntee always said. Later that night, before they went to bed, I saw Mr. Manny take Andria aside and have a talk with her. It turned out he told her to take all her loan letters to his secretary at his law firm when she got home. He told her not to worry, he would see to it she had plenty of money to go to college as long as she was keeping up her grades. He is such a good man. Such a truly fine man. I understood some things after I heard that fight that afternoon. It had been about babies after all. He had wanted Miss Crystal to have more babies and she had refused. That is why their bedrooms were apart and they had turned their marriage into a war. (After everyone blaming it on King cutting off the tops of the Japanese magnolias all these years.)

They went up together that night and the moon was full and they had almost lost their precious child, so I was hopeful something might happen. Not the thing I have with Mark, I guess, where anytime he gets me alone he begins to get that look on his face but whatever it is rich white people do when they stop thinking long enough to smell the roses.

The next morning Mr. Manny announced he had decided to stay two weeks. He called his office and told them to put his calls on hold. Then he put on some casual clothes and went into town and bought a camera and several rolls of film and began to photograph all of us around the house and beside the sea. He had no more than used up his film than things began to happen that required a man's hand.

LYDIA   Manny is here and Crystal has made up with him. I'm glad. I keep telling myself I'm glad. Still, I keep remembering that letter I got from her in 1985, after he threw her down the stairs at that wedding in Memphis. I have it at home in a jewelry box. I don't have it up here or I would give it to her. What if I said, Crystal, do you remember that letter you sent me from the hospital after your fall?

What letter? she might say. What are you talking about?

On the outside of the envelope it said, "Lydia, save this and give it to me if Manny tells me how much he loves me." He had thrown her down the stairs for flirting with a college boy.

The letter was written on small white hospital stationery and mailed in a homemade envelope made of lined graph paper and held together with Scotch tape. By the time I received it she was out of the hospital and Manny had taken her sailing in the B.V.I. Here's the letter.

Dearest Lydia,

I woke up dreaming a recurrent dream I have of you. I decided it was time to tell you about it.

I have suffered a bad fall and a brain concussion. Come see me and I'll tell you the dream. In which you paint a perfect timeless masterpiece. A wonderful dream. I just want you to know about it. So much creativity occurs while our eyes are closed in sleep.

I love you,
Crystal

Manny threw me down the stairs. Give this to me if he tries to tell me how much he loves me.

11

TRACELEEN   Next we got the flu. Influenza B, a terrible epidemic that usually only strikes people in the winter but had gotten a head start up here by flying in on a plane from the north.

A Mr. Arletti from California brought it to us. He stopped by on his way from Nova Scotia to Los Angeles to see the house. He used to visit here when it was full of theater people and he was only a struggling director. Now that he has won two Oscars and can name his own price, he wanted to make a sentimental journey to see where he began his climb. "Noel introduced me to the people who gave me my big chance," he said. "It was the summer of nineteen fifty-nine. It seems a million years ago. Martin Manulis sat right there in that chair and said for me to come and see him in the fall. The rest is history. I made a *Playhouse Ninety* special and the studios started calling." Cough, cough. Cough, cough, cough.

"You need to go to bed, Paulie," Miss Crystal said.

"No, I'm fine. Someone was coughing on the plane from London. What good does it do to fly first class if sick people insist on flying. No, just get me some water." Cough, cough,

cough. "My immune system can deal with it. I never get sick." Cough, cough.

An hour later he was upstairs in bed in the room with the gray-and-white wallpaper. The only time he woke up for two days was to have coughing attacks. Then he began to run a fever.

That was Thursday morning. By Saturday Olivia was down, then Jessie, then King, then Crystal Anne, then Miss Crystal, then Lydia, Mr. Manny went to bed on Monday morning, last of all me. The only person in the whole house who was not sick was Andria.

Mr. Arletti began to recover after four days. He recovered from the coughing spells and his fever was dropping, then the disease spread to his head. He was on the phone every time he woke up talking to doctors in California. They had the drugstore in Rockland delivering supplies and pills five times a day. That is how Andria met her love.

Every time the delivery boy would come Mr. Arletti would hand Andria a twenty-dollar bill to give him for a tip. "I can't take this," the boy said, after the third delivery. "That's sixty dollars today. This man must be out of his mind."

"He's a Hollywood producer," Andria said. "He sat by Princess Anne at a benefit last week. He got the flu on an airplane. Well, how much do we owe you for the vaporizer?"

"I can't take any more tips today."

"Then how much is the bill?" Andria had been running around nursing all of us, her hair tied back with a crimson scarf. She had on those little cutoff blue jeans I hate to see her wear and a tank top. She had been arranging flowers when the doorbell rang. Her arms were full of lilies when she went to the door. No wonder Kale Vito fell in love.

He was not a boy after all. He was twenty-one years old and was a sophomore at Harvard University. Part African and part Italian. Darker than Andria but not as dark as me. The minute I met him I was convinced he was the one for Andria. He has the loveliest manners you can imagine and is on a scholarship to Harvard to learn to be a medical doctor or a physicist, he hasn't made up his mind.

He made up his mind about Andria fast enough. He had never met a black girl from New Orleans and he was captivated by her charm and the legends of our city.

He was also very interested in our flu epidemic, being the son of the pharmacist and going to pre-medical school. He advised Andria to wash her hands every ten minutes as she nursed us. It's the hands that spread it, he told her. Not the air.

"Did he ask you to go anywhere?" I asked. Cough, cough, cough. Andria had come to sit on the side of my bed and tell me about meeting him.

"He asked me to go sailing with him Saturday."

"Oh, no, not out on a sailboat." Cough, cough, cough.

"Aunt Traceleen, take your Robitussin. I can take care of my own private life." She held out the spoon and I tried to swallow it. I cannot think of August in Maine without thinking of the terrible taste of Robitussin mixed with orange juice and crackers and the Whitman's Samplers Mr. Arletti had delivered to make up for giving us the flu.

In the middle of the night, the fifth night of the flu, King began to have terrible stomach pains. Mr. Manny dragged himself out of bed and took him to the hospital. They called back and said it might be his appendix. The next time the phone rang King's appendix was out and Mr. Manny was in an isolation room being treated for pneumonia.

For twenty-four hours it was touch and go. Miss Crystal dragged around in her pajamas putting in calls to the doctors. Finally, after two days, Mr. Manny began to respond to his treatment. On the third day Miss Crystal went into Rockland and brought him home.

"How about King?" I asked. "How is he? Is he doing okay?"

"He's fine," she said. "Only they have had him doped up on shots for pain. After all we went through to get him off of drugs. What if he relapses? What if this gets him back on drugs?"

"He'll never go back on drugs," Jessie said. She was standing in the doorway in her pink pajamas. Her face streaked with the tears she had shed all night. "How could he go back on drugs? He's going to be a father. I'm going to have a baby."

Here is how they knew. They had gone to the drugstore and gotten this kit and taken it to The Hangout and Jessie had tested herself while King played the jukebox. Every now and then I think I have the modern world figured out. I am very interested in inventions and improvements of things and try to keep up. Miss Crystal and Mr. Manny take every magazine known to man and I read them in my spare time. So I always think I have kept up but even I had not known you could find out you were pregnant in a matter of minutes. "Are you sure it worked?" I asked, when she had explained their findings. "Oh, yes," she said. "I did it two days in a row." So there we were no more than coming out of the flu epidemic and an emergency appendectomy and here we were with an unwed mother situation. Life is not a tree that stands out in the yard making nice dependable changes with the seasons. No, it is more like a storm that blows in from the sea, full of rain and sudden surprises. Then the next day as calm as it can be and beautiful and sunlit and blue.

"Oh, my darling, darling child," Miss Crystal kept saying, as if Jessie had handed her a million dollars instead of a problem to be solved.

On the positive side, it was this development that clinched the make-up between Miss Crystal and Mr. Manny. If there is one thing she will always die for it is King. Miss Lydia got drunk later and explained it to me and for once I think she was completely right. "That's it," Lydia said. "Now she'll never leave him. Now she has a whole new set of things for him to solve, money for him to spend. Can you believe it, Traceleen? How people use and drain each other. It drives me nuts. It makes me glad I live alone."

"I want them to love each other," I said. "I want them to make up."

"That isn't making up," Lydia said. "That's using people. She doesn't love him. She doesn't have the hots for him. She never did. She lives with him and spends his money and takes his goodness and his love and in return she despises him."

"Miss Crystal does not despise Mr. Manny."

"Not in the way you mean. Not like you would a criminal. She hates him for what he cannot be. He can't be Big King or Daniel or that football hero she went out with. He's a quiet Jewish intellectual who's a momma's boy. He's an angel and you can't fuck angels no matter how much you like them or think they're wonderful. So now they all go back to New Orleans and she collects a few more lovers and maybe goes back to drinking and he goes back to work and King and Jessie have this baby they don't need and Crystal Anne grows up to do God knows what."

"Nothing will ever happen to her," I said. "She is a blessed child. She will always be a happy person and give happiness to other people. No sadness could destroy her."

"I hope you're right," Miss Lydia said. She poured a glass of gin and drank it off and then she poured another. "God-dammit, these people drive me crazy. They drive me nuts."

"It's not as bad as you think," I said. "Maybe they can go to a counselor. Maybe they can learn to have a stronger love."

"Oh, Traceleen," Miss Lydia goes. "Oh, God, you are so wonderful, and I'll tell you something else." She polished off her drink and leaned across the table at me. "If Crystal Anne's an angel it's because of you. You have done that to her. You have made her safe."

I prayed that night to save me from the sin of pride. I prayed not to want to believe that it was true.

12

TRACELEEN   Olivia and Andria had a fit when they found out about Jessie. They did nothing to hide their disgust. "It doesn't surprise me," Andria said. "She does everything he wants her to. She's his slave."

"Women are always men's slaves," Olivia put in. "They want to keep women down. They know we're smarter than they are. Barefoot and pregnant, that's all they want. Well, it's not King's fault. King isn't bad. He can't help it if he's a man."

"No one will ever knock me up." Andria was preparing their diet breakfast, half a grapefruit and an egg.

"Me either," Olivia agreed. "And if they do I'll get an abortion. I begged her last night to get one. She won't listen to me."

"I know," Andria said. "She wants it. She's going to have it. Can you imagine that."

"Dad's going to kill her. Or he'll kill King. I guess he'll kill King. I hope I'm not there when they tell him." This from Olivia. I was taking a pan of applesauce muffins out of the oven. I put the pan down on the table to cool.

"Oh, God, her father," Andria said. "I'd forgotten about him." Andria picked up a muffin and started eating it, blowing on the pieces as she stuffed them in her mouth. "In this play we saw in Montgomery the king gives this girl the choice of marrying the guy he picks out or going to a nunnery. Or getting killed, that was the third choice. It's just like now. Either you don't do it or you end up as good as dead. This guy at school tried to kill a girl he was screwing because she got an abortion. You can keep all this pussy business as far as I'm concerned."

"Andria," I yelled. I can't bear to hear her talk like that, so common.

"Andria," Olivia yelled. She ran over to her and grabbed the muffin. "Don't eat it. Spit it out. Ten seconds in the mouth. Twenty years on the hips."

Andria ran to the sink and spit out my lovely muffin made with handmade applesauce from apples we picked in the yard. I decided to leave the kitchen. It was too early to be with young people. I started taking off my apron, then they both apologized and settled down. They sat down at the table and began to eat their grapefruit, talking in lower tones.

"My best friend at NOCCA got knocked up last year," Andria said. "Now she's just pitiful. She brings the baby over to see us at school. It's this pitiful little baby. It cries all the time. The guy left her as soon as the baby came. He couldn't stand to hear it cry. Now she doesn't know if she'll ever get back in school."

"What have you said to Jessie?" I asked.

"I told her she didn't have to have a baby if she doesn't want to," Olivia answered. "But she won't even talk about it. She says she's glad. And then she started crying. I guess she's mad at me."

"That's not like you to say mean things to someone," I

said. "King in the hospital and her father in North Carolina and her mother in Europe. You're the only one she has, Olivia. You better go find her and try again."

"I didn't say anything mean. I told her she could count on me if she wants to get rid of it. I know how to find out where to go."

"He only had his appendix out," Andria added. "He'll be home in a couple of days."

Then Jessie appeared in the door, dressed in a light-colored summer dress, ready to go visit the hospital. She didn't look like anything was wrong with her. She sort of floated into the kitchen and sat down beside Olivia and touched her arm. Above the table was a stained-glass picture of Spring as a young girl. It was hanging in the window above the table and the beautiful colored light fell down upon the girls. Andria and Olivia were like a dark sea with Jessie floating above them in the light.

"You feeling okay?" Olivia asked.

"I'm all right. I'm going to see King. Crystal's taking me."

"What did she say?" Andria asked.

"She's happy. She's really happy. She's glad."

"You don't have to have this baby," Olivia said. "It's only a fetus. It's only an eighth of an inch long or even smaller than a bug. It's nothing. You don't have to do this. This is what happened to our mothers. It's nineteen eighty-eight. You don't have to let this happen. It's a trap."

"It isn't a trap."

"It is a trap."

"This friend of mine from NOCCA got knocked up last year." This from Andria. "And it ruined her life. You can get you a baby later on. It's too soon when you just got out of high school."

"I know," she said.

"Know what?" Olivia asked. "That it's a trap?"

"No, that what you say is true but it's not about King and me. We love each other. We want this baby. You don't understand, Olivia." She picked at the muffin I handed her. Andria got up and got a glass and poured her some orange juice. "You ought to drink this, especially after you had the flu. There might be something wrong with it anyway, since you were so sick with the flu. You ought to check on that."

"I don't care, there's nothing wrong with me, or my baby. I'm pregnant and I'm glad I am. As soon as King comes home we'll tell Dad. Dad won't kill anyone, Olivia. Dad loves me. He loves you and me." She drank her orange juice. I was surprised at how strong she seemed. How strong life is when it wishes to be. She floated above the sea of Olivia and Andria.

"Well, I'd better go," Jessie said, and polished off her muffin. "What time is it now?"

"Eight-fifteen."

"I have to see if Crystal's ready."

"Why don't you drive yourself," Olivia said. "You can still drive a car, can't you?"

"Crystal wants to take me."

"You don't have to do this," Olivia said. "I'm not going to stop saying that."

"Then say it all you want. It won't change my mind." Then Miss Crystal appeared and Crystal Anne and the three of them went off to visit the hospital.

"It will never happen to me," Andria said, getting up to put the plates and glasses in the dishwasher. "I'd abort myself in the tub. I'd have an abortion on my way to school. She'll be so sorry."

"Think about me," Olivia added, leaning on the counter to watch Andria work. "Think what it's like to watch your own sister go nuts. I mean, I have to watch her do this." She took her fist and began to bang it on the wall beside the broom closet. Bang, bang, bang. Like an actress in a play. Bang, bang, bang.

"Don't hurt your hand," I said. "That won't do a bit of good."

The next day they brought King home. He came limping up on the porch, bent over, but fine. As soon as he got there we all went into the living room and had a meeting.

"We have to tell her dad," King said. "I was going to go down there but now I can't travel. We are going to get married, Mother."

"Of course you are. How about here, in this room? This would be a beautiful place for a wedding."

"When?" This from Jessie. "When can we do it?"

"We have to tell your father first," Crystal said. "And we have to talk to the minister. There's an Episcopal church in town or do you want a priest?"

"A minister will do," Jessie said. "If it's okay with King."

"Are you sure you want to have a baby?" Miss Lydia got up from her chair and began to pace around. "There are hundreds of eggs in there. Plenty of sperm. You sure you want to hatch this one? What will you do about school?"

All our faces turned her way. She must have felt very lonesome at that moment and wished she had some of her Seattle friends with her.

"We want it," King said. "It's ours."

13

LYDIA I did not stop trying. I am a civilized person and I know my duty when I see it. It is not my job to be popular. It's my job to help the forward progress of civilization, and at this point in history that means the progress of women. A civilization that corrupts or enslaves or weakens its women *in any way* weakens itself and eventually will fall. So I kept on trying.

"How can she be a mother?" I screamed at Crystal. It was after they called Daniel and he had a fit and started flying to Maine in a twin-engine Cessna he's had for twenty years. "She doesn't even have a mother. She doesn't even have herself."

"She has us. All of us. I'll take care of them."

"She's a beautiful young girl at the beginning of her life. She doesn't even know who she is yet. And King certainly doesn't know who he is. Are you going to sacrifice them for the sake of some baby you think will do it for you? That's it? King wouldn't do it for you so you think this baby's going to?"

"It might grow them up."

"Did it grow you up? Hell, no. Did it grow Helen up to be a breed mare? Hell, no. Look what happened when she cut loose. It's a new world, Crystal. New possibilities. We live longer. Everything takes longer. Babies don't die. There doesn't have to be an unending supply at the cost of the mothers' lives, their freedom. Well, goddammit, freedom is worth something. It's priceless. It's beyond price. Just because you traded yours in for Manny's money."

"I don't believe you said that to me. It's over between us, Lydia. That's the last straw."

"No, it isn't. It's true. You've said it to me. I'm just saying it back. So, instead of taking your freedom you will go back to Manny and make up with him and get him to invest fifty thousand dollars in King's and Jessie's education? Well, he's probably pussy enough to do it. He hates being a Jew so much he'll do anything to get to run around with your cousins and brothers. It's pitiful. I don't know how I got mixed up with all of you. I'm going back to Seattle."

"Go on then. I don't care."

"You don't care about the truth anymore?"

"The truth doesn't do me any good. The truth doesn't keep my kids alive. The world is scary, Lydia. Young people have to have something to hang on to. They have to have love. They have to have each other."

"They don't have to have a baby for the glue. It's terrible for those children to have a child. My God, Crystal, have you recanted on everything we knew? It's terrible of you to encourage this."

"What do you suggest? Let her abort it and then she and King would hate each other for the rest of their lives? They might never find each other again. They're made for each other."

"They might find themselves."

She was quiet then. She wasn't even mad anymore. "I

know," she said. "That's the choice, isn't it? But I can't take a chance. He's my son. I have to make sure he has a reason to live."

"Then what about Jessie? You sacrifice her to that?"

"If I have to."

"When is Daniel getting here?"

"I don't know. He's flying in. He's furious."

"I know."

"Don't do anything to make him madder, please."

"Like what?"

"Like say those things to him."

Jessie appeared at the door. She was wearing a little beige linen sundress and sandals. So beautiful. So unearthly beautiful. Anyone would want their son to breed with her. "Dad called," she said. "He's at the airport in Tennant's Harbor. A guy is bringing him here. He'll be here in a minute."

"Get King," Crystal said. "Let's meet him on the porch."

He came tearing up the driveway. He was driving some man's car and when they came to the stairs he got out and handed the man some money. It was Daniel rampant.

"Okay, King," he said, turning to him. "I won't forgive this."

"Oh, Daniel," Crystal said. "Come inside. Let's talk this over." Daniel began to climb the stairs, ignoring Crystal, ignoring Jessie, going straight for King. "You promised me on your honor and now you've ruined my daughter's life," he said. He kept on coming and I'll say this for King, he didn't move. He stood his ground. I guess we all knew Daniel wouldn't really hit him. We hoped he wouldn't anyway. I don't know. Maybe I wanted him to hit him. I'm sick of all the bullshit that goes on in families. Sick of it all. It would have been a relief to see a fight.

"You aren't having a baby at your age." Daniel had turned to Jessie, who wasn't budging either, who was barely scared.

"We told her not to," Olivia chimed in. "We told her to abort it."

"Shut up, Olivia," he said. "You stay out of this." At which point Olivia and Andria kind of faded back. Back toward the little screened-in part of the porch. Daniel was by the door, with King in hitting distance. Manny was moving himself between them. Crystal was on the stairs. I had gone into the hall.

"Please come inside," Crystal said. "We can sort this out."

"You can't sort out a goddamn thing," Daniel said. "I'm taking my little girl to the doctor. Go get your things, Jessie. You too, Olivia."

"I won't do it, Daddy," Jessie said. "I'm in love with him."

"You will do it. You won't ruin your life over this goddamn little bastard."

"I'll make this up to you," King said. "I'll do whatever you want me to."

"I want you to get out of my way." Then Daniel grabbed Jessie by the arm and pulled her into the house and called for Olivia to follow. She hesitated, then whisked past Crystal and Manny, then passed me in the hall and followed her father and her sister up the stairs. WHO ARE WE, ALL OF US, US PEOPLE, US FAMILIES, US UTTERLY NUTS AND CRAZY PIECES OF PROTOPLASM? If you stop for one second and really think about what's going on. A bunch of people inventing themselves every second, making choices no animal or plant has ever made, deciding whether or not to reproduce, flying around in airplanes, being influenced by the dead. I give up. I was being influenced by Daniel being so good-looking and Manny was grabbing a chance to be Crystal's hero and Crystal was stealing Daniel's daughter to save her son and Andria was taking it all in. God help us if she ever does become a writer.

14

OLIVIA   No one will ever know what went on in that goddamn flowered-wallpaper room with those trees outside the windows. I know and Jessie and Dad know and the wallpaper and bed and the iron bedstead painted white and all those chiffoniers or whatever you call those chests and things that are all over this house. "You know I love you, Jess," Dad was saying. "I'm here to help you. I've helped lots of young girls in this kind of trouble. This is nothing new to me." Jessie turned the tape player on right in the middle of him talking. It was this old tape of the Pointer Sisters singing *"I want a man with a slow hand."* I thought Dad might hear the lyrics and go crazy but he was already crazy so what difference does it make? All summer Jessie's been acting like she was this sweet Southern girl that never gets in any trouble and is just this piece of ass for King or something like that. She has changed so much since I first met her. She used to be mean as shit. She hated me so much and she was so mean to me. Then after I went there to live she started being nice to me but she sure wasn't this little sweet girl saying Oh, King, and all that. I sort of liked it when she turned the tape on because I thought she might be turning back into herself. Dad was so mad. I never saw

anybody get that mad. His face was red all the way up into
his blond hair. He has this real light skin with freckles on it.
He looks like that when he plays tennis a long time, only
this time he is standing by the bed hanging on to this fragile
sort of twisted iron bedpost painted white and Jessie is sitting on the bed by the bedside table which is where the tape
player was and I am standing over to the side by this chifforobe with a mirror on it. I can see them and I can see their
reflections in the mirror too and he is going, like, No daughter of mine is going to ruin her life over a goddamn little
dope addict that is about as ready to get married as a dog
and I used to know his daddy and his daddy hasn't ever
grown up and the chances of him growing up are about
zero. Then Dad is crying. He is so tall and good-looking and
it broke my heart. He is just sobbing and wiping his eyes
and nose on this white handkerchief and I'm about to cry
but Jessie just sits there listening to the tape and saying,
Well, Dad, it isn't any of your business. You don't love me
anyway, all you love is your girlfriends and I have to stay
home by myself all the time. Then he goes, You have Olivia
and you have Francine (the maid) and Grandmother and
Granddaddy. Goddammit, honey, I've worked my ass off all
my life to make a good life for you. Please don't have this
baby. Ray (that's his friend who is a doctor and an abor-
tionist) is standing by, all we have to do is fly down there
and it will be over by noon tomorrow and you can see King
all you want, you just can't be fool enough to have a baby
at your age.

"I want it," she says. "I want to have it."

Then he's crying some more and wiping his eyes and
blowing his nose. By then I'm crying too. Only I'm crying
because he loves her so much. If he loved me that much I'd

never get married. I'd stay there and take care of him. I wouldn't even go to college. He hasn't even asked me yet if I heard from Harvard. Which I did. But don't go into that. Who needs those goddamn snobs. This guy Andria met goes there and she says he hasn't got it. She says he doesn't even turn her on.

So Dad says, Don't make up your mind right now. You can think it over and she says, It's over, nothing can change my mind. We are going to get married. Crystal said we could.

So she sort of sinks back into the pillows and reaches over and rewinds the tape but she has turned it down some more. I can barely hear it now. There is half a Hershey bar on the chifforobe and I eat that. I'm thinking, This is just like you read about when someone makes you cry, you grab some candy or something.

"Oh, honey, please listen to me," he says.

"Dad, you can't keep talking to me. I'm sorry I did it after I promised not to but people are human and they can't help it and you go out with everybody and sleep at their apartments, just because you come home at night we know you sleep with them, don't we, Olivia?"

"I don't care," I go. Then Dad sits on the bed with her and tells her this stuff his friend Ray said about how hard it will be on her body and she will lose her gorgeous figure and all this bullshit but she won't budge. I finish off the candy bar.

Then he gives up on her and goes on downstairs to talk to King some more. All this time he hasn't even asked me about college or barely said hello to me. Well, I'm not the bastard at the family reunion. I am the child of his first marriage and the child of his wife and I am myself and that's something and I can do whatever I want in the world like Aunt Anna told me I could. If only she was here. I think I might have to go home for a while and get back into that. Ride my own horse and see Bobby and see Grandmother and Granddaddy and Aunt Mary Lily. I'm about sick of being up here in Maine.

"You have to help me, Olivia," Jessie says after Dad leaves the room. She has turned the music up now. "*I want a lover with a slow hand. I want a lover with an easy touch.*" It gets me thinking about Bobby and what we used to do in the house on the river, especially when it would rain.

"What do you want me to do?" I ask. "I'm not going to say it's a good idea. It sucks to have a baby. I think you're nuts."

Then she starts crying and I don't even care. I just leave the room and go on downstairs to watch Dad talk to King. I'm thinking I wouldn't mind if he beat him up. That's the kind of mood I'm in.

DANIEL   Olivia followed us up there and I was glad she came. At least she's tough enough to live. I don't know if Jessie's tough enough anymore. I used to think she was. I used to think she was tough as shit, tough as Sheila, tough as me, but now I don't know. Ever since she started in with boys, it's been one goddamn thing after the other. She quit playing music, that broke my heart, then she met this goddamn little son-of-a-bitch, then all of this. I got up there as fast as I could. I got into a squall line over Virginia so I went out over the coast and flew at eighteen thousand feet all the way to the Jersey coast. I didn't give a damn if I bought it or not. How much can a man do? I haven't been this mad since some of the stuff Sheila used to pull when we were married.

So I took Jessie upstairs and sat her down on the bed and I said, Goddamn, honey, I'm not letting you ruin your life.

It's my life, she says. It's my own life. I said, Honey, Ray is waiting for us in his office. He's right there. We'll fly to Boston in my plane and go right on down on a commercial jet or we'll fly all the way. How're you feeling?

"I feel fine." She sits on the bed looking me right in the eye just as mean as a snake. She's got her mother in her. Also, she reminds me of Anna when she looks like that, and Helen too. I never could figure out what to do with those goddamn women. I should have cold-cocked one of them years ago. This is what happens when you let a bunch of women run the world.

"You aren't having any baby when you're eighteen years old, that's that."

"Yes, I am. That's that." She turned the radio on.

"Turn off that goddamn radio. I'll kill the little son-of-a-bitch is what I'll do. I can't believe this happened to you, honey. Please listen to me just a minute."

"It won't do any good. I want to have his baby. I love him. He's good, Dad. He's as good as he can be and he's going to take care of me. Crystal said they'd support us until we get out of school."

"Oh, Jesus Christ, honey. Stop a minute." Now she won't even listen to me and the other one is fiddling with things on the dresser.

Then I offered her everything in the world and she still wouldn't budge so I told them to stay right there in that room and I went downstairs and collected Manny and Crystal and King and took them down on the lawn to talk. That came to nothing, so I told Manny and Crystal to leave and I sat King down and tried to reason with him. "I ought to kill you," I said, "but I'd rather try to reason with you."

"I'll take care of her until I die," he answered. "I'll always take care of her and love her. You can depend on me."

"To do what? Goddammit, you don't even have an education or a job. You won't be able to support a wife for years, if you stay sober, which you goddamn well better do."

"I love her. I love her more than life. I'll take care of her until I die. I'd die for her. I swear I will, Daniel. I swear to God."

"Like you weren't going to fuck her, right? Like that oath you swore."

"You can hit me if you need to. Hit me. I don't care."

"I wouldn't waste my time," I said. "I've got better things to do. I'm going and talk to your mother."

So I took Crystal off and I said, Crystal, we've been friends for many years. You cannot do this to me. She's the light of my life. I have lived my life for that little girl. You have to get on my side in this, and she said, No, I want the baby, the baby will be perfect. Okay, I said, then I'll kill your smartass son. She said, You should have known better than to bring her up here. You can't stop them from fucking. They'll never want for anything. We'll take care of them. We'll give them anything they want.

I don't want a baby growing inside my little girl, I said. I don't want a goddamn baby. I want my little girl to finish growing up. I want her to have a decent life.

CRYSTAL   He got me off alone finally. It's the price I have to pay for helping Jessie and King. All those years that he loved me and now it's over. I always thought, At least I have Daniel. Daniel's always there. Daniel will save me if I need him to.

"Crystal," he said, "I have never thought you were as dumb as everyone thinks you are. I never even believed you were crazy."

"Thanks," I said. "I never thought you were dumb either. And I certainly never thought you were mean."

"Am I being mean?"

"Yes. They love each other. They were made for each other. They are what we might have been. They'll be all right, Daniel. King isn't his daddy. He's a good boy. He was okay until he got into drugs. He was okay until I married Manny. He loves her. He will go on loving her. If you make them kill this baby, it will kill it all and then they'll be as lost as we are. No possum, no sop, no taters. Goddammit, you don't have a happy-enough life to give advice."

"Neither do you." He moved closer to me. He took my arm and pulled me so close to him and said, "You're killing my daughter, Crystal. You can't have her. You can't take her away from me. I won't let a goddamn baby grow inside my little girl." Then he started crying. I think he's nuts, I think he's gone completely nuts.

I said, "Daniel, let's go back inside the house. Let's call a gynecologist besides Ray and you ask him if it's going to hurt Jessie to have a baby. Nothing happens to healthy pregnant women who have good care. She'll have everything she needs, everything she wants. Oh, Daniel, please calm down."

"I already talked to Ray," he says. "Ray says it sucks. He said it could warp her life, change her life. He's waiting to abort it and I'm going to talk her into it."

"It isn't you or me or Ray. It's them, your daughter and my son. It's their life."

"Without Manny's money it's not them. If you weren't offering to support them they'd change their minds."

"No, they wouldn't."

"Yes, they goddamn would. Her clothes bill is about five grand a year. You ought to see her charge accounts. I can just see her agreeing to be a welfare mother. She thinks babies come with maids."

"If I didn't help them, you would. Or Mother would or Daddy or Sheila's folks. There's no point in trying to starve them out. They have too many people they can go to."

"It will go bad," he said. "Ray said to stop it. Ray's a genius. A fucking genius. He's the goddamnedest smartest man I ever knew and he said to come up here and stop it."

"No, he's not. He's just sharp. He's made hundreds of thousands of dollars aborting babies and then he pretends it's some sort of crusade. You are totally in his power, Daniel. Everyone knows you believe anything he says because you think he's smart and you're dumb. He's been doing numbers on you since the second grade. He could do numbers on you then. He made you take the blame for that fire we built."

"You can say anything you like about him, Crystal, but he's still a genius. And he said to get Jessie to him pronto and I'm not giving up. You have the goddamn wedding if you want to but it doesn't mean I'm going to give up trying to stop this goddamn baby."

"You hate families," I told him. "I don't think anyone in your whole family knows how to love anyone. Anna hated all of you and Helen won't even see her own kids and now you want your daughter to kill your grandchild."

He gave up then. He shook his head and gave me that ice-cold blue-eyed stare and wandered off. I guess he went off to get drunk. That's usually how Daniel solves his problems.

Anyway, I had stood my ground. I've lost so much the last few years. Lydia's and Manny's love and now Daniel's too. But I don't give a damn. I want that baby. I've been so unhappy, so cheated, and, suddenly, the thought of this child is like the sky has opened up and flooded me with joy. I will give it anything it wants, anything it needs. I couldn't do it for King or even Crystal Anne because by the time she was born I hated Manny and because I almost died and I guess that made me feel funny about her. But this time it will be different. This baby will be blessed. It will belong to me. Oh, thank you, God, if there is a God, I thank you for this one more chance.

DANIEL   That afternoon I tried again with Jessie. I took her off in the car and we sat in the car by the ocean and I said, Honey, look at me. I know King's daddy. His daddy is the worst womanizer in the United States. His daddy would run around on the Queen of England.

"He didn't run around on Crystal. She left him because he drank too much."

"About the time you're getting big he's going to start looking around at other women. He won't be there when you need him. He's a little half-baked kid. I can't believe you'd do this to me, Jessie. I can't believe you'd break my heart."

"It's not your heart. It's my heart and it won't be that way. Just because his dad's that way. Just because that's the way you act. Daddy, you're the one who runs around on everyone, not King. You're the one."

"Oh, baby, you're right." Then I start crying like a god-damn baby. Just sobbing on the wheel. I feel like I've been crying for days and she just sits there cold as ice. Sheila all over and after a few minutes of that I don't care if she does ruin her life. I looked at her and she looked so much like her goddamn mother I almost didn't like her anymore.

"Well, I guess it's good I have a spare," I said.

"What's that supposed to mean?"

"I mean I'll just educate Olivia and have her to be proud of while you're off somewhere with your dope addict."

"I don't believe you said that to me. That's so manipu-lative. That's pitiful, Daddy."

"So go on and have your wedding and your little half-ass teenage husband and your baby. It's okay, Jess, if there's nothing I can do, there's nothing I can do."

But later, when we got home from the drive, I told her one more thing. "Ray's waiting," I said. "He'll be waiting for three more months. If you change your mind, let me know."

"I won't change it."

"He's in the phone book. Ray Farnsworth. 888-8997. You call him any time, day or night. Or call me."

Then I got out of the car and gave up. I walked on into

the house and fixed a drink and went out to sit in the yard under the trees. After a while Olivia came out with her black buddy and they sat around and talked about school and acted like nothing was going on. Then Traceleen called us in to dinner. She'd fixed some barbecue and we ate that and later I went into town and got drunk. I came home about three and climbed in bed and still thought about it. Well, the other one seems to be doing okay. She's surprised me, that's for sure. I figured she was the one that would be handing out pussy. Her mother was a piece for the books. I feel so bad about all that. Every time I look at the little girl I feel bad about it. I can hardly remember that summer out in San Francisco but I remember the fucking. Those blankets Summer had and that great dope. Olivia de Havilland, what a goddamn crazy name. Well, I didn't know about it and I wasn't there.

She stood up for me up there in that room. She's got some iron in her. These girls, these goddamn girls. No wonder my business is going to pot. I used to be able to run the place. Now it's Jessie this and Olivia that. What are they thinking? Who are they fucking? Jesus Christ, what do women want?

15

LYDIA "Helen's coming to the wedding," I told Noel. "Make up your mind what you want to do about that."

"I don't want to do anything. Just bring the letters when you come."

"Well, she'll know they're here. They made all kinds of copies. I know damn well we don't have them all."

"Oh, my. Well, what shall we do?"

"Let me send everything to you and tell Helen you'll write to her. Or sue her if she uses them. Tell her that."

"No, I want you to deliver them to me." (I could see her lying back against the pillows, in one of her incontestable fantasies. I was to deliver the papers to her room, that was that.)

"How did the young girls get involved?" she said. "Tell me again."

"The half-Indian one started a cult and the half-African one lost interest. Crystal Anne told her daddy. Crystal had a fit. Then we collected all the stuff we could and took away the Ouija board."

"The Ouija board?"

"They were trying to talk to her."

"Well, try to keep it from Helen."

"Helen's fucking this Irishman, Noel. Her sole interest in the papers is keeping him on the string."

"Well, she can't have my letters. Hide them good and bring them to me."

"I don't want to hide them anymore, Noel. I read them, by the way. I don't think you have anything to worry about."

"What do you mean?"

"There's nothing damning in them. They aren't even that interesting. I doubt anyone would need them in a book."

"You don't know what they mean. You don't understand. We had to write in shorthand. Because of Francis and because Charles was here with me."

"Noel."

"Yes." Her voice was growing quiet. I had harmed her. I had taken away her letters.

"I'll bring them," I said. "I'll hide them and I'll bring them to you."

"Thank you, my darling. Thank you very much."

So I capitulated. So what? If you take money you pay back thrall. Thrall is always waiting. Like those ice angels Andria wrote that song about. So I got the goddamn letters and locked them in my suitcase and got ready to help out with the wedding. The goddamn teenage bonding pageant. It was going to be a pageant. They only had three days but this vain bunch wasn't going to waste a minute getting everybody dressed.

I knew I would never sleep that night so I didn't even try. Who was it who said three o'clock in the morning is the real dark night of the soul? Around two I gave up on the novel I was reading and went downstairs and got a piece of cold chicken and went out to sit on the front steps. The moon was above the water, perfect and full and round. The giant pine trees on the lawn leaned their shadows toward me. I sat there in that fragrance, nibbling on the chicken and thinking about my womb, my abortions and my womb. My encounters with possible motherhood. If I had had those babies would the world be different? I would never have painted again, real creation does not put up with or wait on art, anyone who ever tried to write or paint around children knows that. It makes me sick to see the slop they write in women's magazines about having it all. You can have one or the other and that's that. Jessie Hand, as beautiful as a young girl could ever be, with an ear for music so divine and Godgiven. She hadn't played the piano five times all summer. A few times on the little organ in the mornings, sometimes the guitar. She was after bigger fish, babies and real drama and terrible flawed human love. The world would have to amuse itself. Having had no mother, she would now be one. Maybe it made sense and I was wrong to rail at Crystal.

I shook my head, picked the last piece of chicken off the bone, wrapped the scraps in a napkin, and laid my head down upon my knees. What good was it doing, all the knowledge McVey had given me, all the knowledge I had gained.

"Lydia." It was Daniel.

"How long have you been here?"

"For a while. I didn't want to disturb you. You seemed so deep in thought."

"I was thinking of Jessie. I'm as disturbed over this as you are, Daniel."

"You couldn't be. I don't know, Lydia. I just lie there in bed and wish she'd lose it."

"Well, nothing physical will happen to her. No one dies in childbirth anymore. You won't lose her."

"I've already lost. Jesus. King Mallison, Junior. I've been out whoring with his dad."

"It might turn out all right."

"It isn't what I planned for her, Lydia, and to have her so far away. I'll be there alone with Olivia. I guess I ought to thank my stars I have a spare. I have Anna to thank for that."

"Daniel, do you mind if I ask you something?"

"No, go ahead."

"Why don't you ever want to fuck me? I'm really curious. I can't believe you don't want to fuck me. Don't you want to?"

"Not with my girls here." He sat down beside me, very close. Our legs were touching. "You're an exciting woman, Lydia. It isn't that. My God, it's all so complicated, isn't it?"

"No. It would be simple if we'd let it be. I think every man wants to fuck every attractive woman he meets and women want to fuck most of the men. I have gotten insanely jealous of a man while looking over his shoulder at his best friend. Our tribal customs do not fit our needs, not at the level where you and I operate. King will never be faithful to Jessie. You know that, don't you? There has never been a man in that family who was faithful to his wife."

"Don't tell me that."

"You ought to tell Jessie."

"I told her. I told her everything a man can say. I can't force her to have an abortion. I can't even find her goddamn mother. She was supposed to be in some place in Provence, but they went off on a motor trip."

"What do you want with Sheila?"

"To get her to talk to her. It's not too late. Even after they get married it might not be too late. How long can they do it?"

"I had one at nine weeks. That was pretty bad. I regret that one. That's the one I hate."

"The one what?"

"The one of four abortions. Five if you count a canoe trip down rapids. Okay, five for sure. And here you see me, aren't I the very model of happiness? Do you want her to end up like me?"

"I don't want her to end up like any of us, like anyone I know." He stretched his arms out over his knees and knotted his hands into fists and began to cry. I comforted him the best I could but he only wanted a very small part of what I had to offer. What are we supposed to do, all of us Homo sapiens. Homo dopes. I didn't have to tell him about those nasty homunculi and their demise. I didn't have to paint myself as the murderer of fetuses. So why did I do it? You know why. Because he was near to me and vulnerable and if I let him get too close I might really fall in love. I don't do that anymore. I don't care how good it feels at first. The aftermath is death and more than death, a hole I don't want to have to crawl out of again.

So the summer moved toward its end. Anna once wrote, "Why must we consume each other? Wouldn't it be enough to know that we were loved? Or do we only love to prove our loneliness and must each time drive away what we desire?"

"No," another character, a physician, answered, "for we come from the womb and only one touch will heal us. We are born jealous and terrified, hungry and greedy. How many mothers can meet such needs? One in ten thousand, perhaps, and her progeny lead happy lives. The rest of us plod along the best we can and pass the sadness on."

"And fury?"

"Yes. Sadness's child."

Helen arrived the next day. She brought the decorations for the wedding cake and a gold bracelet Crystal ordered from Shreve's to give Jessie and a number of other things. The bracelet must have cost two thousand dollars, the first of many bribes. I don't understand how Crystal can be so crazy and so dangerous. She has lived her life in this terrible family dynamic and now will initiate Jessie into it, like a vampire bat. I came to see it as inevitable, finally, but when Helen showed up with that bracelet it drove me nuts. I'll have to see McVey four times a week when I get back to get over this.

Mike Carmichael didn't come with Helen. He was coming on a later plane. So I had a chance to get her off alone. As soon as she got settled, I asked her to go with me to walk upon the beach. I didn't mince words. I was too irritated to be polite. I dove right in.

"Helen, some of Anna's papers were here in a trunk. Letters to Noel. I have sealed them up in a box to take to New Orleans when I go back. Noel said if you won't bother her about it, she'll write to you and talk about them."

"Does that mean I can see them?" We were on these huge granite rocks on a spit of land where the wind comes in. It was almost sundown. Another unbelievable irresistible breathstopping sunset going on. Imagine people *talking* in the midst of that. Hydrogen atoms fusing into helium before our eyes and we take *ourselves seriously* and think we are *important*. Goddamn, it's just too wild. Here was Helen in a white Vittadini bathing suit and dark orange and green and black beach coat (some new Chinese designer), Bernardo sandals. I thought she was supposed to be starving in a garret with the poet. Her hair grown out past her shoulders and pulled back with a black barrette. You would hardly know she is the same startled Charlotte housewife in her Chanel suits who presided over Anna's so-called funeral. She came into the dining room in the middle of the wake and dumped two cartons of cigarettes into a cut-glass punch bowl and wadded up the paper sack and handed it to a maid. It was the rudest thing I have ever seen anyone do. A lot of people were smoking at Anna's funeral. We didn't have a body to bury so we just stayed there for six days and got drunk and smoked. LeLe fucked Anna's old boyfriend. Anna's married lover showed up for the memorial service and sat with Mrs. Hand. Well, that's a long story and I was telling you about Helen's metamorphosis.

"You really look great," I said. "I guess you know that."

"I've never been in love before. I didn't know they had this. This friendship. He's my friend, Lydia. Every day I'm glad he's there. I don't know how to talk about it."

"So you have to have these letters or he won't love you?"

"What's that supposed to mean?" She sat down facing the sea, pulled the beach coat around her and tied the belt.

"Nothing. Just don't go hounding Noel about this and she'll probably give you something in the end. She's the most generous person I know. Don't start getting bootleg copies from Olivia or anything like that."

"Lydia, I am Anna's executor. I'm her closest living relative. I was the nearest thing to, well, I don't know what. I'm her executor. She left it in my hands. I want her memory preserved."

"Oh, Helen."

"You won't let me see them?"

"I can't. They're Noel's."

"All right then. I'll wait. Well, tell me about the summer. Has it been fun? Did you have a good time up here?"

"Yes. I think I did."

"It's ridiculous for Jessie to have this baby. You know that, don't you?"

"Yes. What can I do?"

"Nothing. We have to help with this wedding and keep our mouths shut."

"She could still get an abortion."

"No, it's too late. She's told too many people. King wants it too."

"Then we're off, aren't we? What are you going to wear?"

"You must be kidding."

"No, I really want to know."

"I'm going to wear a little aqua David French. It's real old. I bought it for a wedding in Charlotte two years ago."

"Are your kids okay, Helen?"

"They're fine. They're just like they were when I was there. They've been ruining my life for twenty-seven years, Lydia. Now it's my turn. I quit. They can come up here and live with me if they want. I've invited them. That's all I can do."

"Do you miss them?"

"No. I really don't. Does that shock you?"

"I guess so. A little bit."

"Let's walk," she said. "What happens if you go down that way, around the rocks?"

"It gets wilder. It's windy there in the afternoons. There's a path, but we never go that way. We go down toward the piers."

"Let's go," she said and began to walk from rock to rock. Think about the sky, I told myself, think about the sea, it is all one thing and all this talk and language is just our strange invention. We walked for a while in silence, then stopped where birch trees barred the way.

"Anna once said there are four people involved in any love affair," Helen said. "Do you believe that?"

"Durrell," I said. "That's who said it. Darley said Purse-warden said it. No, I think it may be six, or even eight."

"This is where she died, in this ocean, this part of this sea. She has ruined the ocean for me forever, but everything she wrote about love has turned out to be true. I keep thinking of things she told me.

"Once she said to me, 'When I was a child I was never wrong about love. The first boy I loved would still be right for me. I saw him several years ago on a street in New York City. He was in town on business and we spotted each other and spent an hour in a coffee shop holding hands and talking. I should have married him and had a dozen children. Instead, we had these other lives.'

" 'What does he do?' I asked. 'Who is he?'

" 'He runs a bank in Charlotte. He collects art.'

" 'You recognized each other on the street?'

" 'How could we forget? We loved each other when we were twelve.'

"That was Charles Arthur," Helen said. "He married Sally Brasfield."

We started back. Later, when we were almost to the house, she spoke of Anna again. "She told me not to sacrifice myself," Helen said. "She cried every time I got pregnant. You never had your life, she told me. When will you have your life?"

"What did you say to that?"

"I got mad. I said, You're jealous, Anna. You don't know what my life is like. But she did know. She would look at Spencer with that look, as if nothing he could ever do was good enough for her. My children are not bright, Lydia. They are like their father, plodding. I was a prisoner all those years of plodding. Does everyone think I've lost my mind?"

"No one you should care about. As for me, I wish he had a brother."

"He has four. One is a Jesuit who's about to quit. Do you want to meet him if he quits?" She giggled. Anna's giggle. It undid me. "His name is Thomas," she went on. "He's very handsome and doesn't look repressed. I thought when I met him, Well, if Mike dies maybe I can have his brother."

"Send him on. I'd like an ex-priest."

"Well, look, we better get to the house. Mike is bringing champagne. We might as well celebrate, since they're going to have this wedding."

I called Noel back that night. "It's okay," I said. "She'll wait to hear from you. All she can think about is this guy."

"She's very happy?"

"Oh, you know, the ecstatic state. I wish it was me. Goddamn."

"Lydia."

"Yes."

"Your turn will come."

"I've had some turns. Anyway, it's okay and I found the linens for Jessie. They're gorgeous. She will adore them. I'll give them to her tomorrow. Crystal already gave her a gold bracelet from Shreve's."

"A bribe. I used to do that to Andine until I learned better."

"I don't know if Crystal's going to learn. Well, anyway, Helen's at bay for now."

"Maybe I should pick out parts of the letters and let Helen see some passages. Do you think she would be happy with some passages?"

"You don't owe her anything. They were written to you. Do what you want to do. How are you feeling, by the way? Why don't you have Marissa take you down to Mignon's to see the fall collection. I heard it was marvelous."

"Anna wanted her to be happy. My little Helen, she always called her. How long will she be happy, do you think?"

"Six months, six years. Who knows. At least she will remember it. I was thinking this afternoon, now at least Helen has something to remember."

"Does he love her?"

"It's possible. He's living with her."

"Bring the letters to me, darling girl. I'll decide when I have them. And come home soon. Call and tell me about the wedding." Her voice disappeared into the click. Noel.

Noel. She had power over twenty letters and Helen's happiness might hinge on what she did about them. Is the world composed of traps and quicksand? Is everybody nuts? Will I have to move to Nepal to find somebody living in the present?

I went into the kitchen and found Traceleen and Crystal Anne deep into one of their Monopoly games. Crystal Anne was losing. She was down to five one-dollar bills and a small stack of fives. "Roll the dice," Traceleen said. "Don't look like that. I'll lend you some money if you get in jail again."

16

TRACELEEN We had a meeting to make our plans for the wedding. I made sandwiches and coffee and there were petit fours Miss Lydia had iced. If we were going to have a wedding we were going to do it right and not act like we were ducking our heads. All the young people were eager to help out. The only one of the young people I keep worrying about is Olivia. She has so much nervous energy. She acts like she just might burn herself out.

"She's the one who needs a boyfriend," Andria said. "But she acts so smarty around boys. She never lets them talk. All she does is brag about herself and say what she's going to do." Andria has been pulling away from Olivia ever since we stopped the literary club.

"Olivia wants to be famous," Crystal Anne put in. "That's all she thinks about."

"Then why was she going to jump off a pier?" I asked.

"She was only saying that. She says anything to get attention."

"She can't even swim," Andria put in. "She just paddles around."

"Well, let's don't gossip about someone behind their

back," I said. "We have enough to do getting ready for a wedding."

The young women stayed up night and day for two days making their own bridesmaids' outfits. Yellow for Crystal Anne, blue for Olivia, green for Andria. Jessie wore a long white piqué gown they found for her in town, cut down low in the bosom and with a beautiful long train. Also, they bought her a white silk suit to use for a going-away outfit. She and King left right after the ceremony and went off on a wedding trip to Hilton Head. King's real daddy was paying for all of this. He came in the night before the ceremony. He had left his girlfriend behind (to everyone's relief) and was very nice to Mr. Manny and his son and his new daughter-in-law and me. I began to doubt all the terrible things Miss Crystal has said about him over the years. I now think it was just one more example of two young people caught up in events beyond their control.

Crystal Anne and I were in charge of the flowers. We bought up everything we could find at both the florists in the neighborhood. Lilies and baby's breath and white and yellow tulips and sprays of old-fashioned tea roses. After the flowers were all arranged around the altar Crystal Anne took photographs of them with her Instamatic. She has grown two inches this summer. The light of my life. I cannot imagine my life if it had not been entwined with this little precious girl.

Since Jessie was the bride, we had to hire a lady from town to play the Wedding March. She came out with a harp and set it up beside the flowers and played harp music before, during, and after the ceremony. Mr. Daniel gave the bride away, doing nothing to hide the tears in his eyes.

*   *   *

One more incident. After the wedding was over and the young people had left, Miss Lydia brought out the portraits she had done and gave them to the people they were of. There was a small one of me and one of Crystal Anne but the main one was of Miss Crystal standing underneath a liveoak tree in her yard in Mandeville. Sunlight is falling everywhere. There is moss hanging down from the trees and strands of Miss Crystal's hair hang down from her face. She is dressed in her old lavender polyester robe (which looks much better in the painting than in real life), draped to reveal the lovely soft lines of her body.

"Oh, Lydia," she said when she saw the painting. "You have made me immortal."

"Well, not immortal maybe, but it's acrylic. It will last ten thousand years."

"That is amazing," Mr. Daniel said. He put on his glasses and walked up very close to inspect the painted face. "You have to paint Jessie and Olivia. Name your price. I want you to start painting them today."

"I don't know how long that would take. I'd have to go to New Orleans and Charlotte and do studies. I couldn't do them both at once. Let me think about it." She gives Mr. Daniel this look like she is so hard to get all of a sudden.

"Whatever you want to do," he says. "As long as you paint their portraits."

The next day Andria and I flew back to New Orleans. We had stayed as long as we could stay. Miss Crystal drove us to Portland and put us on a plane, an Eastern Airlines 747. The rest of them were driving home by way of New York

City. They were taking the station wagon and leaving the Peugeot until they could find someone to drive it down.

"There's a boy at the drugstore who might bring it," Olivia said. "He's in love with Andria. He'll probably drive it down."

"Don't go starting that," Andria said. But later she gave Mr. Manny Kale Vito's phone number and when we got to the airport I noticed she called him on the phone.

"What did he say?" I asked, when we had taken our seats on the plane.

"He said if they asked him he would do it. Wait till he meets my momma. That will be a test." She laughed her stage laugh, this sort of cold, devil-may-care laugh she has picked up from Miss Lydia. I guess this is the new women of the world. I guess they think they can pick and choose if they ever do agree to wait on a man. As for me, I was just glad to be home. Mark met me at the airport and took me home and gave me a second honeymoon. After all those love affairs of the summer I had forgotten what I had at home, an abiding goodness of my own.

17

LYDIA   As soon as we got back to New Orleans I went over to Noel's and delivered the letters. Here it is, I said, and put the cardboard box on the table beside the copier. My notebooks and the letters. Noel's room is painted ivory this year. The bed faces the curved dormer windows that look out onto the backyard. Facing the bed is a picnic table covered with plants. The copier is nestled among the plants. Beside the copier is a Mason jar containing a set of Hear-No-Evil, See-No-Evil, Speak-No-Evil monkeys. Noel has broken the monkeys apart and placed them in the jar so their feet are touching. Outside the jar are two more sets of monkeys, still joined, watching the ones in the jar.

"Here they are," I said. "My notes and the letters. Are you going to let Helen see them?"

"I might. I thought about it. No one has any secrets anymore, it seems. But I think I will go on and keep mine, just to be mean." She laughed and came alive at the thought.

"The thought of you being mean is past me. Imagine you being mean."

"I used to play evil roles. I did Medea to the cheers of thousands."

"I love you, Noel." I walked across the room and threw

myself down upon the bed. "I loved your house," I added. "Daniel wants me to paint his girls. Wait till you see the one I did of Crystal. It's fabulous, if I do say so myself."

"Darling girl." She patted me like a child. "Have a cookie." She pointed to the glass jars of Oreos and Peanut Butter Cremes. I opened one and took out a cookie and began to eat. I giggled. I took out another one and came back to the bed. She poured coffee from a Thermos into small white cups and handed one to me. I snuggled down into a sea of pillows. The oak and golden raintree and crepe myrtle trees outside the window made a mosaic of light upon the bed.

"Did you read them all?"

"Yes. I told you that I did." She was waiting for me to tell her that they were the most wonderful letters in the world but I wasn't going to do it. I was tired of thrall. I loved Noel, but I wasn't going to play the games. I loved the room and the oak trees outside the windows and my paintings hanging everywhere and the Oreos and Peanut Butter Cremes but I wasn't going to play Secret Letters anymore.

"Let me see," she said. She opened the envelopes and began to read parts of the letters out loud. Her voice is amazing. What a spell she casts. Her voice is so melodic she can make anything sound mysterious and fraught with meaning. "The mystery of children," she began. "Helen gives her life to her children and they pay her back by making her a slave. The Oedipus Complex, the Electra. In our family power is handed down in a strange and complex way. The most powerful older person keeps it all. To access love you must give your power to that figure. To get love you must steal power from your children. This is achieved by giving and receiving money. The Greeks knew everything. A king sacrifices his daughter to fill the sails of the ships bound for Troy. A boy kills his father and marries his mother. A plague comes."

"Every moment is charged with meaning, each encounter, every act. So the slightest gesture of his hand, his face above me in the shared fantasy of love. Never to be forgotten, never lost. Any moment, these clouds, this dawn, this unending mystery."

"I dreamed I wandered down a sunny hall and found a beautiful Chinese print. It was the cover of a book. Inside were wonderful old photographs of my mother. Before she was married to my father."

"The sunsets are fabulous in your house in Maine. The sunset spreads out across a thousand acres of sky, it encompasses the sea and sky, makes a sunset taco, a sunset shell."

"What a feast we live in. Nationalities, cars, trees, oceans, love affairs, electromagnetic fields. How to write in the face of so much wonder. What to praise."

She looked up. The letters were spread out across her knees. "Pour more coffee, precious," she said. "Wouldn't you like some more?" She began to gather up the letters and fold them back into the envelopes. She wasn't mad at me. She didn't have to have me to play her game. She had Anna and her own imagination. "Where's your painting, my darling?" she added. "You didn't bring it to show to me?"

   "It's at Crystal's house. We had a terrible time getting it

shipped. Manny wanted it shipped in the frame. Well, Federal Express finally did it. It beat us here. You want to see it?"

"Of course I do."

"I could take you over there. You could go in the wheelchair."

"No. I can't do that, Lydia. I can't leave."

"Why not? We'll carry you downstairs."

"Oh, no. Oh, please." Her beautiful old face fell. The face I loved so much. Won't go, won't get in the chair, won't let people look at her, won't leave her domain.

"Okay," I said. "I'll bring it in Crystal's station wagon." I took the Thermos, poured more coffee, got another Peanut Butter Creme, sat on the bed, helped her put the letters back in the box. She had kept one page of a letter. She picked it up and read it while I stirred cream into my coffee. She was giving me one more chance. " 'But if I break the spell, what will there be left? Now, in spring, with flowering plum and apple trees and redbirds mad with sun.' Of course, Millay wrote the best about such things. How much she knew, staying in one place and watching.

> Between the red-top and the rye,
>   Between the buckwheat and the corn,
> The ploughman sees with sullen eye
> The hawkweed licking at the sky:
>
>   Three level acres all forlorn,
>   Unfertile, sour, outrun, outworn,
>   Free as the day that they were born.
>
> Southward and northward, west and east,
>   The sulphate and the lime are spread;

Harrowed and sweetened, urged, increased,
The furrow sprouts for man and beast:

While of the hawkweed's radiant head
No stanchion reeks, no stock is fed.

Triumphant up the taken field
The tractor and the plough advance;
Blest be the healthy germ concealed
In the rich earth, and blest the yield:

And blest be Beauty, that enchants
The frail, the solitary lance.

"I have to be getting back," I said. "I'll bring the painting by this afternoon."

"Will you do me a favor before you leave?" Her head was sinking back into the pillows now. "Hand me those pills in the drawer. All the bottles, please." I took the bottles from the drawer of the little antique bedside table. I handed them to her and picked up a glass to take to the bathroom to get water.

"Use that," she said. "It's water." She pointed to the table. There was a white Thermos nestled among the plants by the Mason jar. I opened it and poured a glass of water for her. "Leave it on the table with the pills," she said. "I'll take them later."

"I'm sorry I have to leave. I have to get back to Crystal's."

"Don't be sorry. There is never any reason to be sorry. We do what we have to do."

"If you say so. I love you, Noel. I hope you know that. I really love you."

"I know you do, darling girl." She held out her hands and I kissed her and let her go.

When I got back to Crystal's there were complications and we couldn't go over to Noel's with the painting until later in the day. "We can't come until tonight," I told Noel on the phone.

"I'll be waiting," she said. "I'll find something to do."

"What did she say?" Crystal asked, when I hung up. "Was she disappointed?"

"I don't think so. She sounded happy. Maybe she's making something. Did you see that thing she did with those monkeys? My God, it should be in the Museum of Modern Art."

"She's amazing. We are lucky to know her, Lydia. No one would believe the things that go on in that room."

"I know. I try to tell people about it but they don't understand. You have to see it to believe it."

What went on that afternoon was really pretty simple. Marissa, the Spanish maid, was outside in the garage apartment with a medical student she had met at the K&B. Noel didn't take the Valium and lithium. Instead she got out of bed and went in the bathroom and burned up all of Anna's letters. With a package of matches and a can of lighter fluid she sat by the tub and burned the letters one by one. She was on the last letter when the cotton shower curtain caught on fire. It caught the peeling wallpaper and the bamboo window shades and made the smoke that brought Marissa and the medical student running out half-dressed to call the fire department. We heard the sirens and got there by the time they had the hoses out.

One result of the afternoon was that the upstairs of the house is being redecorated at the insurance company's expense, including having the hardwood floors bleached, something Noel has always wanted to do. Tell me it doesn't pay to mess around with art.

CRYSTAL ANNE   If Jessie has a girl they're going to name it for me. Crystal Three. No, I'm just kidding. They will name it Anne. Anne Mallison. Isn't that great? There are enough Crystals already and besides it's a tacky name. I used to like it but now I don't. Well, I shouldn't talk like that. It doesn't do any good to hate things. That's what Dad and Traceleen say and they're the nicest people I know.

We came back through New York and saw two plays. We saw *Les Misérables* and *The Tempest*. *The Tempest* was the best. Dad says it is his favorite play in the world. He says he might have named me Ariel. They could name the baby Ariel. They are too young to have a baby but we're going to help them take care of it. I'm the exact right age for babysitting. I can't wait. I'm so sick of being the baby in this family.

I grew two inches this summer. I think I'm going to be pretty tall. Not that it makes much difference. Dad isn't tall and he's perfect. Jessie is tall and Andria is as tall as a queen but look at Olivia, she's only five three and she's the one who is going to be famous. I am going to correspond with Andria and Olivia this year and cheer them up while they are in college. Olivia was going to have Jessie to go to school with but now she will be all alone in Charlotte and Jessie will be here with us. I guess that will be something. Olivia and her dad all alone in Charlotte with plenty to argue about. Jessie says they will fight it out.

I am going to correspond with everyone I saw this summer. Lydia and Olivia and Andria. That way I will keep up my writing skills and not be a couch potato.

Oh, Mrs. Chatevin had a terrible fire the day after we got back from Maine. Two fire trucks came and the sirens were going like mad. Everyone in the neighborhood was there and they saved all the paintings except a watercolor that was over the sink. Mrs. Chatevin doesn't have any towel racks in her house. She took down all the towel racks and put paintings in their place. It was a watercolor by a man who lived a long time ago and she hated to see it go. Still, they saved everything else of value and Momma and Lydia said it will be good for Mrs. Chatevin to have to redecorate her house and will make her live a long time waiting for the plumbers to get through.

Well, that's all for now. If nothing happens I'll be writing some more when I get time. Yours most sincerely, Crystal Anne.

ANDRIA   Let Kale Vito come on down here if he wants to. I'll be in Baton Rouge by then. So let him come on over to the judge's house and get real impressed. I'm not impressed because he goes to Harvard College. No man is going to take over my life and start getting me in the kitchen cooking and washing dishes. All I have to do is get up every morning and walk down the street to Louisiana State University and learn everything I can and I'll be on my way. I'll have a job and a condo and a good car and a new stereo. If I want to get laid, okay. If I get pregnant I'll have an abortion. If they want me to go to Hawaii or England, I pack a bag and get on an airplane and off I go. I saw Jessie Hand the other day. I went around to tell them all goodbye before

I left for school. They are still staying at Crystal's house. They have a couple of rooms downstairs. She's starting to look pregnant and she has this look about her eyes like what did I do to myself. You got fucked, honey, and now you have to pay.

If Kale comes down here and brings their car he can come on over to Baton Rouge. It's okay with me. But he'd better bring a rubber. And I don't think I'd do it to him even then. That reminds me. I have to go to Planned Parenthood tomorrow and get on the pill again. I'm not catching herpes or AIDS or something from anyone and I'm not having any babies. Forget it. That's one thing I like about Olivia. She said she'd take two a day even if they caused cancer rather than turn her body over to a parasite. Excuse me, that's what she said. Excuse me for not wanting to end my life.

CRYSTAL (CALLING HER MOTHER ON A SUNNY DAY) Momma, Momma, is that you? It's so wonderful. It's a whole new world. It's so wonderful to have them here. Jessie is so lovely. I took her shopping and bought her the most divine maternity clothes. Oh, yes, he's fine. He's doing pretty good in all his classes. Well, not perfect, but okay. No, she doesn't want to go anymore. She's going to take some decorating classes at Loyola maybe. Later, after they're settled in an apartment. No, a place around the corner. In a week or two. Sure, sure we'd love it. Come on down. See your beautiful grandson and his bride. Okay, love you, angel darling, love you so much, love you too.

HELEN I woke up dreaming something so profound and visual and true. Only yesterday, *only yesterday*, a woman's body was completely at the mercy of nature. If she married or was fucked then she was impregnated until she died. A few women were able to withstand repeated pregnancies before they died. Some women lived to be forty or fifty years old. An occasional woman lived to be seventy or ninety. I guess those women were widowed or lucky or ugly.

We are vessels for the parasites we create. When the child is born the parents start dying. The parents' wishes and dreams and plans are altered forever. Changed and thwarted.

I hate my children. They have had twenty-seven years of my life. I am so sick of it. So sick of it and now Anna is dead and I might die. Do not let that child have a baby, Crystal. Stop right this minute. Stop those children from doing this to themselves. You are crazy to allow this, encourage this. Stop it, Crystal, stop it, Manny. Stop it, stop it, stop it.

I got this letter from Momma when I got back to Boston after the wedding. She had sent it to me to give to Crystal and it got here too late. Now I'm afraid to send it on. Imagine Momma writing this. Imagine her knowing this.

I saw this terrible sight. It was all in color and the body was a pond, a sea, and in it all the possible eggs were swimming, not hurting the pond. Then this cloud of gnats like white sperm fell on the pond and began to chase me and there was a storm. Afterward, I was upstairs in bed. My eyes were dark and I was sick. Now I was no longer a person. I was a vessel for something I did not understand. It's not fair, Crystal. Don't do this to my beautiful child, my beautiful Jessie. Let me talk to her. Tell her to call me the minute you read this. Yes, I am drinking some sherry.

ANNA HAND   I cannot get you close enough, I said to him, pitiful as a child, and never can and never will. We cannot get from anyone else the things we need to fill the endless terrible need, not to be dissolved, not to sink back into sand, heat, broom, air, thinnest air. And so we revolve around each other and our dreams collide. It is embarrassing that it should be so hard. Look out the window in any weather. We are part of all that glamour, drama, change, and should not be ashamed.

JESSIE   It would be winter now if I were in Charlotte. Instead I'm in New Orleans, with my stomach out to here. I don't care. I did what I wanted to do. King hates me now. He hates the way I look and he doesn't like to go out with me. That's okay. As soon as I get my baby I'll be out of here. I'll get some money from Grandmother and go live in New York. I'll get an apartment like the one Aunt Anna had and get a job or something up there. I told Olivia on the phone about it. She said, okay, she'd been waiting for this to happen. She's doing great in school. She wants to get to New York too. So, in two more months. I can wait. I wonder what it's going to be. I want it to be a girl. I'm sick of men. I'm sick of Manny being so perfect and calling every afternoon to check on us. We live down the street from Crystal now in a house that belongs to Mrs. Chatevin. It's got roaches and they drive me crazy. I never lived in a little house like this. I hate these old houses and all this old stuff in this town. But I love the flowers.

I quit going to Dominican. I got too tired to get up in the

mornings. King comes home any time he wants to. He says he's studying at the Tulane Library but nobody stays at the library until three in the morning. He never touches me now.

Well, I did what I wanted to. I wanted to have the baby and now I'm having it. I won't do it again. Olivia says, Jessie, swear you will never do it again. Okay, I say, I won't. Maybe I'll give it to Crystal. She's the one who wants it so much. I dreamed I left it at a play. I was the star of the play and I put it down backstage and when I went back it wasn't breathing. I haven't been to confession in a year. That's one reason I quit Dominican. I couldn't stand those ugly little nuns giving me those looks. Like they can read my mind.

My baby can read this one day so she'll know not to let it happen to her. I let him do it because he's so good-looking and it felt good. That's it. That's the whole reason. There wasn't anything to do up there all summer anyway. Then I thought I was in love with him. We were starting to argue anyway and so I thought I was depressed the first time I threw up. I guess I got pregnant the first time I let him do it.

When I told him about it he got excited about it. He was the one who wanted to go to the drugstore and get the kit right away and we went to a motel and stayed there all afternoon after we did the test. Crystal gives him too much money. Ever since I first met him at that funeral I have thought that. He gets the most money for nothing of any boy I ever met. That is really nice at first, then you think it over.

So when I woke up the next morning, I thought, I have three choices, get an abortion, get married, run away; Dad will kill me one way or the other. But when Olivia said, Dad will kill you, I said, No, he won't, he loves me. I am a

Hand and we never admit we are scared, never admit we are lonely, never say we are not strong. Our coat of arms says, No One Harms Us And Gets Away With It. Something like that in Latin. Well, King didn't get away with talking me into doing it with him. He is stuck here with me now. I'm stuck too, he thinks. But he's wrong. As soon as I get the baby here I'm gone. I talked to Mother last week. She called me from Athens, Greece. She was going to Venice to meet some friends. She says I could come to Europe. She isn't interested in the baby. She is only interested in me. She is the only person except Olivia who is interested in me. I don't care. I like little kids. At least this one will be good-looking and beautiful. I'll take it to Europe. Oh, no, I forgot. Olivia and I are going to take it and go to New York. She gets out of school the last of May. I'll be okay by then. The baby is coming in March or April. It will be pretty big by May. We'll pack up and leave. I'll get on a 747 and we'll be out of here.

Oh, yeah. This doctor I go to for the baby is a lesbian. I was afraid of her at first then I thought, Well, I don't want to have a relationship with her, I just want her to take care of me. She is very gentle and gray-headed. She sees me every two weeks and she is always worrying about me and asking me questions about how we live and what King does and if he's good to me. She isn't coming on to me. She is just interested in me. She is going to try to make this as easy as possible for me. I am going to Lamaze classes but King never goes. He was too young to deal with this but I am not. I am strong enough. I'll make it. Dr. Cordona is her name. She has opened up my mind about lesbians. I can see why a woman would decide to do that. If she just got tired of putting up with men and all their bullshit. Well, it doesn't scare me to think like that. I told Olivia about it and she said that's the mark of an open mind. She is studying philosophy and biology. They are her favorite subjects. She says the central nervous system is the highest achievement of evolution and she is going to concentrate on it. She says the mind of this baby inside of me is the most important thing and I have to listen to classical music and stay calm because I don't want to pass down the sins of our whole family to this baby in the form of making it a nervous wreck before it's born. She is calling me every other night now. I don't know what I'd do without her.

OLIVIA   I feel so sorry for her. My God, she sounds so bad on the phone. I ought to tell Dad but if I do he'll just go crazy. I'm saving money. I saved sixteen hundred dollars counting the gold coins Dad's dad gave me for Christmas. I keep telling her to save some money. They all give her money all the time. We can't get away unless we have some money. But I don't think she's listening. I'll go down there at spring break. Poor Dad, no one will be here with him. That's okay, I can't worry about all of them at once. Listen, I am going to work on the Human Genome Initiative as soon as I get out. That's my goal now. Listen, it will still be going on. It's going to take them a long time to finish it. Maybe we should go to Washington this summer instead of New York. I could go and visit the labs there. This woman from the National Institutes of Health came to talk to us. It's fabulous. They are going to find the secrets of life and cure all diseases. This is not a joke. I could be the one who writes about what they do. Then I would still be a writer. It's very imaginative, being a biologist. You have to have a good imagination. I have that.

KING   I'm so sick of her crying all the time. She thinks I don't know it. She thinks I believe it when she acts like she likes to cook supper or something like that. It's so god-damn boring, hanging around the house after dinner, trying to study with her moping around. I can't help it if I don't like to fuck somebody that looks like you'd kill the baby if you did. I love Jessie. I told her I did. I just can't stand to stay here.

CRYSTAL   I don't know what went wrong.

LYDIA   I told them so.

TRACELEEN   This too shall pass away.